The Library of Literature

UNDER THE GENERAL EDITORSHIP OF

John Henry Raleigh & Ian Watt

The Marble Faun:

OR,

The Romance of Monte Beni

The Library of Literature

Alinari-Art Reference Bureau

The Faun of Praxiteles
CAPITOLINE MUSEUM, ROME

The Marble Faun:

OR,

The Romance of Monte Beni

A ROMANCE BY

Nathaniel Hawthorne

EDITED, WITH AN INTRODUCTION AND
ANNOTATION, BY

Richard H. Rupp
UNIVERSITY OF MIAMI

The Bobbs-Merrill Company, Inc.
INDIANAPOLIS · NEW YORK

NATHANIEL HAWTHORNE
1804–1864
The Marble Faun was first published in 1860

For Mary

Copyright © 1971 by the Bobbs-Merrill Company, Inc.
Library of Congress Catalog Card Number 73-134464
Printed in the United States of America
First Printing
Designed by Starr Atkinson

Foreword

This edition of Hawthorne's fourth and last completed novel encourages the student to reach his own position regarding *The Marble Faun*, a romance too long neglected in the classroom. The Introduction summarizes Hawthorne's life after 1850, considers the Roman scene in 1860, and presents some thematic considerations.

The map and illustrations give the visual context for Hawthorne's excitement at the discovery of Rome late in his life. Praxiteles' *Faun*, to which Kenyon likens Donatello in the first chapter, and V. Danti's *Pope Julius III*, under whose outstretched arms the sinners repent in Perugia, figure prominently in Hawthorne's sense of Italy. The Appendix shows four manuscript pages in Hawthorne's hand.

The annotated Bibliography should assist the student beginning his own study of the novel. The running notes are intended to identify artists, people, and places. A few critical notes call attention to important moments in the action or to problems in interpretation. Those identified as *NB* refer to the Riverside Edition of the *French and Italian Note-books*, Boston, 1883.

The text of *The Marble Faun* is that of the first Boston edition, third printing, 1860; the text of the Conclusion is that of the Riverside Edition, 1883. I have made 284 corrections to bring the text closer to the manuscript, which is in the British Museum (Add. MSS. 44889 and 44890). This is a classroom text; the textual specialist is referred to the Ohio State Centenary Edition, 1968, for a definitive text and a collation of all variant readings.

I wish to acknowledge the Alinari-Art Reference Bureau for permission to reproduce Praxiteles' *Faun* and V. Danti's *Pope Julius III*, and the Trustees of the British Museum for the manuscript pages in the Appendix.

Finally, I wish to thank all those who have helped me with this pleasant project, especially Ian Watt and John Henry Raleigh, the General Editors; Joseph Jeffs of the Georgetown University Library; Larzer Ziff, for the Chronology and bibliographical matter in the Bobbs-Merrill edition of *The Scarlet Letter*; the Keeper of Manuscripts at the British Museum; my colleagues, Paul Betz, Tom Walsh, Roger Slakey, Duane Koenig, and Bernard Wagner; Ken and Jean Donadio for tramping all over Rome at my request; and Joann Spiegel for her careful and helpful editing.

Contents

Illustrations

Introduction

I. HAWTHORNE IN THE 1850'S

Until the publication of *The Scarlet Letter* in 1850, Nathaniel Hawthorne found little encouragement in his dedication to literature. Twelve years under the eaves of his mother's house were followed by twelve more of relative obscurity. Even his marriage to Sophia Peabody on July 9, 1842, had been postponed until he could find a way to support her. The apprentice and journeyman years were quiet and unrewarding, then. When his somber masterpiece appeared it was the work of a mature man and artist. It was followed in 1851 by *The House of the Seven Gables*, and in 1852 by *The Blithedale Romance*.

But Hawthorne's prolific output in the 1850's should come as no surprise. In 1850 he was at the height of his creative powers. Years of disciplining his art in the gift books and magazines, years of hack work and of civil service had delayed his entry into the full-scale romance until he could bring to it all the resources of his thoughtful, sober experience. Today most novelists have had their say at 45; Hawthorne was just beginning.

Maturity, sobriety, and a melancholy temperament characterize his outlook. Unlike his more exuberant and more unsteady friend Melville, Hawthorne seems never to have been young. True, he wrote *Fanshawe* as a young man, but it mortified him and he suppressed it. Believing that only his best efforts should represent him to his public, he dismissed this first long work as *juvenilia*. Romance-writing was an act of the mature mind.

His maturity and his temperament fitted him for the subject which is uniquely his: the need for human sympathy consequent upon one's discovery of his place among the community of sinners. Unlike the more sunlit world of his fellow townsmen Emerson and Thoreau, Hawthorne's is a dark world. Even so, the darkness is lighted by the sharing of guilt and by the sense of community which give the festivals of that fallen world a dark beauty. His first three romances probe the American community, past and present, for the terms on which its members sympathize with each other. For Hester and Dimmesdale in *The Scarlet Letter*, the terms are tragic. For Clifford, Hepzibah, Phoebe, and Holgrave in *The House of Seven Gables*, they are comic. For Coverdale, Zenobia, Hollingsworth and Priscilla in *The Blithedale Romance*, they are ironic.

All three books, however, are *American* experiences, the result of private reflection on his native land. In 1852 Hawthorne had to forgo the luxury of private citizenship. For one thing, his three romances had won him only a fair-sized although enthusiastic following. For another, the election of his close friend and classmate Franklin Pierce to the Presidency thrust him into the unlikely role of political patron. In return for his services as campaign biographer, Hawthorne was appointed Consul at Liverpool. In July, 1853, the Hawthornes sailed for England with their three children, Una, Julian, and Rose. Four years there and two years of travel in France and Italy would intervene before his fourth romance appeared in 1860. These years made a difference.

The Hawthornes arrived in Rome in January of 1858. Sophia was carried away by the experience. She wrote to her sister: "I am in Rome, Rome, *Rome*! I have stood in the Forum and beneath the Arch of Titus, at the end of the Sacra Via. I have wandered about the Coliseum, the stupendous grandeur of which equals my dream and hope. I have seen the sun kindling the open courts of the Temple of Peace. . . ." Hawthorne was less impressed. He gradually warmed to the monuments and the art treasures, but his chief interest seems to have been the American artists' colony there. His own artistic sense was stirred by the talk and the work of the painters and sculptors he grew to know; he acknowledges his debt to them in his Preface to *The Marble Faun*.

He was closest to William Wetmore Story, wit, genial host, painter, sculptor, and informal dean of the American artists' college in Rome. Henry James wrote a biography of Story—another link between Hawthorne and James—but Story is remembered today chiefly for his *Roba di Roma*, a rambling, discursive autobiography of the Roman years, heavy on local color and folklore. (The book appeared in 1870, ten years after *The Marble Faun*.)

Others who welcomed him in Rome were Cephas Giovanni Thompson, the painter; Harriet Hosmer, painter and free spirit; Thomas Crawford, who carved a monumental figure of Washington on horseback; and Maria Louise Lander of Salem, who made a bust of Hawthorne. Hawthorne liked them all, finding in their company the kind of artistic stimulation he had missed in the attic of his mother's house and in the intervening years.

Hawthorne had carefully saved his salary from the diplomatic post, although he grumbled that he could not save as much as he should have. Originally he thought that the trip to Rome was merely an excursion and that the city was as good a place to write as any. Gradually, however, Rome became more and more real for him, an experience in itself—cultural, artistic, and religious. So Hawthorne came to regard his Roman year as a kind of sabbatical for reeducation in the ways of art. Although he never learned very much about art and preferred statuary to painting, he came back again and again to statues that unlocked his imagination, like Praxiteles' *Faun*.

Hawthorne liked to jot down his reflections on life and art as he went along; he carried this habit with him from Salem to Liverpool and onto the Continent. Most of what we know of his activities in Italy comes from the *French and Italian Note-*

books, edited and published by Sophia after his death. *The Marble Faun* is heavily indebted to this particular journal for material; a few passages appear almost verbatim, and several others are simply reworked to fit the situation. Hawthorne also kept a diary; some of his entries tell us of his daily work record and of his dealings with Smith, Elder and Company, his English publishers.

The whole family left Rome in late May of 1858 for a tour of central Italy. They hired a carriage and packed the three children together with their American governess, Ada Shepard, for a summer in Florence. They went by way of some ancient towns in the Apennines and Tuscany: Civita Castellana, Terni, Spoleto, Foligno, Assisi, Perugia, Lake Trasimeno, Arezzo, and Incisa. In June and July they rented a villa called the Casa del Bello. In August they moved into the Villa Montauto, outside Florence.

This was a happy summer for Hawthorne; according to his son Julian, it was his happiest. He had started work on one of his unfinished romances at the first villa, but the move to the Villa Montauto gave him the tower, the setting, and the atmosphere for his romance of Monte Beni. The rambling villa with its square tower rising toward the heavens was admirably suited for the twilight moods so characteristic of Hawthorne's imagination. From its heights he enjoyed his after-dinner cigar while watching the sunset and the ground fog rolling across the valley.

In addition there was Florence itself, with its galleries and people. Hawthorne was much impressed with the Uffizi, and particularly with its *Venus of Medici.* The people were also important to him. He and Sophia visited the Brownings at Casa Guidi. He found Pennini, their only child, to be a frail boy, and his mother an elfen creature; Browning himself was an emotionless man whose "personal intercourse, though kindly, does not stir one in the least." More important for Hawthorne was the American sculptor Hiram Powers, an energetic, jolly man with

lovely daughters and strong opinions on matters of art. Hawthorne was an apt pupil; Powers' opinions on sculpture found
their way into *The Marble Faun* as Hawthorne's own.

The family returned to Rome in October, spending ten
days in Siena enroute. By now Hawthorne was well launched
into his manuscript, but Una's Roman fever soon dashed any
hopes he may have had of finishing in Rome. The tension was
so great that for four months he could not even keep his notebook. Finally, in April, after a series of advances and relapses,
the malaria broke once and for all. Immensely relieved, Hawthorne planned their return home. On May 25, 1859, they left
Rome for good and went to England.

All along Hawthorne had planned to write an English
romance involving an American's claim to an English legacy
and drawing on his consular experience; this was the work begun at the Casa del Bello and never finished. He had planned
to go directly back to Concord, but Smith, Elder and Company
offered him a contract for his novel at £600—a healthy sum in
1859. He decided to take the contract and to finish his romance
in England. Since the Italian experience was fresher in his mind,
he settled down to write in London, but the social whirl was
too hectic for concentrated work. They moved to Redcar on
the desolate coast of Yorkshire, where the bulk of *The Marble
Faun* was written. After a few weeks in Leamington and a visit
to Bath for the waters (Sophia was not in good health), the
Hawthornes were ready to go home at last. They had been
away for seven years. Before leaving for home, Hawthorne
gave the manuscript of his novel to his friend Henry Bright, an
English social reformer. (In 1931 Bright's daughter gave the
manuscript to the British Museum, where it is catalogued as
Add. MSS. 44889 and 44890. Hawthorne's letter of transmission
is bound with the former volume.)

They returned to the Wayside, their Concord home, in
June of 1860. Hawthorne took up his life there with a greater
sense of possession than he had hitherto shown. At Sophia's sug-

gestion they renovated and enlarged the old house. Hawthorne's new study, high in a turret with windows all around,
was accessible only by a trapdoor on which his chair sat as he
wrote. Here at last he could write undisturbed.

Hawthorne resumed his literary life with Lowell, Longfellow, his publisher, James T. Fields, and others in the Boston-
Concord circle. To a lesser extent he renewed his friendship
with Emerson, Alcott, and the other Transcendentalists. Of
them all he admired Thoreau the most, though he found him
difficult. The renewal of their friendship would be short, however; neither man was to outlive the Civil War.

Financially pressed to write again, Hawthorne's imagination turned back to the days in England. He had a writer's
block on *The Dolliver Romance* and turned to his consular
experience for several essays on the English character, published first in the *Atlantic* and then by Fields as *Our Old Home*
(1863).

Hawthorne's talent and his health flagged together. He
could finish neither *Dr. Grimshawe's Secret* nor *The Ancestral
Footstep*, both concerned with his American home and its
democratic possibilities. Actually, *The Ancestral Footstep* had
reached an impasse in 1858, before he began work on *The Marble Faun.* Two other works of these last years, *Septimus Felton*
and *The Dolliver Romance*, deal with the search for the elixir
of life. Various reasons have been suggested for his failure to
finish any of these four works: he may have lost his will to live;
he was certainly tired and sick after 1861; doubtless the Civil
War depressed him; he may have buckled under psychological
stress. Such is scholarly speculation, at least.

There is no one cause, probably, but there is a further
point. Hawthorne's subjects in these unfinished romances were
the wrong ones for him. All four deal with the rejection of the
past for some brighter future. Yet Hawthorne worked best
when he explored the past, reconstructing history in dramatic,
psychological, and moral terms. The best sequences in *The*

House of the Seven Gables are surely those in which the past impinges profoundly on the present. The weakest sequence is the ending, with its almost operatic quintet singing of future bliss at the new estate in the country. Again, in *The Blithedale Romance*, the future is a delusory utopian dream. As Richard H. Fogle suggests of that romance, "Hawthorne is dealing with contemporary life, and he has the problem of wresting from its confusion and phenomenal chaos the kind of design and meaning which alone interest him. In other novels he escapes through the past, or, as in *The Marble Faun*, through a setting remote from everyday America." If Hawthorne misconceived his subjects, then, we should not be surprised to find them executed badly.

In any event, he never found the crowning success to his life's work. Depressed and frail, he was increasingly unable to write. In the spring of 1864 he took a trip to New Hampshire with Franklin Pierce in hopes that the mountain air would restore him. On May 19 he died in his sleep at a hotel in Plymouth. He was buried four days later in Concord's Sleepy Hollow Cemetery.

II. ROME IN 1860

Rome in 1860 was a restless city, resentful of the French occupation. Pope Pius IX was an unwilling vassal of Napoleon III, tied to the temporal concerns of the Papal States as well as the spiritual cares of the Church. French soldiers were everywhere in Rome, and they appear in the book. In 1870 the French influence and the temporal power of the Papacy crumbled together.

Rome was more papal then than it is today. Pius IX came to the throne in 1846; he was widely heralded as a liberal pontiff who would relax the prohibitions on freedom of movement and freedom of the press. Unfortunately, in the long run, the short-lived Second Roman Republic of 1849 caused Pius to react in a conservative manner when he returned from Neapolitan exile on April 12, 1850. American public opinion, largely Protestant and democratic, lay with Mazzini, a revolutionary leader. Margaret Fuller, the American Transcendentalist, ran a hospital for revolutionaries until the Mazzini-Garibaldi regime collapsed.

Despite the political situation, Americans were coming to Rome in increasing numbers during the 1850's. Numerous travel books whetted the tourist appetite. Hawthorne's friend George S. Hillard wrote the most popular guide, a two-volume memoir called *Six Months in Italy* (1853); Hawthorne used it on his tour. What he found in Rome, however, was a good bit less romantic than Hillard's "Tragical Story of the Savelli Family."

On the other hand, Edward Dicey, an Englishman, gives a blunt and unvarnished account of Roman life during the period in his *Rome in 1860* (London, 1861). Dicey had an ax to grind; his book is an exposé of the abuses Romans suffered under the temporal power of the Papacy. Despite Dicey's prejudices, we learn a good deal about the city as Hawthorne saw it. To begin with, Roman winters are cold, rainy, and inhospitable; Julian Hawthorne's first recollection was of sliding on the ice in St. Peter's Square. The Hawthornes found a city of some 170,000 people who together with the tourists annually purchased 55,000,000 lottery tickets. Unemployment was high; the city swarmed with beggars. Dicey points out, somewhat caustically, that "there were ten thousand persons in holy orders, together with novices, scholars, choristers, beadles, and whole tribes of clerical attendants. . . . probably not far short of forty thousand persons, who in some form or other lived upon and by the church, that is, in plainer words, doing no labour themselves, lived on the labour of others" (pp. 14–15).

Theater censorship was heavy; no public festivals were

allowed except on the last day or two of the Carnival; no gam-
bling other than the papal lottery was permitted; public dress
was rigidly supervised and the nightly curfew enforced; of
greater moment, all the Roman papers were controlled by the
government. To complicate matters, Roman fever (yellow
fever, or malaria, or possibly typhoid) prevailed in warm
weather, driving those who were affluent enough to their villas
in the country. And the Roman economy was so infested with
go-betweens that the tourist could scarcely shop, travel, or
find lodgings without them. Resentment was high against re-
pressive governmental policies; rebellion flared again in 1866,
and was again suppressed.

Of direct relevance to *The Marble Faun* was the system
of papal justice. Trials were held secretly and usually con-
ducted in Latin by the clergy; the accused was held incom-
municado and sometimes languished for years between his
arrest and his trial; no cross-examination by defense counsel
was allowed; there was no court of appeal; and the accused was
punished secretly. Publication of the trial proceedings days or
weeks after the execution of sentence took the form of long
strips of paper pasted on walls and billboards in out-of-the-way
corners of the city. Thus the mysterious disappearance of Hilda
and Donatello at the end of the book is not a bit of gratuitous
mystification on Hawthorne's part, but standard legal pro-
cedure.

The remarkable thing, indeed, is Hawthorne's lack of bias
against the shortcomings of papal Rome. He does criticize
ecclesiastical waste, vanity, and bureaucracy (more often in his
notebook than in his romance), but he is impressed with the
piety of individuals and the practice of confession. Curious,
critical, bemused, respectful—Hawthorne was fascinated with
Rome and the Roman Church. For Hilda, especially, Rome and
the Church are an education, and Hilda reflects Hawthorne's
values throughout the work. For Hawthorne's daughter Rose,
Rome held a more profound meaning. Years after his death she
became a Catholic and a Sister of Charity.

III. AMERICAN ARTISTS IN ROME

The American artists' colony was an enclave with its own rituals. Hawthorne shared them, although he ultimately came to reject them. In *The Flowering of New England*, Van Wyck Brooks describes the expatriate life of the 1850's for us this way: "To warm themselves in one another's presence, the artists in Rome met at the Caffè Grecó, the dark and dirty haunt in former days of Allston, Cooper and Turner. Little groups of aspiring students went for midnight rambles in the Coliseum. They strolled through the Forum, singing 'Hail Columbia' in chorus. They stopped at the Fountain of Trevi, where Lord Neville [Nelvil] had talked with Corinne. They sallied forth with sketch books for picnics on the Appian Way. They pored over one another's portfolios and wrote 'Campagna bits' in their journals and letters. They gathered for musical soirees, perhaps in Charlotte Cushman's rooms, for the great Boston actress with the 'thoughtful' style often spent her winters in Rome. They talked about Guido's 'Aurora' and Canova, who seemed to have brought back the repose of the Greeks, and the mystery of Beatrice Cenci. They sat on ruined columns, with their colours beside them, sketching some model with disheveled hair, and beard that suggested Moses, or a well-turned arm that might have belonged to Apollo" (*The Flowering of New England*, New York: Dutton, 1936, pp. 473–474).

The expatriate American artists of the period went to Rome and to Florence for several reasons. First of all, the art was there. America had no schools, studios, or artistic centers where the artists could learn their craft. Second, living in Rome was cheap, pleasant, and sociable among one's expatriate fellow artists. The first truly American circle of painters and sculptors formed itself in Rome. Third, the wages for stone-cutters, who carved from clay or plaster models, were considerably cheaper in Rome than in America. Ernest Earnest states that "[Hiram] Powers' total bill from workmen came to $15 a day; another American, Harriet Hosmer, kept twenty stone-cutters at work reproducing her designs" (*Expatriates and Patriots*, Durham: Duke University Press, 1968, p. 104).

American artists paid a price for their expatriation, however. Their native themes and materials underwent a change into a stale and imitative classicism. As a result the work of Horatio Greenough, Hiram Powers, W. W. Story, and the rest, is not highly regarded today. Hawthorne's enthusiasm for Story's "Cleopatra" in Chapter 14 of the novel seems excessive now. As Earnest puts it, "In fact Cleopatra looks like nothing so much as a woman who, after a long day of ironing and looking after the youngsters, has sat down and loosened her bra" (p. 123).

Hawthorne had a particular purpose in his association with the American artists: he wanted to have Rome on its own terms; they were artistic terms. Once he learned what he could from his compatriots, he left them to their own pursuits; his concerns were simply other.

As diligently as he studied them, Hawthorne never came to know painting and sculpture. For one thing, his interest was moral, not esthetic. The personal, spiritual content of the work of art was prior to every other consideration. Thus he often responded to the subject matter of a painting like Raphael's *Transfiguration* rather than to its form, color, balance, or technique. Similarly, he disliked Titian's nude Magdalen; "This Magdalen is very coarse and sensual, with only an impudent assumption of penitence and religious sentiment, scarcely so deep as the eyelids; but it is a splendid picture, nevertheless, with those naked, lifelike arms, and the hands that press the rich locks about her, and so carefully permit those voluptuous breasts to be seen. She a penitent! She would shake off all pretence to it as easily as she would shake aside that clustering hair. . . . Titian must have been a very good-for-nothing old man" (*NB*, pp. 330–331).

Julian Hawthorne tells us that his father was a better judge of sculpture that he was of painting. But Hawthorne disapproved of naked statues, especially those by his contemporaries. His chief objection to the English sculptor John Gib-son was his tinting of marble to produce lifelike flesh tones. Hawthorne probably found such statues prurient; they were cheap, in any event. Curiously, he was fascinated by the *Faun* of Praxiteles—surely a sensuous work—but since it stirred his myth-making propensities, the nudity did not matter.

Another seeming contradiction was his attitude toward domestic realism. He liked the Flemish and Dutch painters. The great Italian masters satisfied neither his taste for innocent paganism nor his preference for the prosy actuality of domestic life. His artistic taste combined the romantic and the banal to the exclusion of almost everything else. (He did like painted church windows.)

For Hawthorne, Rome was life, not art. He had found kindred spirits there; he enjoyed the only leisurely period of his life there; his daughter Una almost died and came back to life there. Thus personal realities underlie his response to the gal-leries, churches, villas, gardens, fountains, piazzas, and studios of Rome, all of which he visited with Sophia, an indefatigable tourist. Whatever his esthetic blind spots, Hawthorne saw Rome as a total experience. *The Marble Faun* translates that experience into art.

Other American writers of the time saw Rome in their own way. Howells, American consul in Venice during the Civil War, was overcome by the stench, repelled by the architectural ugliness of modern Rome, and disappointed in the undramatic Tarpeian Rock. Rome was a more prosaic experience for him than it was for Hawthorne—but then Howells was the more prosaic man: "Indeed, it seems to me that all moisture of ro-mance and adventure has been wellnigh sucked out of travel in Italy, and that compared with the old time, when the happy wayfarer journeyed by vettura through the innumerable little states of the Peninsula,—halted every other mile to show his passport, and robbed by customs officers in every colour of shabby uniform and every variety of cocked hat,—the present railroad period is one of but stale and insipid flavour" (*Italian Journeys*, Boston, 1884, pp. 157–158). But even Howells was moved as he stood at the graves of Keats and Shelley in the Protestant Cemetery.

In 1873 Henry James went to Rome, where he found the artists' colony uncongenial. Leon Edel cites a letter to William as evidence: " 'You feel altogether out of the current of modern civilization,' he wrote to his brother in April. 'I often hanker for the high culture and high finish of Paris—the theatres and newspapers and booksellers and restaurants and boulevards' " (*The Conquest of London*, London: Rupert Hart-Davis, 1962, p. 115). Yet Rome cast its spell over him as well. James's most popular novel, *Daisy Miller* (1878), drew on the legends and the atmosphere of the Coliseum and used in its plot the ubiquitous Roman fever. Like Hilda—and many American girls who have since gone to Rome—Daisy fell in love. But unlike Hilda, Daisy did not have the Puritan Code to sustain her, and she could not frame an adequate substitute out of freshness and coquetry.

Mark Twain visited Rome in 1867, enroute to the Holy Land. In *The Innocents Abroad* (1869) he made that visit an occasion for scoring points on the ubiquitous Michelangelo, the local pride of the Roman guides, the anti-Semitism of the Church, and the cruelty of the Coliseum. Despite Twain's burlesques, however, he was undeniably impressed by St. Peter's. For once he found a subject befitting his hyperbole, and he responded to it with uncharacteristic awe. Twain visited Rome only eight years after Hawthorne left it, but the interval marks the end of one era and style in American literature and the beginning of another.

For taken as a whole Hawthorne's Rome and his romance mark the end of the romantic sensibility in the mainstream of American literature. As he says in his Preface, "romance and poetry, like ivy, lichens, and wall-flowers, need Ruin to make them grow." The impact of the Civil War on the American imagination made his work a ruin in a double sense. And for the twentieth-century reader, the basic problem is to recover the romantic sensibility which the ruins in *The Marble Faun* suggest.

IV: NATURE, ART, SIN, AND TRANSFORMATION

What are we to make of this book, finally? To begin with, we can discern at least four subjects. The first of these is Nature, developed in a series of temporal contrasts. At the furthest extreme from the present lies the mythical past. Largely through Donatello, Hawthorne in the early chapters evokes the Golden Age, a time of happy nymphs and satyrs. Again using Donatello, Hawthorne takes us in the middle chapters on a tour of the Renaissance. Only then, beginning in Chapter 36, does he launch directly into the moral complexities of the present.

Nature appears most completely and intensely at Monte Beni, where Donatello vainly tries to recover his lost innocence. We see it around him in old Tomaso and the grape-pickers. Paradoxically, the way to innocence is through repentance, symbolized by the rude wayfarer's cross on the ride to Perugia. (That city, with its marketplace, its vegetable stands, and its simple farmers, seems to prefigure Thomas Hardy's Casterbridge.) At the center of the city we find the dual benediction of nature and God, made manifest by the Bronze Pontiff. His blessing encourages Donatello to repent.

In considering Nature we are already entwined in two other thematic strands of the book, Art and Sin. Art, first of all, is architecture. The Forum, the Coliseum, St. Peter's, the various fountains—all these suggest that the backdrop of man's moral development is the physical record of his noble aspirations. Physical Rome towers over the actors here like the set of a cinema epic. Distances, furthermore, seem to be larger than life. Like the jar in Wallace Stevens's "Anecdote," Rome is the shape that man has imposed on nature.

A series of contrasts helps to reveal that shaping action in architectural terms. The Roman past with its Christian martyrs, its churches and its catacombs, its monuments and its fountains plays against the historical present with French soldiers at every corner. Secondly, Hawthorne juxtaposes the pagan monuments, most often bathed in moonlight and shadows, against the Christian artifacts: large, dead, solemn, yet impressive. A third contrast juxtaposes the towers of the novel—Hilda's and Donatello's—against the public architecture. Each tower reflects the spirit and temperament of its inhabitant; each symbolizes the personal struggle to be played against the public scene.

Like the towers, the studios also reflect their inhabitants. If the towers suggest the penitential isolation of Hilda and Donatello, the studios suggest the artist's connection with sin through his work. Kenyon's statues and Miriam's paintings move them, from different positions, toward Donatello and Hilda.

As with architecture, so with sculpture and painting. The busts of Cleopatra and Donatello suggest the inner truth of art, the truth with which talent must grapple in order to project artistic vision. Kenyon's bust of Donatello reflects the man's transformation: "for here were still the features of the antique Faun, but now illuminated with a higher meaning, such as the old marble never bore." As for painting, Giotto, Fra Angelico, Raphael, and the other Italian masters projected a harmony of art and faith. As their student, Hilda attempts to find that harmony in her own life. Yet she leaves the masters for the confessional, and the confessional for Kenyon. Thus Hawthorne moves from art to life: Kenyon the sculptor and Hilda the copyist are hopeful indicators of a bright future—a future shaped by the art and the sin of the Old World.

Perhaps Sin is not so much a theme as it is the central subject of *The Marble Faun*. The essential contrast between the world made by God (Nature) and the world made by man (Art) is complicated by the evils done by man (Sin). Hawthorne asks a disturbing question: Who is innocent of sin? Isn't innocence, rather than the absence of experience, a quality to be regained through penitential experience? Hilda and Kenyon are involved in the murder only indirectly, but indirect involvement is nonetheless real. In sharing the burden of guilt borne by Miriam and Donatello, they help to lighten it and to regain their innocence as they prepare to marry.

Furthermore, Hawthorne was much impressed with the Catholic practice of confession, penance, and absolution. He adapted it for fictional purposes as he worked out the changing relationships of his four characters to the murder and to each other. The interested reader may wish to relate these changes to changes in physical setting—Chapters 1 to 23 are set in Rome, Chapters 24 to 32 at Monte Beni, Chapters 33 to 35 in Tuscany, and Chapters 36 to 50 in Rome once again.

The effect of performing penance is Transformation. (Hawthorne did not like this title which his English publishers gave to the novel, even though he suggested it himself.) The murder in Chapter 19 begins the transformation of all involved: Donatello falls from primal innocence in murdering the Model; Hilda has a similar fall by witnessing the act. Miriam and Kenyon, more firmly anchored in experience to begin with, are transformed by love. Miriam raises the central question to Kenyon in the end: "Was that very sin—into which Adam precipitated himself and all his race—was it the destined means by which, over a long pathway of toil and sorrow, we are to attain a higher, brighter, and profounder happiness, than our lost birthright gave? Will not this idea account for the permitted existence of sin, as no other theory can?" (p. 419).

There are many questions and answers after this question —too many. But before evaluating *The Marble Faun*—a task which each reader must do for himself—we might note the extraordinary degree to which the book is organized around physical scenes.

Hawthorne uses studio scenes to show us Miriam and Kenyon at work, tower scenes to show us Hilda and Donatello at home, monument scenes to show us Rome and Perugia, church scenes to show us in turn catacomb, chapel, and cathedral, festival scenes to give us the temper of Rome during the Carnival, country scenes (the Medici Gardens, Tuscany, and the Campagna) in contrast to the festival scenes, mythic scenes evoking the Faun, Beatrice Cenci, and Monte Beni, and functional scenes to introduce, connect, and conclude the action. Thus one could, if he wished, classify every chapter in the book to show the impact of Italian places on Hawthorne's imagination.

We might conclude with a few questions: Are art and sin only thematic pegs to hang a story on, or do they have a deeper, more personal meaning?

Second, how much does Hawthorne's slack technique impair the book? All the critics, starting with Hawthorne himself, acknowledge the excessive passages of rambling narrative commentary, the absence of dramatic incident for long stretches, and the inert passages about Rome and art. Does the richly evoked atmosphere compensate for the looseness of structure? One might compare the book to *The House of the Seven Gables* in this respect.

Third, how effective are the deliberate ambiguities: Miriam's dark past and her relationship to the Model and Beatrice Cenci; Donatello's nature (human or faun?) and his ears; the whereabouts of Donatello, Miriam, and Hilda during the last chapters?

Fourth, what is Hawthorne's attitude toward the Church? Unlike Dicey and Story, he was not concerned with its political problems. Though he had strong reservations about it, he was undeniably impressed by its spiritual position. How does he use ecclesiastical material in his book?

Fifth, how completely does Hawthorne endorse the *felix culpa* theme? Is personal sin necessary as a prerequisite for salvation, or is the sin of Adam sufficiently comprehensive to serve as that prerequisite? And how does his treatment of this problem differ from that in *The Scarlet Letter*?

Sixth, what are his sources for the murder and the characters (e.g., is the Praslin murder case a source for the Model's death; how completely does Hawthorne project himself into Kenyon, and Sophia into Hilda)? Like most critical questions, these involve matters of degree which each reader must decide for himself.

If we no longer read *The Marble Faun* as a guidebook to Italy (a Victorian bishop made it required reading before every trip), we read it in other terms—psychological, topical, thematic, historical, or whatever. This is natural and necessary. As Henry James said long ago, there is but one test for a work of fiction: the amount of felt life that it contains. Feeling that life in *The Marble Faun* is a rewarding experience for the modern reader. And the fact that we continue to read the work at all, over a century after its composition, is a testament to the art and the craft of our first great novelist.

Richard H. Rupp   *Coral Gables, Florida*
                                                      October, 1970

Nathaniel Hawthorne Chronology

1804   Born July 4, in Salem, Massachusetts, son of Nathaniel Hathorne, sea captain, and Elizabeth Clarke Manning Hathorne.

1808   His father died in Surinam (Dutch Guiana) while on a voyage.

1818   Moved with his mother and two sisters to Raymond, Maine, where his mother had family and property.

1819   Returned to school in Salem.

1821   Entered Bowdoin College.

1825   Was graduated from Bowdoin and returned to his mother's house in Salem.

1828   Paid to have *Fanshawe* published.

1837   *Twice-Told Tales* published; continued writing stories for magazines and doing hack work for publishers.

1839   Became engaged to marry Sophia Peabody of Salem; took a post in the Boston Custom House.

1841   Joined Brook Farm.

1842   Married Sophia Peabody and settled at the Old Manse.

1844   A daughter, Una, born.

1846   Moved to Salem and became Surveyor of Customs; published *Mosses from an Old Manse;* a son, Julian, born.

1849   Left Custom House and completed *The Scarlet Letter*.

1850   *The Scarlet Letter* published; good critical reception; moved to Tanglewood in Lenox, Massachusetts, where he became friendly with Herman Melville, who lived nearby and was working then on *Moby-Dick*, which he dedicated to Hawthorne.

1851　*The House of the Seven Gables* and *The Snow-Image and Other Twice-Told Tales* published; moved to West Newton, Massachusetts; a daughter, Rose, born.

1852　*The Blithedale Romance* published; moved to the Wayside in Concord.

1853　Went to Liverpool as United States Consul.

1857　Consular appointment ended; traveled on the continent and settled in Italy.

1859　Returned to live for some months in England, where he finished *The Marble Faun* at Royal Leamington Spa, Warwickshire, and at Redcar, Yorkshire, on the North Sea coast.

1860　*The Marble Faun* published; returned to the Wayside.

1863　*Our Old Home*, sketches of England, published.

1864　Died May 19, in Plymouth, New Hampshire, while on a vacation trip with Franklin Pierce; buried May 23, in Concord.

Selected Bibliography

I. HAWTHORNE'S CHIEF WORKS

Fanshawe: A Tale, 1828; *Twice-Told Tales,* 1837; *Mosses from an Old Manse,* 1846; *The Scarlet Letter,* 1850; *The House of the Seven Gables,* 1851; *The Snow-Image and Other Twice-Told Tales,* 1851; *The Blithedale Romance,* 1852; *Tanglewood Tales for Girls and Boys,* 1853; *The Marble Faun,* 1860; *Our Old Home,* 1863; *Septimius Felton: or, The Elixir of Life,* 1872; *The Dolliver Romance and Other Pieces,* 1876; *Dr. Grimshawe's Secret,* 1883.

II. COLLECTED EDITIONS

The Complete Works of Nathaniel Hawthorne. 12 vols. Riverside Edition. Boston, 1883.

The Complete Writings of Nathaniel Hawthorne. 22 vols. "Old Manse Edition." Boston, 1900.

A definitive edition of the complete works of Hawthorne is now in preparation by the Ohio State University Press and the Center for Editions of American Authors. *The Marble Faun* appeared in 1968 in this edition.

III. LETTERS AND NOTEBOOKS

Letters of Hawthorne to William D. Ticknor, 1851–1864. 2 vols. Newark, 1910. Letters to his publisher.

Love Letters of Nathaniel Hawthorne, 1833–41 and 1841–63. Chicago, 1907.

Passages from the French and Italian Note-books, ed. Sophia Hawthorne. Boston, 1872. An expurgated edition by Hawthorne's wife, suppressing personal references, indecorous opinions, and passages used in *The Marble Faun.* This appeared in 1883 as volume 10 of the Riverside Edition, ed. George Parsons Lathrop.

The American Notebooks by Nathaniel Hawthorne, ed. Randall Stewart. New Haven, 1932.

The English Notebooks by Nathaniel Hawthorne, ed. Randall Stewart. New York, 1941, 1962.

IV. BIBLIOGRAPHY

There is no definitive bibliography of Hawthorne's works. A guide to the existing ones appears in Robert E. Spiller and others, *Literary History of the United States: Bibliography* (New York, 1963), pp. 544–553, and *Bibliography Supplement,* pp. 133–136.

The annual *American Literary Scholarship 1963——,* ed. James Woodress and others (Durham, 1964——), contains useful annotated entries.

V. BIOGRAPHY

Stewart, Randall. *Nathaniel Hawthorne: A Biography.* New Haven, 1948. The standard modern biography.

The three most influential critical biographies of Hawthorne are:

James, Henry. *Hawthorne.* London, 1879.
Arvin, Newton. *Hawthorne.* Boston, 1929.
Van Doren, Mark. *Nathaniel Hawthorne.* New York, 1949.

VI. SPECIAL STUDIES OF *The Marble Faun*

Barnett, Gene A. "Hawthorne's Italian Calendar," *ESQ*, No. 43, 68–70. Dates and events of the stories in the 1850's, from March of one year to November of the next. Includes a chronology of each stage in the action.

———. "Hawthorne's Italian Towers," *Studies in Romanticism*, 3 (1964), 252–256. Argues that the towers of Miriam, Hilda, and especially, Donatello, are symbols of spiritual penitence and regeneration.

Bercovitch, Sacvan. "Of Wise and Foolish Virgins: Hilda Versus Miriam in Hawthorne's *Marble Faun*," *NEQ*, 41 (1968), 281–286. Attempts to explain Hilda's partial rejection of Miriam in terms of the parable in Matthew 25; Hilda gently refuses to corrupt Miriam for her own good—she must seek repentence for herself.

Brancaccio, Patrick. "The Ramble and the Pilgrimage: A Critical Reading of Hawthorne's *Marble Faun*," *DA*, 28: 4165A (Rutgers). A doctoral dissertation considering Hawthorne's response to art and artists in Rome, his use of the travel-book genre, pagan and Christian contrasts (Donatello and Hilda), psychological contrasts (Miriam and Kenyon), and the Italian setting and landscape.

Brodtkorb, Paul, Jr. "Art Allegory in *The Marble Faun*," *PMLA*, 77 (1962), 254–267. Reads the books as an insufficiently developed parable of art, concentrating on Hilda and Kenyon as Protestants, artists, and lovers; concludes that Hawthorne rejected the terms with which he began and may have rejected visual art.

Brown, Merle E. "The Structure of *The Marble Faun*," *AL*, 28 (1956), 302–313. Argues a fourfold transformation: of Miriam (chs. 1–23); of Donatello (chs. 24–35); of Hilda (chs. 36–42); and of Kenyon (chs. 43–50), all dramatically interrelated by a similar action—entry into the community of sinners.

Crews, Frederick C. *The Sins of the Fathers: Hawthorne's Psychological Themes.* New York, 1966. A controversial reading of the personal preoccupations and conflicts which undermined Hawthorne as a writer after *The Marble Faun.*

Cronin, Martin. "Hawthorne on Romantic Love and the Status of Women," *PMLA*, 69 (1954), 89–98. A general treatment of Hawthorne's heroines, stressing romantic conventions and attitudes in their make-up.

Davidson, Edward H. *Hawthorne's Last Phase.* New Haven, 1949. Concerned with the problems presented by the unfinished romances which followed *The Marble Faun.*

Earnest, Ernest. *Expatriates and Patriots: American Artists, Scholars, and Writers in Europe.* Durham, North Carolina, 1968. Chapter 4, "The Artists," is an informative historical account of the American artists before and during Hawthorne's stay in Rome. Chapter 6, "The Ambivalent Puritan," argues that Hawthorne remained an American Puritan in Italy.

Fogle, Richard H. *Hawthorne's Fiction: The Light and the Dark.* Norman, Okla., 1952. Chapter 11 discusses the antitheses which Hawthorne projects: "to some extent complexity=humanity=dead matter in *The Marble Faun,* while simplicity=divinity=immortality=life and light." A good analysis of the symbolic function of art and life, Rome and Monte Beni.

Hart, James D. "Hawthorne's Italian Diary," *AL*, 34 (1963), 562–567. A newly discovered diary Hawthorne kept while in Rome fills in gaps during the Roman stay as recorded in the *Note-books,* and dates the beginning of work on the book as Oct. 25, 1858.

Hoeltje, Hubert H. *Inward Sky: The Mind and Art of Nathaniel Hawthorne.* Durham, 1962. Pages 494–515. A biographical approach to the work, arguing the continuity of Hawthorne's literary preoccupations at every stage of his career.

Howard, David. "The Fortunate Fall and Hawthorne's

Marble Faun." In *Romantic Mythologies*, ed. Ian Fletcher. New York, 1967. Pages 97–136. Discusses the characters as Americans vs. Europeans undergoing "the final mockery of the fortunate fall." Treats the unresolved ironies of Hilda's having things both ways and the corruption latent in art.

Levin, Harry. "Statues from Italy: *The Marble Faun.*" In *Hawthorne Centenary Essays*, ed. Roy Harvey Pearce. Columbus, 1964. Pages 119–140. A full analysis of the work, touching on most of the major issues: art, Italy, characterization, the thematic resolution, and the Beatrice Cenci parallel.

Levy, Leo B. "*The Marble Faun:* Hawthorne's Landscape of the Fall," *AL*, 42 (1970), 139–156. Argues that the novel reveals Hawthorne's profound ambivalence regarding America's future. Hilda represents the American Protestant denial of inherent European corruption, but Hawthorne doubted her immunity to sin and America's national innocence, which she represents, even though he apparently endorses it.

Liebman, Sheldon W. "The Design of *The Marble Faun*," *NEQ*, 40 (1967), 61–78. An analysis of motifs in the action: the fortunate fall, transformation, dramatic oppositions within and between chapters, dead bodies, dancing and pilgrimage, all reinforcing "Hawthorne's final comment that life is both absurd and pathetic, both meaningful and meaningless."

Mahan, Helen A. "Hawthorne's *Marble Faun*: A Critical Introduction and Annotations." *DA*, 27 (1966): 1341 A (Rochester). A doctoral dissertation considering Hawthorne's life in Europe, the composition of the novel, its publication history and critical reception, his use of the notebooks in writing the novel, the sources, and a critical evaluation with annotations.

Male, Roy. *Hawthorne's Tragic Vision.* Austin, Texas, 1957. Chapter 9 discusses the transformation effect and the importance of the number 7 in the meaning and structure of the book. Male notes the spiritual significance of painting and sculpture, identifies the Capuchin as Miriam's cousin and ex-fiance, and concludes that "in order to develop his full human potential, man must become fully involved with time yet retain his unique ability to stand aside from its fleeting onrush and contemplate the eternal."

Martin, Terence. *Nathaniel Hawthorne*. New York, 1965. A bio-critical study in the Twayne series, containing an excellent general survey of the theme and characters in Chapter 9. Martin concludes that "Hilda has the final answers."

Matthiessen, F. O. *American Renaissance*. New York, 1941. Pages 179–368. A fine study of the cultural and literary context in which Hawthorne developed. Claims the establishment of "a world of solid moral values" as the principal achievement of the book.

Mills, Barriss. "Hawthorne and Puritanism," *NEQ*, 21 (1948), 78–102. A general survey of Hawthorne's consistently Puritan outlook, emphasizing predestination and education by sin in the book.

Moss, Sidney P. "The Problem of Theme in *The Marble Faun*," *NCF*, 18 (1964), 393–399. A thematic study of the fall of man, stressing Hawthorne's characteristic ambiguity—it is neither fortunate, nor unfortunate, necessarily.

————. "The Symbolism of the Background of *The Marble Faun*," *NCF*, 23 (1968), 332–336. Hawthorne used "mirror images" to develop a moral change in Donatello as he moves from Etruscan (pre-lapsarian) to Roman (pagan) to Christian (penitent) identity.

Pearce, Roy Harvey. "Hawthorne and the Twilight of Romance," *Yale Review*, 37 (1948), 487–506. Suggests that formally speaking, the book is a failure—didactic, forced, and melodramatic. But the form is really the earlier short form or sketch, here transported across the Atlantic and stretched beyond its normal length.

Porte, Joel. *The Romance in America: Studies in Cooper, Poe, Hawthorne, Melville, and James*. Middletown, Conn., 1969. Chapter 3, "Hawthorne," deals with all four novels. In *The Marble Faun*, Porte argues, the characters represent versions of the author's self in varying artistic roles; art, like life, requires a complex awareness of each character.

Scrimgeour, Gary J. "*The Marble Faun*: Hawthorne's Faery Land," *AL*, 36 (1964), 271–287. Argues that art and morality are closely interwoven in the Italian scene, which itself becomes a vital resource for Hawthorne in the novel. Here Hawthorne is closer to James than to Melville.

Ticknor, Caroline. *Hawthorne and His Publisher*. Boston, 1913. Chapter 14 is a log of the circumstances surrounding the writing of the book. Very helpful in assessing Hawthorne's own attitude toward his book.

Voight, Gilbert P. "Hawthorne and the Roman Catholic Church," *NEQ*, 19 (1946), 394–398. An appreciation of Hawthorne's attitude toward the Church, claiming that Hilda speaks for him. Hawthorne liked the Roman liturgy and the practice of confession.

Von Abele, Rudolph. *The Death of the Artist: A Study of Hawthorne's Disintegration*. The Hague, 1955. Chapter 7 argues that the tension in Hawthorne's art between idealism and sex caused the novel to fail.

Waggoner, Hyatt Howe. *Hawthorne: A Critical Study*. Revised edition, Cambridge, 1963. Chapter 8, rewritten for this second edition, discusses the Fortunate Fall, the Kenyon-Hilda, Hawthorne-Sophia parallel, the mythology of the book, and the weakness of the novel as an allegory.

Waples, Dorothy. "Suggestions for Interpreting *The Marble Faun*," *AL*, 13 (1941), 224–239. Approaches the book through Freudian principles, especially those of timelessness, myth and the unconscious, repetition-compulsion, the death wish, and the contest between life and death. Also notes parallel concerns in the work of Thomas Mann.

Wegelin, Christof. "Europe in Hawthorne's Fiction," *ELH*, 14 (1947), 219–245. Draws parallels between the letters and the journals of the Roman period and the text of the novel.

Woodberry, George E. *Nathaniel Hawthorne*. Boston,

1902. An early study of Hawthorne; contains a brief analysis of the novel, pp. 270–278, in the light of the author's imaginative preoccupations in his last years; laments the lack of structure.

Wright, Nathalia. "Hawthorne and the Praslin Murder," *NEQ*, 15 (1942), 5–14. Cites an analogue for the case of Miriam in the murder and suicide of the Duc de Choiseul-Praslin over an affair with his governess, Mlle. Henriette Deluzy-Desportes, a woman whom Hawthorne may have been introduced to in 1851.

The Marble Faun:

OR,

The Romance of Monte Beni

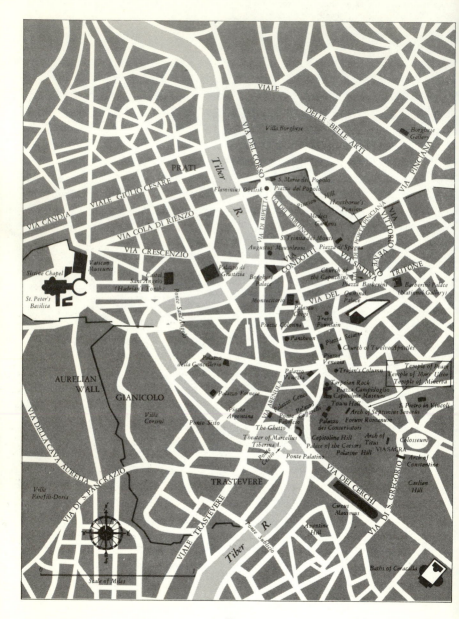

Rome

Preface

It is now seven or eight years (so many, at all events, that I cannot precisely remember the epoch) since the author of this romance last appeared before the Public.[1] It had grown to be a custom with him to introduce each of his humble publications with a familiar kind of preface, addressed nominally to the Public at large, but really to a character with whom he felt entitled to use far greater freedom. He meant it for that one congenial friend,—more comprehensive of his purposes, more appreciative of his success, more indulgent of his short-comings, and, in all respects, closer and kinder than a brother,—that all-sympathizing critic, in short, whom an author never actually meets, but to whom he implicitly makes his appeal whenever he is conscious of having done his best.

The antique fashion of Prefaces recognized this genial personage as the "Kind Reader," the "Gentle Reader," the "Beloved," the "Indulgent," or, at coldest, the "Honored Reader," to whom the prim old author was wont to make his preliminary explanations and apologies, with the certainty that they would be favorably received. I never personally encountered, nor corresponded through the post with this representative essence of all delightful and desirable qualities which a reader can possess. But, fortunately for myself, I never therefore concluded him to be merely a mythic character. I had always a sturdy faith in his actual existence, and wrote for him year after year, during which the great eye of the Public (as well it might) almost utterly overlooked my small productions.

[1] *The Blithedale Romance*, Hawthorne's third novel, appeared in 1852.

Unquestionably, this gentle, kind, benevolent, indulgent, and most beloved and honored Reader did once exist for me, and (in spite of the infinite chances against a letter's reaching its destination without a definite address) duly received the scrolls which I flung upon whatever wind was blowing, in the faith that they would find him out. But, is he extant now? In these many years, since he last heard from me, may he not have deemed his earthly task accomplished, and have withdrawn to the paradise of gentle readers, wherever it may be, to the enjoyments of which his kindly charity on my behalf must surely have entitled him? I have a sad foreboding that this may be the truth. The "Gentle Reader," in the case of any individual author, is apt to be extremely short-lived; he seldom outlasts a literary fashion, and, except in very rare instances, closes his weary eyes before the writer has half done with him. If I find him at all, it will probably be under some mossy gravestone, inscribed with a half-obliterated name which I shall never recognize.

Therefore, I have little heart or confidence (especially, writing as I do, in a foreign land, and after a long, long absence from my own) to presume upon the existence of that friend of friends, that unseen brother of the soul, whose apprehensive sympathy has so often encouraged me to be egotistical in my prefaces, careless though unkindly eyes should skim over what was never meant for them. I stand upon ceremony, now; and, after stating a few particulars about the work which is here offered to the Public, must make my most reverential bow, and retire behind the curtain.

This Romance was sketched out during a residence of considerable length in Italy, and has been re-written and prepared for the press in England. The author proposes to himself merely to write a fanciful story, evolving a thoughtful moral, and did not purpose attempting a portraiture of Italian manners and character. He has lived too long abroad not to be aware that a foreigner seldom acquires that knowledge of a country at once flexible and profound, which may justify him in endeavoring to idealize its traits.

Italy, as the site of his Romance, was chiefly valuable to him as affording a sort of poetic or fairy precinct, where actualities would not be so terribly insisted upon as they are, and must needs be, in America. No author, without a trial, can conceive of the difficulty of writing a romance about a country where there is no shadow, no antiquity, no mystery, no picturesque and gloomy wrong, nor anything but a commonplace prosperity, in broad and simple daylight, as is happily the case with my dear native land. It will be very long, I trust, before romance-writers may find congenial and easily handled themes, either in the annals of our stalwart republic, or in any characteristic and probable events of our individual lives. Romance and poetry, like ivy, lichens, and wall-flowers, need ruin to make them grow.

In re-writing these volumes, the author was somewhat surprised to see the extent to which he had introduced descriptions of various Italian objects, antique, pictorial, and statuesque. Yet these things fill the mind everywhere in Italy, and especially in Rome, and cannot easily be kept from flowing out upon the page when one writes freely, and with self-enjoyment. And, again, while reproducing the book, on the broad and dreary sands of Redcar,[2] with the gray German Ocean tumbling in upon me, and the northern blast always howling in my ears, the complete change of scene made these Italian reminiscences shine out so vividly that I could not find it in my heart to cancel them.

An act of justice remains to be performed towards two men of genius with whose productions the author has allowed himself to use a quite unwarrantable freedom. Having imagined a sculptor in this Romance, it was necessary to provide him with such works in marble as should be in keeping with the artistic ability which he was supposed to possess. With this view, the author laid felonious hands upon a certain bust of Milton, and a statue of a pearl-diver, which he found in the

[2]A small resort town in northeast Yorkshire, on the shores of the North Sea.

studio of Mr. PAUL AKERS,[3] and secretly conveyed them to the premises of his imaginary friend, in the Via Frezza. Not content even with these spoils, he committed a further robbery upon a magnificent statue of Cleopatra, the production of Mr. WILLIAM W. STORY,[4] an artist whom his country and the world will not long fail to appreciate. He had thoughts of appropriating, likewise, a certain door of bronze by Mr. RANDOLPH ROGERS,[5] representing the history of Columbus in a series of admirable bas-reliefs, but was deterred by an unwillingness to meddle with public property. Were he capable of stealing from a lady, he would certainly have made free with Miss HOSMER's[6] admirable statue of Zenobia.

He now wishes to restore the above-mentioned beautiful pieces of sculpture to their proper owners, with many thanks, and the avowal of his sincere admiration. What he has said of them in the Romance, does not partake of the fiction in which they are imbedded, but expresses his genuine opinion, which he has little doubt, will be found in accordance with that of the Public. It is, perhaps, unnecessary to say, that, while stealing their designs, the Author has not taken a similar liberty with the personal characters of either of these gifted sculptors; his own man of marble being entirely imaginary.

Leamington, October 15, 1859

[3]Benjamin Paul Akers (1825–1861), writer and sculptor who received recognition in Rome. He did busts of Hawthorne's two famous classmates, Longfellow and Franklin Pierce.

[4]William Wetmore Story (1819–1895), American classical sculptor who settled in Rome in 1856; his studio was a social and artistic salon.

[5]Randolph Rogers (1825–1892), American sculptor who moved to Italy in 1848 and worked in the classical mode.

[6]Harriet Hosmer (1830–1908), an American sculptress who spent most of her life in Rome. Among her statues are *The Sleeping Faun, The Waking Faun*, and *Beatrice Cenci*, the latter in the St. Louis Mercantile Library.

THE ROMANCE OF MONTE BENI

CHAPTER I. *Miriam, Hilda,
Kenyon, Donatello*

Four individuals, in whose fortunes we should be glad
to interest the reader, happened to be standing in one of the
saloons of the sculpture-gallery in the Capitol at Rome. It was
that room (the first, after ascending the staircase) in the centre
of which reclines the noble and most pathetic figure of the
Dying Gladiator, just sinking into his death-swoon. Around the
walls stand the Antinous, the Amazon, the Lycian Apollo, the
Juno;[1] all famous productions of antique sculpture, and still
shining in the undiminished majesty and beauty of their ideal
life, although the marble that embodies them is yellow with
time, and perhaps corroded by the damp earth in which they
lay buried for centuries. Here, likewise, is seen a symbol (as apt
at this moment as it was two thousand years ago) of the Human

[1]In the Capitoline Museum, *The Dying Gladiator* (properly *The
Dying Gaul*) is a marble copy of an original by the Greek sculptor called
Epigonus (2nd century B.C.), depicting a fallen Galatian warrior. Antinous
(*fl.* A.D. 117–138), who was drowned in the Nile, was a favorite of the
Emperor Hadrian (*fl.* A.D. 117–138); this is one of many statues to his
memory commissioned by Hadrian. The Amazon was a warlike woman of
great size in Greek legend; in the Trojan Wars the Amazons opposed the
Greeks, and the Amazon leader, Penthesilia, was slain by Achilles. Most
statues of Amazons are imitations of that by Polyclitus, who, along with
Phidias and Myron, was the founder of the Greek school. Apollo was the
god of reason and the sun. Hawthorne notes that "the corroded and discolored surfaces of the statues take away from the impression of immortal
youth, and turn Apollo himself into an old stone; unless at rare intervals,
when he appears transfigured by a light gleaming from within." (*NB*, p.
495). Lycia was an ancient country in Asia Minor. Juno was sister and
wife to Jupiter and queen of the gods.

Soul, with its choice of Innocence or Evil close at hand, in the pretty figure of a child, clasping a dove to her bosom, but assaulted by a snake.

From one of the windows of this saloon, we may see a flight of broad stone steps, descending alongside the antique and massive foundation of the Capitol, towards the battered triumphal arch of Septimius Severus, right below. Farther on, the eye skirts along the edge of the desolate Forum,[2] (where Roman washerwomen hang out their linen to the sun,) passing over a shapeless confusion of modern edifices, piled rudely up with ancient brick and stone, and over the domes of Christian churches, built on the old pavements of heathen temples, and supported by the very pillars that once upheld them. At a distance beyond—yet but a little way, considering how much history is heaped into the intervening space—rises the great sweep of the Coliseum, with the blue sky brightening through its upper tier of arches. Far off, the view is shut in by the Alban mountains, looking just the same, amid all this decay and change, as when Romulus[3] gazed thitherward over his half-finished wall.

We glance hastily at these things—at this bright sky, and those blue, distant mountains, and at the ruins, Etruscan, Roman, Christian, venerable with a threefold antiquity, and at the company of world-famous statues in the saloon—in the hope of putting the reader into that state of feeling which is experienced oftenest at Rome. It is a vague sense of ponderous remembrances; a perception of such weight and density in a bygone life, of which this spot was the centre, that the present

[2]The narrator is looking southeast from the window of the Capitoline Museum toward the oldest ruins in Rome. Septimius Severus (*fl.* A.D. 193–211) did much to beautify Rome; he was succeeded by his son, Caracalla. The Forum was an open meeting place, expanded in imperial times and allowed to fall into ruins thereafter.

[3]The Coliseum, marking the end of the ancient quarter in Rome, was much favored by American tourists and British poets. Romulus was the legendary founder of Rome in 753 B.C. Hawthorne is trying to evoke the antiquity of Rome by mentioning him here, as he explains in the next paragraph.

moment is pressed down or crowded out, and our individual affairs and interests are but half as real here as elsewhere. Viewed through this medium, our narrative—into which are woven some airy and unsubstantial threads, intermixed with others, twisted out of the commonest stuff of human existence —may seem not widely different from the texture of all our lives.

Side by side with the massiveness of the Roman Past, all matters that we handle or dream of now-a-days look evanescent and visionary alike.

It might be that the four persons whom we are seeking to introduce, were conscious of this dreamy character of the present, as compared with the square blocks of granite where-with the Romans built their lives. Perhaps it even contributed to the fanciful merriment which was just now their mood. When we find ourselves fading into shadows and unrealities, it seems hardly worth while to be sad, but rather to laugh as gaily as we may, and ask little reason wherefore.

Of these four friends of ours, three were artists, or con-nected with art; and, at this moment, they had been simul-taneously struck by a resemblance between one of the antique statues, a well-known masterpiece of Grecian sculpture, and a young Italian, the fourth member of their party.

"You must needs confess, Kenyon," said a dark-eyed young woman, whom her friends called Miriam, "that you never chiselled out of marble, nor wrought in clay, a more vivid likeness than this, cunning a bust-maker as you think yourself. The portraiture is perfect in character, sentiment, and feature. If it were a picture, the resemblance might be half illusive and imaginary; but here, in this Pentelic marble, it is a substantial fact, and may be tested by absolute touch and meas-urement. Our friend Donatello is the very Faun of Praxiteles.[4] Is it not true, Hilda?"

"Not quite—almost—yes, I really think so," replied Hilda,

[4]Praxiteles, a 4th-century B.C. sculptor, was the acknowledged mas-ter of Athenian marble-workers. The Vatican Museum contains a copy of his *Aphrodite of Cnidus.*

a slender, brown-haired, New England girl, whose perceptions
of form and expression were wonderfully clear and delicate. "If
there is any difference between the two faces, the reason may
be, I suppose, that the Faun dwelt in woods and fields, and
consorted with his like; whereas, Donatello has known cities a
little, and such people as ourselves. But the resemblance is very
close, and very strange."

"Not so strange," whispered Miriam, mischievously; "for
no Faun in Arcadia[5] was ever a greater simpleton than Donatello. He has hardly a man's share of wit, small as that may be.
It is a pity there are no longer any of this congenial race of
rustic creatures for our friend to consort with!"

"Hush, naughty one!" returned Hilda. "You are very
ungrateful, for you well know he has wit enough to worship
you, at all events."

"Then the greater fool he!" said Miriam, so bitterly that
Hilda's quiet eyes were somewhat startled.

"Donatello, my dear friend," said Kenyon, in Italian,
"pray gratify us all by taking the exact attitude of this statue."

The young man laughed, and threw himself into the position in which the statue has been standing for two or three
thousand years. In truth, allowing for the difference of costume, and if a lion's skin could have been substituted for his
modern talma, and a rustic pipe for his stick, Donatello might
have figured perfectly as the marble Faun, miraculously softened into flesh and blood.

"Yes; the resemblance is wonderful," observed Kenyon,
after examining the marble and the man with the accuracy of
a sculptor's eye. "There is one point, however, or, rather, two
points, in respect to which our friend Donatello's abundant
curls will not permit us to say whether the likeness is carried
into minute detail."

And the sculptor directed the attention of the party to

[5]Arcadia, or Arcady, was a landlocked, mountainous area of the
Peloponnesus.

the ears of the beautiful statue which they were contemplating.

But we must do more than merely refer to this exquisite work of art; it must be described, however inadequate may be the effort to express its magic peculiarity in words.

The Faun is the marble image of a young man, leaning his right arm on the trunk or stump of a tree;[6] one hand hangs carelessly by his side; in the other he holds the fragment of a pipe, or some such sylvan instrument of music. His only garment—a lion's skin, with the claw upon his shoulder—falls half way down his back, leaving the limbs and entire front of the figure nude. The form, thus displayed, is marvellously graceful, but has a fuller and more rounded outline, more flesh, and less of heroic muscle than the old sculptors were wont to assign to their types of masculine beauty. The character of the face corresponds with the figure; it is most agreeable in outline and feature, but rounded and somewhat voluptuously developed, especially about the throat and chin; the nose is almost straight,

[6]See the frontispiece. There is some doubt that the statue was actually carved by Praxiteles. The Faun is a Roman woodland deity similar to the Greek Pan. His Festival, the Lupercal, was observed in February and coincides with the Christian Carnival, or Shrove Tuesday celebration. Throughout *The Marble Faun* Hawthorne deliberately mixes pagan and Christian elements. Two notebook entries are relevant here: about the Faun itself Hawthorne says, "The race of fauns was the most delightful of all that antiquity imagined. It seems to me that a story, with all sorts of fun and pathos in it, might be contrived on the idea of their species having become intermingled with the human race; a family with the faun blood in them having prolonged itself from the classic era to our own days. The tail might have disappeared, by dint of constant intermarriages with ordinary mortals; but the pretty hairy ears should occasionally reappear in members of the family; and the moral instincts and intellectual characteristics of the faun might be most picturesquely brought out, without detriment to the human interest of the story. Fancy this combination in the person of a young lady!" (*NB*, p. 173). The second passage is a further reflection on the Faun: "I like these strange, sweet, playful, rustic creatures . . . linked so prettily, without monstrosity, to the lower tribes. . . . The faun is a natural and delightful link betwixt human and brute life, with something of a divine character intermingled" (*NB*, p. 167).

but very slightly curved inward, thereby acquiring an indescribable charm of geniality and humor. The mouth, with its
full yet delicate lips, seems so nearly to smile outright, that it
calls forth a responsive smile. The whole statue—unlike anything else that ever was wrought in that severe material of marble—conveys the idea of an amiable and sensual creature, easy,
mirthful, apt for jollity, yet not incapable of being touched by
pathos. It is impossible to gaze long at this stone image without
conceiving a kindly sentiment towards it, as if its substance were
warm to the touch, and imbued with actual life. It comes very
close to some of our pleasantest sympathies.

Perhaps it is the very lack of moral severity, of any high
and heroic ingredient in the character of the Faun, that makes
it so delightful an object to the human eye and to the frailty of
the human heart. The being here represented is endowed with
no principle of virtue, and would be incapable of comprehending such; but he would be true and honest by dint of his simplicity. We should expect from him no sacrifice nor effort for
an abstract cause; there is not an atom of martyr's stuff in all
that softened marble; but he has a capacity for strong and warm
attachment, and might act devotedly through its impulse, and
even die for it at need. It is possible, too, that the Faun might
be educated through the medium of his emotions, so that the
coarser animal portion of his nature might eventually be
thrown into the background, though never utterly expelled.

The animal nature, indeed, is a most essential part of the
Faun's composition; for the characteristics of the brute creation meet and combine with those of humanity in this strange
yet true and natural conception of antique poetry and art.
Praxiteles has subtly diffused throughout his work that mute
mystery which so hopelessly perplexes us whenever we attempt
to gain an intellectual or sympathetic knowledge of the lower
orders of creation. The riddle is indicated, however, only by
two definite signs: these are the two ears of the Faun, which are
leaf-shaped, terminating in little peaks, like those of some species of animals. Though not so seen in the marble, they are

probably to be considered as clothed in fine, downy fur. In the coarser representations of this class of mythological creatures, there is another token of brute kindred,—a certain caudal appendage; which, if the Faun of Praxiteles must be supposed to possess it at all, is hidden by the lion's skin that forms his garment. The pointed and furry ears, therefore, are the sole indications of his wild, forest nature.

Only a sculptor of the finest imagination, the most delicate taste, the sweetest feeling, and the rarest artistic skill—in a word, a sculptor and a poet too—could have first dreamed of a Faun in this guise, and then have succeeded in imprisoning the sportive and frisky thing in marble. Neither man nor animal, and yet no monster; but a being in whom both races meet on friendly ground! The idea grows coarse as we handle it, and hardens in our grasp. But, if the spectator broods long over the statue, he will be conscious of its spell; all the pleasantness of sylvan life, all the genial and happy characteristics of creatures that dwell in woods and fields, will seem to be mingled and kneaded into one substance, along with the kindred qualities in the human soul. Trees, grass, flowers, woodland streamlets, cattle, deer, and unsophisticated man! The essence of all these was compressed long ago, and still exists within that discolored marble surface of the Faun of Praxiteles.

And, after all, the idea may have been no dream, but rather a poet's reminiscence of a period when man's affinity with nature was more strict, and his fellowship with every living thing more intimate and dear.

CHAPTER 2. *The Faun*

"Donatello," playfully cried Miriam, "do not leave us in this perplexity! Shake aside those brown curls, my friend, and let us see whether this marvellous resemblance extends to the very tips of the ears. If so, we shall like you all the better!"

"No, no, dearest signorina," answered Donatello, laughing, but with a certain earnestness. "I entreat you to take the tips of my ears for granted." As he spoke, the young Italian made a skip and jump, light enough for a veritable faun; so as to place himself quite beyond the reach of the fair hand that was outstretched, as if to settle the matter by actual examination. "I shall be like a wolf of the Apennines," he continued, taking his stand on the other side of the Dying Gladiator, "if you touch my ears ever so softly. None of my race could endure it. It has always been a tender point with my forefathers and me."

He spoke in Italian, with the Tuscan rusticity of accent, and an unshaped sort of utterance, betokening that he must heretofore have been chiefly conversant with rural people.

"Well, well," said Miriam, "your tender point—your two tender points, if you have them—shall be safe, so far as I am concerned. But how strange this likeness is, after all! and how delightful, if it really includes the pointed ears! Oh, it is impossible, of course," she continued, in English, "with a real and commonplace young man like Donatello; but you see how this peculiarity defines the position of the Faun; and, while putting him where he cannot exactly assert his brotherhood, still disposes us kindly towards the kindred creature. He is not supernatural, but just on the verge of nature, and yet within it. What is the nameless charm of this idea, Hilda? You can feel it more delicately than I."

"It perplexes me," said Hilda, thoughtfully, and shrinking a little; "neither do I quite like to think about it."

"But, surely," said Kenyon, "you agree with Miriam and me, that there is something very touching and impressive in this statue of the Faun. In some long-past age, he must really have existed. Nature needed, and still needs, this beautiful creature; standing betwixt man and animal, sympathizing with each, comprehending the speech of either race, and interpreting the whole existence of one to the other. What a pity that he has forever vanished from the hard and dusty paths of life,— unless," added the sculptor, in a sportive whisper, "Donatello be actually he!"

"You cannot conceive how this fantasy takes hold of me," responded Miriam, between jest and earnest. "Imagine, now, a real being, similar to this mythic Faun; how happy, how genial, how satisfactory would be his life, enjoying the warm, sensuous, earthy side of nature; revelling in the merriment of woods and streams; living as our four-footed kindred do,—as mankind did in its innocent childhood; before sin, sorrow, or morality itself had ever been thought of! Ah! Kenyon, if Hilda and you and I—if I, at least,—had pointed ears! For I suppose the Faun had no conscience, no remorse, no burthen on the heart, no troublesome recollections of any sort; no dark future neither."

"What a tragic tone was that last, Miriam!" said the sculptor; and, looking into her face, he was startled to behold it pale and tear-stained. "How suddenly this mood has come over you!"

"Let it go as it came," said Miriam, "like a thundershower in this Roman sky. All is sunshine again, you see!"

Donatello's refractoriness as regarded his ears had evidently cost him something, and he now came close to Miriam's side, gazing at her with an appealing air, as if to solicit forgiveness. His mute, helpless gesture of entreaty had something pathetic in it, and yet might well enough excite a laugh, so like it was to what you may see in the aspect of a hound when he thinks himself in fault or disgrace. It was difficult to make out the character of this young man. So full of animal life as he was, so joyous in his deportment, so handsome, so physically well developed, he made no impression of incompleteness, of maimed or stinted nature. And yet, in social intercourse, these familiar friends of his habitually and instinctively allowed for him, as for a child or some other lawless thing, exacting no strict obedience to conventional rules, and hardly noticing his eccentricities enough to pardon them. There was an indefinable characteristic about Donatello that set him outside of rules.

He caught Miriam's hand, kissed it, and gazed into her eyes without saying a word. She smiled, and bestowed on him a little careless caress, singularly like what one would give to a pet dog when he puts himself in the way to receive it. Not that it was so decided a caress neither, but only the merest touch, somewhere between a pat and a tap of the finger; it might be a mark of fondness, or perhaps a playful pretense of punishment. At all events, it appeared to afford Donatello exquisite pleasure; insomuch that he danced quite round the wooden railing that fences in the Dying Gladiator.

"It is the very step of the Dancing Faun," said Miriam apart to Hilda. "What a child, or what a simpleton, he is! I continually find myself treating Donatello as if he were the merest unfledged chicken; and yet he can claim no such privileges in the right of his tender age; for he is at least—how old should you think him, Hilda?"

"Twenty years, perhaps," replied Hilda, glancing at Donatello; "but, indeed, I cannot tell; hardly so old, on second thoughts, or possibly older. He has nothing to do with time, but has a look of eternal youth in his face."

"All underwitted people have that look," said Miriam, scornfully.

"Donatello has certainly the gift of eternal youth, as Hilda suggests," observed Kenyon, laughing; "for, judging by the date of this statue, which, I am more and more convinced, Praxiteles carved on purpose for him, he must be at least twenty-five centuries old, and he still looks as young as ever."

"What age have you, Donatello?" asked Miriam.

"Signorina, I do not know," he answered; "no great age, however; for I have only lived since I met you."

"Now, what old man of society could have turned a silly compliment more smartly than that!" exclaimed Miriam. "Nature and art are just at one sometimes. But what a happy ignorance is this of our friend Donatello! Not to know his own age! It is equivalent to being immortal on earth. If I could only forget mine!"

"It is too soon to wish that," observed the sculptor; "you are scarcely older than Donatello looks."

"I should be content, then," rejoined Miriam, "if I could only forget one day of all my life." Then she seemed to repent of this allusion, and hastily added, "A woman's days are so tedious that it is a boon to leave even one of them out of the account."

The foregoing conversation had been carried on in a mood in which all imaginative people, whether artists or poets, love to indulge. In this frame of mind, they sometimes find their profoundest truths side by side with the idlest jest, and utter one or the other, apparently without distinguishing which is the most valuable, or assigning any considerable value to either. The resemblance between the marble Faun and their living companion had made a deep, half-serious, half-mirthful impression on these three friends, and had taken them into a certain airy region, lifting up, as it is so pleasant to feel them lifted, their heavy earthly feet from the actual soil of life. The world had been set afloat, as it were, for a moment, and relieved them for just so long of all customary responsibility for what they thought and said.

It might be under this influence—or, perhaps, because sculptors always abuse one another's works—that Kenyon threw in a criticism upon the Dying Gladiator.

"I used to admire this statue exceedingly," he remarked, "but, latterly, I find myself getting weary and annoyed that the man should be such a length of time leaning on his arm in the very act of death. If he is so terribly hurt, why does he not sink down and die without further ado? Flitting moments, imminent emergencies, imperceptible intervals between two breaths, ought not to be encrusted with the eternal repose of marble; in any sculptural subject, there should be a moral standstill, since there must of necessity be a physical one. Otherwise, it is like flinging a block of marble up into the air, and by some trick or enchantment, causing it to stick there. You feel that it ought to come down, and are dissatisfied that it does not obey the natural law."

"I see," said Miriam, mischievously. "You think that sculpture should be a sort of fossilizing process. But, in truth, your frozen art has nothing like the scope and freedom of Hilda's and mine. In painting there is no similar objection to the representation of brief snatches of time; perhaps, because a story can be so much more fully told in picture, and buttressed about with circumstances that give it an epoch. For instance, a painter never would have sent down yonder Faun out of his far antiquity, lonely and desolate, with no companion to keep his simple heart warm."

"Ah, the Faun!" cried Hilda, with a little gesture of impatience; "I have been looking at him too long; and now, instead of a beautiful statue, immortally young, I see only a corroded and discolored stone. This change is very apt to occur in statues."

"And a similar one in pictures, surely," retorted the sculptor. "It is the spectator's mood that transfigures the Transfiguration[1] itself. I defy any painter to move and elevate me without my own consent and assistance."

---

[1]A celebrated painting by Raphael (1483–1520), depicting the Transfiguration of Christ on the mountain before Peter, James, and John. See Luke 9:28–36. The original hangs in the Vatican. Hawthorne saw it on April 25, 1858, and wrote in his notebook: "Approaching it, I felt that the picture was worthy of its fame, and was far better than I could at once appreciate; admirably preserved, too, though I fully believe it must have possessed a charm when it left Raphael's hand that has now vanished forever" (NB, p. 177).

"Then you are deficient of a sense," said Miriam.

The party now strayed onward from hall to hall of that rich gallery, pausing here and there, to look at the multitude of noble and lovely shapes, which have been dug up out of the deep grave in which old Rome lies buried. And, still, the realization of the antique Faun, in the person of Donatello, gave a more vivid character to all these marble ghosts. Why should not each statue grow warm with life! Antinous might lift his brow, and tell us why he is forever sad. The Lycian Apollo might strike his lyre; and, at the first vibration, that other Faun in red marble, who keeps up a motionless dance, should frisk gayly forth, leading yonder Satyrs, with shaggy goat-shanks, to clatter their little hoofs upon the floor, and all join hands with Donatello! Bacchus, too, a rosy flush diffusing itself over his time-stained surface, would come down from his pedestal, and offer a cluster of purple grapes to Donatello's lips: because the god recognizes him as the woodland elf who so often shared his revels. And here, on this sarcophagus, the exquisitely carved figures might assume life, and chase one another round its verge with that wild merriment which is so strangely represented on those old burial coffers; though still with some subtle allusion to death, carefully veiled, but forever peeping forth amid emblems of mirth and riot.

As the four friends descended the stairs, however, their play of fancy subsided into a much more sombre mood; a result apt to follow upon such exhilaration as that which had so recently taken possession of them.

"Do you know," said Miriam confidentially to Hilda, "I doubt the reality of this likeness of Donatello to the Faun, which we have been talking so much about? To say the truth, it never struck me so forcibly as it did Kenyon and yourself, though I gave in to whatever you were pleased to fancy, for the sake of a moment's mirth and wonder."

"I was certainly in earnest, and you seemed equally so," replied Hilda, glancing back at Donatello, as if to reassure herself of the resemblance. "But faces change so much, from hour

to hour, that the same set of features has often no keeping with
itself; to an eye, at least, which looks at expression more than
outline. How sad and sombre he has grown, all of a sudden!"

"Angry too, methinks! nay, it is anger much more than
sadness," said Miriam. "I have seen Donatello in this mood once
or twice before. If you consider him well, you will observe an
odd mixture of the bull-dog, or some other equally fierce brute,
in our friend's composition; a trait of savageness hardly to be
expected in such a gentle creature as he usually is. Donatello is
a very strange young man. I wish he would not haunt my footsteps so continually."

"You have bewitched the poor lad," said the sculptor
laughing. "You have a faculty of bewitching people, and it is
providing you with a singular train of followers. I see another
of them behind yonder pillar; and it is his presence that has
aroused Donatello's wrath."

They had now emerged from the gateway of the palace;
and partly concealed by one of the pillars of the portico, stood
a figure such as may often be encountered in the streets and
piazzas of Rome, and nowhere else. He looked as if he might
just have stepped out of a picture, and, in truth, was likely
enough to find his way into a dozen pictures; being no other
than one of those living models, dark, bushy-bearded, wild of
aspect and attire, whom artists convert into saints or assassins,
according as their pictorial purposes demand.

"Miriam," whispered Hilda, a little startled, "it is your
model!"

CHAPTER 3. *Subterranean Reminiscences*

Miriam's model has so important a connection with our story, that it is essential to describe the singular mode of his first appearance, and how he subsequently became a self-appointed follower of the young female artist. In the first place, however, we must devote a page or two to certain peculiarities in the position of Miriam herself.

There was an ambiguity about this young lady, which, though it did not necessarily imply anything wrong, would have operated unfavorably as regarded her reception in society, anywhere but in Rome. The truth was, that nobody knew anything about Miriam, either for good or evil. She had made her appearance without introduction, had taken a studio, put up her card upon the door, and shown very considerable talent as a painter in oils. Her fellow-professors of the brush, it is true, showered abundant criticisms upon her pictures, allowing them to be well enough for the idle half-efforts of an amateur, but lacking both the trained skill and the practice that distinguish the works of a true artist.

Nevertheless, be their faults what they might, Miriam's pictures met with good acceptance among the patrons of modern art. Whatever technical merit they lacked, its absence was more than supplied by a warmth and passionateness, which she had the faculty of putting into her productions, and which all the world could feel. Her nature had a great deal of color, and, in accordance with it, so likewise had her pictures.

Miriam had great apparent freedom of intercourse; her manners were so far from evincing shyness, that it seemed easy to become acquainted with her, and not difficult to develop a casual acquaintance into intimacy. Such, at least, was the impression which she made, upon brief contact, but not such the ultimate conclusion of those who really sought to know her. So airy, free, and affable was Miriam's deportment towards all who came within her sphere, that possibly they might never be conscious of the fact; but so it was, that they did not get on, and were seldom any further advanced into her good graces to-day than yesterday. By some subtle quality, she kept people at a distance, without so much as letting them know that they were excluded from her inner circle. She resembled one of those images of light, which conjurors evoke and cause to shine before us, in apparent tangibility, only an arm's length beyond our grasp: we make a step in advance, expecting to seize the illusion, but find it still precisely so far out of our reach. Finally, society began to recognize the impossibility of getting nearer to Miriam, and gruffly acquiesced.

There were two persons, however, whom she appeared to acknowledge as friends in the closer and truer sense of the word; and both of these more favored individuals did credit to Miriam's selection. One was a young American sculptor, of high promise and rapidly increasing celebrity; the other, a girl of the same country, a painter like Miriam herself, but in a widely different sphere of art. Her heart flowed out towards these two; she requited herself by their society and friendship (and especially by Hilda's) for all the loneliness with which, as regarded the rest of the world, she chose to be surrounded. Her two friends were conscious of the strong, yearning grasp which Miriam laid upon them, and gave her their affection in full measure; Hilda, indeed, responding with the fervency of a girl's first friendship, and Kenyon with a manly regard, in which there was nothing akin to what is distinctively called love.

A sort of intimacy subsequently grew up between these three friends and a fourth individual; it was a young Italian, who, casually visiting Rome, had been attracted by the beauty which Miriam possessed in a remarkable degree. He had sought her, followed her, and insisted, with simple perseverance, upon

being admitted at least to her acquaintance; a boon which had
been granted, when a more artful character, seeking it by a
more subtile mode of pursuit, would probably have failed to
obtain it. This young man, though anything but intellectually
brilliant, had many agreeable characteristics which won him the
kindly and half-contemptuous regard of Miriam and her two
friends. It was he whom they called Donatello, and whose wonderful resemblance to the Faun of Praxiteles forms the key-
note of our narrative.

Such was the position in which we find Miriam some few
months after her establishment at Rome. It must be added,
however, that the world did not permit her to hide her ante-
cedents without making her the subject of a good deal of conjecture; as was natural enough, considering the abundance of
her personal charms, and the degree of notice that she attracted
as an artist. There were many stories about Miriam's origin and
previous life, some of which had a very probable air, while
others were evidently wild and romantic fables. We cite a few,
leaving the reader to designate them either under the probable
or the romantic head.

It was said, for example, that Miriam was the daughter
and heiress of a great Jewish banker, (an idea perhaps suggested
by a certain rich Oriental character in her face,) and had fled
from her paternal home to escape a union with a cousin, the
heir of another of that golden brotherhood; the object being,
to retain their vast accumulation of wealth within the family.
Another story hinted, that she was a German princess, whom,
for reasons of state, it was proposed to give in marriage either
to a decrepit sovereign, or a prince still in his cradle. According
to a third statement, she was the offspring of a Southern American planter, who had given her an elaborate education and
endowed her with his wealth; but the one burning drop of
African blood in her veins so affected her with a sense of igno-
miny, that she relinquished all, and fled her country. By still
another account she was the lady of an English nobleman; and,
out of mere love and honor of art, had thrown aside the splen-

dor of her rank, and come to seek a subsistence by her pencil
in a Roman studio.

In all the above cases, the fable seemed to be instigated by
the large and bounteous impression which Miriam invariably
made, as if necessity and she could have nothing to do with
one another. Whatever deprivations she underwent must needs
be voluntary. But there were other surmises, taking such a
commonplace view as that Miriam was the daughter of a
merchant or financier, who had been ruined in a great commer-
cial crisis; and, possessing a taste for art, she had attempted to
support herself by the pencil, in preference to the alternative of
going out as governess.

Be these things how they might, Miriam, fair as she
looked, was plucked up out of a mystery, and had its roots
still clinging to her. She was a beautiful and attractive woman,
but based, as it were, upon a cloud, and all surrounded with
misty substance; so that the result was to render her sprite-like
in her most ordinary manifestations. This was the case even in
respect to Kenyon and Hilda, her especial friends. But such was
the effect of Miriam's natural language, her generosity, kindliness, and native truth of character, that these two received her
as a dear friend into their hearts, taking her good qualities as
evident and genuine, and never imagining that what was hidden
must be therefore evil.

We now proceed with our narrative.

The same party of friends, whom we have seen at the
sculpture gallery of the Capitol, chanced to have gone together,
some months before, to the catacomb of St. Calixtus.[1] They

[1]The Catacomb of St. Calixtus is the largest catacomb in Rome.
Hawthorne and his wife visited the monument on March 11, 1859. He
noted: "We descended not a very great way under ground, by a broad
flight of stone steps, and, lighting some wax tapers, with which we had
provided ourselves, we followed the guide through a great many intricate
passages, which mostly were just wide enough for me to touch the wall on
each side, while keeping my elbows close to my body; and as to height,
they were from seven to ten feet, and sometimes a good deal higher. . . . It

went joyously down into that vast tomb, and wandered by
torchlight through a sort of dream, in which reminiscences of
church-aisles and grimy cellars—and chiefly the latter—seemed
to be broken into fragments, and hopelessly intermingled. The
intricate passages along which they followed their guide had
been hewn, in some forgotten age, out of a dark-red, crumbly
stone. On either side were horizontal niches, where, if they
held their torches closely, the shape of a human body was discernible in white ashes, into which the entire mortality of a
man or woman had resolved itself. Among all this extinct dust,
there might perchance be a thighbone, which crumbled at a
touch; or possibly a skull, grinning at its own wretched plight,
as is the ugly and empty habit of the thing.

Sometimes their gloomy pathway tended upward, so that,
through a crevice, a little daylight glimmered down upon them,
or even a streak of sunshine peeped into a burial niche; then
again, they went downward by gradual descent, or by abrupt,
rudely hewn steps, into deeper and deeper recesses of the earth.
Here and there the narrow and tortuous passages widened somewhat, developing themselves into small chapels; which once, no
doubt, had been adorned with marble-work and lighted with
ever-burning lamps and tapers. All such illumination and ornament, however, had long since been extinguished and stript
away; except, indeed, that the low roofs of a few of these
ancient sites of worship were covered with dingy stucco, and
frescoed with scriptural scenes and subjects, in the dreariest
stage of ruin.

In one such chapel, the guide showed them a low arch,
beneath which the body of St. Cecilia had been buried after

---

was rather picturesque, when we saw the long line of our tapers, for another party had joined us, twinkling along the dark passage, and it was
interesting to think of the former inhabitants of these caverns. . . . In one or
two places there was the round mark in the stone or plaster where a bottle
had been deposited. This was said to have been the token of a martyr's
burial-place, and to have contained his blood" (*NB*, p. 491).

her martyrdom, and where it lay till a sculptor saw it, and rendered it forever beautiful in marble.[2]

In a similar spot they found two sarcophagi, one containing a skeleton, and the other a shrivelled body, which still wore the garments of its former lifetime.

"How dismal all this is!" said Hilda, shuddering. "I do not know why we came here, nor why we should stay a moment longer."

"I hate it all!" cried Donatello, with peculiar energy. "Dear friends, let us hasten back into the blessed daylight!"

From the first, Donatello had shown little fancy for the expedition; for, like most Italians, and in especial accordance with the law of his own simple and physically happy nature, this young man had an infinite repugnance to graves and skulls, and to all that ghastliness which the Gothic mind loves to associate with the idea of death. He shuddered, and looked fearfully round, drawing nearer to Miriam, whose attractive influence alone had enticed him into that gloomy region.

"What a child you are, my poor Donatello!" she observed, with the freedom which she always used towards him. "You are afraid of ghosts!"

"Yes, signorina; terribly afraid!" said the truthful Donatello.

"I also believe in ghosts," answered Miriam, "and could tremble at them, in a suitable place. But these sepulchres are so old, and these skulls and white ashes so very dry, that methinks they have ceased to be haunted. The most awful idea connected with the catacombs is their interminable extent, and the possibility of going astray into this labyrinth of darkness, which broods around the little glimmer of our tapers."

---

[2]Virgin and martyr, one of the most popular saints in Rome. According to legend, she was martyred during the 3rd century. Her body was discovered in 821 and removed to the church in the Trastevere which bears her name (hence the empty niche here). See also Hawthorne's reference to the Roman matron Cecilia Metella, whose tomb Kenyon passes in Chapter 46—another example of his merging Christian and pagan references.

"Has any one ever been lost here?" asked Kenyon of the guide.

"Surely, signor; one, no longer ago than my father's time," said the guide; and he added, with the air of a man who believed what he was telling, "but the first that went astray here was a pagan of old Rome, who hid himself in order to spy out and betray the blessed saints, who then dwelt and worshipped in these dismal places. You have heard the story, signor? A miracle was wrought upon the accursed one; and, ever since (for fifteen centuries at least), he has been groping in the darkness, seeking his way out of the catacomb."

"Has he ever been seen?" asked Hilda, who had great and tremulous faith in marvels of this kind.

"These eyes of mine never beheld him, signorina; the saints forbid!" answered the guide. "But it is well known that he watches near parties that come into the catacomb, especially if they be heretics, hoping to lead some straggler astray. What this lost wretch pines for, almost as much as for the blessed sunshine, is a companion to be miserable with him."

"Such an intense desire for sympathy indicates something amiable in the poor fellow, at all events," observed Kenyon.

They had now reached a larger chapel than those heretofore seen; it was of a circular shape, and though hewn out of the solid mass of red sandstone, had pillars, and a carved roof, and other tokens of a regular architectural design. Nevertheless, considered as a church, it was exceedingly minute, being scarcely twice a man's stature in height, and only two or three paces from wall to wall; and while their collected torches illuminated this one, small, consecrated spot, the great darkness spread all around it, like that immenser mystery which envelops our little life, and into which friends vanish from us, one by one.

"Why, where is Miriam?" cried Hilda.

The party gazed hurriedly from face to face, and became aware than one of their party had vanished into the great darkness, even while they were shuddering at the remote possibility of such a misfortune.

"Surely, she cannot be lost!" exclaimed Kenyon. "It is but a moment since she was speaking."

"No, no!" said Hilda, in great alarm. "She was behind us all; and it is a long while since we have heard her voice!"

"Torches! torches!" cried Donatello, desperately. "I will seek her, be the darkness ever so dismal!"

But the guide held him back, and assured them all, that there was no possibility of assisting their lost companion, unless by shouting at the very top of their voices. As the sound would go very far along these close and narrow passages, there was a fair probability that Miriam might hear the call, and be able to retrace her steps.

Accordingly, they all—Kenyon with his bass voice; Donatello with his tenor; the guide with that high and hard Italian cry, which makes the streets of Rome so resonant; and Hilda with her slender scream, piercing farther than the united uproar of the rest—began to shriek, halloo, and bellow, with the uttermost force of their lungs. And, not to prolong the reader's suspense, (for we do not particularly seek to interest him in this scene, telling it only on account of the trouble and strange entanglement which followed,) they soon heard a responsive call, in a female voice.

"It was the signorina!" cried Donatello, joyfully.

"Yes; it was certainly dear Miriam's voice," said Hilda. "And here she comes! Thank Heaven! Thank Heaven!"

The figure of their friend was now discernible by her own torchlight, approaching out of one of the cavernous passages. Miriam came forward, but not with the eagerness and tremulous joy of a fearful girl, just rescued from a labyrinth of gloomy mystery. She made no immediate response to their inquiries and tumultuous congratulations; and, as they afterwards remembered, there was something absorbed, thoughtful, and self-concentrated in her deportment. She looked pale, as well she might, and held her torch with a nervous grasp, the tremor of which was seen in the irregular twinkling of the flame. This last was the chief perceptible sign of any recent agitation or alarm.

"Dearest, dearest Miriam," exclaimed Hilda, throwing her arms about her friend, "where have you been straying from us? Blessed be Providence, which has rescued you out of that miserable darkness!"

"Hush, dear Hilda!" whispered Miriam, with a strange little laugh. "Are you quite sure that it was Heaven's guidance which brought me back? If so, it was by an odd messenger, as you will confess. See; there he stands."

Startled at Miriam's words and manner, Hilda gazed into the duskiness whither she pointed, and there beheld a figure standing just on the doubtful limit of obscurity, at the threshold of the small, illuminated chapel. Kenyon discerned him at the same instant, and drew nearer with his torch; although the guide attempted to dissuade him, averring that, once beyond the consecrated precincts of the chapel, the apparition would have power to tear him limb from limb. It struck the sculptor, however, when he afterwards recurred to these circumstances, that the guide manifested no such apprehension on his own account as he professed on behalf of others; for he kept pace with Kenyon as the latter approached the figure, though still endeavoring to restrain him.

In fine, they both drew near enough to get as good a view of the spectre as the smoky light of their torches, struggling with the massive gloom, could supply.

The stranger was of exceedingly picturesque, and even melodramatic aspect. He was clad in a voluminous cloak, that seemed to be made of a buffalo's hide, and a pair of those goat-skin breeches, with the hair outward, which are still commonly

worn by the peasants of the Roman Campagna.[1] In this garb,
they look like antique Satyrs;[2] and, in truth, the Spectre of the
Catacomb might have represented the last survivor of that
vanished race, hiding himself in sepulchral gloom, and mourning over his lost life of woods and streams.

Furthermore, he had on a broad-brimmed, conical hat,
beneath the shadow of which a wild visage was indistinctly
seen, floating away, as it were, into a dusky wilderness of mous-
tache and beard. His eyes winked, and turned uneasily from the
torches, like a creature to whom midnight would be more
congenial than noonday.

On the whole, the spectre might have made a considerable
impression on the sculptor's nerves, only that he was in the habit
of observing similar figures, almost every day, reclining on the
Spanish steps, and waiting for some artist to invite them within
the magic realm of picture. Nor, even thus familiarized with
the stranger's peculiarities of appearance, could Kenyon help
wondering to see such a personage, shaping himself so suddenly
out of the void darkness of the catacomb.

"What are you?" said the sculptor, advancing his torch
nearer. "And how long have you been wandering here?"

"A thousand and five hundred years!" muttered the guide,
loud enough to be heard by all the party. "It is the old pagan
phantom[3] that I told you of, who sought to betray the blessed
saints!"

"Yes; it is a phantom!" cried Donatello, with a shudder.
"Ah, dearest signorina, what fearful thing has beset you, in
those dark corridors!"

[1]A plain surrounding Rome; a wild and arid country littered with
aqueducts and tombs; used for sheep-grazing. See Browning's poem, "Two
in the Campagna."

[2]In Greek mythology, a tribe of hairy little men with tails and goat-
like ears. Note the link here between the goat-herding peasant and Donatello.

[3]Working for a good tip, the guide is trying to impress the tourists
here; actually the shadowy figure is Miriam's Model. See note 7, p. 32.

"Nonsense, Donatello," said the sculptor. "The man is no more a phantom than yourself. The only marvel is, how he comes to be hiding himself in the catacomb. Possibly, our guide might solve the riddle."

The spectre himself here settled the point of his tangibility, at all events, and physical substance, by approaching a step nearer, and laying his hand on Kenyon's arm.

"Inquire not what I am, nor wherefore I abide in the darkness," said he, in a hoarse, harsh voice, as if a great deal of damp were clustering in his throat. "Henceforth, I am nothing but a shadow behind her footsteps. She came to me when I sought her not. She has called me forth, and must abide the consequences of my reappearance in the world."

"Holy Virgin! I wish the signorina joy of her prize," said the guide, half to himself. "And in any case, the catacomb is well rid of him."

We need follow the scene no farther. So much is essential to the subsequent narrative, that, during the short period while astray in those tortuous passages, Miriam had encountered an unknown man, and led him forth with her, or was guided back by him, first into the torchlight, thence into the sunshine.

It was the further singularity of this affair, that the connection, thus briefly and casually formed, did not terminate with the incident that gave it birth. As if her service to him, or his service to her, whichever it might be, had given him an indefeasible claim on Miriam's regard and protection, the Spectre of the Catacomb never long allowed her to lose sight of him, from that day forward. He haunted her footsteps with more than the customary persistency of Italian mendicants,[4] when

[4]Hawthorne frequently remarked on the numerous beggars who crowded around the tourists at the entrances of Roman monuments. Generally the Roman beggars were better behaved than those he encountered elsewhere in Italy. He resolved his own attitude in a note for Oct. 15, 1858: "To beggars—after my much experience both in England and Italy—I give very little, though I am not certain that it would not often be real beneficence in the latter country. There being little or no provision for poverty

once they have recognized a benefactor. For days together, it is true, he occasionally vanished, but always reappeared, gliding after her through the narrow streets, or climbing the hundred steps of her staircase and sitting at her threshold.

Being often admitted to her studio, he left his features, or some shadow or reminiscence of them, in many of her sketches and pictures. The moral atmosphere of these productions was thereby so influenced, that rival painters pronounced it a case of hopeless mannerism, which would destroy all Miriam's prospects of true excellence in art.

The story of this adventure spread abroad, and made its way beyond the usual gossip of the Forestieri,[5] even into Italian circles, where, enhanced by a still potent spirit of superstition, it grew far more wonderful than as above recounted. Thence, it came back among the Anglo-Saxons, and was communicated to the German artists, who so richly supplied it with romantic ornaments and excrescences, after their fashion, that it became a fantasy worthy of Tieck or Hoffmann.[6] For nobody has any conscience about adding to the improbabilities of a marvellous tale.

The most reasonable version of the incident, that could anywise be rendered acceptable to the auditors, was substantially the one suggested by the guide of the catacomb, in his allusion to the legend of Memmius.[7] This man, or demon, or

---

and age, the poor must often suffer. Nothing can be more earnest than their gratitude when they receive it. They return you the value of their alms in prayers, and say, 'God will accompany you.' Many of them have a professional whine, and a certain doleful twist of the neck and turn of the head, which hardens my heart against them at once" (*NB*, pp. 477–478).

[5]Strangers; foreign tourists.

[6]Ludwig Tieck (1773–1853), a well-esteemed German romantic novelist; E. T. A. Hoffmann (1776–1822), a German composer, writer, and illustrator, known today principally through Jacques Offenbach's opera, *The Tales of Hoffmann*.

[7]Diocletian (*fl.* A.D. 284–305) was the last Roman emperor to persecute the Christians; thus the guide's earlier allusion to "fifteen hundred years" puts the Model in the context of Diocletian's persecution. The le-

man-demon, was a spy during the persecutions of the early
Christians, probably under the Emperor Diocletian, and penetrated into the catacombs of St. Calixtus, with the malignant
purpose of tracing out the hiding-places of the refugees. But,
while he stole craftily through those dark corridors, he chanced
to come upon a little chapel, where tapers were burning before
an altar and a crucifix, and a priest was in the performance of
his sacred office. By divine indulgence, there was a single moment's grace allowed to Memmius, during which, had he been
capable of Christian faith and love, he might have knelt before
the cross, and received the holy light into his soul, and so have
been blest forever. But he resisted the sacred impulse. As soon,
therefore, as that one moment had glided by, the light of the
consecrated tapers, which represent all truth, bewildered the
wretched man with everlasting error, and the blessed cross
itself was stamped as a seal upon his heart, so that it should
never open to receive conviction.

Thenceforth, this heathen Memmius has haunted the wide
and dreary precincts of the catacomb, seeking, as some say, to
beguile new victims into his own misery; but, according to
other statements, endeavoring to prevail on any unwary visitor
to take him by the hand, and guide him out into the daylight.
Should his wiles and entreaties take effect, however, the man-
demon would remain only a little while above ground. He
would gratify his fiendish malignity by perpetrating signal
mischief on his benefactor, and perhaps bringing some old
pestilence or other forgotten and long-buried evil on society;
or, possibly, teaching the modern world some decayed and
dusty kind of crime, which the antique Romans knew; and then
would hasten back to the catacomb, which, after so long haunting it, has grown his most congenial home.

---

gend of Memmius is a good example of Hawthorne's gothic tactics with
overlaying allusions. Memmius and the Model have obvious parallels with
the Wandering Jew, the Flying Dutchman, and the Demon Lover in
European folklore.

Miriam herself, with her chosen friends, the sculptor and the gentle Hilda, often laughed at the monstrous fictions that had gone abroad in reference to her adventure. Her two confidants (for such they were, on all ordinary subjects) had not failed to ask an explanation of the mystery, since undeniably a mystery there was, and one sufficiently perplexing itself, without any help from the imaginative faculty. And, sometimes responding to their inquiries with a melancholy sort of playfulness, Miriam let her fancy run off into wilder fables than any which German ingenuity or Italian superstition had contrived.

For example, with a strange air of seriousness over all her face, only belied by a laughing gleam in her dark eyes, she would aver that the spectre (who had been an artist in his mortal lifetime) had promised to teach her a long lost, but invaluable secret of old Roman fresco-painting.[8] The knowledge of this process would place Miriam at the head of modern art; the sole condition being agreed upon, that she should return with him into his sightless gloom, after enriching a certain extent of stuccoed wall with the most brilliant and lovely designs. And what true votary of art would not purchase unrivalled excellence, even at so vast a sacrifice!

Or, if her friends still solicited a soberer account, Miriam replied, that, meeting the old infidel in one of the dismal passages of the catacomb, she had entered into controversy with him, hoping to achieve the glory and satisfaction of converting him to the Christian faith. For the sake of so excellent a result, she had even staked her own salvation against his, binding herself to accompany him back into his penal gloom, if, within a twelvemonth's space, she should not have convinced him of the errors through which he had so long groped and stumbled. But, alas! up to the present time, the controversy had gone direfully in favor of the man-demon; and Miriam (as she whispered in

[8]Old Roman fresco painting, or *buon fresco*, was an art requiring quick work with wet plaster; the lime formed a binder for the pigment. In Hawthorne's time fresco painting was performed on dry plaster with a glue or casein base (*fresco secco*).

Hilda's ear) had awful forebodings, that, in a few more months, she must take an eternal farewell of the sun!

It was somewhat remarkable, that all her romantic fantasies arrived at this selfsame dreary termination; it appeared impossible for her even to imagine any other than a disastrous result from her connection with her ill-omened attendant.

This singularity might have meant nothing, however, had it not suggested a despondent state of mind, which was likewise indicated by many other tokens. Miriam's friends had no difficulty in perceiving that, in one way or another, her happiness was very seriously compromised. Her spirits were often depressed into deep melancholy. If ever she was gay, it was seldom with a healthy cheerfulness. She grew moody, moreover, and subject to fits of passionate ill-temper; which usually wreaked itself on the heads of those who loved her best. Not that Miriam's indifferent acquaintances were safe from similar outbreaks of her displeasure, especially if they ventured upon any allusion to the model. In such cases, they were left with little disposition to renew the subject, but inclined, on the other hand, to interpret the whole matter as much to her discredit as the least favorable coloring of the facts would allow.

It may occur to the reader, that there was really no demand for so much rumor and speculation in regard to an incident, which might well enough have been explained without going many steps beyond the limits of probability. The spectre might have been merely a Roman beggar, whose fraternity often harbor in stranger shelters than the catacombs; or one of those pilgrims, who still journey from remote countries to kneel and worship at the holy sites, among which these haunts of the early Christians are esteemed especially sacred. Or, as was perhaps a more plausible theory, he might be a thief of the city, a robber of the Campagna, a political offender, or an assassin, with blood upon his hand; whom the negligence or connivance of the police allowed to take refuge in those subterranean fastnesses, where such outlaws have been accustomed to hide themselves from a far antiquity downward. Or he might have been a lunatic, fleeing instinctively from man, and making it his dark pleasure to dwell among the tombs, like him whose awful cry echoes afar to us from Scripture times.

And, as for the stranger's attaching himself so devotedly to Miriam, her personal magnetism might be allowed a certain weight in the explanation. For what remains, his pertinacity need not seem so very singular to those who consider how slight a link serves to connect these vagabonds of idle Italy with any person that may have the ill-hap to bestow charity, or be otherwise serviceable to them, or betray the slightest interest in their fortunes.

Thus, little would remain to be accounted for, except the deportment of Miriam herself; her reserve, her brooding melancholy, her petulance, and moody passion. If generously interpreted, even these morbid symptoms might have sufficient cause in the stimulating and exhausting influencies of an imaginative art, exercised by a delicate young woman, in the nervous and unwholesome atmosphere of Rome. Such, at least, was the view of the case which Hilda and Kenyon endeavored to impress on their own minds, and impart to those whom their opinions might influence.

One of Miriam's friends took the matter sadly to heart. This was the young Italian. Donatello, as we have seen, had been an eye-witness of the stranger's first appearance, and had ever since nourished a singular prejudice against the mysterious, dusky, death-scented apparition. It resembled not so much a human dislike or hatred, as one of those instinctive, unreasoning antipathies which the lower animals sometimes display, and which generally prove more trustworthy than the acutest insight into character. The shadow of the model, always flung into the light which Miriam diffused around her, caused no slight trouble to Donatello. Yet he was of a nature so remarkably genial and joyous, so simply happy, that he might well afford to have something subtracted from his comfort, and make tolerable shift to live upon what remained.

CHAPTER 5

Miriam's Studio

The courtyard and staircase of a palace built three hundred years ago, are a peculiar feature of modern Rome, and interest the stranger more than many things of which he has heard loftier descriptions. You pass through the grand breadth and height of a squalid entrance-way, and perhaps see a range of dusky pillars, forming a sort of cloister round the court, and in the intervals, from pillar to pillar, are strewn fragments of antique statues, headless and legless torsos, and busts that have have invariably lost—what it might be well if living men could lay aside in that unfragrant atmosphere—the nose. Bas-reliefs, the spoil of some far elder palace, are set in the surrounding walls, every stone of which has been ravished from the Coliseum, or any other imperial ruin which earlier barbarism had not already levelled with the earth. Between two of the pillars, moreover, stands an old sarcophagus without its lid, and with all its more prominently projecting sculptures broken off; perhaps it once held famous dust, and the bony framework of some historic man, although now only a receptacle for the rubbish of the courtyard, and a half-worn broom.

In the centre of the court, under the blue Italian sky, and with the hundred windows of the vast palace gazing down upon it, from four sides, appears a fountain. It brims over from one stone basin to another, or gushes from a Naiad's[1] urn, or spirts its many little jets from the mouths of nameless monsters, which were merely grotesque and artificial when Bernini,[2] or whoever

[1] A water nymph.
[2] Giovanni Lorenzo Bernini (1598–1680) was the leading sculptor of Italian Baroque style and architect of St. Peter's. He designed the Trevi Fountain, which Hawthorne describes in his note for April 25, 1858:

was their unnatural father, first produced them; but now the patches of moss, the tufts of grass, the trailing maidenhair, and all sorts of verdant weed that thrive in the cracks and crevices of moist marble, tell us that Nature takes the fountain back into her great heart, and cherishes it as kindly as if it were a woodland spring. And, hark, the pleasant murmur, the gurgle, the plash! You might hear just those tinkling sounds from any tiny waterfall in the forest, though here they gain a delicious pathos from the stately echoes that reverberate their natural language. So the fountain is not altogether glad, after all its three centuries of play!

In one of the angles of the courtyard, a pillared doorway gives access to the staircase, with its spacious breadth of low, marble steps, up which, in former times, have gone the princes and cardinals of the great Roman family who built this palace. Or they have come down, with still grander and loftier mien, on their way to the Vatican or the Quirinal, there to put off their scarlet hats in exchange for the triple crown.[3] But, in fine, all these illustrious personages have gone down their hereditary staircase for the last time, leaving it to be the thoroughfare of ambassadors, English noblemen, American millionnaires, artists, tradesmen, washerwomen, and people of every degree; all of whom find such gilded and marble-panelled saloons as their

---

"Night before last, my wife and I took a moonlight ramble through Rome, it being a very beautiful night, warm enough for comfort, and with no perceptible dew or dampness. We set out at about nine o'clock, and, our general direction being towards the Coliseum, we soon came to the Fountain of Trevi, full on the front of which the moonlight fell, making Bernini's sculptures look stately and beautiful, though the semicircular gush and fall of the cascade, and the many jets of the water, pouring and bubbling into the great marble basin, are of far more account than Neptune and his steeds, and the rest of the figures . . ." (*NB*, p. 173).

[3]An allusion to the election of a Pope. The triple crown, or tiara, represents the three kingdoms of God: The Church Suffering (in Purgatory), the Church Militant (on Earth), and the Church Triumphant (in Heaven). The Quirinal is one of Rome's seven hills. In Hawthorne's time the palace at its base was used as the summer residence of the Pope.

pomp and luxury demand, or such homely garrets as their necessity can pay for, within this one multifarious abode. Only,
in not a single nook of the palace (built for splendor, and the
accommodation of a vast retinue, but with no vision of a happy
fireside or any mode of domestic enjoyment) does the humblest
or the haughtiest occupant find comfort.

Up such a staircase, on the morning after the scene at the
sculpture gallery, sprang the light foot of Donatello. He ascended from story to story, passing lofty doorways, set within
rich frames of sculptured marble, and climbing unweariedly
upward, until the glories of the first piano and the elegance of
the middle height were exchanged for a sort of Alpine region,
cold and naked in its aspect. Steps of rough stone, rude wooden
balustrades, a brick pavement in the passages, a dingy whitewash on the walls; these were here the palatial features. Finally,
he paused before an oaken door, on which was pinned a card,
bearing the name of Miriam Schaefer, artist in oils. Here Donatello knocked, and the door immediately fell somewhat ajar; its
latch having been pulled up by means of a string on the inside.
Passing through a little anteroom, he found himself in Miriam's
presence.

"Come in, wild Faun," she said, "and tell me the latest
news from Arcady!"

The artist was not just then at her easel, but was busied
with the feminine task of mending a pair of gloves.

There is something extremely pleasant, and even touching
—at least, of very sweet, soft, and winning effect—in this peculiarity of needle-work, distinguishing women from men. Our
own sex is incapable of any such by-play aside from the main
business of life; but women—be they of what earthly rank they
may, however gifted with intellect or genius, or endowed with
awful beauty—have always some little handiwork ready to fill
the tiny gap of every vacant moment. A needle is familiar to
the fingers of them all. A queen, no doubt, plies it on occasion;
the woman-poet can use it as adroitly as her pen; the woman's
eye, that has discovered a new star, turns from its glory to send

the polished little instrument gleaming along the hem of her kerchief, or to darn a casual fray in her dress. And they have greatly the advantage of us in this respect. The slender thread of silk or cotton keeps them united with the small, familiar, gentle interests of life, the continually operating influences of which do so much for the health of the character, and carry off what would otherwise be a dangerous accumulation of morbid sensibility. A vast deal of human sympathy runs along this electric line, stretching from the throne to the wicker-chair of the humblest seamstress, and keeping high and low in a species of communion with their kindred beings. Methinks it is a token of healthy and gentle characteristics, when women of high thoughts and accomplishments love to sew; especially as they are never more at home with their own hearts than while so occupied.[4]

And when the work falls in a woman's lap, of its own accord, and the needle involuntarily ceases to fly, it is a sign of trouble, quite as trustworthy as the throb of the heart itself. This was what happened to Miriam. Even while Donatello stood gazing at her, she seemed to have forgotten his presence, allowing him to drop out of her thoughts, and the torn glove to fall from her idle fingers. Simple as he was, the young man knew by his sympathies that something was amiss.

"Dear lady, you are sad," said he, drawing close to her.

"It is nothing, Donatello," she replied, resuming her work: "yes; a little sad, perhaps; but that is not strange for us people of the ordinary world, especially for women. You are of a cheerfuller race, my friend, and know nothing of this disease of sadness. But why do you come into this shadowy room of mine?"

"Why do you make it so shadowy?" asked he.

"We artists purposely exclude sunshine, and all but a partial light," said Miriam, "because we think it necessary to put

---

[4]Cf. Hawthorne's treatment of Hester in Chapter 5 of *The Scarlet Letter*, "Hester at Her Needle."

ourselves at odds with Nature before trying to imitate her. That strikes you very strangely, does it not? But we make very pretty pictures sometimes, with our artfully arranged lights and shadows. Amuse yourself with some of mine, Donatello, and by and by I shall be in the mood to begin the portrait we were talking about."

The room had the customary aspect of a painter's studio; one of those delightful spots that hardly seem to belong to the actual world, but rather to be the outward type of a poet's haunted imagination, where there are glimpses, sketches, and half-developed hints of beings and objects grander and more beautiful than we can anywhere find in reality. The windows were closed with shutters, or deeply curtained, except one, which was partly open to a sunless portion of the sky, admitting only from high upward that partial light which, with its strongly marked contrast of shadow, is the first requisite towards seeing objects pictorially. Pencil-drawings were pinned against the wall or scattered on the tables. Unframed canvases turned their backs on the spectator, presenting only a blank to the eye, and churlishly concealing whatever riches of scenery or human beauty Miriam's skill had depicted on the other side.

In the obscurest part of the room Donatello was half startled at perceiving duskily a woman with long dark hair, who threw up her arms with a wild gesture of tragic despair, and appeared to beckon him into the darkness along with her.

"Do not be afraid, Donatello," said Miriam, smiling to see him peering doubtfully into the mysterious dusk. "She means you no mischief, nor could perpetrate any if she wished it ever so much. It is a lady of exceedingly pliable disposition; now a heroine of romance, and now a rustic maid; yet all for show; being created, indeed, on purpose to wear rich shawls and other garments in a becoming fashion. This is the true end of her being, although she pretends to assume the most varied duties and perform many parts in life, while really the poor puppet has nothing on earth to do. Upon my word, I am satirical unawares, and seem to be describing nine women out of ten in the person of my lay-figure. For most purposes she has the advantage of the sisterhood. Would I were like her!"

"How it changes her aspect," exclaimed Donatello, "to know that she is but a jointed figure. When my eyes first fell upon her, I thought her arms moved, as if beckoning me to help her in some direful peril."

"Are you often troubled with such sinister freaks of fancy?" asked Miriam. "I should not have supposed it."

"To tell you the truth, dearest signorina," answered the young Italian, "I am apt to be fearful in old, gloomy houses, and in the dark. I love no dark or dusky corners, except it be in a grotto, or among the thick green leaves of an arbor, or in some nook of the woods, such as I know many in the neighborhood of my home. Even there, if a stray sunbeam steal in, the shadow is all the better for its cheerful glimmer."

"Yes; you are a Faun, you know," said the fair artist, laughing at the remembrance of the scene of the day before. "But the world is sadly changed now-a-days; grievously changed, poor Donatello, since those happy times when your race used to dwell in the Arcadian woods, playing hide-and-seek with the nymphs in grottoes and nooks of shrubbery. You have reappeared on earth some centuries too late."

"I do not understand you now," answered Donatello, looking perplexed; "only, signorina, I am glad to have my lifetime while you live; and where you are, be it in cities or fields, I would fain be there too."

"I wonder whether I ought to allow you to speak in this way," said Miriam, looking thoughtfully at him. "Many young women would think it behoved them to be offended. Hilda would never let you speak so, I dare say. But he is a mere boy," she added, aside, "a simple boy, putting his boyish heart to the proof on the first woman whom he chances to meet. If yonder lay-figure had had the luck to meet him first, she would have smitten him as deeply as I."

"Are you angry with me?" asked Donatello, dolorously.

"Not in the least," answered Miriam, frankly giving him

her hand. "Pray look over some of these sketches till I have leisure to chat with you a little. I hardly think I am in spirits enough to begin your portrait today."

Donatello was as gentle and docile as a pet spaniel; as playful, too, in his general disposition, or saddening with his mistress's variable mood like that of any other kindly animal which has the faculty of bestowing its sympathies more completely than man or woman can ever do. Accordingly, as Miriam bade him, he tried to turn his attention to a great pile and confusion of pen-and-ink sketches and pencil-drawings which lay tossed together on a table. As it chanced, however, they gave the poor youth little delight.

The first that he took up was a very impressive sketch, in which the artist had jotted down her rough ideas for a picture of Jael driving the nail through the temples of Sisera.[5] It was dashed off with remarkable power, and showed a touch or two that were actually life-like and death-like, as if Miriam had been standing by when Jael gave the first stroke of her murderous hammer, or as if she herself were Jael, and felt irresistibly impelled to make her bloody confession in this guise.

Her first conception of the stern Jewess had evidently been that of perfect womanhood, a lovely form, and a high, heroic face of lofty beauty; but, dissatisfied either with her own work or the terrible story itself, Miriam had added a certain wayward quirk of her pencil, which at once converted the heroine into a vulgar murderess. It was evident that a Jael like this would be sure to search Sisera's pockets as soon as the breath was out of his body.

In another sketch she had attempted the story of Judith,[6] which we see represented by the old masters so often, and in

---

[5] Jael was a Jewish heroine in the time of Deborah; she murdered Sisera, a Canaanite captain who led an army against the Israelites. See Judges 4:17–24. Hawthorne uses Jael as a type for Miriam.

[6] A brave and resourceful Jewish widow who rescued her besieged city by sleeping with the enemy general, Holofernes, and cutting off his head. See Judith 13:1–12.

such various styles. Here, too, beginning with a passionate and fiery conception of the subject in all earnestness, she had given the last touches in utter scorn, as it were, of the feeling which at first took such powerful possession of her hand. The head of Holofernes (which, by and by, had a pair of twisted moustachios, like those of a certain potentate of the day) being fairly cut off, was screwing its eyes upward and twirling its features into a diabolical grin of triumphant malice, which it flung right at Judith's face. On her part, she had the startled aspect that might be conceived of a cook if a calf's head should sneer at her when about to be popped into the dinner-pot.

Over and over again, there was the idea of woman, acting the part of a revengeful mischief towards man. It was, indeed, very singular to see how the artist's imagination seemed to run on these stories of bloodshed, in which woman's hand was crimsoned by the stain; and how, too,—in one form or another, grotesque or sternly sad,—she failed not to bring out the moral, that woman must strike through her own heart to reach a human life, whatever were the motive that impelled her.

One of the sketches represented the daughter of Herodias receiving the head of John the Baptist in a charger. The general conception appeared to be taken from Bernardo Luini's picture, in the Uffizi gallery at Florence;[7] but Miriam had imparted to the saint's face a look of gentle and heavenly reproach, with sad and blessed eyes fixed upward at the maiden; by the force of which miraculous glance, her whole womanhood was at once awakened to love and endless remorse.

These sketches had a most disagreeable effect on Donatello's peculiar temperament. He gave a shudder; his face assumed a look of trouble, fear, and disgust; he snatched up one sketch after another, as if about to tear it in pieces. Finally, shoving away the pile of drawings, he shrank back from the table and clasped his hands over his eyes.

[7]Bernardino Luini (ca. 1480–1532), a disciple of Leonardo da Vinci, who painted largely religious subjects.

"What is the matter, Donatello?" asked Miriam, looking up from a letter which she was now writing. "Ah! I did not mean you to see those drawings. They are ugly phantoms that stole out of my mind; not things that I created, but things that haunt me. See! here are some trifles that perhaps will please you better."

She gave him a portfolio, the sketches in which indicated a happier mood of mind, and one, it is to be hoped, more truly characteristic of the artist. Supposing neither of these classes of subject to show anything of her own individuality, Miriam had evidently a great scope of fancy, and a singular faculty of putting what looked like heart into her productions. The latter sketches were domestic and common scenes, so finely and subtly idealized that they seemed such as we may see at any moment, and everywhere; while still there was the indefinable something added, or taken away, which makes all the difference between sordid life and an earthly paradise. The feeling and sympathy in all of them were deep and true. There was the scene, that comes once in every life, of the lover winning the soft and pure avowal of bashful affection from the maiden, whose slender form half leans towards his arm, half shrinks from it, we know not which. There was wedded affection in its successive stages, represented in a series of delicately conceived designs, touched with a holy fire, that burned from youth to age in those two hearts, and gave one identical beauty to the faces, throughout all the changes of feature.

There was a drawing of an infant's shoe, half worn out, with the airy print of the blessed foot within; a thing that would make a mother smile or weep out of the very depths of her heart; and yet an actual mother would not have been likely to appreciate the poetry of the little shoe, until Miriam revealed it to her. It was wonderful, the depth and force with which the above, and other kindred subjects were depicted, and the profound significance which they often acquired. The artist, still in her fresh youth, could not probably have drawn any of these dear and rich experiences from her own life; unless, perchance, that first sketch of all, the avowal of maiden affection, were a remembered incident, and not a prophecy. But it is more delightful to believe, that, from first to last, they were the productions of a beautiful imagination, dealing with the warm and pure suggestions of a woman's heart, and thus idealizing a truer and lovelier picture of the life that belongs to woman, than an actual acquaintance with some of its hard and dusty facts could have inspired. So considered, the sketches intimated such a force and variety of imaginative sympathies as would enable Miriam to fill her life richly with the bliss and suffering of womanhood, however barren it might individually be.

There was one observable point, indeed, betokening that the artist relinquished, for her personal self, the happiness which she could so profoundly appreciate for others. In all those sketches of common life, and the affections that spiritualize it, a figure was portrayed apart; now it peeped between the branches of a shrubbery, amid which two lovers sat; now it was looking through a frosted window, from the outside, while a young wedded pair sat at their new fireside, within; and once it leaned from a chariot, which six horses were whirling onward in pomp and pride, and gazed at a scene of humble enjoyment by a cottage-door. Always it was the same figure, and always depicted with an expression of deep sadness; and in every instance, slightly as they were brought out, the face and form had the traits of Miriam's own.

"Do you like these sketches better, Donatello?" asked Miriam.

"Yes," said Donatello, rather doubtfully.

"Not much, I fear," responded she, laughing. "And what should a boy like you—a Faun, too—know about the joys and sorrows, the intertwining light and shadow, of human life? I forgot that you were a Faun. You cannot suffer deeply; therefore you can but half enjoy. Here, now, is a subject which you can better appreciate."

The sketch represented merely a rustic dance, but with such extravagance of fun as was delightful to behold; and here there was no drawback, except that strange sigh and sadness which always come when we are merriest.

"I am going to paint the picture in oils," said the artist; "and I want you, Donatello, for the wildest dancer of them all. Will you sit for me, some day?—or, rather, dance for me?"

"Oh! most gladly, signorina!" exclaimed Donatello. "See; it shall be like this."

And forthwith he began to dance, and flit about the studio, like an incarnate sprite of jollity, pausing at last on the extremity of one toe, as if that were the only portion of himself, whereby his frisky nature could come in contact with the earth. The effect in that shadowy chamber, whence the artist had so carefully excluded the sunshine, was as enlivening as if one bright ray had contrived to shimmer in and frolic around the walls, and finally rest just in the centre of the floor.

"That was admirable!" said Miriam, with an approving smile. "If I can catch you on my canvas, it will be a glorious picture; only I am afraid you will dance out of it, by the very truth of the representation, just when I shall have given it the last touch. We will try it one of these days. And now, to reward you for that jolly exhibition, you shall see what has been shown to no one else."

She went to her easel, on which was placed a picture with its back turned towards the spectator. Reversing the position, there appeared the portrait of a beautiful woman, such as one sees only two or three, if even so many, in all a lifetime; so beautiful, that she seemed to get into your consciousness and memory, and could never afterwards be shut out, but haunted your dreams, for pleasure or for pain; holding your inner realm as a conquered territory, though without deigning to make herself at home there.

She was very youthful, and had what was usually thought to be a Jewish aspect; a complexion in which there was no roseate bloom, yet neither was it pale; dark eyes, into which you might look as deeply as your glance would go, and still be conscious of a depth that you had not sounded, though it lay open to the day. She had black, abundant hair, with none of the vulgar glossiness of other women's sable locks; if she were really of Jewish blood, then this was Jewish hair, and a dark glory such as crowns no Christian maiden's head. Gazing at this portrait, you saw what Rachel might have been, when Jacob deemed her worth the wooing seven years, and seven more;[8] or perchance she might ripen to be what Judith was, when she vanquished Holofernes with her beauty, and slew him for too much adoring it.[9]

[8] Jacob loved Rachel and asked her father Laban for her hand; Laban consented if Jacob would work for him seven years. Jacob did so, but on the wedding night Laban substituted Leah, his unattractive older daughter. When Jacob complained of the trick the next morning, Laban granted him Rachel in addition, provided Jacob would work for him seven more years. The Twelve Tribes of Israel are descended from Leah and Rachel, and from their two serving maids, who also bore Jacob sons. See Genesis 29: 18–30.

[9] Hawthorne makes the portrait of Judith a means of describing Miriam (see below). Physically at least, Miriam is based on a young Jewish woman Hawthorne faced across a banquet table at the Lord Mayor's House in London on April 13, 1856. Here is the entry from the *English Notebooks:* "The band kept playing, at intervals, all the time; and, when not talking with Mrs. Hall, or my neighbor on the other side (some city dignitary) my eyes were mostly drawn to a young lady who sat nearly opposite me, across the table. She was, I suppose, dark, and yet not dark, but rather seemed to be of pure white marble, yet not white; but the purest and finest complexion, (without a shade of color in it, yet anything but sallow or sickly) that I ever beheld. Her hair was a wonderful deep, raven black, black as night, black as death; *not* raven black, for that has a shiny gloss, and her's [sic] had not; but it was hair never to be painted, nor described—wonderful hair, Jewish hair. Her nose had a beautiful outline, though I could see that it was Jewish too; and that, and all her features, were so fine that sculpture seemed a despicable art beside her; and certainly my pen is good for nothing. If any likeness of her could be given, it must be by sculpture, not painting. She was slender, and youthful, but yet had a stately and cold, though soft and womanly grace; and, looking at her, I saw what were the wives of the old patriarchs, in their maiden or early married days—what Rachel was, when Jacob wooed her seven years, and seven more—what Judith was; for, womanly as she looked, I doubt not she could have slain a man, in a good cause—what Bathsheba was; only she

Miriam watched Donatello's contemplation of the picture, and seeing his simple rapture, a smile of pleasure brightened on her face, mixed with a little scorn; at least, her lips curled and her eyes gleamed, as if she disdained either his admiration or her own enjoyment of it.

"Then you like the picture, Donatello?" she asked.

"Oh, beyond what I can tell!" he answered. "So beautiful!—so beautiful!"

"And do you recognize the likeness?"

"Signorina," exclaimed Donatello, turning from the picture to the artist, in astonishment that she should ask the question, "the resemblance is as little to be mistaken as if you had bent over the smooth surface of a fountain, and possessed the witchcraft to call forth the image that you made there! It is yourself!"

Donatello said the truth; and we forbore to speak descriptively of Miriam's beauty earlier in our narrative, because we foresaw this occasion to bring it perhaps more forcibly before the reader.

We know not whether the portrait were a flattered likeness; probably not, regarding it merely as the delineation of a lovely face; although Miriam, like all self-painters, may have endowed herself with certain graces which other eyes might not discern. Artists are fond of painting their own portraits; and, in Florence, there is a gallery of hundreds of them, including the most illustrious, in all of which there are autobiographical characteristics, so to speak; traits, expressions, loftinesses, and amenities, which would have been invisible, had they not been painted from within. Yet their reality and truth is none

---

seemed to have no sin in her—perhaps what Eve was, though one could hardly think her weak enough to eat the apple. I never should have thought of touching her, nor desired to touch her; for, whether owing to distinctness of race, my sense that she was a Jewess, or whatever else, I felt a sort of repugnance, simultaneously with my perception that she was an admirable creature." *The English Notebooks*, ed. Randall Stewart (New York: Russell and Russell, 1962), p. 321.

the less. Miriam, in like manner, had doubtless conveyed some of the intimate results of her heart-knowledge into her own portrait, and perhaps wished to try whether they would be perceptible to so simple and natural an observer as Donatello.

"Does the expression please you?" she asked.

"Yes," said Donatello, hesitatingly; "if it would only smile so like the sunshine as you sometimes do. No, it is sadder than I thought at first. Cannot you make yourself smile a little, signorina?"

"A forced smile is uglier than a frown," said Miriam, a bright, natural smile breaking out over her face, even as she spoke.

"Oh! catch it now!" cried Donatello, clapping his hands. "Let it shine upon the picture! There! it has vanished already! And you are sad again, very sad; and the picture gazes sadly forth at me, as if some evil had befallen it in the little time since I looked last."

"How perplexed you seem, my friend!" answered Miriam. "I really half believe you are a Faun, there is such a mystery and terror for you in these dark moods, which are just as natural as daylight to us people of ordinary mould. I advise you, at all events, to look at other faces with those innocent and happy eyes, and never more to gaze at mine!"

"You speak in vain," replied the young man, with a deeper emphasis than she had ever before heard in his voice; "shroud yourself in what gloom you will, I must needs follow you."

"Well, well, well," said Miriam, impatiently: "but leave me now; for, to speak plainly, my good friend, you grow a little wearisome. I walk this afternoon in the Borghese grounds. Meet me there, if it suits your pleasure."

CHAPTER 6.   *The Virgin's Shrine*

After Donatello had left the studio, Miriam herself came forth, and taking her way through some of the intricacies of the city, entered what might be called either a widening of a street, or a small piazza. The neighborhood comprised a baker's oven, emitting the usual fragrance of sour bread; a shoe shop; a linen-draper's shop; a pipe and cigar shop; a lottery office; a station for French soldiers, with a sentinel pacing in front; and a fruit stand, at which a Roman matron was selling the dried kernels of chestnuts, wretched little figs, and some bouquets of yesterday. A church, of course, was near at hand, the façade of which ascended into lofty pinnacles, whereon were perched two or three winged figures of stone, either angelic or allegorical, blowing stone trumpets in close vicinity to the upper windows of an old and shabby palace. This palace was distinguished by a feature not very common in the architecture of Roman edifices; that is to say, a mediæval tower, square, massive, lofty, and battlemented and machicolated at the summit.[1]

[1]Hilda's tower, like most of the physical settings in this romance, is drawn from life: "Mr. [C. G.] Thompson took me into the Via Portoghese, and showed me an old palace, above which rose—not a very customary feature of the architecture of Rome—a tall, battlemented bower. At one angle of the tower we saw a shrine of the Virgin, with a lamp, and all the appendages of those numerous shrines which we see at the street corners, and in hundreds of places about the city. Three or four centuries ago this palace was inhabited by a nobleman who had an only son, and a large, pet monkey, and one day the monkey caught the infant up and clambered to this lofty turret, and sat there with him in his arms grinning and chattering like the Devil himself. The father was in despair, but was afraid to pursue the monkey lest he should fling down the child from the height of the tower and make his escape. At last he vowed that if the boy were safely

At one of the angles of the battlements stood a shrine of the Virgin, such as we see everywhere at the street-corners of Rome, but seldom or never, except in this solitary instance, at a height above the ordinary level of men's views and aspirations. Connected with this old tower and its lofty shrine, there is a legend which we cannot here pause to tell; but for centuries a lamp has been burning before the Virgin's image, at noon, at midnight, and at all hours of the twenty-four, and must be kept burning forever, as long as the tower shall stand; or else the tower itself, the palace, and whatever estate belongs to it, shall pass from its hereditary possessor, in accordance with an ancient vow, and become the property of the Church.

As Miriam approached, she looked upward, and saw—not, indeed, the flame of the never-dying lamp, which was swallowed up in the broad sunlight that brightened the shrine—but a flock of white doves, skimming, fluttering, and wheeling about the topmost height of the tower, their silver wings flashing in the pure transparency of the air. Several of them sat on the ledge of the upper window, pushing one another off by their eager struggle for this favorite station, and all tapping their beaks and flapping their wings tumultuously against the panes; some had alighted in the street, far below, but flew hastily upward, at the sound of the window being thrust ajar, and opening in the middle, on rusty hinges, as Roman windows do.

----

restored to him he would build a shrine at the summit of the tower, and cause it to be kept as a sacred place forever. By and by the monkey came down and deposited the child on the ground; the father fulfilled his vow, built the shrine, and made it obligatory on all future possessors of the palace to keep the lamp burning before it. Centuries have passed, the property has changed hands; but still there is the shrine on the giddy top of the tower, far aloft over the street, on the very spot where the monkey sat, and there burns the lamp, in memory of the father's vow. This being the tenure by which the estate is held, the extinguishment of that flame might yet turn the present owner out of the palace" (*NB,* pp. 206–207). Note, in this context, the significance of the title of Chapter 43, "The Extinction of a Lamp."

A fair young girl, dressed in white, showed herself at the aperture for a single instant, and threw forth as much as her two small hands could hold of some kind of food, for the flock of eleemosynary doves. It seemed greatly to the taste of the feathered people; for they tried to snatch beaksful of it from her grasp, caught it in the air, and rustled downward after it upon the pavement.

"What a pretty scene this is," thought Miriam, with a kindly smile, "and how like a dove she is herself, the fair, pure creature! The other doves know her for a sister, I am sure."

Miriam passed beneath the deep portal of the palace, and turning to the left, began to mount flight after flight of a staircase, which, for the loftiness of its aspiration, was worthy to be Jacob's ladder, or, at all events, the staircase of the Tower of Babel.[2] The city bustle, which is heard even in Rome, the rumble of wheels over the uncomfortable paving-stones, the hard harsh cries reëchoing in the high and narrow streets, grew faint and died away; as the turmoil of the world will always die, if we set our faces to climb heavenward. Higher, and higher still; and now, glancing through the successive windows that threw in their narrow light upon the stairs, her view stretched across the roofs of the city, unimpeded even by the stateliest palaces. Only the domes of churches ascend into this airy region, and hold up their golden crosses on a level with her eye; except, that, out of the very heart of Rome, the column of Antoninus[3]

[2]On a journey, Jacob became tired and slept in open country. While asleep he dreamed of a ladder leading from earth to heaven, and of angels going up and down upon it. God appeared to him on the ladder and promised his descendants a homeland. Jacob awoke and built a temple on the spot, calling it Bethel (note the religious parallel in this chapter title). See Genesis 28:10-22. The Tower of Babel, in contrast to Jacob's temple, was a profanation to God, built to reach heaven and establish man there. God punished the builders by multiplying the languages in which they spoke so that they could not cooperate. See Genesis 11:1-9. Note Hawthorne's wry humor in pairing these allusions incongruously.

[3]Antonnius Pius (*fl.* A.D. 138-161) was the first of the Antonine emperors. The column of Antonnius stands in the Piazza Colonna.

thrusts itself upward, with St. Paul upon its summit, the sole human form that seems to have kept her company.

Finally, the staircase came to an end; save that, on one side of the little entry where it terminated, a flight of a dozen steps gave access to the roof of the tower and the legendary shrine. On the other side was a door, at which Miriam knocked, but rather as a friendly announcement of her presence than with any doubt of hospitable welcome; for, awaiting no response, she lifted the latch and entered.

"What a hermitage you have found for yourself, dear Hilda!" she exclaimed. "You breathe sweet air, above all the evil scents of Rome; and even so, in your maiden elevation, you dwell above our vanities and passions, our moral dust and mud, with the doves and the angels for your nearest neighbors. I should not wonder if the Catholics were to make a saint of you, like your namesake of old; especially as you have almost avowed yourself of their religion, by undertaking to keep the lamp alight before the Virgin's shrine."

"No, no, Miriam!" said Hilda, who had come joyfully forward to greet her friend. "You must not call me a Catholic. A Christian girl—even a daughter of the Puritans—may surely pay honor to the idea of divine Womanhood, without giving up the faith of her forefathers. But how kind you are to climb into my dove-cote!"

"It is no trifling proof of friendship, indeed," answered Miriam; "I should think there were three hundred stairs at least."

"But it will do you good," continued Hilda. "A height of some fifty feet above the roofs of Rome gives me all the advantages that I could get from fifty miles of distance. The air so exhilarates my spirits, that sometimes I feel half inclined to attempt a flight from the top of my tower, in the faith that I should float upward."

"Oh, pray don't try it!" said Miriam, laughing. "If it should turn out that you are less than an angel, you would find the stones of the Roman pavement very hard; and if an angel, indeed, I am afraid you would never come down among us again."

This young American girl was an example of the freedom of life which it is possible for a female artist to enjoy at Rome. She dwelt in her tower, as free to descend into the corrupted atmosphere of the city beneath, as one of her companion doves to fly downward into the street;—all alone, perfectly independent, under her own sole guardianship, unless watched over by the Virgin, whose shrine she tended; doing what she liked, without a suspicion or a shadow upon the snowy whiteness of her fame. The customs of artist life bestow such liberty upon the sex, which is elsewhere restricted within so much narrower limits; and it is perhaps an indication that, whenever we admit woman to a wider scope of pursuits and professions, we must also remove the shackles of our present conventional rules, which would then become an insufferable restraint on either maid or wife. The system seems to work unexceptionably in Rome; and in many other cases, as in Hilda's, purity of heart and life are allowed to assert themselves, and to be their own proof and security, to a degree unknown in the society of other cities.

Hilda, in her native land, had early shown what was pronounced by connoisseurs a decided genius for the pictorial art. Even in her school days—still not so very distant—she had produced sketches that were seized upon by men of taste, and hoarded as among the choicest treasures of their portfolios; scenes delicately imagined, lacking, perhaps, the reality which comes only from a close acquaintance with life, but so softly touched with feeling and fancy that you seemed to be looking at humanity with angel's eyes. With years and experience she might be expected to attain a darker and more forcible touch, which would impart to her designs the relief they needed. Had Hilda remained in her own country it is not improbable that she might have produced original works worthy to hang in that gallery of native art which, we hope, is destined to extend its rich length through many future centuries. An orphan,

however, without near relatives, and possessed of a little property, she had found it within her possibilities to come to Italy;
that central clime, whither the eyes and the heart of every
artist turn, as if pictures could not be made to glow in any
other atmosphere, as if statues could not assume grace and expression save in that land of whitest marble.

Hilda's gentle courage had brought her safely over land
and sea; her mild, unflagging perseverence had made a place
for her in the famous city, even like a flower that finds a chink
for itself, and a little earth to grow in, on whatever ancient
wall its slender roots may fasten. Here she dwelt, in her tower,
possessing a friend or two in Rome, but no home companion
except the flock of doves, whose cote was in a ruinous chamber
contiguous to her own. They soon became as familiar with the
fairhaired Saxon girl as if she were a born sister of their brood;
and her customary white robe bore such an analogy to their
snowy plumage that the confraternity of artists called Hilda
the Dove, and recognized her aërial apartment as the Dove-cote.
And while the other doves flew far and wide in quest of what
was good for them, Hilda likewise spread her wings, and sought
such ethereal and imaginative sustenance as God ordains for
creatures of her kind.

We know not whether the result of her Italian studies, so
far is it could yet be seen, will be accepted as a good or desirable one. Certain it is, that, since her arrival in the pictorial
land, Hilda seemed to have entirely lost the impulse of original
design, which brought her thither. No doubt the girl's early
dreams had been of sending forms and hues of beauty into the
visible world out of her own mind; of compelling scenes of
poetry and history to live before men's eyes, through con-
ceptions and by methods individual to herself. But more and
more, as she grew familiar with the miracles of art that enrich
so many galleries in Rome, Hilda had ceased to consider herself as an original artist. No wonder that this change should
have befallen her. She was endowed with a deep and sensitive
faculty of appreciation; she had the gift of discerning and

worshipping excellence in a most unusual measure. No other person, it is probable, recognized so adequately, and enjoyed with such deep delight, the pictorial wonders that were here displayed. She saw—no, not saw, but felt—through and through a picture; she bestowed upon it all the warmth and richness of a woman's sympathy; not by any intellectual effort, but by this strength of heart, and this guiding light of sympathy, she went straight to the central point, in which the master had conceived his work. Thus, she viewed it, as it were, with his own eyes, and hence her comprehension of any picture that interested her was perfect.

This power and depth of appreciation depended partly upon Hilda's physical organization, which was at once health-ful and exquisitely delicate; and, connected with this advan-tage, she had a command of hand, a nicety and force of touch, which is an endowment separate from pictorial genius, though indispensable to its exercise.

It has probably happened in many other instances, as it did in Hilda's case, that she ceased to aim at original achieve-ment in consequence of the very gifts which so exquisitely fitted her to profit by familiarity with the works of the mighty old masters. Reverencing these wonderful men so deeply, she was too grateful for all they bestowed upon her, too loyal, too humble, in their awful presence, to think of enrolling herself in their society. Beholding the miracles of beauty which they had achieved, the world seemed already rich enough in original designs, and nothing now was so desirable as to diffuse those selfsame beauties more widely among mankind. All the youth-ful hopes and ambitions, the fanciful ideas which she had brought from home, of great pictures to be conceived in her feminine mind, were flung aside, and, so far as those most intimate with her could discern, relinquished without a sigh. All that she would henceforth attempt—and that most rever-ently, not to say religiously—was to catch and reflect some of the glory which had been shed upon canvas from the immortal pencils of old.

So Hilda became a copyist: in the Pinacotheca of the Vatican,[4] in the galleries of the Pamfili-Doria palace, the Borghese, the Corsini, the Sciarra, her easel was set up before many a famous picture of Guido, Domenichino, Raphael, and the devout painters of earlier schools than these. Other artists, and visitors from foreign lands, beheld her slender, girlish figure in front of some world-known work, absorbed, unconscious of everything around her, seeming to live only in what she sought to do. They smiled, no doubt, at the audacity which led her to dream of copying those mighty achievements. But, if they paused to look over her shoulder, and had sensibility enough to understand what was before their eyes, they soon felt inclined to believe that the spirits of the old masters were hovering over Hilda, and guiding her delicate white hand. In truth, from whatever realm of bliss and many-colored beauty those spirits might descend, it would have been no unworthy errand to help so gentle and pure a worshipper of their genius in giving the last divine touch to her repetitions of their works.

Her copies were indeed marvellous. Accuracy was not the phrase for them; a Chinese copy is accurate. Hilda's had that evanescent and ethereal life—that flitting fragrance, as it were, of the originals—which it is as difficult to catch and retain as it would be for a sculptor to get the very movement and varying color of a living man into his marble bust. Only by watching the efforts of the most skilful copyists—men who spend a lifetime, as some of them do, in multiplying copies of a single picture—and observing how invariably they leave out just the indefinable charm that involves the last, inestimable

[4]A small Vatican art gallery established by Pius VII (*fl.* 1800–1823) after the fall of Napoleon I. The gallery contains Raphael's *Transfiguration*. Raphael, Leonardo da Vinci (1452–1519), and Michelangelo (1474–1564) were the three greatest painters of the Italian Renaissance. Guido Reni (1575–1642) was a baroque painter, somewhat voluptuous and sentimental in style. Domenichino (1581–1641) worked largely in frescoes for Roman churches; among his works is the *Assumption of the Virgin*, finished on the ceiling of Santa Maria in Trastevere in 1617.

value, can we understand the difficulties of the task which they undertake.

It was not Hilda's general practice to attempt reproducing the whole of a great picture, but to select some high, noble, and delicate portion of it, in which the spirit and essence of the picture culminated: the Virgin's celestial sorrow, for example, or a hovering angel, imbued with immortal light, or a saint with the glow of heaven in his dying face;—and these would be rendered with her whole soul. If a picture had darkened into an indistinct shadow through time and neglect, or had been injured by cleaning, or retouched by some profane hand, she seemed to possess the faculty of seeing it in its pristine glory. The copy would come from her hands with what the beholder felt must be the light which the old master had left upon the original in bestowing his final and most ethereal touch. In some instances even (at least, so those believed who best appreciated Hilda's power and sensibility,) she had been enabled to execute what the great master had conceived in his imagination, but had not so perfectly succeeded in putting upon canvas; a result surely not impossible when such depth of sympathy as she possessed was assisted by the delicate skill and accuracy of her slender hand. In such cases the girl was but a finer instrument, a more exquisitely effective piece of mechanism, by the help of which the spirit of some great departed painter now first achieved his ideal, centuries after his own earthly hand, that other tool, had turned to dust.

Not to describe her as too much a wonder, however, Hilda, or the Dove, as her well-wishers half laughingly delighted to call her, had been pronounced by good judges incomparably the best copyist in Rome. After minute examination of her works, the most skilful artists declared that she had been led to her results by following precisely the same processes step by step through which the original painter had trodden to the development of his idea. Other copyists—if such they are worthy to be called—attempt only a superficial imitation. Copies of the old masters in this sense are produced by thousands; there are artists, as we have said, who spend their lives in painting the works, or perhaps one single work of one illustrious painter over and over again: thus they convert themselves into Guido machines, or Raphaelic machines. Their performances, it is true, are often wonderfully deceptive to a careless eye; but working entirely from the outside, and seeking only to reproduce the surface, these men are sure to leave out that indefinable nothing, that inestimable something, that constitutes the life and soul through which the picture gets its immortality. Hilda was no such machine as this; she wrought religiously, and therefore wrought a miracle.

It strikes us that there is something far higher and nobler in all this, in her thus sacrificing herself to the devout recognition of the highest excellence in art, than there would have been in cultivating her not inconsiderable share of talent for the production of works from her own ideas. She might have set up for herself, and won no ignoble name; she might have helped to fill the already crowded and cumbered world with pictures, not destitute of merit, but falling short, if by ever so little, of the best that has been done; she might thus have gratified some tastes that were incapable of appreciating Raphael. But this could be done only by lowering the standard of art to the comprehension of the spectator. She chose the better and loftier and more unselfish part, laying her individual hopes, her fame, her prospects of enduring remembrance, at the feet of those great departed ones, whom she so loved and venerated; and therefore the world was the richer for this feeble girl. Since the beauty and glory of a great picture are confined within itself, she won out that glory by patient faith and self-devotion, and multiplied it for mankind. From the dark, chill corner of a gallery—from some curtained chapel in a church, where the light came seldom and aslant—from the prince's carefully guarded cabinet, where not one eye in thousands was permitted to behold it—she brought the wondrous picture into daylight, and gave all its magic splendor for the enjoyment of the world. Hilda's faculty of genuine admiration is one of the rarest to be found in human nature; and let us try to recompense her in kind by adducing her generous self-surrender, and her brave, humble magnanimity in choosing to be the handmaid of those old magicians, instead of a minor enchantress within a circle of her own.

The handmaid of Raphael, whom she loved with a virgin's love! Would it have been worth Hilda's while to relinquish this office for the sake of giving the world a picture or two which it would call original; pretty fancies of snow and moonlight; the counterpart in picture of so many feminine achievements in literature!

CHAPTER 7. *Beatrice*

Miriam was glad to find the Dove in her turret-home; for being endowed with an infinite activity, and taking exquisite delight in the sweet labor of which her life was full, it was Hilda's practice to flee abroad betimes and haunt the galleries till dusk. Happy were those (but they were very few) whom she ever chose to be the companions of her day; they saw the art-treasures of Rome, under her guidance, as they had never seen them before. Not that Hilda could dissertate, or talk learnedly about pictures; she would probably have been puzzled by the technical terms of her own art. Not that she had much to say about what she most profoundly admired; but even her silent sympathy was so powerful that it drew your own along with it, endowing you with a second-sight that enabled you to see excellencies with almost the depth and delicacy of her own perceptions.

All the Anglo-Saxon denizens of Rome, by this time, knew Hilda by sight. Unconsciously, the poor child had become one of the spectacles of the Eternal City, and was often pointed out to strangers, sitting at her easel among the wild-bearded young men, the white-haired old ones, and the shabbily dressed, painfully plain women, who make up the throng of copyists. The old custodes knew her well, and watched over her as their own child. Sometimes, a young artist, instead of going on with a copy of the picture before which he had placed his easel, would enrich his canvas with an original portrait of Hilda at her work. A lovelier subject could not have been selected, nor one which required nicer skill and insight in doing it anything like justice. She was pretty at all times, in our native New England style, with her light-brown ringlets, her delicately tinged, but healthful cheek, her sensitive, intelligent, yet most feminine and kindly face. But, every few moments, this pretty and girlish face grew beautiful and striking, as some inward thought and feeling brightened, rose to the surface, and then, as it were, passed out of sight again; so that, taking into view this constantly recurring change, it really seemed as if Hilda were only visible by the sunshine of her soul.

In other respects, she was a good subject for a portrait, being distinguished by a gentle picturesqueness, which was perhaps unconsciously bestowed by some minute peculiarity of dress, such as artists seldom fail to assume. The effect was to make her appear like an inhabitant of picture-land, a partly ideal creature, not to be handled, nor even approached too closely. In her feminine self, Hilda was natural, and of pleasant deportment, endowed with a mild cheerfulness of temper, not overflowing with animal spirits, but never long despondent. There was a certain simplicity that made every one her friend, but it was combined with a subtle attribute of reserve, that insensibly kept those at a distance who were not suited to her sphere.

Miriam was the dearest friend whom she had ever known. Being a year or two the elder, of longer acquaintance with Italy, and better fitted to deal with its crafty and selfish inhabitants, she had helped Hilda to arrange her way of life, and had encouraged her through those first weeks, when Rome is so dreary to every newcomer.

"But how lucky that you are at home to-day," said Miriam, continuing the conversation which was begun, many pages back. "I hardly hoped to find you, though I had a favor to ask—a commission to put into your charge. But what picture is this?"

"See!" said Hilda, taking her friend's hand and leading her in front of the easel. "I wanted your opinion of it."

"If you have really succeeded," observed Miriam, recognizing the picture at the first glance, "it will be the greatest miracle you have yet achieved."

The picture represented simply a female head; a very youthful, girlish, perfectly beautiful face, enveloped in white drapery, from beneath which strayed a lock or two of what seemed a rich, though hidden luxuriance of auburn hair. The eyes were large and brown, and met those of the spectator, but evidently with a strange, ineffectual effort to escape. There was a little redness about the eyelids, very slightly indicated, so that you would question whether or no the girl had been weeping. The whole face was quiet; there was no distortion or disturbance of any single feature; nor was it easy to see why the expression was not cheerful, or why a single touch of the artist's pencil should not brighten it into joyousness. But, in fact, it was the very saddest picture ever painted or conceived; it involved an unfathomable depth of sorrow, the sense of which came to the observer by a sort of intuition. It was a sorrow that removed this beautiful girl out of the sphere of humanity, and set her in a far-off region, the remoteness of which —while yet her face is so close before us—makes us shiver as at a spectre.

"Yes, Hilda," said her friend, after closely examining the picture, "you have done nothing else so wonderful as this. But by what unheard-of solicitations or secret interest have you obtained leave to copy Guido's Beatrice Cenci?[1] It is an unexampled favor; and the impossibility of getting a genuine copy

---

[1]Beatrice Cenci (1577–1599) was imprisoned by her vicious father, an Italian nobleman. She had him murdered and was executed together with her stepmother, brothers, and lover for the crime. Shelley's play *The Cenci* postulated that the murder was her revenge on her father for raping her; historically this is doubtful. But Hawthorne uses the incest-rape-patricide motif to draw Miriam, who has a dark past. He was powerfully moved by Guido's portrait of Beatrice: "It is the most profoundly wrought picture in the world; no artist did it, nor could do it again. Guido may have held the brush, but he painted better than he knew. I wish, however, it were possible for some spectator, of deep sensibility, to see the picture without knowing anything of its subject or history; for, no doubt, we bring all our knowledge of the Cenci tragedy to the interpretation of it" (*NB*, pp. 89–90).

has filled the Roman picture-shops with Beatrices, gay, grievous, or coquettish, but never a true one among them."

"There has been one exquisite copy, I have heard," said Hilda, "by an artist capable of appreciating the spirit of the picture. It was Thompson,[2] who brought it away piecemeal, being forbidden (like the rest of us) to set up his easel before it. As for me, I knew the Prince Barberini would be deaf to all entreaties; so I had no resource but to sit down before the picture, day after day, and let it sink into my heart. I do believe it is now photographed there. It is a sad face to keep so close to one's heart; only, what is so very beautiful can never be quite a pain. Well; after studying it in this way, I know not how many times, I came home, and have done my best to transfer the image to canvas."

"Here it is then," said Miriam, contemplating Hilda's work with great interest and delight, mixed with the painful sympathy that the picture excited. "Everywhere we see oil-paintings, crayon sketches, cameos, engravings, lithographs, pretending to be Beatrice, and representing the poor girl with blubbered eyes, a leer of coquetry, a merry look as if she were dancing, a piteous look as if she were beaten, and twenty other modes of fantastic mistake. But here is Guido's very Beatrice; she that slept

[2]Cephas Giovanni Thompson (1809–1888), an American artist who painted Hawthorne's portrait in 1850, helped the Hawthornes rent a carriage for their tour of northern Italy in the summer of 1858, and helped them find lodgings on their return to Rome in the fall. Hawthorne admired his sharp bargaining with the vetturini, the Hertz and Avis men of that day. He wrote of Thompson on March 11, 1858, "I do not think there is a better painter than Mr. Thompson living—among Americans at least; not one so earnest, faithful, and religious in his worship of art. I had rather look at his pictures than at any except the very finest of the old masters, and, taking into consideration only the comparative pleasure to be derived, I would not except more than one or two of those" (*NB*, p. 123).

Guido's *Beatrice* hung in the gallery of the Palazzo Barberini, which was designed by Bernini. The Prince Barberini was the scion of an aristocratic Italian family who patronized Roman art and literature in the 17th century.

in the dungeon, and awoke betimes, to ascend the scaffold. And now that you have done it, Hilda, can you interpret what the feeling is, that gives this picture such a mysterious force? For my part, though deeply sensible of its influence, I cannot seize it."

"Nor can I, in words," replied her friend. "But while I was painting her, I felt all the time as if she were trying to escape from my gaze. She knows that her sorrow is so strange and so immense, that she ought to be solitary forever, both for the world's sake and her own; and this is the reason we feel such a distance between Beatrice and ourselves, even when our eyes meet hers. It is infinitely heart-breaking to meet her glance, and to feel that nothing can be done to help or comfort her; neither does she ask help or comfort, knowing the hopelessness of her case better than we do. She is a fallen angel—fallen, and yet sinless; and it is only this depth of sorrow, with its weight and darkness, that keeps her down upon earth, and brings her within our view even while it sets her beyond our reach."

"You deem her sinless?" asked Miriam; "that is not so plain to me. If I can pretend to see at all into that dim region, whence she gazes so strangely and sadly at us, Beatrice's own conscience does not acquit her of something evil, and never to be forgiven!"

"Sorrow so black as hers oppresses her very nearly as sin would," said Hilda.

"Then," inquired Miriam, "do you think that there was no sin in the deed for which she suffered?"

"Ah!" replied Hilda, shuddering, "I really had quite forgotten Beatrice's history, and was thinking of her only as the picture seems to reveal her character. Yes, yes; it was terrible guilt, an inexpiable crime, and she feels it to be so. Therefore it is that the forlorn creature so longs to elude our eyes, and forever vanish away into nothingness! Her doom is just!"

"Oh! Hilda, your innocence is like a sharp steel sword," exclaimed her friend. "Your judgments are often terribly severe, though you seem all made up of gentleness and mercy. Beatrice's

sin may not have been so great: perhaps it was no sin at all, but
the best virtue possible in the circumstances. If she viewed it as
a sin, it may have been because her nature was too feeble for
the fate imposed upon her. Ah!" continued Miriam, passionately, "if I could only get within her consciousness!—if I could
but clasp Beatrice Cenci's ghost, and draw it into myself! I
would give my life to know whether she thought herself
innocent, or the one great criminal since time began."

As Miriam gave utterance to these words, Hilda looked
from the picture into her face, and was startled to observe that
her friend's expression had become almost exactly that of the
portrait; as if her passionate wish and struggle to penetrate
poor Beatrice's mystery had been successful.

"Oh! for Heaven's sake, Miriam, do not look so!" she
cried. "What an actress you are! And I never guessed it before.
Ah! now you are yourself again," she added, kissing her. "Leave
Beatrice to me in future."

"Cover up your magical picture, then," replied her friend,
"else I never can look away from it. It is strange, dear Hilda,
how an innocent, delicate, white soul like yours has been able
to seize the subtle mystery of this portrait; as you surely must,
in order to reproduce it so perfectly. Well; we will not talk of
it any more. Do you know, I have come to you this morning on
a small matter of business. Will you undertake it for me?"

"Oh, certainly," said Hilda, laughing; "if you choose to
trust me with business."

"Nay, it is not a matter of any difficulty," answered
Miriam; "merely to take charge of this packet, and keep it for
me awhile."

"But why not keep it yourself?" asked Hilda.

"Partly because it will be safer in your charge," said her
friend. "I am a careless sort of person in ordinary things; while
you, for all you dwell so high above the world, have certain
good little housewifely ways of accuracy and order. The packet
is of some slight importance; and yet, it may be, I shall not ask
you for it again. In a week or two, you know, I am leaving

Rome. You, setting at defiance the malaria fever, mean to stay here and haunt your beloved galleries through the summer. Now, four months hence, unless you hear more from me, I would have you deliver the packet according to its address."

Hilda read the direction: it was to Signore Luca Barboni, at the Palazzo Cenci, third piano.[3]

"I will deliver it with my own hand," said she, "precisely four months from to-day, unless you bid me to the contrary. Perhaps I shall meet the ghost of Beatrice in that grim old palace of her forefathers."

"In that case," rejoined Miriam, "do not fail to speak to her, and try to win her confidence. Poor thing! she would be all the better for pouring her heart out freely, and would be glad to do it, if she were sure of sympathy. It irks my brain and heart to think of her, all shut up within herself." She withdrew the cloth that Hilda had drawn over the picture, and took another long look at it,—"Poor sister Beatrice! for she was still a woman, Hilda, still a sister, be her sin or sorrow what they might. How well you have done it, Hilda! I know not whether Guido will thank you, or be jealous of your rivalship."

"Jealous, indeed!" exclaimed Hilda. "If Guido had not wrought through me, my pains would have been thrown away."

"After all," resumed Miriam, "if a woman had painted the original picture, there might have been something in it which we miss now. I have a great mind to undertake a copy myself, and try to give it what it lacks. Well; good bye. But, stay! I am going for a little airing to the grounds of the Villa Borghese this afternoon. You will think it very foolish, but I always feel the safer in your company, Hilda, slender little maiden as you are. Will you come?"

"Ah, not to-day, dearest Miriam," she replied, "I have set my heart on giving another touch or two to this picture, and shall not stir abroad till nearly sunset."

"Farewell, then," said her visitor. "I leave you in your

[3] I.e., on the third floor.

dove-cote. What a sweet, strange life you lead here; conversing with the souls of the old masters, feeding and fondling your sister-doves, and trimming the Virgin's lamp! Hilda, do you ever pray to the Virgin while you tend her shrine?"

"Sometimes I have been moved to do so," replied the Dove, blushing and lowering her eyes; "she was a woman once. Do you think it would be wrong?"

"Nay, that is for you to judge," said Miriam; "but when you pray next, dear friend, remember me!"

She went down the long descent of the tower staircase, and just as she reached the street the flock of doves again took their hurried flight from the pavement to the topmost window. She threw her eyes upward and beheld them hovering about Hilda's head; for after her friend's departure the girl had been more impressed than before by something very sad and troubled in her manner. She was, therefore, leaning forth from her airy abode, and flinging down a kind, maidenly kiss, and a gesture of farewell, in the hope that these might alight upon Miriam's heart and comfort its unknown sorrow a little. Kenyon the sculptor, who chanced to be passing the head of the street, took note of that ethereal kiss, and wished that he could have caught it in the air and got Hilda's leave to keep it.

CHAPTER 8. *The Suburban Villa*

Donatello, while it was still a doubtful question betwixt afternoon and morning, set forth to keep the appointment which Miriam had carelessly tendered him in the grounds of the Villa Borghese.[1]

The entrance to these grounds (as all my readers know, for everybody now-a-days has been in Rome) is just outside of the Porta del Popolo. Passing beneath that not very impressive specimen of Michael Angelo's architecture, a minute's walk will transport the visitor from the small, uneasy lava stones of the Roman pavement into broad, gravelled carriage-drives, whence a little farther stroll brings him to the soft turf of a beautiful seclusion. A seclusion, but seldom a solitude; for priest, noble, and populace, stranger and native, all who breathe Roman air, find free admission, and come hither to taste the languid enjoyment of the daydream that they call life.

But Donatello's enjoyment was of a livelier kind. He soon began to draw long and delightful breaths among those shadowy walks. Judging by the pleasure which the sylvan character of the scene excited in him, it might be no merely fanciful theory to set him down as the kinsman, not far remote, of that wild, sweet, playful, rustic creature, to whose marble image he bore so striking a resemblance. How mirthful a discovery would it be (and yet with a touch of pathos in it), if the breeze which sported fondly with his clustering locks were to waft them sud-

[1]A large and lovely garden, a favorite spot for Roman strollers. When Pope Paul V, Camillo Borghese (*fl.* 1605–1621), named his young nephew Scipio to the Sacred College of Cardinals, Scipio had Van Zans design the villa for him.

denly aside, and show a pair of leaf-shaped, furry ears! What an honest strain of wildness would it indicate! and into what regions of rich mystery would it extend Donatello's sympathies, to be thus linked (and by no monstrous chain) with what we call the inferior tribes of being, whose simplicity, mingled with his human intelligence, might partly restore what man has lost of the divine!

The scenery amid which the youth now strayed was such as arrays itself in the imagination when we read the beautiful old myths, and fancy a brighter sky, a softer turf, a more picturesque arrangement of venerable trees, than we find in the rude and untrained landscapes of the Western world. The ilex-trees, so ancient and time-honored were they, seemed to have lived for ages undisturbed, and to feel no dread of profanation by the axe any more than overthrow by the thunder-stroke. It had already passed out of their dreamy old memories that only a few years ago they were grievously imperilled by the Gaul's last assault upon the walls of Rome.[2] As if confident in the long peace of their lifetime, they assumed attitudes of indolent repose. They leaned over the green turf in ponderous grace, throwing abroad their great branches without danger of interfering with other trees, though other majestic trees grew near enough for dignified society, but too distant for constraint. Never was there a more venerable quietude than that which slept among their sheltering boughs; never a sweeter sunshine than that now gladdening the gentle gloom which these leafy patriarchs strove to diffuse over the swelling and subsiding lawns.

In other portions of the grounds the stone-pines lifted their dense clump of branches upon a slender length of stem, so high that they looked like green islands in the air, flinging down a shadow upon the turf so far off that you hardly knew what tree had made it. Again, there were avenues of cypress, resembling dark flames of huge funereal candles, which spread dusk and twilight round about them instead of cheerful radiance. The

[2]Alaric and his Visigoths sacked Rome A.D. 410.

more open spots were all a-bloom, even so early in the season, with anemones of wondrous size, both white and rose-colored, and violets that betrayed themselves by their rich fragrance, even if their blue eyes failed to meet your own. Daisies, too, were abundant, but larger than the modest little English flower, and therefore of small account.

These wooded and flowery lawns are more beautiful than the finest of English park-scenery, more touching, more impressive, through the neglect that leaves nature so much to her own ways and methods. Since man seldom interferes with her, she sets to work in her quiet way and makes herself at home. There is enough of human care, it is true, bestowed long ago, and still bestowed, to prevent wildness from growing into deformity; and the result is an ideal landscape, a woodland scene that seems to have been projected out of a poet's mind. If the ancient Faun were other than a mere creation of old poetry, and could have reappeared anywhere, it must have been in such a scene as this.

In the openings of the wood there are fountains plashing into marble basins, the depths of which are shaggy with water-weeds; or they tumble like natural cascades from rock to rock, sending their murmur afar, to make the quiet and silence more appreciable. Scattered here and there with careless artifice, stand old altars bearing Roman inscriptions. Statues, gray with the long corrosion of even that soft atmosphere, half hide and half reveal themselves, high on pedestals, or perhaps fallen and broken on the turf. Terminal figures, columns of marble or granite, porticoes, arches, are seen in the vistas of the wood-paths, either veritable relics of antiquity, or with so exquisite a touch of artful ruin on them that they are better than if really antique. At all events, grass grows on the tops of the shattered pillars, and weeds and flowers root themselves in the chinks of the massive arches and fronts of temples, and clamber at large over their pediments, as if this were the thousandth summer since their winged seeds alighted there.

What a strange idea—what a needless labor—to construct artificial ruins in Rome, the native soil of ruin! But even these

sportive imitations, wrought by man in emulation of what time
has done to temples and palaces, are perhaps centuries old, and,
beginning as illusions, have grown to be venerable in sober earnest. The result of all is a scene, pensive, lovely, dream-like,
enjoyable and sad, such as is to be found nowhere save in these
princely villa-residences in the neighborhood of Rome; a scene
that must have required generations and ages, during which
growth, decay, and man's intelligence wrought kindly together,
to render it so gently wild as we behold it now.

The final charm is bestowed by the malaria. There is a
piercing, thrilling, delicious kind of regret in the idea of so
much beauty thrown away, or only enjoyable at its half-
development, in winter and early spring, and never to be dwelt
amongst, as the home-scenery of any human being. For if you
come hither in summer, and stray through these glades in the
golden sunset, fever walks arm in arm with you, and death
awaits you at the end of the dim vista. Thus the scene is like
Eden in its loveliness; like Eden, too, in the fatal spell that removes it beyond the scope of man's actual possessions. But
Donatello felt nothing of this dream-like melancholy that haunts
the spot. As he passed among the sunny shadows, his spirit
seemed to acquire new elasticity. The flicker of the sunshine,
the sparkle of the fountain's gush, the dance of the leaf upon the
bough, the woodland fragrance, the green freshness, the old
sylvan peace and freedom, were all intermingled in those long
breaths which he drew.

The ancient dust, the mouldiness of Rome, the dead
atmosphere in which he had wasted so many months, the hard
pavements, the smell of ruin and decaying generations, the chill
palaces, the convent-bells, the heavy incense of altars, the life
that he had led in those dark, narrow streets, among priests,
soldiers, nobles, artists, and women—all the sense of these things
rose from the young man's consciousness like a cloud which
had darkened over him without his knowing how densely.

He drank in the natural influences of the scene, and was
intoxicated as by an exhilarating wine. He ran races with him-

self along the gleam and shadow of the wood-paths. He leapt
up to catch the overhanging bough of an ilex, and swinging himself by it alighted far onward, as if he had flown thither through
the air. In a sudden rapture he embraced the trunk of a sturdy
tree, and seemed to imagine it a creature worthy of affection
and capable of a tender response; he clasped it closely in his
arms, as a Faun might have clasped the warm, feminine grace
of the nymph, whom antiquity supposed to dwell within that
rough, encircling rind. Then, in order to bring himself closer
to the genial earth, with which his kindred instincts linked him
so strongly, he threw himself at full length on the turf, and
pressed down his lips, kissing the violets and daisies, which kissed
him back again, though shyly, in their maiden fashion.

While he lay there, it was pleasant to see how the green
and blue lizards, who had been basking on some rock or on a
fallen pillar that absorbed the warmth of the sun, scrupled not
to scramble over him with their small feet; and how the birds
alighted on the nearest twigs and sang their little roundelays
unbroken by any chirrup of alarm; they recognized him, it may
be, as something akin to themselves, or else they fancied that
he was rooted and grew there; for these wild pets of nature
dreaded him no more in his buoyant life than if a mound of soil
and grass and flowers had long since covered his dead body,
converting it back to the sympathies from which human existence had estranged it.

All of us, after long abode in cities, have felt the blood
gush more joyously through our veins with the first breath of
rural air; few could feel it so much as Donatello, a creature of
simple elements, bred in the sweet sylvan life of Tuscany, and
for months back dwelling amid the mouldy gloom and dim
splendor of old Rome. Nature has been shut out for numberless
centuries from those stony-hearted streets, to which he had
latterly grown accustomed; there is no trace of her, except for
what glades of grass spring out of the pavements of the less
trodden piazzas, or what weeds cluster and tuft themselves on
the cornices of ruins. Therefore his joy was like that of a child

that had gone astray from home, and finds him suddenly in his mother's arms again.

At last, deeming it full time for Miriam to keep her tryst, he climbed to the tiptop of the tallest tree, and thence looked about him, swaying to and fro in the gentle breeze, which was like the respiration of that great leafy, living thing. Donatello saw beneath him the whole circuit of the enchanted ground; the statues and columns pointing upward from among the shrubbery, the fountains flashing in the sunlight, the paths winding hither and thither, and continually finding out some nook of new and ancient pleasantness. He saw the villa, too, with its marble front incrusted all over with bas-reliefs, and statues in its many niches. It was as beautiful as a fairy palace, and seemed an abode in which the lord and lady of this fair domain might fitly dwell, and come forth each morning to enjoy as sweet a life as their happiest dreams of the past night could have depicted. All this he saw, but his first glance had taken in too wide a sweep, and it was not till his eyes fell almost directly beneath him, that Donatello beheld Miriam just turning into the path that led across the roots of his very tree.

He descended among the foliage, waiting for her to come close to the trunk, and then suddenly dropped from an impending bough, and alighted at her side. It was as if the swaying of the branches had let a ray of sunlight through. The same ray likewise glimmered among the gloomy meditations that encompassed Miriam, and lit up the pale, dark beauty of her face, while it responded pleasantly to Donatello's glance.

"I hardly know," said she, smiling, "whether you have sprouted out of the earth, or fallen from the clouds. In either case, you are welcome."

And they walked onward together.

Miriam's sadder mood, it might be, had at first an effect on Donatello's spirits. It checked the joyous ebullition into which they would otherwise have effervesced when he found himself in her society, not, as heretofore, in the old gloom of Rome, but under that bright soft sky and in those Arcadian woods. He was silent for awhile; it being, indeed, seldom Donatello's impulse to express himself copiously in words. His usual modes of demonstration were by the natural language of gesture, the instinctive movement of his agile frame, and the unconscious play of his features, which, within a limited range of thought and emotion, could speak volumes in a moment.

By-and-by, his own mood seemed to brighten Miriam's, and was reflected back upon himself. He began inevitably, as it were, to dance along the woodpath, flinging himself into attitudes of strange comic grace. Often, too, he ran a little way in advance of his companion, and then stood to watch her as she approached along the shadowy and sun-flickered path. With every step she took, he expressed his joy at her nearer and nearer presence by what might be thought an extravagance of gesticulation, but which doubtless was the language of the natural man, though laid aside and forgotten by other men, now that words have been feebly substituted in the place of signs and symbols. He gave Miriam the idea of a being not precisely man, nor yet a child, but, in a high and beautiful sense, an animal—a creature in a state of development less than what mankind has attained, yet the more perfect within itself for that very deficiency. This idea filled her mobile imagination with agreeable fantasies, which, after smiling at them herself, she tried to convey to the young man.

"What are you, my friend?" she exclaimed, always keeping in mind his singular resemblance to the Faun of the Capitol. "If you are, in good truth, that wild and pleasant creature whose face you wear, pray make me known to your kindred. They will be found hereabouts, if anywhere. Knock at the rough rind of this ilex-tree, and summon forth the Dryad![1] Ask the water-nymph to rise dripping from yonder fountain, and exchange a moist pressure of the hand with me! Do not fear that I shall shrink, even if one of your rough cousins, a hairy Satyr, should come capering on his goat-legs out of the haunts of far antiquity, and propose to dance with me among these lawns! And will not Bacchus—with whom you consorted so familiarly of old, and who loved you so well—will he not meet us here, and squeeze rich grapes into his cup for you and me?"

Donatello smiled; he laughed heartily, indeed, in sympathy with the mirth that gleamed out of Miriam's deep, dark eyes. But he did not seem quite to understand her mirthful talk, nor to be disposed to explain what kind of creature he was, or to inquire with what divine or poetic kindred his companion feigned to link him. He appeared only to know that Miriam was beautiful, and that she smiled graciously upon him; that the present moment was very sweet, and himself most happy with the sunshine, the sylvan scenery, and woman's kindly charm, which it enclosed within its small circumference. It was delightful to see the trust which he reposed in Miriam, and his pure joy in her propinquity; he asked nothing, sought nothing, save to be near the beloved object, and brimmed over with ecstasy at that simple boon. A creature of the happy tribes below us sometimes shows the capacity of this enjoyment; a man, seldom or never.

"Donatello," said Miriam, looking at him thoughtfully, but amused, yet not without a shadow of sorrow, "you seem very happy; what makes you so?"

[1]A nymph who lives in a tree; Bacchus, below, is the Roman god of wine.

"Because I love you!" answered Donatello.

He made this momentous confession as if it were the most natural thing in the world; and, on her part—such was the contagion of his simplicity—Miriam heard it without anger or disturbance, though with no responding emotion. It was as if they had strayed across the limits of Arcadia, and come under a civil polity where young men might avow their passion with as little restraint as a bird pipes its notes to a similar purpose.

"Why should you love me, foolish boy?" said she. "We have no points of sympathy at all. There are not two creatures more unlike, in this wide world, than you and I!"

"You are yourself, and I am Donatello," replied he. "Therefore I love you! There needs no other reason."

Certainly, there was no better or more explicable reason. It might have been imagined that Donatello's unsophisticated heart would be more readily attracted to a feminine nature of clear simplicity like his own, than to one already turbid with grief or wrong, as Miriam's seemed to be. Perhaps, on the other hand, his character needed the dark element, which it found in her. The force and energy of will, that sometimes flashed through her eyes, may have taken him captive; or, not improbably, the varying lights and shadows of her temper, now so mirthful, and anon so sad with mysterious gloom, had bewitched the youth. Analyze the matter as we may, the reason assigned by Donatello himself was as satisfactory as we are likely to attain.

Miriam could not think seriously of the avowal that had passed. He held out his love so freely, in his open palm, that she felt it could be nothing but a toy, which she might play with for an instant, and give back again. And yet Donatello's heart was so fresh a fountain, that, had Miriam been more world-worn than she was, she might have found it exquisite to slake her thirst with the feelings that welled up and brimmed over from it. She was far, very far, from the dusty mediæval epoch, when some women had a taste for such refreshment. Even for her, however, there was an inexpressible charm in the simplicity that prompted Donatello's words and deeds; though, unless she caught them in precisely the true light, they seemed but folly, the offspring of a maimed or imperfectly developed intellect. Alternately, she almost admired, or wholly scorned him, and knew not which estimate resulted from the deeper appreciation. But it could not, she decided for herself, be other than an innocent pastime, if they two—sure to be separated by their different paths in life, to-morrow—were to gather up some of the little pleasures that chanced to grow about their feet, like the violets and wood-anemones, to-day.

Yet an impulse of rectitude impelled Miriam to give him what she still held to be a needless warning against an imaginary peril.

"If you were wiser, Donatello, you would think me a dangerous person," said she. "If you follow my footsteps, they will lead you to no good. You ought to be afraid of me."

"I would as soon think of fearing the air we breathe," he replied.

"And well you may, for it is full of malaria," said Miriam; she went on, hinting at an intangible confession, such as persons with overburdened hearts often make to children or dumb animals, or to holes in the earth, where they think their secrets may be at once revealed and buried. "Those who come too near me are in danger of great mischiefs, I do assure you. Take warning therefore! It is a sad fatality that has brought you from your home among the Apennines—some rusty old castle, I suppose, with a village at its foot, and an Arcadian environment of vine-yards, fig-trees, and olive-orchards—a sad mischance, I say, that has transported you to my side. You have had a happy life hitherto—have you not, Donatello?"

"Oh, yes," answered the young man; and, though not of a retrospective turn, he made the best effort he could to send his mind back into the past. "I remember thinking it happiness to dance with the contadinas at a village feast; to taste the new, sweet wine at vintage-time, and the old, ripened wine, which our podere[2] is famous for in the cold winter evenings; and to devour great, luscious figs, and apricots, peaches, cherries, and

[2]Contadinas are peasant girls; a podere is an estate.

melons. I was often happy in the woods, too, with hounds and horses, and very happy in watching all sorts of creatures and birds that haunt the leafy solitudes. But never half so happy as now!"

"In these delightful groves?" she asked.

"Here, and with you," answered Donatello. "Just as we are now."

"What a fulness of content in him! How silly, and how delightful!" said Miriam to herself. Then addressing him again: "But, Donatello, how long will this happiness last?"

"How long!" he exclaimed; for it perplexed him even more to think of the future than to remember the past. "Why should it have any end? How long! Forever! forever! forever!"

"The child! the simpleton!" said Miriam, with sudden laughter, and checking it as suddenly. "But is he a simpleton indeed? Here, in those few natural words, he has expressed that deep sense, that profound conviction of its own immortality, which genuine love never fails to bring. He perplexes me,—yes, and bewitches me,—wild, gentle, beautiful creature that he is! It is like playing with a young greyhound!"

Her eyes filled with tears, at the same time that a smile shone out of them. Then first she became sensible of a delight and grief at once in feeling this zephyr of a new affection, with its untainted freshness, blow over her weary, stifled heart, which had no right to be revived by it. The very exquisiteness of the enjoyment made her know that it ought to be a forbidden one.

"Donatello," she hastily exclaimed, "for your own sake, leave me! It is not such a happy thing as you imagine it, to wander in these woods with me, a girl from another land, burdened with a doom that she tells to none. I might make you dread me, —perhaps hate me,—if I chose; and I must choose, if I find you loving me too well!"

"I fear nothing!" said Donatello, looking into her unfathomable eyes with perfect trust. "I love always!"

" I speak in vain," thought Miriam within herself. "Well, then, for this one hour, let me be such as he imagines me. To-morrow will be time enough to come back to my reality. My reality! what is it? Is the past so indestructible? the future so immitigable? Is the dark dream, in which I walk, of such solid, stony substance, that there can be no escape out of its dungeon? Be it so! There is, at least, that ethereal quality in my spirit, that it can make me as gay as Donatello himself—for this one hour!"

And immediately she brightened up, as if an inward flame, heretofore stifled, were now permitted to fill her with its happy lustre, glowing through her cheeks and dancing in her eyebeams.

Donatello, brisk and cheerful as he seemed before, showed a sensibility to Miriam's gladdened mood by breaking into still wilder and ever-varying activity. He frisked around her, bubbling over with joy, which clothed itself in words that had little individual meaning, and in snatches of song that seemed as natural as bird-notes. Then they both laughed together, and heard their own laughter returning in the echoes, and laughed again at the response; so that the ancient and solemn grove became full of merriment for these two blithe spirits. A bird happening to sing cheerily, Donatello gave a peculiar call, and the little feathered creature came fluttering about his head, as if it had known him through many summers.

"How close he stands to nature!" said Miriam, observing this pleasant familiarity between her companion and the bird. "He shall make me as natural as himself for this one hour."

As they strayed through that sweet wilderness, she felt more and more the influence of his elastic temperament. Miriam was an impressible and impulsive creature, as unlike herself, in different moods, as if a melancholy maiden and a glad one were both bound within the girdle about her waist, and kept in magic thraldom by the brooch that clasped it. Naturally, it is true, she was the more inclined to melancholy, yet fully capable of that high frolic of the spirits which richly compensates for many gloomy hours; if her soul was apt to lurk in the darkness of a cavern, she could sport madly in the sunshine before the cavern's mouth. Except the freshest mirth of animal spirits, like Dona-

tello's, there is no merriment, no wild exhilaration, comparable
to that of melancholy people escaping from the dark region in
which it is their custom to keep themselves imprisoned.

So the shadowy Miriam almost outdid Donatello, on his
own ground. They ran races with each other, side by side, with
shouts and laughter; they pelted one another with early flowers,
and gathering them up again, they twined them with green
leaves into garlands for both their heads. They played together
like children, or creatures of immortal youth; for (so much had
they flung aside the sombre habitudes of daily life) that they
seemed born to be sportive forever, and endowed with eternal
mirthfulness instead of any deeper joy. It was a glimpse far
backward into Arcadian life, or, farther still, into the Golden
Age, before mankind was burdened with sin and sorrow, and
before pleasure had been darkened with those shadows that
bring it into high relief, and make it happiness.[3]

"Hark!" cried Donatello, stopping short, as he was about
to bind Miriam's fair hands with flowers, and lead her along in
triumph, "there is music somewhere in the grove!"

"It is your kinsman, Pan, most likely," said Miriam, "playing on his pipe.[4] Let us go seek him, and make him puff out his
rough cheeks and pipe his merriest air! Come; the strain of music
will guide us onward like a gayly colored thread of silk."

"Or like a chain of flowers," responded Donatello, drawing
her along by that which he had twined. "This way!—Come!"

[3]Here Miriam mingles two myths, Christian and Greek. The Christian myth reflects Donatello in a pre-lapsarian, Edenic state. The Golden
Age, according to Hesiod and Ovid, was a period of tranquility and eternal
spring, ruled by Cronus.

[4]Pan (the Roman Faunus) was a god of fertility; his pipes are an
allusion to his amorous pursuit of the nymph Syrinx, who was changed into
a reed by her sister nymphs to avoid capture. Pan played on reed pipes
in her memory. Hawthorne carries the Donatello-Pan analogy through the
following chapter.

CHAPTER 10. *The Sylvan Dance*

As the music came fresher on their ears, they danced to its cadence, extemporizing new steps and attitudes. Each varying movement had a grace which might have been worth putting into marble, for the long delight of days to come, but vanished with the moment that gave it birth, and was effaced from memory by another. In Miriam's motion, freely as she flung herself into the frolic of the hour, there was still an artful beauty; in Donatello's, there was a charm of indescribable grotesqueness, hand in hand with grace; sweet, bewitching, most provocative of laughter, and yet akin to pathos, so deeply did it touch the heart. This was the ultimate peculiarity, the final touch, distinguishing between the sylvan creature and the beautiful companion at his side. Setting apart only this, Miriam resembled a Nymph, as much as Donatello did a Faun.

There were flitting moments, indeed, when she played the sylvan character as perfectly as he. Catching glimpses of her, then, you would have fancied that an oak had sundered its rough bark to let her dance freely forth, endowed with the same spirit in her human form as that which rustles in the leaves; or that she had emerged through the pebbly bottom of a fountain, a waternymph to play and sparkle in the sunshine, flinging a quivering light around her, and suddenly disappearing in a shower of rainbow drops.

As the fountain sometimes subsides into its basin, so in Miriam there were symptoms that the frolic of her spirits would at last tire itself out.

"Ah! Donatello," cried she, laughing, as she stopped to take breath; "you have an unfair advantage over me! I am no true creature of the woods; while you are a real Faun, I do believe. When your curls shook just now, methought I had a peep at the pointed ears."

Donatello snapped his fingers above his head, as fauns and satyrs taught us first to do, and seemed to radiate jollity out of his whole nimble person. Nevertheless, there was a kind of dim apprehension in his face, as if he dreaded that a moment's pause might break the spell, and snatch away the sportive companion whom he had waited for through so many dreary months.

"Dance! dance!" cried he, joyously. "If we take breath, we shall be as we were yesterday. Here, now, is the music, just beyond this clump of trees. Dance, Miriam dance!"

They had now reached an open, grassy glade (of which there are many in that artfully constructed wilderness,) set round with stone seats, on which the aged moss had kindly essayed to spread itself instead of cushions. On one of the stone benches sat the musicians, whose strains had enticed our wild couple thitherward. They proved to be a vagrant band, such as Rome, and all Italy, abounds with; comprising a harp, a flute, and a violin, which, though greatly the worse for wear, the performers had skill enough to provoke and modulate into tolerable harmony. It chanced to be a feast-day; and, instead of playing in the sun-scorched piazzas of the city, or beneath the windows of some unresponsive palace, they had bethought themselves to try the echoes of these woods; for, on the festas[1] of the Church, Rome scatters its merry-makers all abroad, ripe for the dance or any other pastime.

As Miriam and Donatello emerged from among the trees the musicians scraped, tinkled, or blew, each according to his various kind of instrument, more inspiringly than ever. A dark-cheeked little girl, with bright black eyes, stood by, shaking a tambourine set round with tinkling bells, and thumping it on its parchment head. Without interrupting his brisk, though measured movement, Donatello snatched away this unmelodious contrivance, and flourishing it above his head, produced music

---

[1]Feast-days.

of indescribable potency, still dancing with frisky step, and striking the tambourine, and ringing its little bells, all in one jovial act.

It might be that there was magic in the sound, or contagion, at least, in the spirit which had got possession of Miriam and himself, for very soon a number of festal people were drawn to the spot, and struck into the dance, singly, or in pairs, as if they were all gone mad with jollity. Among them were some of the plebeian damsels whom we meet bareheaded in the Roman streets, with silver stilettos thrust through their glossy hair; the contadinas, too, from the Campagna and the villages, with their rich and picturesque costumes of scarlet and all bright hues, such as fairer maidens might not venture to put on. Then came the modern Roman from Trastevere,[2] perchance, with his old cloak drawn about him like a toga, which anon, as his active motion heated him, he flung aside. Three French soldiers capered freely into the throng, in wide scarlet trousers, their short swords dangling at their sides; and three German artists in gray flaccid hats and flaunting beards; and one of the Pope's Swiss guardsmen[3] in the strange motley garb which Michael Angelo contrived for them. Two young English tourists (one of them a lord) took contadine partners and dashed in, as did also a shaggy man in goat-skin breeches, who looked like rustic Pan in person, and footed it as merrily as he. Besides the above there was a herdsman or two from the Campagna, and a few peasants in sky-blue jackets, and small-clothes tied with ribbons at the knees; haggard and sallow were these last, poor serfs, having little to eat and nothing but the malaria to breathe; but still they plucked up a momentary spirit and joined hands in Donatello's dance.

[2]That section of Rome just west from the Circus Maximus and across the Tiber; see map. The Trastevere is a residential section where a typical Roman might live.

[3]The Swiss Guard, largely ceremonial, are charged with the duty of protecting the Pope. Michelangelo did indeed design the uniform, a vivid gold and red doublet over pantaloons to the knee. The uniform has been worn, unchanged, since the 16th century.

Here, as it seemed, had the Golden Age come back again within the precincts of this sunny glade, thawing mankind out of their cold formalities, releasing them from irksome restraint, mingling them together in such child-like gayety that new flowers (of which the old bosom of the earth is full) sprang up beneath their footsteps. The sole exception to the geniality of the moment, as we have understood, was seen in a countryman of our own, who sneered at the spectacle, and declined to compromise his dignity by making part of it.

The harper thrummed with rapid fingers; the violin-player flashed his bow back and forth across the strings; the flautist poured his breath in quick puffs of jollity, while Donatello shook the tambourine above his head, and led the merry throng with unweariable steps. As they followed one another in a wild ring of mirth, it seemed the realization of one of those bas-reliefs where a dance of nymphs, satyrs, or bacchanals is twined around the circle of an antique vase; or it was like the sculptured scene on the front and sides of a sarcophagus, where, as often as any other device, a festive procession mocks the ashes and white bones that are treasured up within. You might take it for a marriage-pageant; but, after a while, if you look attentively at these merry-makers, following them from end to end of the marble coffin, you doubt whether their gay movement is leading them to a happy close. A youth has suddenly fallen in the dance; a chariot is overturned and broken, flinging the charioteer headlong on the ground; a maiden seems to have grown faint or weary and is drooping on the bosom of a friend. Always some tragic incident is shadowed forth or thrust sidelong into the spectacle; and when once it has caught your eye you can look no more at the festal portions of the scene except with reference to this one slightly suggested doom and sorrow.

As in its mirth, so in the darker characteristic here alluded to, there was an analogy between the sculptured scene on the sarcophagus and the wild dance which we have been describing. In the midst of its madness and riot Miriam found herself suddenly confronted by a strange figure that shook its fantastic garments in the air, and pranced before her on its tiptoes, almost vying with the agility of Donatello himself. It was the model.

A moment afterwards Donatello was aware that she had retired from the dance. He hastened towards her, and flung himself on the grass beside the stone bench on which Miriam was sitting. But a strange distance and unapproachableness had all at once enveloped her; and though he saw her within reach of his arm, yet the light of her eyes seemed as far off as that of a star, nor was there any warmth in the melancholy smile with which she regarded him.

"Come back!" cried he. "Why should this happy hour end so soon?"

"It must end here, Donatello," said she, in answer to his words and outstretched hand; "and such hours, I believe, do not often repeat themselves in a lifetime. Let me go, my friend; let me vanish from you quietly among the shadows of these trees. See, the companions of our pastime are vanishing already!"

Whether it was that the harp-strings were broken, the violin out of tune, or the flautist out of breath, so it chanced that the music had ceased, and the dancers come abruptly to a pause. All that motley throng of rioters was dissolved as suddenly as it had been drawn together. In Miriam's remembrance the scene had a character of fantasy. It was as if a company of satyrs, fauns, and nymphs, with Pan in the midst of them, had been disporting themselves in these venerable woods only a moment ago; and now in another moment, because some profane eye had looked at them too closely, or some intruder had cast a shadow on their mirth, the sylvan pageant had utterly disappeared. If a few of the merry-makers lingered among the trees, they had hidden their racy peculiarities under the garb and aspect of ordinary people, and sheltered themselves in the weary commonplace of daily life. Just an instant before it was Arcadia and the Golden Age. The spell being broken, it was now only that old tract of pleasure-ground, close by the people's gate of Rome, —a tract where the crimes and calamities of ages, the many battles, blood recklessly poured out, and deaths of myriads, have corrupted all the soil, creating an influence that makes the air deadly to human lungs.

"You must leave me," said Miriam to Donatello, more imperatively than before: "have I not said it? Go; and look not behind you."

"Miriam," whispered Donatello, grasping her hand forcibly, "who is it that stands in the shadow yonder, beckoning you to follow him?"

"Hush; leave me!" repeated Miriam. "Your hour is past; his hour has come."

Donatello still gazed in the direction which he had indicated, and the expression of his face was fearfully changed, being so disordered, perhaps with terror—at all events with anger and invincible repugnance—that Miriam hardly knew him. His lips were drawn apart so as to disclose his set teeth, thus giving him a look of animal rage, which we seldom see except in persons of the simplest and rudest natures. A shudder seemed to pass through his very bones.

"I hate him!" muttered he.

"Be satisfied; I hate him too!" said Miriam.

She had no thought of making this avowal, but was irresistibly drawn to it by the sympathy of the dark emotion in her own breast with that so strongly expressed by Donatello. Two drops of water or of blood do not more naturally flow into each other than did her hatred into his.

"Shall I clutch him by the throat?" whispered Donatello, with a savage scowl. "Bid me do so, and we are rid of him forever."

"In Heaven's name, no violence!" exclaimed Miriam, affrighted out of the scornful control which she had hitherto held over her companion, by the fierceness that he so suddenly developed. 'Oh, have pity on me, Donatello, if for nothing else, yet because in the midst of my wretchedness I let myself be your playmate for this one wild hour. Follow me no farther. Henceforth, leave me to my doom. Dear friend,—kind, simple, loving friend,—make me not more wretched by the remembrance of having thrown fierce hates or loves into the wellspring of your happy life!"

"Not follow you!" repeated Donatello, soothed from anger into sorrow, less by the purport of what she said, than by the melancholy sweetness of her voice. "Not follow you! What other path have I?"

"We will talk of it once again," said Miriam, still soothingly; "soon—to-morrow—when you will; only leave me now."

CHAPTER 11. *Fragmentary Sentences*

In the Borghese Grove, so recently uproarious with merriment and music, there remained only Miriam and her strange follower.

A solitude had suddenly spread itself around them. It perhaps symbolized a peculiar character in the relation of these two, insulating them, and building up an insuperable barrier between their life-streams and other currents, which might seem to flow in close vicinity. For it is one of the chief earthly incommodities of some species of misfortune, or of a great crime, that it makes the actor in the one, or the sufferer of the other, an alien in the world, by interposing a wholly unsympathetic medium betwixt himself and those whom he yearns to meet.

Owing, it may be, to this moral estrangement,—this chill remoteness of their position,—there have come to us but a few vague whisperings of what passed in Miriam's interview that afternoon with the sinister personage who had dogged her footsteps ever since the visit to the catacomb. In weaving these mystic utterances into a continuous scene, we undertake a task resembling in its perplexity that of gathering up and piecing together the fragments of a letter which has been torn and scattered to the winds. Many words of deep significance, many entire sentences, and those possibly the most important ones, have flown too far on the winged breeze to be recovered. If we insert our own conjectural amendments, we perhaps give a purport utterly at variance with the true one. Yet unless we attempt something in this way, there must remain an unsightly gap, and a lack of continuousness and dependence in our narrative; so that it would arrive at certain inevitable catastrophes without due warning of their imminence.

Of so much we are sure, that there seemed to be a sadly mysterious fascination in the influence of this ill-omened person over Miriam; it was such as beasts and reptiles of subtle and evil nature sometimes exercise upon their victims. Marvellous it was to see the hopelessness with which—being naturally of so courageous a spirit—she resigned herself to the thraldom in which he held her. That iron chain, of which some of the massive links were round her feminine waist, and the others in his ruthless hand,—or which, perhaps, bound the pair together by a bond equally torturing to each,—must have been forged in some such unhallowed furnace as is only kindled by evil passions and fed by evil deeds.

Yet, let us trust, there may have been no crime in Miriam, but only one of those fatalities which are among the most insoluble riddles propounded to mortal comprehension; the fatal decree by which every crime is made to be the agony of many innocent persons, as well as of the single guilty one.

It was, at any rate, but a feeble and despairing kind of remonstrance which she had now the energy to oppose against his persecution.

"You follow me too closely," she said, in low, faltering accents; "you allow me too scanty room to draw my breath. Do you know what will be the end of this?"

"I know well what must be the end," he replied.

"Tell me, then," said Miriam, "that I may compare your foreboding with my own. Mine is a very dark one."

"There can be but one result, and that soon," answered the model. "You must throw off your present mask and assume another. You must vanish out of the scene: quit Rome with me, and leave no trace whereby to follow you. It is in my power, as you well know, to compel your acquiescence in my bidding. You are aware of the penalty of a refusal."

"Not that penalty with which you would terrify me," said Miriam; "another there may be, but not so grievous."

"What is that other?" he inquired.

"Death! simply, death!" she answered.

"Death," said her persecutor, "is not so simple and opportune a thing as you imagine. You are strong and warm with life. Sensitive and irritable as your spirit is, these many months of trouble, this latter thraldom in which I hold you, have scarcely made your cheek paler than I saw it in your girlhood. Miriam,—for I forbear to speak another name, at which these leaves would shiver above our heads,—Miriam, you cannot die!"

"Might not a dagger find my heart?" said she, for the first time meeting his eyes. "Would not poison make an end of me? Will not the Tiber drown me?"

"It might," he answered; "for I allow that you are mortal. But, Miriam, believe me, it is not your fate to die while there remains so much to be sinned and suffered in the world. We have a destiny which we must needs fulfil together. I, too, have struggled to escape it. I was as anxious as yourself to break the tie between us—to bury the past in a fathomless grave—to make it impossible that we should ever meet, until you confront me at the bar of Judgment! You little can imagine what steps I took to render all this secure; and what was the result? Our strange interview in the bowels of the earth convinced me of the futility of my design."

"Ah, fatal chance!" cried Miriam, covering her face with her hands.

"Yes, your heart trembled with horror when you recognized me," rejoined he; "but you did not guess that there was an equal horror in my own!"

"Why could not the weight of earth, above our heads, have crumbled down upon us both, forcing up apart, but burying us equally?" cried Miriam, in a burst of vehement passion. "Oh, that we could have wandered in those dismal passages till we both perished, taking opposite paths in the darkness, so that when we lay down to die our last breaths might not mingle!"

"It were vain to wish it," said the model. "In all that labyrinth of midnight paths, we should have found one another out to live or die together. Our fates cross and are entangled. The threads are twisted into a strong cord, which is dragging us to an evil doom. Could the knots be severed, we might escape. But neither can your slender fingers untie those knots, nor my masculine force break them. We must submit!"

"Pray for rescue, as I have," exclaimed Miriam. "Pray for deliverance from me, since I am your evil genius, as you mine. Dark as your life has been, I have known you to pray in times past!"

At these words of Miriam, a tremor and horror appeared to seize upon her persecutor, insomuch that he shook and grew ashy pale before her eyes. In this man's memory, there was something that made it awful for him to think of prayer; nor could any torture be more intolerable, than to be reminded of such divine comfort and succor as await pious souls merely for the asking. This torment was perhaps the token of a native temperament deeply susceptible of religious impressions, but which had been wronged, violated, and debased, until, at length, it was capable only of terror from the sources that were intended for our purest and loftiest consolation. He looked so fearfully at her, and with such intense pain struggling in his eyes, that Miriam felt pity.

And, now, all at once, it struck her that he might be mad. It was an idea that had never before seriously occurred to her mind, although, as soon as suggested, it fitted marvellously into many circumstances that lay within her knowledge. But, alas! such was her evil fortune, that, whether mad or no, his power over her remained the same, and was likely to be used only the more tyrannously, if exercised by a lunatic.

"I would not give you pain," she said, soothingly; "your faith allows you the consolations of penance and absolution. Try what help there may be in these, and leave me to myself."

"Do not think it, Miriam," said he; "we are bound together, and can never part again."

"Why should it seem so impossible?" she rejoined. "Think how I had escaped from all the past! I had made for myself a new sphere, and found new friends, new occupations, new hopes and enjoyments. My heart, methinks, was almost as un-burdened as if there had been no miserable life behind me. The human spirit does not perish of a single wound, nor exhaust itself in a single trial of life. Let us but keep asunder, and all may go well for both."

"We fancied ourselves forever sundered," he replied. "Yet we met once, in the bowels of the earth; and, were we to part now, our fates would fling us together again in a desert, on a mountain-top, or in whatever spot seemed safest. You speak in vain, therefore."

"You mistake your own will for an iron necessity," said Miriam; "otherwise, you might have suffered me to glide past you like a ghost, when we met among those ghosts of ancient days. Even now you might bid me pass as freely."

"Never!" said he, with immitigable will; "your reappear-ance has destroyed the work of years. You know the power that I have over you. Obey my bidding; or, within short time it shall be exercised: nor will I cease to haunt you till the moment comes."

"Then," said Miriam, more calmly, "I foresee the end, and have already warned you of it. It will be death!"

"Your own death, Miriam—or mine?" he asked, looking fixedly at her.

"Do you imagine me a murderess?" said she, shuddering; "you, at least, have no right to think me so!"

"Yet," rejoined he, with a glance of dark meaning, "men have said that this white hand had once a crimson stain." He took her hand as he spoke, and held it in his own, in spite of the repugnance, amounting to nothing short of agony, with which she struggled to regain it. Holding it up to the fading light, (for there was already dimness among the trees,) he appeared to examine it closely, as if to discover the imaginary blood-stain with which he taunted her. He smiled as he let it go. "It looks very white," said he; "but I have known hands as white, which all the water in the ocean could not have washed clean."[1]

"It had no stain," retorted Miriam, bitterly, "until you grasped it in your own."

The wind has blown away whatever else they may have spoken.

They went together towards the town, and, on their way, continued to make reference, no doubt, to some strange and dreadful history of their former life, belonging equally to this dark man and to the fair and youthful woman, whom he perse-cuted. In their words, or in the breath that uttered them, there seemed to be an odor of guilt, and a scent of blood. Yet, how can we imagine that a stain of ensanguined crime should attach to Miriam! Or, how, on the other hand, should spotless inno-cence be subjected to a thraldom like that which she endured from the spectre, whom she herself had evoked out of the dark-ness! Be this as it might, Miriam, we have reason to believe, still continued to beseech him, humbly, passionately, wildly, only to go his way, and leave her free to follow her own sad path.

Thus they strayed onward through the green wilderness of the Borghese grounds, and soon came near the city wall, where, had Miriam raised her eyes, she might have seen Hilda and the sculptor leaning on the parapet. But she walked in a mist of trouble, and could distinguish little beyond its limits. As they

[1]Hawthorne paraphrases Macbeth's speech after the murder of Duncan:

> Will all great Neptune's ocean wash this blood
> Clean from my hand? No. This my hand will rather
> The multitudinous seas incarnadine,
> Making the green one red.

SHAKESPEARE, *Macbeth*, II.ii.60–64.

This scene with the sinister Model also may be compared to Chilling-worth's interview with Hester in Chapter 4 of *The Scarlet Letter;* Wester-velt's hypnotism of Priscilla in Chapter 23 of *The Blithedale Romance;* and, by contrast, Holgrave's refusal to hypnotize Phoebe in Chapter 14 of *The House of the Seven Gables.* Hawthorne considered hypnotism a seri-ous violation of another's moral integrity.

came within public observation, her persecutor fell behind,
throwing off the imperious manner which he had assumed during their solitary interview. The Porta del Popolo swarmed with
life. The merry-makers, who had spent the feast-day outside
the walls, were now thronging in; a party of horsemen were entering beneath the arch; a travelling-carriage had been drawn up
just within the verge, and was passing through the villanous
ordeal of the papal custom-house. In the broad piazza, too, there
was a motley crowd.

But the stream of Miriam's trouble kept its way through
this flood of human life, and neither mingled with it nor was
turned aside. With a sad kind of feminine ingenuity, she found
a way to kneel before her tyrant, undetected, though in full
sight of all the people, still beseeching him for freedom, and in
vain.

CHAPTER 12. *A Stroll on the Pincian*

Hilda, after giving the last touches to the picture of Beatrice Cenci, had flown down from her dove-cote, late in the afternoon, and gone to the Pincian Hill, in the hope of hearing a strain or two of exhilarating music. There, as it happened, she met the sculptor; for, to say the truth, Kenyon had well noted the fair artist's ordinary way of life, and was accustomed to shape his own movements so as to bring him often within her sphere.

The Pincian Hill is the favorite promenade of the Roman aristocracy. At the present day, however, like most other Roman possessions, it belongs less to the native inhabitants than to the barbarians from Gaul, Great Britain, and beyond the sea, who have established a peaceful usurpation over whatever is enjoyable or memorable in the Eternal City. These foreign guests are indeed ungrateful, if they do not breathe a prayer for Pope Clement, or whatever Holy Father it may have been, who levelled the summit of the mount so skilfully, and bounded it with the parapet of the city wall; who laid out those broad walks and drives, and overhung them with the deepening shade of many kinds of tree; who scattered the flowers of all seasons, and of every clime, abundantly over those green, central lawns; who scooped out hollows, in fit places, and setting great basins of marble in them, caused ever-gushing fountains to fill them to the brim; who reared up the immemorial obelisk out of the soil that had long hidden it; who placed pedestals along the borders of the avenues, and crowned them with busts of that multitude of worthies—statesmen, heroes, artists, men of letters, and of song —whom the whole world claims as its chief ornaments, though Italy produced them all. In a word, the Pincian garden is one of the things that reconcile the stranger (since he fully appreciates the enjoyment, and feels nothing of the cost) to the rule of an irresponsible dynasty of Holy Fathers, who seem to have aimed at making life as agreeable an affair as it can well be.

In this pleasant spot the red-trousered French soldiers are always to be seen; bearded and grizzled veterans, perhaps, with medals of Algiers or the Crimea[1] on their breasts. To them is assigned the peaceful duty of seeing that children do not trample on the flower-beds, nor any youthful lover rifle them of their fragrant blossoms to stick in the beloved one's hair. Here sits (drooping upon some marble bench, in the treacherous sunshine) the consumptive girl, whose friends have brought her, for cure, to a climate that instils poison into its very purest breath. Here, all day, come nursery-maids, burdened with rosy English babies, or guiding the footsteps of little travellers from the far Western world. Here, in the sunny afternoons, roll and rumble all kinds of equipages, from the cardinal's old-fashioned and gorgeous purple carriage to the gay barouche of modern date. Here horsemen gallop on thorough-bred steeds. Here, in short, all the transitory population of Rome, the world's great watering-place, rides, drives, or promenades! Here are beautiful sunsets; and here, whichever way you turn your eyes, are scenes as well worth gazing at, both in themselves and for their historic interest, as any that the sun ever rose and set upon. Here, too, on certain afternoons of the week, a French military band flings out rich music over the poor old city, floating her with strains as loud as those of her own echoless triumphs.

Hilda and the sculptor (by the contrivance of the latter, who loved best to be alone with his young countrywoman) had wandered beyond the throng of promenaders, whom they left in a dense cluster around the music. They strayed, indeed, to the

---

[1]Allusions to military campaigns in which the French participated and for which they would presently (in 1859) be wearing ribbons. Algiers, a center of piracy, was captured by the French in 1830. The Crimean War (1853-1856) was a joint venture with the British against the Russians.

farthest point of the Pincian Hill, and leaned over the parapet,
looking down upon the Muro Torto, a massive fragment of the
oldest Roman wall, which juts over, as if ready to tumble down
by its own weight, yet seems still the most indestructible piece
of work that men's hands ever piled together. In the blue distance, rose Soracte,[2] and other heights, which have gleamed afar,
to our imaginations, but look scarcely real to our bodily eyes,
because, being dreamed about so much, they have taken the
aërial tints which belong only to a dream. These, nevertheless,
are the solid framework of hills that shut in Rome, and its wide
surrounding Campagna; no land of dreams, but the broadest
page of history, crowded so full with memorable events that one
obliterates another; as if Time had crossed and recrossed his own
records till they grew illegible.

But, not to meddle with history—with which our narrative is no otherwise concerned, than that the very dust of Rome
is historic, and inevitably settles on our page and mingles with
our ink—we will return to our two friends, who were still leaning over the wall. Beneath them lay the broad sweep of the
Borghese grounds, covered with trees, amid which appeared the
white gleam of pillars and statues, and the flash of an upspringing
fountain, all to be overshadowed at a later period of the year, by
the thicker growth of foliage.

The advance of vegetation, in this softer climate, is less
abrupt than the inhabitant of the cold North is accustomed to
observe. Beginning earlier—even in February—Spring is not
compelled to burst into Summer with such headlong haste; there
is time to dwell upon each opening beauty, and to enjoy the
budding leaf, the tender green, the sweet youth and freshness
of the year; it gives us its maiden charm, before settling into the
married Summer, which, again, does not so soon sober itself into
matronly Autumn. In our own country, the virgin Spring has-
tens to its bridal too abruptly. But, here, after a month or two of
kindly growth, the leaves of the young trees, which cover that

[2]An isolated peak north of Rome, 2267 feet high.

portion of the Borghese grounds nearest the city wall, were still in their tender half-development.

In the remoter depths, among the old groves of ilex-trees, Hilda and Kenyon heard the faint sound of music, laughter, and mingling voices. It was probably the uproar—spreading even so far as the walls of Rome, and growing faded and melancholy in its passage—of that wild sylvan merriment, which we have already attempted to describe. By and by, it ceased; although the two listeners still tried to distinguish it between the bursts of nearer music from the military band. But there was no renewal of that distant mirth. Soon afterwards, they saw a solitary figure, advancing along one of the paths that lead from the obscurer part of the grounds, towards the gateway.

"Look! is it not Donatello?" said Hilda.

"He it is, beyond a doubt," replied the sculptor. "But how gravely he walks, and with what long looks behind him! He seems either very weary, or very sad. I should not hesitate to call it sadness, if Donatello were a creature capable of the sin and folly of low spirits. In all these hundred paces, while we have been watching him, he has not made one of those little caprioles[3] in the air, which are a characteristic of his natural gait. I begin to doubt whether he is a veritable Faun."

"Then," said Hilda, with perfect simplicity, "you have thought him—and do think him—one of that strange, wild, happy race of creatures, that used to laugh and sport in the woods, in the old, old times? So do I, indeed! But I never quite believed, till now, that fauns existed anywhere but in poetry."

The sculptor at first merely smiled. Then, as the idea took further possession of his mind, he laughed outright, and wished from the bottom of his heart (being in love with Hilda, though he had never told her so) that he could have rewarded or punished her for its pretty absurdity with a kiss.

"Oh, Hilda, what a treasure of sweet faith and pure imagination you hide under that little straw hat!" cried he, at length.

[3]Playful leaps; a capriolo is a stag.

"A Faun! a Faun! Great Pan is not dead, then, after all! The whole tribe of mythical creatures yet live in the moonlit seclusion of a young girl's fancy, and find it a lovelier abode and play-place, I doubt not, than their Arcadian haunts of yore. What bliss, if a man of marble, like myself, could stray thither too!"

"Why do you laugh so?" asked Hilda, reddening; for she was a little disturbed at Kenyon's ridicule, however kindly expressed. "What can I have said, that you think so very foolish?"

"Well, not foolish, then," rejoined the scupltor, "but wiser, it may be, than I can fathom. Really, however, the idea does strike one as delightfully fresh, when we consider Donatello's position and external environment. Why, my dear Hilda, he is a Tuscan born, of an old noble race in that part of Italy; and he has a moss-grown tower among the Apennines, where he and his forefathers have dwelt, under their own vines and fig-trees, from an unknown antiquity. His boyish passion for Miriam has introduced him familiarly to our little circle; and our republican and artistic simplicity of intercourse has included this young Italian, on the same terms as one of ourselves. But, if we paid due respect to rank and title, we should bend reverentially to Donatello, and salute him as his Excellency the Count di Monte Beni."

"That is a droll idea—much droller than his being a Faun!" said Hilda, laughing in her turn. "This does not quite satisfy me, however, especially as you yourself recognized and acknowledged his wonderful resemblance to the statue."

"Except as regards the pointed ears," said Kenyon; adding, aside—"and one other little peculiarity, generally observable in the statues of fauns."

"As for his Excellency the Count di Monte Beni's ears," replied Hilda, smiling again at the dignity with which this title invested their playful friend, "you know we could never see their shape, on account of his clustering curls. Nay, I remember, he once started back, as shyly as a wild deer, when Miriam made a pretence of examining them. How do you explain that?"

"Oh, I certainly shall not contend against such a weight of evidence; the fact of his faunship being otherwise so probable," answered the sculptor, still hardly retaining his gravity. "Faun or not, Donatello—or the Count di Monte Beni—is a singularly wild creature, and as I have remarked on other occasions, though very gentle, does not love to be touched. Speaking in no harsh sense, there is a great deal of animal nature in him, as if he had been born in the woods, and had run wild all his childhood, and were as yet but imperfectly domesticated. Life, even in our day, is very simple and unsophisticated in some of the shaggy nooks of the Apennines."

"It annoys me very much," said Hilda, "this inclination, which most people have, to explain away the wonder and the mystery out of everything. Why could not you allow me—and yourself, too—the satisfaction of thinking him a Faun?"

"Pray keep your belief, dear Hilda, if it makes you any happier," said the sculptor; "and I shall do my best to become a convert. Donatello has asked me to spend the summer with him, in his ancestral tower, where I purpose investigating the pedigree of these sylvan counts, his forefathers; and if their shadows beckon me into dreamland, I shall willingly follow. By the by, speaking of Donatello, there is a point on which I should like to be enlightened."

"Can I help you, then?" said Hilda, in answer to his look.

"Is there the slightest chance of his winning Miriam's affection?" suggested Kenyon.

"Miriam! she, so accomplished and gifted!" exclaimed Hilda—"and he, a rude, uncultivated boy! No, no, no!"

"It would seem impossible," said the sculptor. "But, on the other hand, a gifted woman flings away her affections so unaccountably, sometimes! Miriam, of late, has been very morbid and miserable, as we both know. Young as she is, the morning light seems already to have faded out of her life; and now comes Donatello, with natural sunshine enough for himself and her, and offers her the opportunity of making her heart and life all new and cheery again. People of high intellectual endowments do not require similar ones in those they love. They are just the persons to appreciate the wholesome gush of natural feeling, the honest affection, the simple joy, the fulness of contentment with what he loves, which Miriam sees in Donatello. True; she may call him a simpleton. It is a necessity of the case; for a man loses the capacity for this kind of affection, in proportion as he cultivates and refines himself."

"Dear me!" said Hilda, drawing imperceptibly away from her companion. "Is this the penalty of refinement? Pardon me; I do not believe it. It is because you are a sculptor, that you think nothing can be finely wrought, except it be cold and hard, like the marble in which your ideas take shape. I am a painter, and know that the most delicate beauty may be softened and warmed throughout."

"I said a foolish thing, indeed," answered the sculptor. "It surprises me, for I might have drawn a wiser knowledge out of my own experience. It is the surest test of genuine love, that it brings back our early simplicity to the worldliest of us."

Thus talking, they loitered slowly along beside the parapet which borders the level summit of the Pincian with its irregular sweep. At intervals they looked through the lattice-work of their thoughts at the varied prospect that lay before and beneath them.

From the terrace where they now stood there is an abrupt descent towards the Piazza del Popolo; and looking down into its broad space they beheld the tall palatial edifices, the church-domes, and the ornamented gateway, which grew and were consolidated out of the thought of Michael Angelo. They saw, too, the red granite obelisk, eldest of things, even in Rome, which rises in the centre of the piazza, with a fourfold fountain at its base.[4] All Roman works and ruins (whether of the empire, the far-off republic, or the still more distant kings) assume a transient, visionary, and impalpable character when we think that this indestructible monument supplied one of the recollections which Moses and the Israelites bore from Egypt into the desert. Perchance, on beholding the cloudy pillar and the fiery column,

---

[4]The Flaminius obelisk, 66 feet high, is the second oldest in Rome, after the Lateran obelisk; see map. On the edge of the People's Square stands a huge gate, the Porta del Popolo, designed by Michelangelo.

they whispered awe-stricken to one another, "In its shape it is like that old obelisk which we and our fathers have so often seen on the borders of the Nile."[5] And now that very obelisk, with hardly a trace of decay upon it, is the first thing that the modern traveller sees after entering the Flaminian Gate!

Lifting their eyes, Hilda and her companion gazed westward, and saw beyond the invisible Tiber the Castle of St. Angelo; that immense tomb of a pagan emperor, with the archangel at its summit. Still farther off appeared a mighty pile of building, surmounted by the vast dome, which all of us have shaped and swelled outward, like a huge bubble, to the utmost scope of our imaginations, long before we see it floating over the worship of the city. It may be most worthily seen from precisely the point where our two friends were now standing. At any nearer view the grandeur of St. Peter's hides itself behind the immensity of its separate parts, so that we see only the front, only the sides, only the pillared length and loftiness of the portico, and not the mighty whole. But at this distance the entire outline of the world's cathedral, as well as that of the palace of the world's chief priest, is taken in at once. In such remoteness, moreover, the imagination is not debarred from lending its assistance, even while we have the reality before our eyes, and helping the weakness of human sense to do justice to so grand an object. It requires both faith and fancy to enable us to feel, what is nevertheless so true, that yonder, in front of the purple outline of hills, is the grandest edifice ever built by man, painted against God's loveliest sky.

After contemplating a little while a scene which their long residence in Rome had made familiar to them, Kenyon and Hilda again let their glances fall into the piazza at their feet.

[5]A cloud covered the Ark of the Covenant by day, and a pillar of fire by night. Thus Moses and the Israelites were led through Sinai toward the Promised Land. See Exodus 40:32–36.

The Egyptians dedicated their obelisks to Osiris, god of the sun and the Nile. Note how Hawthorne juxtaposes Jewish, Egyptian, and Roman sacred allusions here.

They there beheld Miriam, who had just entered the Porta del Popolo, and was standing by the obelisk and fountain. With a gesture that impressed Kenyon as at once suppliant and imperious, she seemed to intimate to a figure which had attended her thus far, that it was now her desire to be left alone. The pertinacious model, however, remained immovable.

And the sculptor here noted a circumstance, which, according to the interpretation he might put upon it, was either too trivial to be mentioned, or else so mysteriously significant that he found it difficult to believe his eyes. Miriam knelt down on the steps of the fountain; so far there could be no question of the fact. To other observers, if any there were, she probably appeared to take this attitude merely for the convenience of dipping her fingers into the gush of water from the mouth of one of the stone lions. But as she clasped her hands together after thus bathing them, and glanced upward at the model, an idea took strong possession of Kenyon's mind that Miriam was kneeling to this dark follower there in the world's face!

"Do you see it?" he said to Hilda.

"See what?" asked she, surprised at the emotion in his tone. "I see Miriam, who has just bathed her hands in that delightfully cool water. I often dip my fingers into a Roman fountain, and think of the brook that used to be one of my playmates in my New England village."

"I fancied I saw something else," said Kenyon; "but it was doubtless a mistake."

But,—allowing that he had caught a true glimpse into the hidden significance of Miriam's gesture,—what a terrible thraldom did it suggest! Free as she seemed to be—beggar as he looked—the nameless vagrant must then be dragging the beautiful Miriam through the streets of Rome, fettered and shackled more cruelly than any captive queen of yore following in an emperor's triumph. And was it conceivable that she could have been thus enthralled unless some great error—how great Kenyon dared not think—or some fatal weakness had given this dark adversary a vantage-ground?

"Hilda," said he, abruptly, "who and what is Miriam? Pardon me; but are you sure of her?"

"Sure of her!" repeated Hilda, with an angry blush, for her friend's sake. "I am sure that she is kind, good, and generous; a true and faithful friend, whom I love dearly, and who loves me as well! What more than this need I be sure of?"

"And your delicate instincts say all this in her favor?—nothing against her?" continued the sculptor, without heeding the irritation of Hilda's tone. "These are my own impressions, too. But she is such a mystery! We do not even know whether she is a countrywoman of ours, or an Englishwoman, or a German. There is Anglo-Saxon blood in her veins, one would say, and a right English accent on her tongue, but much that is not English breeding, nor American. Nowhere else but in Rome, and as an artist, could she hold a place in society without giving some clue to her past life."

"I love her dearly," said Hilda, still with displeasure in her tone, "and trust her most entirely."

"My heart trusts her at least, whatever my head may do," rejoined Kenyon; "and Rome is not like one of our New England villages, where we need the permission of each individual neighbor for every act that we do, every word that we utter, and every friend that we make or keep. In these particulars the papal despotism allows us freer breath than our native air; and if we like to take generous views of our associates, we can do so, to a reasonable extent, without ruining ourselves."

"The music has ceased," said Hilda; "I am going now."

There are three streets that, beginning close beside each other, diverge from the Piazza del Popolo towards the heart of Rome: on the left, the Via del Babuino; on the right, the Via di Ripetta; and between these two that world-famous avenue, the Corso.[6] It appeared that Miriam and her strange companion were passing up the first-mentioned of these three, and were soon hidden from Hilda and the sculptor.

The two latter left the Pincian by the broad and stately

[6]See map.

walk that skirts along its brow. Beneath them, from the base of
the abrupt descent, the city spread wide away in a close contiguity of red-earthen roofs, above which rose eminent the domes
of a hundred churches, besides here and there a tower, and the
upper windows of some taller or higher situated palace, looking
down on a multitude of palatial abodes. At a distance, ascending
out of the central mass of edifices, they could see the top of the
Antonine column, and near it the circular roof of the Pantheon,
looking heavenward with its ever-open eye. Except these two
objects, almost everything that they beheld was mediæval,
though built, indeed, of the massive old stones and indestructible
bricks of imperial Rome; for the ruin of the Coliseum, the
Golden House, and innumerable temples of Roman gods, and
mansions of Cæsars and senators, had supplied the material for
all these gigantic hovels, and their walls were cemented with
mortar of inestimable cost, being made of precious antique statues, burnt long ago for this petty purpose.

Rome, as it now exists, has grown up under the Popes,
and seems like nothing but a heap of broken rubbish, thrown
into the great chasm between our own days and the Empire,
merely to fill it up; and, for the better part of two thousand
years, its annals of obscure policies, and wars, and continually
recurring misfortunes, seem also but broken rubbish, as compared with its classic history.

If we consider the present city as at all connected with
the famous one of old, it is only because we find it built over its
grave. A depth of thirty feet of soil has covered up the Rome
of ancient days, so that it lies like the dead corpse of a giant,
decaying for centuries, with no survivor mighty enough even
to bury it, until the dust of all those years has gathered slowly
over its recumbent form and made a casual sepulchre.

We know not how to characterize, in any accordant and
compatible terms, the Rome that lies before us; its sunless alleys,
and streets of palaces; its churches, lined with the gorgeous
marbles that were originally polished for the adornment of
pagan temples; its thousands of evil smells, mixed up with fragrance of rich incense, diffused from as many censers; its little

life, deriving feeble nutriment from what has long been dead. Everywhere, some fragment of ruin suggesting the magnificence of a former epoch; everywhere, moreover, a Cross—and nasti- ness at the foot of it. As the sum of all, there are recollections that kindle the soul, and a gloom and languor that depress it beyond any depth of melancholic sentiment that can be else- where known.

Yet how is it possible to say an unkind or irreverential word of Rome? The city of all time, and of all the world! The spot for which man's great life and deeds have done so much, and for which decay has done whatever glory and dominion could not do! At this moment, the evening sunshine is flinging its golden mantle over it, making all that we thought mean mag- nificent; the bells of all the churches suddenly ring out, as if it were a peal of triumph because Rome is still imperial.

"I sometimes fancy," said Hilda, on whose susceptibility the scene always made a strong impression, "that Rome—mere Rome—will crowd everything else out of my heart."

"Heaven forbid!" ejaculated the sculptor.

They had now reached the grand stairs that ascend from the Piazza di Spagna to the hither brow of the Pincian Hill. Old Beppo, the millionaire of his ragged fraternity—it is a wonder that no artist paints him as the cripple whom St. Peter heals at the Beautiful Gate of the Temple—was just mounting his donkey to depart, laden with the rich spoil of the day's beggary.[7]

[7]Hawthorne's notebook entry on this beggar for February 15, 1858: "Yesterday was a bright day, but I did not go out till the afternoon, when I took an hour's walk along the Pincian, stopping a good while to look at the old beggar who, for many years past, has occupied one of the platforms of the flight of steps leading from the Piazza di Spagna to the Trinita di Monti. Hillard commemorates him in his book. He is an unlovely object, moving about on his hands and knees, principally by aid of his hands, which are fortified with a sort of wooden shoes; while his poor, wasted lower shanks stick up in the air behind him, loosely vibrating as he pro- gresses. He is gray, old, ragged, a pitiable sight, but seems very active in his own fashion, and bestirs himself on the approach of his visitors with the alacrity of a spider when a fly touches the remote circumference of his web . . ." (*NB*, p. 75). For St. Peter and the beggar, see Acts 3:1-11.

Up the stairs, drawing his tattered cloak about his face, came the model, at whom Beppo looked askance, jealous of an encroacher on his rightful domain. The figure passed away, however, up the Via Sistina. In the piazza below, near the foot of the magnificent steps, stood Miriam, with her eyes bent on the ground, as if she were counting those little, square, uncomfortable paving-stones, that make it a penitential pilgrimage to walk in Rome. She kept this attitude for several minutes, and when, at last, the importunities of a beggar disturbed her from it, she seemed bewildered, and pressed her hand upon her brow.

"She has been in some sad dream or other, poor thing!" said Kenyon, sympathizingly; "and even now, she is imprisoned there in a kind of cage, the iron bars of which are made of her own thoughts."

"I fear she is not well," said Hilda. "I am going down the stairs, and will join Miriam."

"Farewell, then," said the sculptor. "Dear Hilda, this is a perplexed and troubled world! It soothes me inexpressibly to think of you in your tower, with white doves and white thoughts for your companions, so high above us all, and with the Virgin for your household friend. You know not how far it throws its light, that lamp, which you keep burning at her shrine! I passed beneath the tower last night, and the ray cheered me—because you lighted it."

"It has for me a religious significance," replied Hilda, quietly, "and yet I am no Catholic."

They parted, and Kenyon made haste along the Via Sistina, in the hope of overtaking the model, whose haunts and character he was anxious to investigate, for Miriam's sake. He fancied that he saw him a long way in advance, but before he reached the Fountain of the Triton,[8] the dusky figure had vanished.

[8]Kenyon pursues the Model down the Via Sistina to the Piazza Barberini, before the Barberini Palace (the National Gallery); see map. The Fountain of the Triton, carved by Bernini, is in the middle of this piazza.

CHAPTER 13. *A Sculptor's Studio*

About this period, Miriam seems to have been goaded by a weary restlessness, that drove her abroad on any errand or none. She went one morning to visit Kenyon in his studio, whither he had invited her to see a new statue, on which he staked many hopes, and which was now almost completed in the clay. Next to Hilda, the person for whom Mirian felt most affection and confidence was Kenyon; and in all the difficulties that beset her life, it was her impulse to draw near Hilda for feminine sympathy, and the sculptor for brotherly counsel.

Yet it was to little purpose that she approached the edge of the voiceless gulf between herself and them. Standing on the utmost verge of that dark chasm, she might stretch out her hand, and never clasp a hand of theirs; she might strive to call out, "Help, friends! help!" but, as with dreamers when they shout, her voice would perish inaudibly in the remoteness that seemed such a little way. This perception of an infinite, shivering solitude, amid which we cannot come close enough to human beings to be warmed by them, and where they turn to cold, chilly shapes of mist, is one of the most forlorn results of any accident, misfortune, crime, or peculiarity of character, that puts an individual ajar with the world. Very often, as in Miriam's case, there is an insatiable instinct that demands friendship, love, and intimate communion, but is forced to pine in empty forms; a hunger of the heart, which finds only shadows to feed upon.

Kenyon's studio was in a cross-street, or, rather, an ugly and dirty little lane, between the Corso and the Via di Ripetta; and though chill, narrow, gloomy, and bordered with tall and shabby structures, the lane was not a whit more disagreeable than nine tenths of the Roman streets. Over the door of one of the houses was a marble tablet, bearing an inscription, to the purport that the sculpture-rooms within had formerly been occupied by the illustrious artist Canova.[1] In these precincts (which Canova's genius was not quite of a character to render sacred, though it certainly made them interesting) the young American sculptor had now established himself.

The studio of a sculptor is generally but a rough and dreary-looking place, with a good deal the aspect, indeed, of a stone-mason's workshop. Bare floors of brick or plank, and plastered walls; an old chair or two, or perhaps only a block of marble (containing, however, the possibility of ideal grace within it) to sit down upon; some hastily scrawled sketches of nude figures on the whitewash of the wall. These last are probably the sculptor's earliest glimpses of ideas that may hereafter be solidified into imperishable stone, or perhaps may remain as impalpable as a dream. Next there are a few very roughly modelled little figures in clay or plaster, exhibiting the second stage of the idea as it advances towards a marble immortality; and then is seen the exquisitely designed shape of clay, more interesting than even the final marble, as being the intimate production of the sculptor himself, moulded throughout with his loving hands, and nearest to his imagination and heart. In the plaster-cast, from this clay model, the beauty of the statue strangely disappears, to shine forth again with pure, white radiance, in the precious marble of Carrara. Works in all these stages of advancement, and some with the final touch upon them, might be found in Kenyon's studio.

Here might be witnessed the process of actually chiselling the marble, with which (as it is not quite satisfactory to think) a sculptor, in these days, has very little to do. In Italy, there is a class of men whose merely mechanical skill is perhaps more exquisite than was possessed by the ancient artificers, who wrought out the designs of Praxiteles; or, very possibly, by

[1]Antonio Canova (1757–1822), Italian sculptor who led the classical revival in Italy. He carved statues of Napoleon and his family.

Praxiteles himself. Whatever of illusive representation can be effected in marble, they are capable of achieving, if the object be before their eyes. The sculptor has but to present these men with a plaster-cast of his design, and a sufficient block of marble, and tell them that the figure is imbedded in the stone, and must be freed from its encumbering superfluities; and, in due time, without the necessity of his touching the work with his own finger, he will see before him the statue that is to make him renowned. His creative power has wrought it with a word.

In no other art, surely, does genius find such effective instruments, and so happily relieve itself of the drudgery of actual performance; doing wonderfully nice things by the hands of other people, when it may be suspected they could not always be done by the sculptor's own. And how much of the admiration which our artists get for their buttons and buttonholes, their shoeties, their neckcloths,—and these, at our present epoch of taste, make a large share of the renown,—would be abated, if we were generally aware that the sculptor can claim no credit for such pretty performances, as immortalized in marble! They are not his work, but that of some nameless machine in human shape.

Miriam stopped an instant in an antechamber, to look at a half-finished bust, the features of which seemed to be struggling out of the stone; and, as it were, scattering and dissolving its hard substance by the glow of feeling and intelligence. As the skilful workman gave stroke after stroke of the chisel with apparent carelessness, but sure effect, it was impossible not to think that the outer marble was merely an extraneous environment; the human countenance within its embrace must have existed there since the limestone ledges of Carrara were first made. Another bust was nearly completed, though still one of Kenyon's most trustworthy assistants was at work, giving delicate touches, shaving off an impalpable something, and leaving little heaps of marble-dust to attest it.

"As these busts in the block of marble," thought Miriam, "so does our individual fate exist in the limestone of time. We fancy that we carve it out; but its ultimate shape is prior to all our action."

Kenyon was in the inner room, but, hearing a step in the antechamber, he threw a veil over what he was at work upon, and came out to receive his visitor. He was dressed in a gray blouse, with a little cap on the top of his head; a costume which became him better than the formal garments which he wore, whenever he passed out of his own domains. The sculptor had a face which, when time had done a little more for it, would offer a worthy subject for as good an artist as himself; features finely cut, as if already marble; an ideal forehead, deeply set eyes, and a mouth much hidden in a light-brown beard, but apparently sensitive and delicate.

"I will not offer you my hand," said he; "it is grimy with Cleopatra's clay."

"No; I will not touch clay; it is earthy and human," answered Miriam. "I have come to try whether there is any calm and coolness among your marbles. My own art is too nervous, too passionate, too full of agitation, for me to work at it whole days together, without intervals of repose. So, what have you to show me?"

"Pray look at everything here," said Kenyon. "I love to have painters see my work. Their judgment is unprejudiced, and more valuable than that of the world generally, from the light which their own art throws on mine. More valuable, too, than that of my brother sculptors, who never judge me fairly—nor I them, perhaps."

To gratify him, Miriam looked round at the specimens in marble or plaster, of which there were several in the room, comprising originals or casts of most of the designs that Kenyon had thus far produced. He was still too young to have accumulated a large gallery of such things. What he had to show were chiefly the attempts and experiments, in various directions, of a beginner in art, acting as a stern tutor to himself, and profiting more by his failures than by any successes of which he was yet capable. Some of them, however, had great merit; and, in the pure, fine glow of the new marble, it may be, they dazzled the judgment into awarding them higher praise than they deserved. Miriam admired the statue of a beautiful youth, a pearl-fisher, who had got entangled in the weeds at the bottom of the sea, and lay dead among the pearl-oysters, the rich shells, and the sea-weeds, all of like value to him now.

"The poor young man has perished among the prizes that he sought," remarked she. "But what a strange efficacy there is in death! If we cannot all win pearls, it causes an empty shell to satisfy us just as well. I like this statue, though it is too cold and stern in its moral lesson; and, physically, the form has not settled itself into sufficient repose."

In another style, there was a grand, calm head of Milton, not copied from any one bust or picture, yet more authentic than any of them, because all known representations of the poet had been profoundly studied, and solved in the artist's mind. The bust over the tomb in Grey Friars Church, the original minia-tures and pictures, wherever to be found, had mingled each its special truth in this one work; wherein, likewise, by long perusal and deep love of the *Paradise Lost,* the *Comus,* the *Lycidas,* and *L'Allegro,* the sculptor had succeeded even better than he knew, in spiritualizing his marble with the poet's mighty genius. And this was a great thing to have achieved, such a length of time after the dry bones and dust of Milton were like those of any other dead man.

There were also several portrait-busts, comprising those of two or three of the illustrious men of our own country, whom Kenyon, before he left America, had asked permission to model. He had done so, because he sincerely believed that, whether he wrought the busts in marble or bronze, the one would corrode and the other crumble, in the long lapse of time, beneath these great men's immortality. Possibly, however, the young artist may have under-estimated the durability of his material. Other faces there were, too, of men who (if the brevity of their remem-brance, after death, can be argued from their little value in life) should have been represented in snow rather than marble. Posterity will be puzzled what to do with busts like these, the concretions and petrifactions of a vain self-estimate; but will find, no doubt, that they serve to build into stone walls, or burn into quicklime, as well as if the marble had never been blocked into the guise of human heads.

But it is an awful thing, indeed, this endless endurance, this almost indestructibility, of a marble bust! Whether in our own case, or that of other men, it bids us sadly measure the little, little time, during which our lineaments are likely to be of interest to any human being. It is especially singular that Americans should care about perpetuating themselves in this mode. The brief duration of our families, as a hereditary household, renders it next to a certainty that the great-grandchildren will not know their father's grandfather, and that half a century hence, at farthest, the hammer of the auctioneer will thump its knock-down blow against his blockhead, sold at so much for the pound of stone! And it ought to make us shiver, the idea of leaving our features to be a dusty-white ghost among strangers of another generation, who will take our nose between their thumb and fingers (as we have seen men do by Cæsar's), and infallibly break it off, if they can do so without detection!

"Yes," observed Miriam, who had been revolving some such thoughts as the above, "it is a good state of mind for mortal man, when he is content to leave no more definite memorial than the grass, which will sprout kindly and speedily over his grave, if we do not make the spot barren with marble. Methinks, too, it will be a fresher and better world, when it flings off this great burthen of stony memories, which the ages have deemed it a piety to heap upon its back."

"What you say," remarked Kenyon, "goes against my whole art. Sculpture, and the delight which men naturally take in it, appear to me a proof that it is good to work with all time before our view."

"Well, well," answered Miriam, "I must not quarrel with you for flinging your heavy stones at poor Posterity; and, to say the truth, I think you are as likely to hit the mark as anybody. These busts, now, much as I seem to scorn them, make me feel as if you were a magician. You turn feverish men into cool, quiet marble. What a blessed change for them! Would you could do as much for me!"

"Oh, gladly!" cried Kenyon, who had long wished to model that beautiful and most expressive face. "When will you begin to sit?"

"Poh! that was not what I meant," said Miriam. "Come, show me something else."

"Do you recognize this?" asked the sculptor.

He took out of his desk a little old-fashioned ivory coffer, yellow with age; it was richly carved with antique figures and foliage; and had Kenyon thought fit to say that Benvenuto Cellini wrought this precious box, the skill and elaborate fancy of the work would by no means have discredited his word, nor the old artist's fame. At least, it was evidently a production of Benvenuto's school and century, and might once have been the jewel-case of some grand lady at the court of the De' Medici.[2]

Lifting the lid, however, no blaze of diamonds was disclosed, but only, lapped in fleecy cotton, a small, beautifully-shaped hand, most delicately sculptured in marble. Such loving care and nicest art had been lavished here, that the palm really seemed to have a tenderness in its very substance. Touching those lovely fingers—had the jealous sculptor allowed you to touch—you could hardly believe that a virgin warmth would not steal from them into your heart.

"Ah, this is very beautiful!" exclaimed Miriam, with a genial smile. "It is as good in its way as Loulie's hand with its

[2]Cellini, famous 16th-century Florentine sculptor (1500-1571) and metalworker, worked for Pope Clement VII and later for the great French patron of the arts, Francis I. His *Autobiography* is a classic. Hawthorne saw examples of the goldsmith's art (quite possibly Cellini's) at the Uffizi Gallery in Florence. The De' Medici, of whom Clement VII, Giulio de' Medici, was one, were wealthy merchants and patrons of art in Florence.

baby-dimples, which Powers showed me at Florence,[3] evidently valuing it as must as if he had wrought it out of a piece of his great heart. As good as Harriet Hosmer's clasped hands of Browning and his wife, symbolizing the individuality and heroic union of two high, poetic lives! Nay, I do not question that it is better than either of those, because you must have wrought it passionately, in spite of its maiden palm and dainty finger-tips."

"Then you do recognize it?" asked Kenyon.

"There is but one right hand on earth that could have supplied the model," answered Miriam; "so small and slender, so perfectly symmetrical, and yet with a character of delicate energy. I have watched it a hundred times at its work; but I did not dream that you had won Hilda so far! How have you persuaded that shy maiden to let you take her hand in marble?"

"Never! She never knew it!" hastily replied Kenyon, anxious to vindicate his mistress's maidenly reserve. "I stole it from her. The hand is a reminiscence. After gazing at it so often, and even holding it once for an instant when Hilda was not thinking of me, I should be a bungler indeed, if I could not now reproduce it to something like the life."

"May you win the original one day!" said Miriam, kindly.

"I have little ground to hope it," answered the sculptor, despondingly; "Hilda does not dwell in our mortal atmosphere; and gentle and soft as she appears, it will be as difficult to win her heart as to entice down a white bird from its sunny freedom

[3]Loulie, or Luly, was the daughter of the American sculptor Hiram Powers (1805–1873), whom Hawthorne met and liked in Florence. Powers carved her fist when she was a baby and showed it to Hawthorne, who remarked in his notebook for June 13, 1858: "At sixty years Luly ought to have her hand sculptured again, and give it to her grandchildren with the baby's hand of five months old. The baby-hand that had done nothing and felt only its mother's kiss; the old lady's hand that had exchanged the love-pressure, worn the marriage-ring, closed dead eyes,—done a lifetime's work, in short. The sentiment is rather obvious, but true nevertheless" (*NB*, pp. 308–309). Note that Hawthorne here put his experience through Miriam, not Kenyon.

in the sky. It is strange, with all her delicacy and fragility, the impression she makes of being utterly sufficient to herself. No; I shall never win her. She is abundantly capable of sympathy, and delights to receive it, but she has no need of love."

"I partly agree with you," said Miriam. "It is a mistaken idea, which men generally entertain, that nature has made women especially prone to throw their whole being into what is technically called love. We have, to say the least, no more necessity for it than yourselves; only we have nothing else to do with our hearts. When women have other objects in life, they are not apt to fall in love. I can think of many women distinguished in art, literature, and science,—and multitudes whose hearts and minds find good employment in less ostentatious ways,—who lead high, lonely lives, and are conscious of no sacrifice so far as your sex is concerned."

"And Hilda will be one of these!" said Kenyon, sadly; "the thought makes me shiver for myself, and—and for her, too."

"Well," said Miriam, smiling, "perhaps she may sprain the delicate wrist which you have sculptured to such perfection. In that case you may hope. These old masters to whom she has vowed herself, and whom her slender hand and woman's heart serve so faithfully, are your only rivals."

The sculptor sighed as he put away the treasure of Hilda's marble hand into the ivory coffer, and thought how slight was the probability that he should ever feel responsive to his own the tender clasp of the original. He dared not even kiss the image that he himself had made; it had assumed its share of Hilda's remote and shy divinity.

"And now," said Miriam, "show me the new statue which you asked me hither to see."

CHAPTER 14. *Cleopatra*

"My new statue!" said Kenyon, who had positively forgotten it in the thought of Hilda; "here it is under this veil."

"Not a nude figure, I hope," observed Miriam. "Every young sculptor seems to think that he must give the world some specimen of indecorous womanhood, and call it Eve, Venus, a Nymph, or any name that may apologize for a lack of decent clothing. I am weary, even more than I am ashamed, of seeing such things. Now-a-days people are as good as born in their clothes, and there is practically not a nude human being in existence. An artist, therefore, as you must candidly confess, cannot sculpture nudity with a pure heart, if only because he is compelled to steal guilty glimpses at hired models. The marble inevitably loses its chastity under such circumstances. An old Greek sculptor, no doubt, found his models in the open sunshine, and among pure and princely maidens, and thus the nude statues of antiquity are as modest as violets, and sufficiently draped in their own beauty. But as for Mr. Gibson's colored Venuses,[1] (stained, I believe, with tobacco-juice,) and all other nudities of to-day, I really do not understand what they have to say to this generation, and would be glad to see as many heaps of quick-lime in their stead."

"You are severe upon the professors of my art," said Ken-

[1]John Gibson (1790–1866), an English sculptor whom Hawthorne met on March 14, 1858, at a party given by T. B. Read, American poet and artist. Hawthorne visited Gibson's studio where he saw various nude statues in tinted marble. He noted on April 22, 1858: "I have spoken of Mr. Gibson's colored statues. It seems (at least Mr. Nichols tells me) that he stains them with tobacco juice. . . . Were he to send a Cupid to America, he need not trouble himself to stain it beforehand" (*NB*, p. 173). Gibson disliked clothed figures and insisted on carving the statue of Sir Robert Peel in classical drape. He also instructed Harriet Hosmer.

yon, half smiling, half seriously; "not that you are wholly wrong, neither. We are bound to accept drapery of some kind, and make the best of it. But what are we to do? Must we adopt the costume of to-day, and carve, for example, a Venus in a hoop-petticoat?"

"That would be a boulder, indeed!" rejoined Miriam, laughing. "But the difficulty goes to confirm me in my belief that, except for portrait-busts, sculpture has no longer a right to claim any place among living arts. It has wrought itself out, and come fairly to an end. There is never a new group now-a-days; never even so much as a new attitude. Greenough (I take my examples among men of merit) imagined nothing new; nor Crawford either, except in the tailoring line.[2] There are not, as you will own, more than half a dozen positively original statues or groups in the world, and these few are of immemorial antiquity. A person familiar with the Vatican, the Uffizi Gallery, the Naples Gallery, and the Louvre, will at once refer any modern production to its antique prototype; which, moreover, had begun to get out of fashion, even in old Roman days."

"Pray stop, Miriam," cried Kenyon, "or I shall fling away the chisel forever!"

"Fairly own to me, then, my friend," rejoined Miriam, whose disturbed mind found a certain relief in this declamation, "that you sculptors are, of necessity, the greatest plagiarists in the world."

[2]Horatio Greenough (1805–1852), "The Divine Mechanic," Boston-born sculptor and student of Thorwaldsen in Rome. He executed the gigantic and controversial statue of Washington as a Roman Emperor in 1843. The statue, too heavy for the Rotunda floor, now rests in the basement of the Capitol in Washington, D.C.

Thomas Crawford (1813–1857) was an American sculptor who worked in Rome. His son was the romantic novelist Francis Marion Crawford. Hawthorne is following the opinion of his friend Powers on the worth of these sculptors and puts that opinion into the mouth of Miriam here: "He [Powers] seemed to think the faculty of making a bust an extremely rare one. Canova puts his own likeness into all the busts he made. Greenough could not make a good one; nor Crawford, nor Gibson" (NB, p. 284).

"I do not own it," said Kenyon, "yet cannot utterly contradict you, as regards the actual state of the art. But as long as the Carrara quarries[3] still yield pure blocks, and while my own country has marble mountains, probably as fine in quality, I shall steadfastly believe that future sculptors will revive this noblest of the beautiful arts, and people the world with new shapes of delicate grace and massive grandeur. Perhaps," he added, smiling, "mankind will consent to wear a more manageable costume; or, at worst, we sculptors shall get the skill to make broadcloth transparent, and render a majestic human character visible through the coats and trousers of the present day."

"Be it so!" said Miriam; "you are past my counsel. Show me the veiled figure, which, I am afraid, I have criticized beforehand. To make amends, I am in the mood to praise it now."

But, as Kenyon was about to take the cloth off the clay model, she laid her hand on his arm.

"Tell me first what is the subject," said she, "for I have sometimes incurred great displeasure from members of your brotherhood by being too obtuse to puzzle out the purport of their productions. It is so difficult, you know, to compress and define a character or story, and make it patent at a glance, within the narrow scope attainable by sculpture! Indeed, I fancy it is still the ordinary habit with sculptors, first to finish their group of statuary—in such development as the particular block of marble will allow—and then to choose the subject; as John of Bologna did with his 'Rape of the Sabines.'[4] Have you followed that good example?"

"No; my statue is intended for Cleopatra," replied Kenyon, a little disturbed by Miriam's raillery. "The special epoch of her history you must make out for yourself."

He drew away the cloth that had served to keep the moisture of the clay model from being exhaled. The sitting figure of

[3]Carrara, in Tuscany (central Italy), has over four hundred quarries with the finest marble in the world.

[4]John of Bologna (1524–1608), Flemish sculptor who settled in Florence in 1553; his most famous works are a bronze Mercury resting on one foot and the marble group called *The Rape of the Sabines*.

a woman was seen. She was draped from head to foot in a costume minutely and scrupulously studied from that of ancient Egypt, as revealed by the strange sculpture of that country, its coins, drawings, painted mummy-cases, and whatever other tokens have been dug out of its pyramids, graves, and catacombs. Even the stiff Egyptian head-dress was adhered to, but had been softened into a rich feminine adornment, without losing a particle of its truth. Difficulties that might well have seemed insurmountable, had been courageously encountered and made flexible to purposes of grace and dignity; so that Cleopatra sat attired in a garb proper to her historic and queenly state, as a daughter of the Ptolemies, and yet such as the beautiful woman would have put on as best adapted to heighten the magnificence of her charms, and kindle a tropic fire in the cold eyes of Octavius.[5]

A marvellous repose—that rare merit in statuary, except it be the lumpish repose native to the block of stone—was diffused throughout the figure. The spectator felt that Cleopatra

---

[5]Octavius Caesar Augustus (63 B.C.–A.D. 14), grand-nephew of Julius Caesar, defeated the forces of Marc Antony and Cleopatra at Actium in 31 B.C. Shakespeare portrays him as considerate but invulnerable to Cleopatra's charms, largely owing to Antony's neglect of his wife Octavia, the sister of Octavius. See *Antony and Cleopatra*, V. ii.111–191.

This particular Cleopatra was actually the work of William Story. In draping his statue from head to foot, Kenyon echoes Hawthorne's own preference for clothed figures: "We have likewise been to Mr. B——'s studio, where we saw several pretty statues and busts, and among them an Eve, with her wreath of fig-leaves lying across her poor nudity; comely in some points, but with a frightful volume of thighs and calves. I do not altogether see the necessity of ever sculpturing another nakedness. Man is no longer a naked animal; his clothes are as natural to him as his skin, and sculptors have no more right to undress him than to flay him.

"Also, we have seen again William Story's Cleopatra—a work of genuine thought and energy, representing a terribly dangerous woman; quiet enough for the moment, but very likely to spring upon you like a tigress. It is delightful to escape to his creations from this universal prettiness, which seems to be the highest conception of the crowd of modern sculptors, and which they almost invariably attain" (*NB*, pp. 170–171).

had sunk down out of the fever and turmoil of her life, and for one instant—as it were, between two pulse-throbs—had relinquished all activity, and was resting throughout every vein and muscle. It was the repose of despair, indeed; for Octavius had seen her, and remained insensible to her enchantments. But still there was a great smouldering furnace deep down in the woman's heart. The repose, no doubt, was as complete as if she were never to stir hand or foot again; and yet, such was the creature's latent energy and fierceness, she might spring upon you like a tigress, and stop the very breath that you were now drawing midway in your throat.

The face was a miraculous success. The sculptor had not shunned to give the full, Nubian lips, and other characteristics of the Egyptian physiognomy. His courage and integrity had been abundantly rewarded; for Cleopatra's beauty shone out richer, warmer, more triumphantly beyond comparison, than if, shrinking timidly from the truth, he had chosen the tame Grecian type. The expression was of profound, gloomy, heavily revolving thought; a glance into her past life and present emergencies, while her spirit gathered itself up for some new struggle, or was getting sternly reconciled to impending doom. In one view, there was a certain softness and tenderness—how breathed into the statue, among so many strong and passionate elements, it is impossible to say. Catching another glimpse, you beheld her as implacable as a stone and cruel as fire.

In a word, all Cleopatra—fierce, voluptuous, passionate, tender, wicked, terrible, and full of poisonous and rapturous enchantment—was kneaded into what, only a week or two before, had been a lump of wet clay from the Tiber. Soon, apotheosized in an indestructible material, she would be one of the images that men keep forever, finding a heat in them which does not cool down, throughout the centuries.

"What a woman is this!" exclaimed Miriam, after a long pause. "Tell me, did she never try, even while you were creating her, to overcome you with her fury, or her love? Were you not afraid to touch her, as she grew more and more towards hot life beneath your hand? My dear friend, it is a great work! How have you learned to do it?"

"It is the concretion of a good deal of thought, emotion, and toil of brain and hand," said Kenyon, not without a perception that his work was good; "but I know not how it came about at last. I kindled a great fire within my mind, and threw in the material,—as Aaron threw the gold of the Israelites into the furnace,[6]—and in the midmost heat uprose Cleopatra, as you see her."

"What I most marvel at," said Miriam, "is the womanhood that you have so thoroughly mixed up with all those seemingly discordant elements. Where did you get that secret? You never found it in your gentle Hilda: yet I recognize its truth."

"No, surely, it was not in Hilda," said Kenyon. "Her womanhood is of the ethereal type, and incompatible with any shadow of darkness or evil."

"You are right," rejoined Miriam; "there are women of that ethereal type, as you term it, and Hilda is one of them. She would die of her first wrong-doing—supposing for a moment that she could be capable of doing wrong. Of sorrow, slender as she seems, Hilda might bear a great burden; of sin, not a feather's weight. Methinks now, were it my doom, I could bear either, or both at once; but my conscience is still as white as Hilda's. Do you question it?"

"Heaven forbid, Miriam!" exclaimed the sculptor.

He was startled at the strange turn which she had so suddenly given to the conversation. Her voice, too—so much emotion was stifled rather than expressed in it—sounded unnatural.

"Oh, my friend," cried she, with sudden passion, "will you be my friend indeed? I am lonely, lonely, lonely! There is a secret in my heart that burns me—that tortures me! Sometimes

[6]While Moses went up to the mountain to receive the Ten Commandments, Aaron humored the rebellious Israelites by melting their gold and making the Golden Calf to amuse them. See Exodus 32:24.

I fear to go mad of it; sometimes I hope to die of it; but neither of the two happens. Ah, if I could but whisper it to only one human soul! And you—you see far into womanhood; you receive it widely into your large view! Perhaps—perhaps, but Heaven only knows, you might understand me! Oh, let me speak!"

"Miriam, dear friend," replied the sculptor, "if I can help you, speak freely, as to a brother."

"Help me? No!" said Miriam.

Kenyon's response had been perfectly frank and kind; and yet the subtlety of Miriam's emotion detected a certain reserve and alarm in his warmly expressed readiness to hear her story. In his secret soul, to say the truth, the sculptor doubted whether it were well for this poor, suffering girl to speak what she so yearned to say, or for him to listen. If there were any active duty of friendship to be performed, then, indeed, he would joyfully have come forward to do his best. But if it were only a pent-up heart that sought an outlet? in that case it was by no means so certain that a confession would do good. The more her secret struggled and fought to be told, the more certain would it be to change all former relations that had subsisted between herself and the friend to whom she might reveal it. Unless he could give her all the sympathy, and just the kind of sympathy that the occasion required, Miriam would hate him by and by, and herself still more, if he let her speak.

This was what Kenyon said to himself; but his reluctance, after all, and whether he were conscious of it or no, resulted from a suspicion that had crept into his heart and lay there in a dark corner. Obscure as it was, when Miriam looked into his eyes, she detected it at once.

"Ah, I shall hate you!" cried she, echoing the thought which he had not spoken; she was half choked with the gush of passion that was thus turned back upon her. "You are as cold and pitiless as your own marble."

"No; but full of sympathy, God knows!" replied he.

In truth his suspicions, however warranted by the mystery in which Miriam was enveloped, had vanished in the earnestness of his kindly and sorrowful emotion. He was now ready to receive her trust.

"Keep your sympathy, then, for sorrows that admit of such solace," said she, making a strong effort to compose herself. "As for my griefs, I know how to manage them. It was all a mistake: you can do nothing for me, unless you petrify me into a marble companion for your Cleopatra there; and I am not of her sisterhood, I do assure you. Forget this foolish scene, my friend, and never let me see a reference to it in your eyes when they meet mine hereafter."

"Since you desire it, all shall be forgotten," answered the sculptor, pressing her hand as she departed; "or, if ever I can serve you, let my readiness to do so be remembered. Meanwhile, dear Miriam, let us meet in the same clear, friendly light as heretofore."

"You are less sincere than I thought you," said Miriam, "if you try to make me think that there will be no change."

As he attended her through the antechamber, she pointed to the statue of the pearl-diver.

"My secret is not a pearl," said she; "yet a man might drown himself in plunging after it."

After Kenyon had closed the door, she went wearily down the staircase, but paused midway, as if debating with herself whether to return.

"The mischief was done," thought she; "and I might as well have had the solace that ought to come with it. I have lost— by staggering a little way beyond the mark, in the blindness of my distress—I have lost, as we shall hereafter find, the genuine friendship of this clear-minded, honorable, truehearted young man, and all for nothing. What if I should go back this moment and compel him to listen?"

She ascended two or three of the stairs, but again paused, murmured to herself, and shook her head.

"No, no, no," she thought; "and I wonder how I ever came to dream of it. Unless I had his heart for my own,—and that is Hilda's, nor would I steal it from her,—it should never be the treasure-place of my secret. It is no precious pearl, as I just now told him; but my dark-red carbuncle—red as blood—is too rich a gem to put into a stranger's casket."

She went down the stairs and found her Shadow waiting for her in the street.

CHAPTER 15. *An Æsthetic Company*

On the evening after Miriam's visit to Kenyon's studio, there was an assemblage composed almost entirely of Anglo-Saxons, and chiefly of American artists, with a sprinkling of their English brethren; and some few of the tourists who still lingered in Rome, now that Holy Week was past. Miriam, Hilda, and the sculptor, were all three present, and, with them, Donatello, whose life was so far turned from its natural bent, that, like a pet spaniel, he followed his beloved mistress wherever he could gain admittance.

The place of meeting was in the palatial, but somewhat faded and gloomy apartment of an eminent member of the æsthetic body. It was no more formal an occasion than one of those weekly receptions, common among the foreign residents of Rome, at which pleasant people—or disagreeable ones, as the case may be—encounter one another with little ceremony.

If anywise interested in art, a man must be difficult to please who cannot find fit companionship among a crowd of persons, whose ideas and pursuits all tend towards the general purpose of enlarging the world's stock of beautiful productions.[1]

One of the chief causes that make Rome the favorite residence of artists—their ideal home which they sigh for in advance, and are so loth to migrate from, after once breathing its enchanted air—is, doubtless, that they there find themselves in force, and are numerous enough to create a congenial atmo-

[1]Randall Stewart comments: "He cultivated the artistic fraternity [in Rome] with more than ordinary interest. He was a frequent visitor at the studios. He enjoyed the talk about art, some of which he used in the chapter 'An Aesthetic Company' in *The Marble Faun*." *Hawthorne* (New Haven: Yale University Press, 1948), p. 194.

sphere. In every other clime they are isolated strangers; in this land of art, they are free citizens.

Not that, individually, or in the mass, there appears to be any large stock of mutual affection among the brethren of the chisel and the pencil. On the contrary, it will impress the shrewd observer that the jealousies and petty animosities, which the poets of our day have flung aside, still irritate and gnaw into the hearts of this kindred class of imaginative men. It is not difficult to suggest reasons why this should be the fact. The public, in whose good graces lie the sculptor's or the painter's prospects of success, is infinitely smaller than the public to which literary men make their appeal. It is composed of a very limited body of wealthy patrons; and these, as the artist well knows, are but blind judges in matters that require the utmost delicacy of perception. Thus, success in art is apt to become partly an affair of intrigue; and it is almost inevitable that even a gifted artist should look askance at his gifted brother's fame, and be chary of the good word that might help him to sell still another statue or picture. You seldom hear a painter heap generous praise on anything in his special line of art; a sculptor never has a favorable eye for any marble but his own.

Nevertheless, in spite of all these professional grudges, artists are conscious of a social warmth from each other's presence and contiguity. They shiver at the remembrance of their lonely studios in the unsympathizing cities of their native land. For the sake of such brotherhood as they can find, more than for any good that they get from galleries, they linger year after year in Italy, while their originality dies out of them, or is polished away as a barbarism.

The company this evening included several men and women whom the world has heard of, and many others, beyond all question, whom it ought to know. It would be a pleasure to introduce them upon our humble pages, name by name, and— had we confidence enough in our own taste—to crown each well-deserving brow according to its deserts. The opportunity is tempting, but not easily manageable, and far too perilous, both in respect to those individuals whom we might bring forward, and the far greater number that must needs be left in the shade. Ink, moreover, is apt to have a corrosive quality, and might chance to raise a blister, instead of any more agreeable titillation, on skins so sensitive as those of artists. We must therefore forego the delight of illuminating this chapter with personal allusions to men whose renown glows richly on canvas, or gleams in the white moonlight of marble.

Otherwise we might point to an artist who has studied nature with such tender love that she takes him to her intimacy, enabling him to reproduce her in landscapes that seem the reality of a better earth, and yet are but the truth of the very scenes around us, observed by the painter's insight and interpreted for us by his skill. By his magic, the moon throws her light far out of the picture, and the crimson of the summer night absolutely glimmers on the beholder's face. Or we might indicate a poet-painter, whose song has the vividness of picture, and whose canvas is peopled with angels, fairies, and water-sprites, done to the ethereal life, because he saw them face to face in his poetic mood. Or we might bow before an artist, who has wrought too sincerely, too religiously, with too earnest a feeling, and too delicate a touch, for the world at once to recognize how much toil and thought are compressed into the stately brow of Prospero, and Miranda's maiden loveliness; or from what a depth within this painter's heart the Angel is leading forth St. Peter.[2]

Thus it would be easy to go on, perpetrating a score of little

---

[2]The landscape artist alluded to here is George L. Brown (1814–1889), an American wood-engraver and oil painter active in Italy, 1839–1859. He painted picturesque Italian landscapes in the style of Claude Lorrain for sale to American tourists. Hawthorne says of Brown in his notebook entry for April 22, 1858: "We have been recently to the studio of Mr. Brown, the American landscape-painter, and were altogether surprised and delighted with his pictures. . . . His pictures were views of Swiss and Italian scenery, and were really magical, beautiful and true. One of them, a moonlight picture, was really magical,—the moon shining so brightly that it seemed to throw a light even beyond the limits of the picture,—and yet his sunrises and sunsets, and noontides too, were nowise inferior to this,

epigrammatical allusions, like the above, all kindly meant, but none of them quite hitting the mark, and often striking where they were not aimed. It may be allowable to say, however, that American art is much better represented at Rome in the pictorial than in the sculpturesque department. Yet the men of marble appear to have more weight with the public than the men of canvas; perhaps on account of the greater density and solid substance of the material in which they work, and the sort of physical advantage which their labors thus acquire over the illusive unreality of color. To be a sculptor, seems a distinction in itself; whereas, a painter is nothing, unless individually eminent.

One sculptor there was, an Englishman,[3] endowed with a beautiful fancy, and possessing at his fingers' ends the capability of doing beautiful things. He was a quiet, simple, elderly personage, with eyes brown and bright, under a slightly impending brow, and a Grecian profile, such as he might have cut with his own chisel. He had spent his life, for forty years, in making Venuses, Cupids, Bacchuses, and a vast deal of other marble progeny of dream-work, or rather frost-work: it was all a vapory exhalation out of the Grecian mythology, crystallizing on the dull window-panes of to-day. Gifted with a more delicate power than any other man alive, he had foregone to be a Christian reality, and perverted himself into a Pagan idealist, whose business or efficacy, in our present world, it would be exceedingly difficult to define. And, loving and reverencing the pure material in which he wrought, as surely this admirable sculptor did, he had nevertheless robbed the marble of its chastity, by giving it an artificial warmth of hue. Thus it became a sin and shame to look at his nude goddesses. They had revealed them-

---

although their excellence required somewhat longer study to be appreciated . . ." (*NB*, pp. 169–170).

The poet-painter is probably W. W. Story; see note 4, p. 6. The painter of the angel with St. Peter is C. G. Thompson; see note 2, p. 65.

Prospero is the exiled Duke of Milan in Shakespeare's *The Tempest*; Miranda is his daughter.

[3] John Gibson; see note 1, p. 119.

selves to his imagination, no doubt, with all their deity about them; but, bedaubed with buff-color, they stood forth to the eyes of the profane in the guise of naked women. But, whatever criticism may be ventured on his style, it was good to meet a man so modest, and yet imbued with such thorough and simple conviction of his own right principles and practice, and so quietly satisfied that his kind of antique achievement was all that sculpture could effect for modern life.

This eminent person's weight and authority among his artistic brethren were very evident; for beginning unobtrusively to utter himself on a topic of art, he was soon the centre of a little crowd of younger sculptors. They drank in his wisdom, as if it would serve all the purposes of original inspiration; he, meanwhile, discoursing with gentle calmness, as if there could possibly be no other side, and often ratifying, as it were, his own conclusions by a mildly emphatic—"Yes."

The veteran sculptor's unsought audience was composed mostly of our own countrymen. It is fair to say, that they were a body of very dexterous and capable artists, each of whom had probably given the delighted public a nude statue, or had won credit for even higher skill by the nice carving of buttonholes, shoeties, coat-seams, shirt-bosoms, and other such graceful peculiarities of modern costume. Smart, practical men they doubtless were, and some of them far more than this, but, still, not precisely what an uninitiated person looks for in a sculptor. A sculptor, indeed, to meet the demands which our preconceptions make upon him, should be even more indispensably a poet than those who deal in measured verse and rhyme. His material, or instrument, which serves him in the stead of shifting and transitory language, is a pure, white, undecaying substance. It insures immortality to whatever is wrought in it, and therefore makes it a religious obligation to commit no idea to its mighty guardianship, save such as may repay the marble for its faithful care, its incorruptible fidelity, by warming it with an ethereal life. Under this aspect, marble assumes a sacred character; and no man should dare to touch it unless he feels within himself a certain consecration and a priesthood, the only evidence of which, for the public eye, will be the high treatment of heroic subjects, or the delicate evolution of spiritual, through material beauty.

No ideas such as the foregoing—no misgivings suggested by them—probably troubled the self-complacency of most of these clever sculptors. Marble, in their view, had no such sanctity as we impute to it. It was merely a sort of white limestone from Carrara, cut into convenient blocks, and worth, in that state, about two or three dollars per pound; and it was susceptible of being wrought into certain shapes (by their own mechanical ingenuity, or that of artisans in their employment) which would enable them to sell it again at a much higher figure. Such men, on the strength of some small knack in handling clay, which might have been fitly employed in making waxwork, are bold to call themselves sculptors. How terrible should be the thought, that the nude woman whom the modern artist patches together, bit by bit, from a dozen heterogeneous models, meaning nothing by her, shall last as long as the Venus of the Capitol! —that his group of—no matter what, since it has no moral or intellectual existence—will not physically crumble any sooner than the immortal agony of the Laocoön!

Yet we love the artists, in every kind; even these, whose merits we are not quite able to appreciate. Sculptors, painters, crayon sketchers, or whatever branch of æsthetics they adopted, were certainly pleasanter people, as we saw them that evening, than the average whom we meet in ordinary society. They were not wholly confined within the sordid compass of practical life; they had a pursuit which, if followed faithfully out, would lead them to the beautiful, and always had a tendency thitherward, even if they lingered to gather up golden dross by the wayside. Their actual business (though they talked about it very much as other men talk of cotton, politics, flour barrels, and sugar) necessarily illuminated their conversation with something akin to the ideal. So, when the guests collected themselves in little groups, here and there, in the wide saloon, a cheerful and airy gossip began to be heard. The atmosphere ceased to be precisely that of common life; a faint, mellow tinge, such as we see in pictures, mingled itself with the lamplight.

This good effect was assisted by many curious little treasures of art, which the host had taken care to strew upon his tables. They were principally such bits of antiquity as the soil of Rome and its neighborhood is still rich in; seals, gems, small figures of bronze, mediæval carvings in ivory; things which had been obtained at little cost, yet might have borne no inconsiderable value in the museum of a virtuoso.

As interesting as any of these relics was a large portfolio of old drawings, some of which, in the opinion of their possessor, bore evidence on their faces of the touch of master-hands. Very ragged and ill-conditioned they mostly were, yellow with time, and tattered with rough usage; and, in their best estate, the designs had been scratched rudely with pen and ink, on coarse paper, or, if drawn with charcoal or a pencil, were now half rubbed out. You would not anywhere see rougher and homelier things than these. But this hasty rudeness made the sketches only the more valuable; because the artist seemed to have bestirred himself at the pinch of the moment, snatching up whatever material was nearest, so as to seize the first glimpse of an idea that might vanish in the twinkling of an eye. Thus, by the spell of a creased, soiled, and discolored scrap of paper, you were enabled to steal close to an old master, and watch him in the very effervescence of his genius.

According to the judgment of several connoisseurs Raphael's own hand had communicated its magnetism to one of these sketches; and, if genuine, it was evidently his first conception of a favorite Madonna, now hanging in the private apartment of the Grand Duke, at Florence. Another drawing was attributed to Leonardo da Vinci, and appeared to be a somewhat varied design for his picture of Modesty and Vanity, in the Sciarra Palace.[4] There were at least half a dozen others, to which the

---

[4]A small gallery on the Corso, nearly opposite the Piazza Colonna.

owner assigned as high an origin. It was delightful to believe in
their authenticity, at all events; for these things make the spectator more vividly sensible of a great painter's power, than the
final glow and perfected art of the most consummate picture
that may have been elaborated from them. There is an effluence
of divinity in the first sketch; and there, if anywhere, you find
the pure light of inspiration, which the subsequent toil of the
artist serves to bring out in stronger lustre, indeed, but likewise
adulterates it with what belongs to an inferior mood. The aroma
and fragrance of new thought were perceptible in these designs,
after three centuries of wear and tear. The charm lay partly in
their very imperfection; for this is suggestive, and sets the
imagination at work; whereas, the finished picture, if a good one,
leaves the spectator nothing to do, and, if bad, confuses, stupe-
fies, disenchants, and disheartens him.

Hilda was greatly interested in this rich portfolio. She
lingered so long over one particular sketch, that Miriam asked
her what discovery she had made.

"Look at it carefully," replied Hilda, putting the sketch
into her hands. "If you take pains to disentangle the design
from those pencil-marks, that seem to have been scrawled over
it, I think you will see something very curious."

"It is a hopeless affair, I am afraid," said Miriam. "I have
neither your faith, dear Hilda, nor your perceptive faculty. Fie!
what a blurred scrawl it is indeed!"

The drawing had originally been very slight, and had suffered more from time and hard usage than almost any other in
the collection; it appeared, too, that there had been an attempt
(perhaps by the very hand that drew it) to obliterate the design.
By Hilda's help, however, Miriam pretty distinctly made out a
winged figure with a drawn sword, and a dragon, or a demon,
prostrate at his feet.

"I am convinced," said Hilda, in a low reverential tone,
"that Guido's own touches are on that ancient scrap of paper!
If so, it must be his original sketch for the picture of the Archangel Michael, setting his foot upon the demon, in the Church

of the Cappuccini.[5] The composition and general arrangement
of the sketch are the same with those of the picture; the only
difference being, that the demon has a more upturned face, and
scowls vindictively at the Archangel, who turns away his eyes
in painful disgust."

"No wonder!" responded Miriam. "The expression suits
the daintiness of Michael's character, as Guido represents him.
He never could have looked the demon in the face!"

"Miriam!" exclaimed her friend, reproachfully, "you
grieve me, and you know it, by pretending to speak contemp-
tuously of the most beautiful and the divinest figure that mortal
painter ever drew."

"Forgive me, Hilda!" said Miriam. "You take these matters
more religiously than I can, for my life. Guido's Archangel is a
fine picture, of course, but it never impressed me as it does you."

"Well; we will not talk of that," answered Hilda. "What
I wanted you to notice, in this sketch, is the face of the demon.
It is entirely unlike the demon of the finished picture. Guido,
you know, always affirmed that the resemblance to Cardinal
Pamfili was either casual or imaginary.[6] Now, here is the face as
he first conceived it."

"And a more energetic demon, altogether, than that of the
finished picture," said Kenyon, taking the sketch into his hand.
"What a spirit is conveyed into the ugliness of this strong, writhing, squirming dragon, under the Archangel's foot! Neither is
the face an impossible one. Upon my word, I have seen it somewhere, and on the shoulders of a living man!"

"And so have I," said Hilda. "It was what struck me from
the first."

"Donatello, look at this face!" cried Kenyon.

[6]See note 2, p. 180. Of this painting Hawthorne said: "This is surely
one of the most beautiful things in the world, one of the human concep-
tions that are imbued most deeply with the celestial" (*NB*, p. 96).

The Capuchins, an independent branch of the Franciscans, were
founded by Matteo di Bascio as a missionary group in 1525. Their brown
hood, or capuch, and their beards (after St. Francis) are distinctive insignia.

[6]Camilo Cardinal Pamfili (1622–1666) was a powerful Florentine
churchman.

The young Italian, as may be supposed, took little interest in matters of art, and seldom or never ventured an opinion respecting them. After holding the sketch a single instant in his hand, he flung it from him with a shudder of disgust and repugnance, and a frown that had all the bitterness of hatred.

"I know the face well!" whispered he. "It is Miriam's model!"

It was acknowledged both by Kenyon and Hilda that they had detected, or fancied, the resemblance which Donatello so strongly affirmed; and it added not a little to the grotesque and weird character which, half playfully, half seriously, they assigned to Miriam's attendant, to think of him as personating the demon's part in a picture of more than two centuries ago. Had Guido, in his effort to imagine the utmost of sin and misery, which his pencil could represent, hit ideally upon just this face? Or was it an actual portrait of somebody that haunted the old master, as Miriam was haunted now? Did the ominous shadow follow him through all the sunshine of his earlier career, and into the gloom that gathered about its close? And when Guido died, did the spectre betake himself to those ancient sepulchres, there awaiting a new victim, till it was Miriam's ill-hap to encounter him?

"I do not acknowledge the resemblance at all," said Miriam, looking narrowly at the sketch; "and, as I have drawn the face twenty times, I think you will own that I am the best judge."

A discussion here arose, in reference to Guido's Archangel, and it was agreed that these four friends should visit the Church of the Cappuccini the next morning, and critically examine the picture in question; the similarity between it and the sketch being, at all events, a very curious circumstance.

It was now a little past ten o'clock, when some of the company, who had been standing in a balcony, declared the moonlight to be resplendent. They proposed a ramble through the streets, taking in their way some of those scenes of ruin, which produced their best effects under the splendor of the Italian moon.

CHAPTER 16. *A Moonlight Ramble*

The proposal for a moonlight ramble was received with acclamation by all the younger portion of the company.[1] They immediately set forth and descended from story to story, dimly lighting their way by waxen tapers, which are a necessary equipment to those whose thoroughfare, in the night-time, lies up and down a Roman staircase. Emerging from the courtyard of the edifice, they looked upward and saw the sky full of light, which seemed to have a delicate purple or crimson lustre, or, at least, some richer tinge than the cold, white moonshine of other skies. It gleamed over the front of the opposite palace, showing the architectural ornaments of its cornice and pillared portal, as

[1]The action of the next four chapters follows a walk that Hawthorne and his wife took on the evening of April 23, 1858, from their lodgings at 37 Palezzo Larazani, Via di Porta Pinciana, to the Capitoline Hill; see map: "Night before last, my wife and I took a moonlight ramble through Rome, it being a very beautiful night, warm enough for comfort, and with no perceptible dew or dampness. We set out about nine o'clock, and, our general direction being towards the Coliseum, we soon came to the Fountain of Trevi, full on the front of which the moonlight fell, making Bernini's sculptures look stately and beautiful, though the semicircular gush and fall of the cascade, and the many jets of water, pouring and bubbling into the great marble basin, are of far more account than Neptune and his steeds, and the rest of the figures. . . .

"We ascended the Capitoline Hill, and I felt a satisfaction in placing my hands on those immense blocks of stone, the remains of the ancient Capitol, which form the foundation of the present edifice, and will make a sure basis for as many edifices as posterity may choose to rear upon it, till the end of the world. . . .

"Reaching the top of the Capitoline Hill, we ascended the steps of the portal of the Palace of the Senator, and looked down into the piazza, with the equestrian statue of Marcus Aurelius in the centre of it. The archiwell as the iron-barred basement windows, that gave such a prison-like aspect to the structure, and the shabbiness and squalor that lay along its base. A cobbler was just shutting up his little shop, in the basement of the palace; a cigar vendor's lantern flared in the blast that came through the archway; a French sentinel paced to and fro before the portal; a homeless dog, that haunted thereabouts, barked as obstreperously at the party as if he were the domestic guardian of the precincts.

The air was quietly full of the noise of falling water, the cause of which was nowhere visible, though apparently near at hand. This pleasant, natural sound, not unlike that of a distant cascade in the forest, may be heard in many of the Roman streets and piazzas, when the tumult at the city is hushed; for consuls, emperors, and popes, the great men of every age, have found no better way of immortalizing their memories, than by the shifting, indestructible, ever new, yet unchanging, up-gush and downfall of water. They have written their names in that unstable element, and proved it a more durable record than brass or marble.

"Donatello, you had better take one of those gay, boyish artists for your companion," said Miriam, when she found the Italian youth at her side. "I am not now in a merry mood, as when we set all the world a-dancing the other afternoon, in the Borghese grounds."

---

tecture that surrounds the piazza is very ineffective; and so, in my opinion, are all the other architectural works of Michel Angelo, including St. Peter's itself, of which he has made as little as could possibly be made of such a vast pile of material. He balances everything in such a way that it seems but half of itself.

"We soon descended into the piazza, and walked round and round the statue of Marcus Aurelius, contemplating it from every point and admiring it in all. . . . On these beautiful moonlight nights, Rome appears to keep awake and stirring, though in a quiet and decorous way. It is, in fact, the pleasantest time for promenades, and we both felt less wearied than by any promenade in the daytime, of similar extent, since our residence in Rome. In future, I mean to walk often after nightfall" (*NB*, pp. 173–174).

"I never wish to dance any more," answered Donatello.

"What a melancholy was in that tone!" exclaimed Miriam. "You are getting spoilt, in this dreary Rome, and will be as wise and as wretched as all the rest of mankind, unless you go back soon to your Tuscan vineyards. Well; give me your arm then! But take care that no friskiness comes over you. We must walk evenly and heavily to-night!"

The party arranged itself according to its natural affinities or casual likings; a sculptor generally choosing a painter, and a painter a sculptor, for his companion, in preference to brethren of their own art. Kenyon would gladly have taken Hilda to himself, and have drawn her a little aside from the throng of merry wayfarers. But she kept near Miriam, and seemed, in her gentle and quiet way, to decline a separate alliance either with him or any other of her acquaintances.

So they set forth, and had gone but a little way, when the narrow street emerged into a piazza, on one side of which, glistening, and dimpling in the moonlight, was the most famous fountain in Rome. Its murmur—not to say its uproar—had been in the ears of the company, ever since they came into the open air. It was the Fountain of Trevi, which draws its precious water from a source far beyond the walls, whence it flows hitherward through old subterranean aqueducts, and sparkles forth as pure as the virgin who first led Agrippa to its wellspring, by her father's door.[2]

"I shall sip as much of this water as the hollow of my hand will hold," said Miriam. "I am leaving Rome in a few days; and the tradition goes, that a parting draught at the Fountain of

[2]The waters of the Fountain of Trevi were brought to Rome via an aqueduct built by Agrippa. According to legend, his soldiers were looking for water in the Via Collatina in the country and met a maiden who showed them where to find pure water, which was subsequently called the Virgin Water. The bas-relief on the right of the fountain explains this event; that on the left depicts Agrippa explaining his plan for the aqueduct to Augustus.

Trevi insures the traveller's return, whatever obstacles and improbabilities may seem to beset him. Will you drink, Donatello?"

"Signorina, what you drink, I drink," said the youth.

They and the rest of the party, descended some steps to
the water's brim, and, after a sip or two, stood gazing at the absurd design of the fountain, where some sculptor of Bernini's
school had gone absolutely mad, in marble. It was a great palace-
front, with niches and many bas-reliefs, out of which looked
Agrippa's legendary virgin, and several of the allegoric sisterhood; while, at the base, appeared Neptune, with his floundering
steeds and Tritons blowing their horns about him, and twenty
other artificial fantasies, which the calm moonlight soothed into
better taste than was native to them.

And, after all, it was as magnificent a piece of work as ever
human skill contrived. At the foot of the palatial façade, was
strown, with careful art and ordered irregularity, a broad and
broken heap of massive rock, looking as if it might have lain
there since the deluge. Over a central precipice fell the water,
in a semicircular cascade; and from a hundred crevices, on all
sides, snowy jets gushed up, and streams spouted out of the
mouths and nostrils of stone monsters, and fell in glistening
drops; while other rivulets, that had run wild, came leaping from
one rude step to another, over stones that were mossy, slimy, and
green with sedge, because, in a century of this wild play, Nature
had adopted the Fountain of Trevi, with all its elaborate devices,
for her own. Finally, the water, tumbling, sparkling, and dash-
ing, with joyous haste and never-ceasing murmur, poured itself
into a great marble-brimmed reservoir, and filled it with a
quivering tide; on which was seen, continually, a snowy semi-
circle of momentary foam from the principal cascade, as well as
a multiude of snow-points from smaller jets. The basin occupied
the whole breadth of the piazza, whence flights of steps descended to its border. A boat might float, and make voyages
from one shore to another, in this mimic lake.

In the daytime, there is hardly a livelier scene in Rome than the neighborhood of the Fountain of Trevi; for the piazza is then filled with the stalls of vegetable and fruit dealers, chestnut roasters, cigar vendors, and other people, whose petty and wandering traffic is transacted in the open air. It is likewise thronged with idlers, lounging over the iron railing, and with Forestieri,[3] who come hither to see the famous fountain. Here, also, are seen men with buckets, urchins with cans, and maidens (a picture as old as the patriarchal times) bearing their pitchers upon their heads. For the water of Trevi is in request, far and wide, as the most refreshing draught for feverish lips, the pleasantest to mingle with wine, and the wholesomest to drink, in its native purity, that can anywhere be found. But, now, at nearly midnight, the piazza was a solitude; and it was a delight to behold this untamable water, sporting by itself in the moonshine, and compelling all the elaborate trivialities of art to assume a natural aspect, in accordance with its own powerful simplicity.

"What would be done with this water-power," suggested an artist, "if we had it in one of our American cities? would they employ it to turn the machinery of a cotton-mill, I wonder?"

"The good people would pull down those rampant marble deities," said Kenyon, "and possibly they would give me a commission to carve the one-and-thirty (is that the number?)[4] sister States, each pouring a silver stream from a separate can into one vast basin, which should represent the grand reservoir of national prosperity."

"Or, if they wanted a bit of satire," remarked an English artist, "you could set those same one-and-thirty States to cleansing the national flag of any stains that it may have incurred. The Roman washerwomen at the lavatory yonder, plying their labor in the open air, would serve admirably as models."

"I have often intended to visit this fountain by moonlight," said Miriam, "because it was here that the interview took place

[3]Strangers; foreigners.
[4]California, the thirty-first state, was admitted to the Union in 1850; Minnesota, the thirty-second state, on May 11, 1858—eighteen days after the Hawthornes' own moonlight ramble.

between Corinne and Lord Nelvil, after their separation and temporary estrangement.[5] Pray come behind me, one of you, and let me try whether the face can be recognized in the water."

Leaning over the stone brim of the basin, she heard footsteps stealing behind her, and knew that somebody was looking over her shoulder. The moonshine fell directly behind Miriam, illuminating the palace-front and the whole scene of statues and rocks, and filling the basin, as it were, with tremulous and palpable light. Corinne, it will be remembered, knew Lord Nelvil by the reflection of his face in the water. In Miriam's case, however, (owing to the agitation of the water, its transparency, and the angle at which she was compelled to lean over,) no reflected image appeared; nor, from the same causes, would it have been possible for the recognition between Corinne and her lover to take place. The moon, indeed, flung Miriam's shadow at the bottom of the basin, as well as two more shadows of persons who had followed her, on either side.

"Three shadows!" exclaimed Miriam. "Three separate shadows, all so black and heavy that they sink in the water! There they lie on the bottom, as if all three were drowned together. This shadow on my right is Donatello; I know him by his curls, and the turn of his head. My left-hand companion puzzles me; a shapeless mass, as indistinct as the premonition of calamity! Which of you can it be? Ah!"

She had turned round, while speaking, and saw beside her the strange creature, whose attendance on her was already familiar, as a marvel and a jest, to the whole company of artists. A general burst of laughter followed the recognition; while the model leaned towards Miriam, as she shrank from him, and muttered something that was inaudible to those who witnessed

[5]An allusion to Mme. de Staël's romance, *Corinne* (1807), in which an Englishman, Lord Nelvil, visiting Rome, meets and falls in love with Corinne, a beautiful Frenchwoman. Duty forces his return to England and to his fiancée, Corinne's half-sister. Corinne thereupon dies of a broken heart. The romance was quite popular in Hawthorne's day; Hillard alludes to it in his guidebook, *Six Months in Italy*.

the scene. By his gestures, however, they concluded that he was inviting her to bathe her hands.

"He cannot be an Italian; at least, not a Roman," observed an artist. "I never knew one of them to care about ablution. See him now! It is as if he were trying to wash off the time-stains and earthy soil of a thousand years!"

Dipping his hands into the capacious washbowl before him, the model rubbed them together with the utmost vehemence. Ever and anon, too, he peeped into the water, as if expecting to see the whole Fountain of Trevi turbid with the results of his ablution. Miriam looked at him, some little time, with an aspect of real terror, and even imitated him by leaning over to peep into the basin. Recovering herself, she took up some of the water in the hollow of her hand, and practised an old form of exorcism by flinging it in her persecutor's face.

"In the name of all the Saints," cried she, "vanish, Demon, and let me be free of you, now and forever!"

"It will not suffice," said some of the mirthful party, "unless the Fountain of Trevi gushes with holy water."

In fact, the exorcism was quite ineffectual upon the pertinacious demon, or whatever the apparition might be. Still he washed his brown, bony talons; still he peered into the vast basin, as if all the water of that great drinking-cup of Rome must needs be stained black or sanguine; and still he gesticulated to Miriam to follow his example. The spectators laughed loudly, but yet with a kind of constraint; for the creature's aspect was strangely repulsive and hideous.

Miriam felt her arm seized violently by Donatello. She looked at him, and beheld a tiger-like fury gleaming from his wild eyes.

"Bid me drown him!" whispered he, shuddering between rage and horrible disgust. "You shall hear his death-gurgle in another instant!"

"Peace, peace, Donatello!" said Miriam, soothingly; for this naturally gentle and sportive being seemed all aflame with animal rage. "Do him no mischief! He is mad; and we are as

mad as he, if we suffer ourselves to be disquieted by his antics.
Let us leave him to bathe his hands till the fountain run dry, if
he find solace and pastime in it. What is it to you or me, Donatello? There, there! Be quiet, foolish boy!"

Her tone and gesture were such as she might have used in
taming down the wrath of a faithful hound, that had taken upon
himself to avenge some supposed affront to his mistress. She
smoothed the young man's curls (for his fierce and sudden fury
seemed to bristle among his hair), and touched his cheek with
her soft palm, till his angry mood was a little assuaged.

"Signorina, do I look as when you first knew me?" asked
he, with a heavy, tremulous sigh, as they went onward, somewhat apart from their companions. "Methinks there has been
a change upon me, these many months; and more and more,
these last few days. The joy is gone out of my life; all gone! all
gone! Feel my hand! Is it not very hot? Ah; and my heart burns
hotter still!"

"My poor Donatello, you are ill!" said Miriam, with deep
sympathy and pity. "This melancholy and sickly Rome is stealing away the rich, joyous life that belongs to you. Go back, my
dear friend, to your home among the hills, where (as I gather
from what you have told me) your days were filled with simple
and blameless delights. Have you found aught in the world that
is worth what you there enjoyed? Tell me truly, Donatello!"

"Yes!" replied the young man.

"And what, in Heaven's name?" asked she.

"This burning pain in my heart," said Donatello; "for you
are in the midst of it."

By this time, they had left the Fountain of Trevi considerably behind them. Little farther allusion was made to the scene
at its margin; for the party regarded Miriam's persecutor as
diseased in his wits, and were hardly to be surprised by any ec-
centricity in his deportment.

Threading several narrow streets, they passed through the
Piazza of the Holy Apostles, and soon came to Trajan's forum.
All over the surface of what once was Rome, it seems to be the

effort of Time to bury up the ancient city, as if it were a corpse, and he the sexton; so that, in eighteen centuries, the soil over its grave has grown very deep, by the slow scattering of dust, and the accumulation of more modern decay upon elder ruin.

This was the fate, also, of Trajan's forum, until some papal antiquary, a few hundred years ago, began to hollow it out again, and disclosed the full height of the gigantic column, wreathed round with bas-reliefs of the old Emperor's warlike deeds.[6] In the area before it, stands of grove of stone, consisting of the broken and unequal shafts of a vanished temple, still holding a majestic order, and apparently incapable of further demolition. The modern edifices of the piazza (wholly built, no doubt, out of the spoil of its old magnificence) look down into the hollow space whence these pillars rise.

One of the immense gray granite shafts lay in the piazza, on the verge of the area. It was a great, solid fact of the Past, making old Rome actually sensible to the touch and eye; and no study of history, nor force of thought, nor magic of song, could so vitally assure us that Rome once existed, as this sturdy specimen of what its rulers and people wrought.

"And, see!" said Kenyon, laying his hand upon it, "there is still a polish remaining on the hard substance of the pillar; and even now, late as it is, I can feel very sensibly the warmth of the noonday sun, which did its best to heat it through. This shaft will endure forever! The polish of eighteen centuries ago, as yet but half rubbed off, and the heat of to-day's sunshine, lingering into the night, seem almost equally ephemeral in relation to it."

"There is comfort to be found in the pillar," remarked Miriam, "hard and heavy as it is. Lying here forever, as it will, it makes all human trouble appear but a momentary annoyance."

"And human happiness as evanescent too," observed Hilda, sighing; "and beautiful art hardly less so! I do not love

[6]Trajan, Roman emperor (*fl.* A.D. 98–117) subdued much of Rumania and Parthia (the region southeast of the Caspian Sea).

to think that this dull stone, merely by its massiveness, will last infinitely longer than any picture, in spite of the spiritual life that ought to give it immortality!"

"My poor little Hilda," said Miriam, kissing her compassionately, "would you sacrifice this greatest mortal consolation, which we derive from the transitoriness of all things—from the right of saying, in every conjuncture. 'This, too, will pass away' —would you give up this unspeakable boon, for the sake of making a picture eternal?"

Their moralizing strain was interrupted by a demonstration from the rest of the party, who, after talking and laughing together, suddenly joined their voices, and shouted at full pitch,—

"Trajan! Trajan!"

"Why do you deafen us with such an uproar?" inquired Miriam.

In truth, the whole piazza had been filled with their idle vociferation; the echoes from the surrounding houses reverberating the cry of "Trajan," on all sides; as if there was a great search for that imperial personage, and not so much as a handful of his ashes to be found.

"Why, it was a good opportunity to air our voices in this resounding piazza," replied one of the artists. "Besides, we had really some hopes of summoning Trajan to look at his column, which, you know, he never saw in his lifetime. Here is your model (who, they say, lived and sinned before Trajan's death) still wandering about Rome; and why not the Emperor Trajan?"

"Dead emperors have very little delight in their columns, I am afraid," observed Kenyon. "All that rich sculpture of Trajan's bloody warfare, twining from the base of the pillar to its capital, may be but an ugly spectacle for his ghostly eyes, if he considers that this huge, storied shaft must be laid before the judgment-seat, as a piece of the evidence of what he did in the flesh. If ever I am employed to sculpture a hero's monument, I shall think of this, as I put in the bas-reliefs of the pedestal!"

"There are sermons in stones," said Hilda, thoughtfully, smiling at Kenyon's morality; "and especially in the stones of Rome."

The party moved on, but deviated a little from the straight way, in order to glance at the ponderous remains of the Temple of Mars Ultor,[7] within which a convent of nuns is now established,—a dove-cote, in the war-god's mansion. At only a little distance, they passed the portico of a Temple of Minerva,[8] most rich and beautiful in architecture, but wofully gnawed by time and shattered by violence, besides being buried midway in the accumulation of soil, that rises over dead Rome like a flood-tide. Within this edifice of antique sanctity, a baker's shop was now established, with an entrance on one side; for, everywhere, the remnants of old grandeur and divinity have been made available for the meanest necessities of to-day.

"The baker is just drawing his loaves out of the oven," remarked Kenyon. "Do you smell how sour they are? I should fancy that Minerva (in revenge for the desecration of her temple) had slily poured vinegar into the batch, if I did not know that the modern Romans prefer their bread in the acetous fermentation."

They turned into the Via Alessandrina, and thus gained the rear of the Temple of Peace, and passing beneath its great arches, pursued their way along a hedge-bordered lane. In all probability, a stately Roman street lay buried beneath that rustic-looking pathway; for they had now emerged from the close and narrow avenues of the modern city, and were treading on a soil where the seeds of antique grandeur had not yet produced the

[7]A temple to the Roman god of war in the Forum Augustum; two of the statues before this temple once supported the tent of Alexander the Great in his warring expeditions (see Pliny *Natural History* 36. 18, 8).

[8]A picturesque ruin in the Forum; Minerva was the Roman goddess of wisdom, said to have sprung fully grown from the brow of Jove. Pope Clement VIII used stone from this temple to build the high altar in St. Peter's, which he dedicated in 1594. The rest of the temple disappeared in 1606.

squalid crop that elsewhere sprouts from them. Grassy as the
lane was, it skirted along heaps of shapeless ruin, and the bare
site of the vast temple that Hadrian[9] planned and built. It terminated on the edge of a somewhat abrupt descent, at the foot of
which, with a muddy ditch between, rose, in the bright moonlight, the great curving wall and multitudinous arches of the
Coliseum.

[9]Roman emperor (*fl.* A.D. 117–138) who succeeded Trajan; a strong
commander, able administrator, and patron of the arts; known best today
for the great wall he built in northeast England to contain the Picts and
the Scots, invading from the north.

CHAPTER 17. *Miriam's Trouble*

As usual of a moonlight evening, several carriages stood at the entrance of this famous ruin, and the precincts and interior were anything but a solitude. The French sentinel on duty beneath the principal archway eyed our party curiously, but offered no obstacle to their admission. Within, the moonlight filled and flooded the great empty space; it glowed upon tier above tier of ruined, grass-grown arches, and made them even too distinctly visible. The splendor of the revelation took away that inestimable effect of dimness and mystery by which the imagination might be assisted to build a grander structure than the Coliseum, and to shatter it with a more picturesque decay. Byron's celebrated description is better than the reality. He beheld the scene in his mind's eye, through the witchery of many intervening years, and faintly illuminated it as if with starlight instead of this broad glow of moonshine.[1]

The party of our friends sat down, three or four of them on a prostrate column, another on a shapeless lump of marble, once a Roman altar; others on the steps of one of the Christian shrines. Goths and barbarians though they were, they chatted as gayly together as if they belonged to the gentle and pleasant race of people who now inherit Italy. There was much pastime and gayety just then in the area of the Coliseum, where so many gladiators and wild beasts had fought and died, and where so much blood of Christian martyrs had been lapped up by that fiercest of wild beasts, the Roman populace of yore. Some youths and maidens were running merry races across the open

[1]Cf. Byron's *Childe Harold*, Canto IV, stanzas 128–151, especially stanza 144, which Hawthorne probably had in mind.

space, and playing at hide-and-seek a little way within the duskiness of the ground-tier of arches, whence now and then you
could hear the half-shriek, half-laugh of a frolicsome girl, whom
the shadow had betrayed into a young man's arms. Elder groups
were seated on the fragments of pillars and blocks of marble
that lie round the verge of the area, talking in the quick, short
ripple of the Italian tongue. On the steps of the great black cross
in the centre of the Coliseum, sat a party singing scraps of song,
with much laughter and merriment between the stanzas.

It was a strange place for song and mirth. That black cross
marks one of the especial blood-spots of the earth, where
thousands of times over the dying gladiator fell, and more of
human agony has been endured for the mere pastime of the
multitude than on the breadth of many battle-fields. From all
this crime and suffering, however, the spot has derived a more
than common sanctity. An inscription promises seven years'
indulgence, seven years of remission from the pains of purgatory, and earlier enjoyment of heavenly bliss, for each separate
kiss imprinted on the black cross. What better use could be made
of life, after middle-age, when the accumulated sins are many
and the remaining temptations few, than to spend it all in kissing
the black cross of the Coliseum!

Besides its central consecration, the whole area has been
made sacred by a range of shrines, which are erected round the
circle, each commemorating some scene or circumstance of the
Saviour's passion and suffering. In accordance with an ordinary
custom, a pilgrim was making his progress from shrine to shrine
upon his knees, and saying a penitential prayer at each. Light-
footed girls ran across the path along which he crept, or sported
with their friends close by the shrines where he was kneeling.
The pilgrim took no heed, and the girls meant no irreverence;
for in Italy religion jostles along side by side with business and
sport, after a fashion of its own, and people are accustomed to
kneel down and pray, or see others praying between two fits
of merriment, or between two sins.

To make an end of our description, a red twinkle of light

was visible amid the breadth of shadow that fell across the upper part of the Coliseum. Now it glimmered through a line of arches, or threw a broader gleam as it rose out of some profound abyss of ruin; now it was muffled by a heap of shrubbery which had adventurously clambered to that dizzy height; and so the red light kept ascending to loftier and loftier ranges of the structure until it stood like a star where the blue sky rested against the Coliseum's topmost wall. It indicated a party of English or Americans paying the inevitable visit by moonlight, and exalting themselves with raptures that were Byron's, not their own.

Our company of artists sat on the fallen column, the pagan altar, and the steps of the Christian shrine, enjoying the moonlight and shadow, the present gayety and the gloomy reminiscences of the scene, in almost equal share. Artists, indeed, are lifted by the ideality of their pursuits a little way off the earth, and are therefore able to catch the evanescent fragrance that floats in the atmosphere of life above the heads of the ordinary crowd. Even if they seem endowed with little imagination individually, yet there is a property, a gift, a talisman, common to their class, entitling them to partake somewhat more bountifully than other people in the thin delights of moonshine and romance.

"How delightful this is!" said Hilda; and she sighed for very pleasure.

"Yes," said Kenyon, who sat on the column, at her side. "The Coliseum is far more delightful, as we enjoy it now, than when eighty thousand persons sat squeezed together, row above row, to see their fellow-creatures torn by lions and tigers limb from limb. What a strange thought that the Coliseum was really built for us, and has not come to its best uses till almost two thousand years after it was finished!"

"The Emperor Vespasian[2] scarcely had us in his mind," said Hilda, smiling; "but I thank him none the less for building it."

"He gets small thanks, I fear, from the people whose bloody instincts he pampered," rejoined Kenyon. "Fancy a

[2]Roman emperor (*fl.* A.D. 69–79) who built the Coliseum.

nightly assemblage of eighty thousand melancholy and remorseful ghosts, looking down from those tiers of broken arches, striving to repent of the savage pleasures which they once enjoyed, but still longing to enjoy them over again."

"You bring a Gothic horror into this peaceful moonlight scene," said Hilda.

"Nay, I have good authority for peopling the Coliseum with phantoms," replied the sculptor. "Do you remember that veritable scene in Benvenuto Cellini's autobiography, in which a necromancer of his acquaintance draws a magic circle—just where the black cross stands now, I suppose—and raises myriads of demons? Benvenuto saw them with his own eyes—giants, pigmies, and other creatures of frightful aspect—capering and dancing on yonder walls. Those spectres must have been Romans, in their lifetime, and frequenters of this bloody amphitheatre."

"I see a spectre now!" said Hilda, with a little thrill of uneasiness. "Have you watched that pilgrim, who is going round the whole circle of shrines, on his knees, and praying with such fervency at every one? Now that he has revolved so far in his orbit, and has the moonshine on his face as he turns towards us, methinks I recognize him!"

"And so do I," said Kenyon. "Poor Miriam! Do you think she sees him?"

They looked around, and perceived that Miriam had risen from the steps of the shrine and disappeared. She had shrunk back, in fact, into the deep obscurity of an arch that opened just behind them.

Donatello (whose faithful watch was no more to be eluded than that of a hound) had stolen after her, and became the innocent witness of a spectacle that had its own kind of horror. Unaware of his presence, and fancying herself wholly unseen, the beautiful Miriam began to gesticulate extravagantly, gnashing her teeth, flinging her arms wildly abroad, stamping with her foot. It was as if she had stepped aside for an instant, solely to snatch the relief of a brief fit of madness. Persons in acute trouble, or labouring under strong excitement, with a necessity for concealing it, are prone to relieve the nerves in this wild way; although, when practicable, they find a more effectual solace in shrieking aloud.

Thus, as soon as she threw off her self-control, under the dusky arches of the Coliseum, we may consider Miriam as a mad woman, concentrating the elements of a long insanity into that instant.

"Signorina! signorina! have pity on me!" cried Donatello, approaching her—"this is too terrible!"

"How dare you look at me?" exclaimed Miriam, with a start; then, whispering below her breath, "men have been struck dead for a less offence!"

"If you desire it, or need it," said Donatello, humbly, "I shall not be loth to die."

"Donatello," said Miriam, coming close to the young man, and speaking low, but still with the almost insanity of the moment vibrating in her voice, "if you love yourself—if you desire those earthly blessings, such as you, of all men, were made for; if you would come to a good old age among your olive-orchards and your Tuscan vines, as your forefathers did; if you would leave children to enjoy the same peaceful, happy, innocent life, then flee from me. Look not behind you! Get you gone without another word." He gazed sadly at her, but he did not stir. "I tell you," Miriam went on, "there is a great evil hanging over me! I know it; I see it in the sky; I feel it in the air! It will overwhelm me as utterly as if this arch should crumble down upon our heads! It will crush you, too, if you stand at my side! Depart, then; and make the sign of the cross, as your faith bids you, when an evil spirit is nigh. Cast me off, or you are lost forever."

A higher sentiment brightened upon Donatello's face, than had hitherto seemed to belong to its simple expression and sensuous beauty.

"I will never quit you," he said; "you cannot drive me from you."

"Poor Donatello!" said Miriam, in a changed tone, and

rather to herself than him. "Is there no other that seeks me out—
follows me—is obstinate to share my affliction and my doom—
but only you! They call me beautiful; and I used to fancy that,
at my need, I could bring the whole world to my feet. And lo!
here is my utmost need; and my beauty and my gifts have
brought me only this poor, simple boy. Half-witted, they call
him; and surely fit for nothing but to be happy. And I accept
his aid! To-morrow, to-morrow, I will tell him all! Ah! what a
sin to stain his joyous nature with the blackness of a woe like
mine!"

She held out her hand to him, and smiled sadly as Donatello
pressed it to his lips. They were now about to emerge from the
depth of the arch; but, just then, the kneeling pilgrim, in his
revolution round the orbit of the shrines, had reached the one
on the steps of which Miriam had been sitting. There, as at the
other shrines, he prayed, or seemed to pray. It struck Kenyon,
however,—who sat close by, and saw his face distinctly,—that
the suppliant was merely performing an enjoined penance, and
without the penitence that ought to have given it effectual life.
Even as he knelt, his eyes wandered, and Miriam soon felt that
he had detected her, half hidden as she was within the obscurity
of the arch.

"He is evidently a good Catholic, however," whispered
one of the party. "After all, I fear we cannot identify him with
the ancient pagan who haunts the catacombs."

"The doctors of the Propaganda may have converted
him," said another; "they have had fifteen hundred years to
perform the task."[3]

The company now deemed it time to continue their ramble. Emerging from a side entrance of the Coliseum, they had
on their left the Arch of Constantine, and, above it, the shapeless
ruins of the Palace of the Cæsars; portions of which have taken

[3]The Propaganda, or Congregation for the Propagation of the
Faith, is charged with directing the missionary efforts of the Catholic
Church.

shape anew, in mediæval convents and modern villas. They turned their faces cityward, and, treading over the broad flagstones of the old Roman pavement, passed through the Arch of Titus.[4] The moon shone brightly enough within it, to show the seven-branched Jewish candlestick, cut in the marble of the interior. The original of that awful trophy lies buried, at this moment, in the yellow mud of the Tiber; and, could its gold of Ophir again be brought to light, it would be the most precious relic of past ages, in the estimation of both Jew and Gentile.[5]

Standing amid so much ancient dust, it is difficult to spare the reader the commonplaces of enthusiasm, on which hundreds of tourists have already insisted. Over this half-worn pavement, and beneath this Arch of Titus, the Roman armies had trodden in their outward march, to fight battles, a world's width away. Returning victorious, with royal captives and inestimable spoil, a Roman triumph, that most gorgeous pageant of earthly pride, had streamed and flaunted in hundred-fold succession over these same flagstones, and through this yet stalwart archway. It is politic, however, to make few allusions to such a past; nor, if we would create an interest in the characters of our story, is it wise to suggest how Cicero's foot may have stepped on yonder stone, nor how Horace was wont to stroll near by, making his footsteps chime with the measure of the ode that was ringing in his mind. The very ghosts of that massive and stately epoch have so much density that the actual people of to-day seem the thin-

[4]Constantine (*fl.* A.D. 312–337), son of St. Helena, was the first Christian emperor. Titus was the Roman emperor (*fl.* A.D. 78–81) who destroyed Jerusalem and finished the Coliseum. The Arch of Titus was built in his memory by his successor, Domitian (*fl.* A.D. 81–96).

[5]The menorah, as described in Exodus 25:31, was a seven-branched candlestick made of pure hammered gold. The allusion here is to the candelabrum in the second Temple which was carried off by the soldiers of Titus, A.D. 70, after the destruction of Jerusalem. The earliest and most authentic reproduction of the menorah is carved on the Arch of Titus; the original presumably lies buried in the mud of the Tiber. Ophir was a seaport in the Bible from which Solomon's ships brought gold, jewels, and exotic animals to Israel; its exact location is unknown.

ner of the two, and stand more ghostlike by the arches and columns, letting the rich sculpture be discerned through their ill-compacted substance.

The party kept onward, often meeting pairs and groups of midnight strollers like themselves. On such a moonlight night as this, Rome keeps itself awake and stirring, and is full of song and pastime, the noise of which mingles with your dreams, if you have gone betimes to bed. But it is better to be abroad, and take our own share of the enjoyable time; for the languor that weighs so heavily in the Roman atmosphere by day, is lightened beneath the moon and stars.

They had now reached the precincts of the Forum.

CHAPTER 18. *On the Edge of a Precipice*

"Let us settle it," said Kenyon, stamping his foot firmly down, "that this is precisely the spot where the chasm opened, into which Curtius precipitated his good steed and himself.[1] Imagine the great, dusky gap, impenetrably deep, and with half-shaped monsters and hideous faces looming upward out of it, to the vast affright of the good citizens who peeped over the brim! There, now, is a subject, hitherto unthought of, for a grim and ghastly story, and, methinks, with a moral as deep as the gulf itself. Within it, beyond a question, there were prophetic visions—intimations of all the future calamities of Rome—shades of Goths and Gauls, and even of the French soldiers of to-day. It was a pity to close it up so soon! I would give much for a peep into such a chasm."

"I fancy," remarked Miriam, "that every person takes a peep into it in moments of gloom and despondency; that is to say, in his moments of deepest insight."

"Where is it, then?" asked Hilda. "I never peeped into it."

"Wait, and it will open for you," replied her friend. "The chasm was merely one of the orifices of that pit of blackness that lies beneath us, everywhere. The firmest substance of human happiness is but a thin crust spread over it, with just reality enough to bear up the illusive stage-scenery amid which we tread. It needs no earthquake to open the chasm. A footstep, a little heavier than ordinary, will serve; and we must step very

[1]Marcus Curtius, a legendary Roman hero. In about 326 B.C., according to legend, a gulf opened in the Forum. The seers declared that it would never close until Rome's most valuable possession was thrown into it. Curtius, inspired by civic love, galloped into the chasm fully armed. The abyss closed immediately.

daintily, not to break through the crust at any moment. By-and-by, we inevitably sink! It was a foolish piece of heroism in Curtius to precipitate himself there, in advance; for all Rome, you see, has been swallowed up in that gulf, in spite of him. The Palace of the Cæsars has gone down thither, with a hollow, rumbling sound of its fragments! All the temples have tumbled into it; and thousands of statues have been thrown after! All the armies and the triumphs have marched into the great chasm, with their martial music playing, as they stept over the brink. All the heroes, the statesmen, and the poets! All piled upon poor Curtius, who thought to have saved them all! I am loth to smile at the self-conceit of that gallant horseman, but cannot well avoid it."

"It grieves me to hear you speak thus, Miriam," said Hilda, whose natural and cheerful piety was shocked by her friend's gloomy view of human destinies. "It seems to me that there is no chasm, nor any hideous emptiness under our feet, except what the evil within us digs. If there be such a chasm, let us bridge it over with good thoughts and deeds, and we shall tread safely to the other side. It was the guilt of Rome, no doubt, that caused this gulf to open; and Curtius filled it up with his heroic self-sacrifice and patriotism, which was the best virtue that the old Romans knew. Every wrong thing makes the gulf deeper; every right one helps to fill it up. As the evil of Rome was far more than its good, the whole commonwealth finally sank into it, indeed, but of no original necessity."

"Well, Hilda, it came to the same thing at last," answered Miriam, despondingly.

"Doubtless, too," resumed the sculptor (for his imagination was greatly excited by the idea of this wondrous chasm), "all the blood that the Romans shed, whether on battle-fields, or in the Coliseum, or on the cross,—in whatever public or private murder,—ran into this fatal gulf, and formed a mighty subterranean lake of gore, right beneath our feet. The blood from the thirty wounds in Cæsar's breast flowed hitherward, and that pure little rivulet from Virginia's bosom, too! Virginia, beyond all question, was stabbed by her father, precisely where we are standing."[2]

"Then the spot is hallowed forever!" said Hilda.

"Is there such blessed potency in bloodshed?" asked Miriam. "Nay, Hilda, do not protest! I take your meaning rightly."

They again moved forward. And still, from the Forum and the Via Sacra, from beneath the arches of the Temple of Peace on one side, and the acclivity of the Palace of the Cæsars on the other, there arose singing voices of parties that were strolling through the moonlight. Thus, the air was full of kindred melodies that encountered one another, and twined themselves into a broad, vague music, out of which no single strain could be disentangled. These good examples, as well as the harmonious influences of the hour, incited our artist-friends to make proof of their own vocal powers. With what skill and breath they had, they set up a choral strain,—"Hail, Columbia!" we believe,— which those old Roman echoes must have found it exceedingly difficult to repeat aright. Even Hilda poured the slender sweetness of her note into her country's song. Miriam was at first silent, being perhaps unfamiliar with the air and burden. But, suddenly, she threw out such a swell and gush of sound, that it seemed to pervade the whole choir of other voices, and then to rise above them all, and become audible in what would else have been the silence of an upper region. That volume of melodious voice was one of the tokens of a great trouble. There had long been an impulse upon her—amounting, at last, to a necessity— to shriek aloud; but she had struggled against it, till the thunderous anthem gave her an opportunity to relieve her heart by a great cry.

They passed the solitary column of Phocas,[3] and looked

---

[2]In Roman legend, Virginia was the daughter of the centurion Virginius. In 449 B.C. her father stabbed her to save her from the lust of the decemvir Appius Claudius Crassus.

[3]Erected in gratitude to an eccentric Byzantine emperor (*fl.* A.D. 602–610) who allowed Pope Boniface IV to change the Pantheon into a Christian church.

down into the excavated space, where a confusion of pillars, arches, pavements, and shattered blocks and shafts—the crumbs of various ruin dropped from the devouring maw of Time—stand, or lie, at the base of the Capitoline Hill. That renowned hillock (for it is little more) now rose abruptly above them. The ponderous masonry, with which the hill-side is built up, is as old as Rome itself, and looks likely to endure while the world retains any substance or permanence. It once sustained the Capitol, and now bears up the great pile which the mediæval builders raised on the antique foundation, and that still loftier tower, which looks abroad upon a larger page, of deeper historic interest, than any other scene can show. On the same pedestal of Roman masonry, other structures will doubtless rise, and vanish like ephemeral things.

To a spectator on the spot, it is remarkable that the events of Roman history, and Roman life itself, appear not so distant as the Gothic ages which succeeded them. We stand in the Forum, or on the height of the Capitol, and seem to see the Roman epoch close at hand. We forget that a chasm extends between it and ourselves, in which lie all those dark, rude, unlettered centuries, around the birth-time of Christianity, as well as the age of chivalry and romance, the feudal system, and the infancy of a better civilization than that of Rome. Or, if we remember these mediæval times, they look farther off than the Augustan age. The reason may be, that the old Roman literature survives, and creates for us an intimacy with the classic ages, which we have no means of forming with the subsequent ones.

The Italian climate, moreover, robs age of its reverence, and makes it look newer than it is. Not the Coliseum, nor the tombs of the Appian Way, nor the oldest pillar in the Forum, nor any other Roman ruin, be it as dilapidated as it may, ever give the impression of venerable antiquity which we gather, along with the ivy, from the gray walls of an English abbey or castle. And yet every brick or stone, which we pick up among the former, had fallen, ages before the foundation of the latter was begun. This is owing to the kindliness with which Nature takes an English ruin to her heart, covering it with ivy, as ten-

derly as Robin Redbreast covered the dead babes with forest
leaves.[4] She strives to make it a part of herself, gradually obliter-
ating the handiwork of man, and supplanting it with her own
mosses and trailing verdure, till she has won the whole structure
back. But, in Italy, whenever man has once hewn a stone, Nature
forthwith relinquishes her right to it, and never lays her finger
on it again. Age after age finds it bare and naked, in the barren
sunshine, and leaves it so. Besides this natural disadvantage, too,
each succeeding century, in Rome, has done its best to ruin the
very ruins, so far as their picturesque effect is concerned, by
stealing away the marble and hewn stone, and leaving only yellow bricks, which never can look venerable.

The party ascended the winding way that leads from the
Forum to the Piazza of the Campidoglio on the summit of the
Capitoline Hill. They stood awhile to contemplate the bronze
equestrian statue of Marcus Aurelius.[5] The moonlight glistened
upon traces of the gilding which had once covered both rider
and steed; these were almost gone, but the aspect of dignity was

---

[4]A children's nursery tale, going back at least as far as the 18th-
century chapbooks. Note the popular Victorian version by Randolph
Caldecott, in *Babes in the Wood* (1879):

> Now ponder well, you parents deare
> A doleful story you shall heare,
> In time brought forth to light
>
> .   .   .   .
>
> No burial these prettye babes
> Of any man receives,
> Till Robin-red-breast painfully
> Did cover them with leaves.

[5]One of the Antonine emperors (*fl.* A.D. 161–180) who defended the
Empire against the barbarians; known principally for his stoic *Meditations*,
a gathering of philosophical reflections. The bronze statue, carved by an
unknown Roman, is the oldest of its kind and the only one to survive the
barbarian invasions. In 1538 Michelangelo removed it from the Palace of
Varus and carved a pedestal for it. For centuries Italian peasants believed
that when the gilt on the emperor's horse became bright again, the world
would end.

still perfect, clothing the figure as it were with an imperial robe of light. It is the most majestic representation of the kingly character that ever the world has seen. A sight of this old Heathen Emperor is enough to create an evanescent sentiment of loyalty even in a democratic bosom, so august does he look, so fit to rule, so worthy of man's profoundest homage and obedience, so inevitably attractive of his love. He stretches forth his hand with an air of grand beneficence and unlimited authority, as if uttering a decree from which no appeal was permissible, but in which the obedient subject would find his highest interests consulted; a command that was in itself a benediction.

"The sculptor of this statue knew what a king should be," observed Kenyon, "and knew likewise, the heart of mankind, and how it craves a true ruler, under whatever title, as a child its father."

"Oh, if there were but one such man as this!" exclaimed Miriam. "One such man in an age, and one in all the world; then how speedily would the strife, wickedness, and sorrow of us poor creatures be relieved. We would come to him with our griefs, whatever they might be,—even a poor, frail woman burdened with her heavy heart,—and lay them at his feet and never need to take them up again. The rightful king would see to all."

"What an idea of the regal office and duty!" said Kenyon, with a smile. "It is a woman's idea of the whole matter to perfection. It is Hilda's too, no doubt?"

"No," answered the quiet Hilda; "I should never look for such assistance from an earthly king."

"Hilda, my religious Hilda," whispered Miriam, suddenly drawing the girl close to her, "do you know how it is with me? I would give all I have or hope—my life, oh how freely—for one instant of your trust in God! You little guess my need of it. You really think, then, that He sees and cares for us?"

"Miriam, you frighten me."

"Hush, hush! do not let them hear you!" whispered Miriam. "I frighten you, you say; for Heaven's sake, how? Am I strange? is there anything wild in my behavior?"

"Only for that moment," replied Hilda, "because you seemed to doubt God's providence."

"We will talk of that another time," said her friend. "Just now it is very dark to me."

On the left of the Piazza of the Campidoglio, as you face cityward, and at the head of the long and stately flight of steps descending from the Capitoline Hill to the level of lower Rome, there is a narrow lane or passage. Into this the party of our friends now turned. The path ascended a little and ran along under the walls of a palace, but soon passed through a gateway, and terminated in a small paved courtyard. It was bordered by a low parapet.

The spot, for some reason or other, impressed them as exceedingly lonely. On one side was the great height of the palace, with the moonshine falling over it, and showing all the windows barred and shuttered. Not a human eye could look down into the little courtyard, even if the seemingly deserted palace had a tenant. On all other sides of its narrow compass there was nothing but the parapet, which as it now appeared was built right on the edge of a steep precipice. Gazing from its imminent brow, the party beheld a crowded confusion of roofs spreading over the whole space between them and the line of hills that lay beyond the Tiber. A long, misty wreath, just dense enough to catch a little of the moonshine, floated above the houses, midway towards the hilly line, and showed the course of the unseen river. Far away on the right, the moon gleamed on the dome of St. Peter's as well as on many lesser and nearer domes.

"What a beautiful view of the city!" exclaimed Hilda; "and I never saw Rome from this point before."

"It ought to afford a good prospect," said the sculptor; "for it was from this point—at least we are at liberty to think so, if we choose—that many a famous Roman caught his last glimpse of his native city, and of all other earthly things. This is one of the sides of the Tarpeian Rock. Look over the parapet and see what a sheer tumble there might still be for a traitor, in spite of the thirty feet of soil that have accumulated at the foot of the precipice."[6]

They all bent over, and saw that the cliff fell perpendicularly downward to about the depth, or rather more, at which the tall palace rose in height above their heads. Not that it was still the natural, shaggy front of the original precipice; for it appeared to be cased in ancient stonework, through which the primeval rock showed its face here and there grimly and doubtfully. Mosses grew on the slight projections, and little shrubs sprouted out of the crevices, but could not much soften the stern aspect of the cliff. Brightly as the Italian moonlight fell a-down the height, it scarcely showed what portion of it was man's work, and what was Nature's, but left it all in very much the same kind of ambiguity and half-knowledge in which antiquarians generally leave the identity of Roman remains.

The roofs of some poor-looking houses which had been built against the base and sides of the cliff, rose nearly midway to the top; but from an angle of the parapet there was a precipitous plunge straight downward into a stone-paved court.

"I prefer this to any other site as having been veritably the Traitor's Leap," said Kenyon, "because it was so convenient to the Capitol. It was an admirable idea of those stern old fellows to fling their political criminals down from the very summit on which stood the Senate House and Jove's Temple, emblems of the institutions which they sought to violate. It symbolizes how sudden was the fall in those days from the utmost height of ambition to its profoundest ruin."

[6]Hawthorne visited the Tarpeian Rock on the evening of May 21, 1858. It stood behind the garden of a Swedish lady, a Miss Bremer: "As [the sun's] lovely hues died slowly away, the half-moon shone brighter and brighter; for there was not a cloud in the sky, and it seemed like the moonlight of my younger days. In the garden, beneath her window, verging on the Tarpeian Rock, there was shrubbery and one large tree, softening the brow of the famous precipice, adown which the old Romans used to fling their traitors, or sometimes, indeed, their patriots" (*NB*, pp. 213–214). For Capitoline Hill, see the map.

"Come, come; it is midnight," cried another artist, "too late to be moralizing here. We are literally dreaming on the edge of a precipice. Let us go home."

"It is time, indeed," said Hilda.

The sculptor was not without hopes that he might be favored with the sweet charge of escorting Hilda to the foot of her tower. Accordingly, when the party prepared to turn back, he offered her his arm. Hilda at first accepted it; but when they had partly threaded the passage between the little courtyard and the Piazza del Campidoglio, she discovered that Miriam had remained behind.

"I must go back," said she, withdrawing her arm from Kenyon's; "but pray do not come with me. Several times this evening I have had a fancy that Miriam has something on her mind, some sorrow or perplexity, which, perhaps, it would relieve her to tell me about. No, no; do not turn back! Donatello will be a sufficient guardian for Miriam and me."

The sculptor was a good deal mortified, and perhaps a little angry; but he knew Hilda's mood of gentle decision and independence too well not to obey her. He therefore suffered the fearless maiden to return alone.

Meanwhile, Miriam had not noticed the departure of the rest of the company; she remained on the edge of the precipice, and Donatello along with her.

"It would be a fatal fall, still," she said to herself, looking over the parapet, and shuddering as her eye measured the depth. "Yes; surely yes! Even without the weight of an overburdened heart, a human body would fall heavily enough upon those stones to shake all its joints asunder. How soon it would be over!"

Donatello, of whose presence she was possibly not aware, now pressed closer to her side; and he, too, like Miriam, bent over the low parapet and trembled violently. Yet he seemed to feel that perilous fascination which haunts the brow of precipices, tempting the unwary one to fling himself over for the very horror of the thing, for after drawing hastily back, he again looked down, thrusting himself out farther than before. He then stood silent a brief space, struggling, perhaps, to make himself conscious of the historic associations of the scene.

"What are you thinking of, Donatello?" asked Miriam.

"Who were they," said he, looking earnestly in her face, "who have been flung over here in days gone by?"

"Men that cumbered the world," she replied. "Men whose lives were the bane of their fellow-creatures. Men who poisoned the air, which is the common breath of all, for their own selfish purposes. There was short work with such men in old Roman times. Just in the moment of their triumph a hand, as of an avenging giant, clutched them, and dashed the wretches down this precipice."

"Was it well done?" asked the young man.

"It was well done," answered Miriam; "innocent persons were saved by the destruction of a guilty one, who deserved his doom."

While this brief conversation passed, Donatello had once or twice glanced aside with a watchful air, just as a hound may often be seen to take sidelong note of some suspicious object, while he gives his more direct attention to something nearer at hand. Miriam seemed now first to become aware of the silence that had followed upon the cheerful talk and laughter of a few moments before. Looking round, she perceived that all her company of merry friends had retired, and Hilda, too, in whose soft and quiet presence she had always an indescribable feeling of security. All gone; and only herself and Donatello left hanging over the brow of the ominous precipice.

Not so, however; not entirely alone! In the basement wall of the palace, shaded from the moon, there was a deep, empty niche, that had probably once contained a statue; not empty, neither; for a figure now came forth from it and approached Miriam. She must have had cause to dread some unspeakable evil from this strange persecutor, and to know that this was the very crisis of her calamity; for, as he drew near, such a cold, sick despair crept over her, that it impeded her breath, and benumbed her natural promptitude of thought. Miriam seemed dreamily to remember falling on her knees; but, in her whole recollection of that wild moment, she beheld herself as in a dim show, and could not well distinguish what was done and suffered; no, not even whether she were really an actor and sufferer in the scene.

Hilda, meanwhile, had separated herself from the sculptor, and turned back to rejoin her friend. At a distance, she still heard the mirth of her late companions, who were going down the cityward descent of the Capitoline Hill; they had set up a new stave of melody, in which her own soft voice, as well as the powerful sweetness of Miriam's, was sadly missed.

The door of the little courtyard had swung upon its hinges, and partly closed itself. Hilda (whose native gentleness pervaded all her movements) was quietly opening it, when she was startled, midway, by the noise of a struggle within, beginning and ending all in one breathless instant. Along with it, or closely succeeding it, was a loud, fearful cry, which quivered upward through the air, and sank quivering downward to the earth. Then, a silence! Poor Hilda had looked into the courtyard, and saw the whole quick passage of a deed, which took but that little time to grave itself in the eternal adamant.

CHAPTER 19. *The Faun's Transformation*

The door of the courtyard swang slowly, and closed itself of its own accord. Miriam and Donatello were now alone there. She clasped her hands, and looked wildly at the young man, whose form seemed to have dilated, and whose eyes blazed with the fierce energy that had suddenly inspired him. It had kindled him into a man; it had developed within him an intelligence which was no native characteristic of the Donatello whom we have heretofore known. But that simple and joyous creature was gone forever.

"What have you done?" said Miriam, in a horror-stricken whisper.

The glow of rage was still lurid on Donatello's face, and now flashed out again from his eyes.

"I did what ought to be done to a traitor!" he replied. "I did what your eyes bade me do, when I asked them with mine, as I held the wretch over the precipice!"

These last words struck Miriam like a bullet. Could it be so? Had her eyes provoked or assented to this deed? She had not known it. But, alas! looking back into the frenzy and turmoil of the scene just acted, she could not deny—she was not sure whether it might be so, or no—that a wild joy had flamed up in her heart, when she beheld her persecutor in his mortal peril. Was it horror?—or ecstasy?—or both in one? Be the emotion what it might, it had blazed up more madly, when Donatello flung his victim off the cliff, and more and more, while his shriek went quivering downward. With the dead thump upon the stones below, had come an unutterable horror.[1]

"And my eyes bade you do it!" repeated she.

They both leaned over the parapet, and gazed downward as earnestly as if some inestimable treasure had fallen over, and were yet recoverable. On the pavement, below, was a dark mass, lying in a heap, with little or nothing human in its appearance, except that the hands were stretched out, as if they might have clutched, for a moment, at the small square stones. But there was no motion in them, now. Miriam watched the heap of mortality while she could count a hundred, which she took pains to do. No stir; not a finger moved!

"You have killed him, Donatello! He is quite dead!" said she. "Stone dead! Would I were so, too!"

"Did you not mean that he should die?" sternly asked Donatello, still in the glow of that intelligence which passion had developed in him. "There was short time to weigh the matter; but he had his trial in that breath or two while I held him over the cliff, and his sentence in that one glance, when your eyes responded to mine! Say that I have slain him against your will—say that he died without your whole consent—and, in another breath, you shall see me lying beside him."

"Oh, never!" cried Miriam. "My one, own friend! Never, never, never!"

She turned to him—the guilty, blood-stained, lonely woman—she turned to her fellow-criminal, the youth, so lately innocent, whom she had drawn into her doom. She pressed him close, close to her bosom, with a clinging embrace that brought their two hearts together, till the horror and agony of each was combined into one emotion, and that, a kind of rapture.

"Yes, Donatello, you speak the truth!" said she; "my heart consented to what you did. We two slew yonder wretch. The deed knots us together for time and eternity, like the coil of a serpent!"

---

[1]Hawthorne exaggerates the actual distance of the drop here. Howells, for one, complained that the Tarpeian Rock was not the precipice that Hawthorne made it out to be. See the Introduction, p. xxiv.

They threw one other glance at the heap of death below, to assure themselves that it was there; so like a dream was the whole thing. Then they turned from that fatal precipice, and came out of the courtyard, arm in arm, heart in heart. Instinctively, they were heedful not to sever themselves so much as a pace or two from one another, for fear of the terror and deadly chill that would thenceforth wait for them in solitude. Their deed—the crime which Donatello wrought, and Miriam accepted on the instant—had wreathed itself, as she said, like a serpent, in inextricable links about both their souls, and drew them into one, by its terrible contractile power. It was closer than a marriage-bond. So intimate, in those first moments, was the union, that it seemed as if their new sympathy annihilated all other ties, and that they were released from the chain of humanity; a new sphere, a special law, had been created for them alone. The world could not come near them; they were safe!

When they reached the flight of steps, leading downward from the Capitol, there was a far-off noise of singing and laughter. Swift, indeed, had been the rush of the crisis that was come and gone! This was still the merriment of the party that had so recently been their companions; they recognized the voices which, a little while ago, had accorded and sung in cadence with their own. But they were familiar voices no more; they sounded strangely, and, as it were, out of the depths of space; so remote was all that pertained to the past life of these guilty ones, in the moral seclusion that had suddenly extended itself around them. But how close, and ever closer, did the breadth of the immeasurable waste, that lay between them and all brotherhood or sisterhood, now press them one within the other!

"Oh, friend," cried Miriam, so putting her soul into that word that it took a heavy richness of meaning, and seemed never to have been spoken before. "Oh, friend, are you conscious, as I am, of this companionship that knits our heart-strings together?"

"I feel it, Miriam," said Donatello. "We draw one breath; we live one life!"

"Only yesterday," continued Miriam; "nay, only a short half-hour ago, I shivered in an icy solitude. No friendship, no sisterhood, could come near enough to keep the warmth within my heart. In an instant, all is changed! There can be no more loneliness!"

"None, Miriam!" said Donatello.

"None, my beautiful one!" responded Miriam, gazing in his face, which had taken a higher, almost an heroic aspect from the strength of passion. "None, my innocent one! Surely, it is no crime that we have committed. One wretched and worthless life has been sacrificed, to cement two other lives forevermore."

"Forevermore, Miriam!" said Donatello; "cemented with his blood!"

The young man started at the word which he had himself spoken; it may be that it brought home, to the simplicity of his imagination, what he had not before dreamed of—the ever-increasing loathsomeness of a union that consists in guilt. Cemented with blood, which would corrupt and grow more noisome forever and forever, but bind them none the less strictly for that!

"Forget it! Cast it all behind you!" said Miriam, detecting, by her sympathy, the pang that was in his heart. "The deed has done its office, and has no existence any more."

They flung the past behind them, as she counselled, or else distilled from it a fiery intoxication, which sufficed to carry them triumphantly through those first moments of their doom. For, guilt has its moment of rapture too. The foremost result of a broken law is ever an ecstatic sense of freedom. And thus there exhaled upward (out of their dark sympathy, at the base of which lay a human corpse) a bliss, or an insanity, which the unhappy pair imagined to be well worth the sleepy innocence that was forever lost to them.

As their spirits rose to the solemn madness of the occasion, they went onward—not stealthily, not fearfully—but with a stately gait and aspect. Passion lent them (as it does to meaner shapes) its brief nobility of carriage. They trod through the streets of Rome, as if they, too, were among the majestic and guilty shadows, that, from ages long gone by, have haunted the blood-stained city. And, at Miriam's suggestion, they turned aside, for the sake of treading loftily past the old site of Pompey's forum.

"For there was a great deed done here!" she said—"a deed of blood, like ours! Who knows, but we may meet the high and ever-sad fraternity of Cæsar's murderers, and exchange a salutation?"

"Are they our brethren, now?" asked Donatello.

"Yes; all of them," said Miriam; "and many another, whom the world little dreams of, has been made our brother or our sister, by what we have done within this hour!"

And, at the thought, she shivered. Where, then, was the seclusion, the remoteness, the strange, lonesome Paradise, into which she and her one companion had been transported by their crime? Was there, indeed, no such refuge, but only a crowded thoroughfare and jostling throng of criminals? And was it true, that whatever hand had a blood-stain on it—or had poured out poison—or strangled a babe at its birth—or clutched a grandsire's throat, he sleeping, and robbed him of his few last breaths—had now the right to offer itself in fellowship with their two hands? Too certainly, that right existed. It is a terrible thought, that an individual wrong-doing melts into the great mass of human crime, and makes us—who dreamed only of our own little separate sin—makes us guilty of the whole. And thus Miriam and her lover were not an insulated pair, but members of an innumerable confraternity of guilty ones, all shuddering at each other.

"But not now; not yet," she murmured to herself. "To-night, at least, there shall be no remorse!"

Wandering without a purpose, it so chanced that they turned into a street, at one extremity of which stood Hilda's tower. There was a light in her high chamber; a light, too, at the Virgin's shrine; and the glimmer of these two was the loftiest light beneath the stars. Miriam drew Donatello's arm to make him stop, and while they stood at some distance looking at Hilda's window, they beheld her approach and throw it open.

She leaned far forth, and extended her clasped hands towards the sky.

"The good, pure child! She is praying, Donatello," said Miriam, with a kind of simple joy at witnessing the devoutness of her friend. Then her own sin rushed upon her, and she shouted, with the rich strength of her voice, "Pray for us, Hilda; we need it!"

Whether Hilda heard and recognized the voice we cannot tell. The window was immediately closed, and her form disappeared from behind the snowy curtain. Miriam felt this to be a token that the cry of her condemned spirit was shut out of heaven.

CHAPTER 20

The Burial Chant

The Church of the Capuchins (where, as the reader may remember, some of our acquaintances had made an engagement to meet) stands a little aside from the Piazza Barberini. Thither, at the hour agreed upon on the morning after the scenes last described, Miriam and Donatello directed their steps. At no time are people so sedulously careful to keep their trifling appointments, attend to their ordinary occupations, and thus put a commonplace aspect on life, as when conscious of some secret that if suspected would make them look monstrous in the general eye.

Yet how tame and wearisome is the impression of all ordinary things in the contrast with such a fact! How sick and tremulous, the next morning, is the spirit that has dared so much, only the night before! How icy cold is the heart, when the fervor, the wild ecstacy of passion has faded away, and sunk down among the dead ashes of the fire that blazed so fiercely, and was fed by the very substance of its life! How faintly does the criminal stagger onward, lacking the impulse of that strong madness that hurried him into guilt, and treacherously deserts him in the midst of it!

When Miriam and Donatello drew near the church, they found only Kenyon awaiting them on the steps. Hilda had likewise promised to be of the party, but had not yet appeared. Meeting the sculptor, Miriam put a force upon herself and succeeded in creating an artificial flow of spirits, which to any but the nicest observation was quite as effective as a natural one. She spoke sympathizingly to the sculptor on the subject of Hilda's absence, and somewhat annoyed him by alluding in Donatello's hearing to an attachment which had never been openly avowed, though perhaps plainly enough betrayed. He fancied that

Miriam did not quite recognize the limits of the strictest delicacy; he even went so far as to generalize, and conclude within himself that this deficiency is a more general failing in woman than in man, the highest refinement being a masculine attribute.

But the idea was unjust to the sex at large, and especially so to this poor Miriam, who was hardly responsible for her frantic efforts to be gay. Possibly, moreover, the nice action of the mind is set ajar by any violent shock as of great misfortune or great crime, so that the finer perceptions may be blurred thenceforth, and the effect be traceable in all the minutest conduct of life.

"Did you see anything of the dear child after you left us?" asked Miriam, still keeping Hilda as her topic of conversation. "I missed her sadly on my way homeward; for nothing insures me such delightful and innocent dreams (I have experienced it twenty times) as a talk late in the evening with Hilda."

"So I should imagine," said the sculptor, gravely; "but it is an advantage that I have little or no opportunity of enjoying. I know not what became of Hilda after my parting from you. She was not especially my companion in any part of our walk. The last I saw of her she was hastening back to rejoin you in the courtyard of the Palazzo Caffarelli."

"Impossible!" cried Miriam, starting.

"Then did you not see her again?" inquired Kenyon, in some alarm.

"Not there," answered Miriam, quietly; "indeed, I followed pretty closely on the heels of the rest of the party. But do not be alarmed on Hilda's account; the Virgin is bound to watch over the good child, for the sake of the piety with which she keeps the lamp alight at her shrine. And, besides, I have always felt that Hilda is just as safe in these evil streets of Rome, as her white doves, when they fly downward from the tower-top, and run to and fro among the horses' feet. There is certainly a Providence on purpose for Hilda, if for no other human creature."

"I religiously believe it," rejoined the sculptor; "and yet my mind would be the easier, if I knew that she had returned safely to her tower."

"Then make yourself quite easy," answered Miriam. "I saw her (and it is the last sweet sight that I remember) leaning from her window midway between earth and sky!"

Kenyon now looked at Donatello.

"You seem out of spirits, my dear friend," he observed. "This languid Roman atmosphere is not the airy wine that you were accustomed to breathe at home. I have not forgotten your hospitable invitation to meet you this summer at your castle among the Apennines. It is my fixed purpose to come, I assure you. We shall both be the better for some deep draughts of the mountain-breezes."

"It may be," said Donatello, with unwonted sombreness; "the old house seemed joyous when I was a child. But as I remember it now it was a grim place, too."

The sculptor looked more attentively at the young man, and was surprised and alarmed to observe how entirely the fine, fresh glow of animal spirits had departed out of his face. Hitherto, moreover, even while he was standing perfectly still, there had been a kind of possible gambol indicated in his aspect. It was quite gone now. All his youthful gayety, and with it his simplicity of manner, was eclipsed, if not utterly extinct.

"You are surely ill, my dear fellow," exclaimed Kenyon.

"Am I? Perhaps so," said Donatello, indifferently; "I never have been ill, and know not what it may be."

"Do not make the poor lad fancy-sick," whispered Miriam, pulling the sculptor's sleeve. "He is of a nature to lie down and die at once, if he finds himself drawing such melancholy breaths as we ordinary people are enforced to burden our lungs withal. But we must get him away from this old, dreamy, and dreary Rome, where nobody but himself ever thought of being gay. Its influences are too heavy to sustain the life of such a creature."

The above conversation had passed chiefly on the steps of the Cappuccini; and, having said so much, Miriam lifted the leathern curtain that hangs before all church doors in Italy.

"Hilda has forgotten her appointment," she observed, "or else her maiden slumbers are very sound this morning. We will wait for her no longer."

They entered the nave. The interior of the church was of moderate compass, but of good architecture, with a vaulted roof over the nave, and a row of dusky chapels on either side of it instead of the customary side-aisles. Each chapel had its saintly shrine, hung round with offerings; its picture above the altar, although closely veiled, if by any painter of renown; and its hallowed tapers, burning continually, to set alight the devotion of the worshippers. The pavement of the nave was chiefly of marble, and looked old and broken, and was shabbily patched here and there with tiles of brick; it was inlaid, moreover, with tombstones of the mediæval taste, on which were quaintly sculptured borders, figures, and portraits in bas-relief, and Latin epitaphs, now grown illegible by the tread of footsteps over them. The church appertains to a convent of Capuchin monks; and, as usually happens when a reverend brotherhood have such an edifice in charge, the floor seemed never to have been scrubbed or swept, and had as little the aspect of sanctity as a kennel; whereas, in all churches of nunneries, the maiden sisterhood invariably show the purity of their own hearts by the virgin cleanliness and visible consecration of the walls and pavement.

As our friends entered the church, their eyes rested at once on a remarkable object in the centre of the nave. It was either the actual body—or, as might rather have been supposed at first glance, the cunningly wrought waxen face and suitably draped figure—of a dead monk. This image of wax or clay-cold reality, whichever it might be, lay on a slightly elevated bier, with three tall candles burning on each side, another tall candle at the head, and another at the foot. There was music, too, in harmony with so funereal a spectacle. From beneath the pavement of the church came the deep, lugubrious strain of a De Profundis,[1] which sounded like an utterance of the tomb itself; so dismally did it rumble through the burial-vaults, and ooze up among the

[1]The great penitential Psalm 29 (30), "Out of the depths," is part of the Roman Catholic burial liturgy.

flat gravestones and sad epitaphs, filling the church as with a gloomy mist.

"I must look more closely at that dead monk before we leave the church," remarked the sculptor. "In the study of my art, I have gained many a hint from the dead, which the living could never have given me."

"I can well imagine it," answered Miriam. "One clay image is readily copied from another. But let us first see Guido's picture. The light is favorable now."

Accordingly, they turned into the first chapel on the right hand, as you enter the nave; and there they beheld—not the picture, indeed—but a closely drawn curtain. The churchmen of Italy make no scruple of sacrificing the very purpose for which a work of sacred art has been created; that of opening the way for religious sentiment through the quick medium of sight, by bringing angels, saints, and martyrs, down visibly upon earth; of sacrificing this high purpose, and, for aught they know, the welfare of many souls along with it, to the hope of a paltry fee. Every work by an artist of celebrity is hidden behind a veil, and seldom revealed, except to Protestants, who scorn it as an object of devotion, and value it only for its artistic merit.

The sacristan was quickly found, however, and lost no time in disclosing the youthful Archangel, setting his divine foot on the head of his fallen adversary. It was an image of that greatest of future events, which we hope for so ardently,—at least, while we are young,—but find so very long in coming,— the triumph of goodness over the evil principle.

"Where can Hilda be?" exclaimed Kenyon. "It is not her custom ever to fail in an engagement; and the present one was made entirely on her account. Except herself, you know, we were all agreed in our recollection of the picture."

"But we were wrong, and Hilda right, as you perceive," said Miriam, directing his attention to the point on which their dispute of the night before had arisen. "It is not easy to detect her astray, as regards any picture on which those clear, soft eyes of hers have ever rested."

"And she has studied and admired few pictures so much as
this," observed the sculptor. "No wonder; for there is hardly
another so beautiful in the world.² What an expression of heavenly severity in the Archangel's face! There is a degree of pain,
trouble, and disgust at being brought in contact with sin, even
for the purpose of quelling and punishing it; and yet a celestial
tranquility pervades his whole being."

"I have never been able," said Miriam, "to admire this
picture nearly so much as Hilda does, in its moral and intellectual
aspect. If it cost her more trouble to be good, if her soul were less
white and pure, she would be a more competent critic of this
picture, and would estimate it not half so high. I see its defects
to-day more clearly than ever before."

"What are some of them?" asked Kenyon.

"That Archangel, now," Miriam continued; "how fair he
looks, with his unruffled wings, with his unhacked sword, and
clad in his bright armor, and that exquisitely fitting sky-blue
tunic, cut in the latest Paradisiacal mode! What a dainty air of
the first celestial society! With what half-scornful delicacy he
sets his prettily sandalled foot on the head of his prostrate foe!
But, is it thus that virtue looks, the moment after its death-
struggle with evil? No, no; I could have told Guido better. A
full third of the Archangel's feathers should have been torn from

²On May 14, 1859, Hawthorne and Sophia visited the Church of the
Capuchins to see Guido's *Archangel Michael:* "I have been several times to
this church, but never saw the picture before, though I am familiar with
the mosaic copy at St. Peter's, and had supposed the latter to be an equivalent representation of the original. It is nearly or quite so as respects the
general effect but there is a beauty in the Archangel's face that immeasurably surpasses the copy—the expression of heavenly severity, and a
degree of pain, trouble, or disgust, at being brought in contact with sin,
even for the purpose of quelling and punishing it. There is something fini-
cal in the copy, which I do not find in the original. The sandalled feet are
here those of an angel; in the mosaic they are those of a celestial coxcomb,
treading daintily, as if he were afraid they would be soiled by the touch
of Lucifer" (*NB*, pp. 505–506).

his wings; the rest all ruffled, till they looked like Satan's own!
His sword should be streaming with blood, and perhaps broken
half way to the hilt; his armor crushed, his robes rent, his breast
gory; a bleeding gash on his brow, cutting right across the stern
scowl of battle! He should press his foot hard down upon the
old serpent, as if his very soul depended upon it, feeling him
squirm mightily, and doubting whether the fight were half over
yet, and how the victory might turn! And, with all this fierceness, this grimness, this unutterable horror, there should still be
something high, tender, and holy, in Michael's eyes, and around
his mouth. But the battle never was such child's play as Guido's
dapper Archangel seems to have found it."

"For Heaven's sake, Miriam," cried Kenyon, astonished
at the wild energy of her talk; "paint the picture of man's struggle against sin according to your own idea! I think it will be a
masterpiece."

"The picture would have its share of truth, I assure you,"
she answered; "but I am sadly afraid the victory would fall on
the wrong side. Just fancy a smoke-blackened, fiery-eyed
demon, bestriding that nice young angel, clutching his white
throat with one of his hinder claws; and giving a triumphant
whisk of his scaly tail, with a poisonous dart at the end of it!
That is what they risk, poor souls, who do battle with Michael's
enemy."

It now, perhaps, struck Miriam that her mental disquietude
was impelling her to an undue vivacity; for she paused, and
turned away from the picture, without saying a word more
about it. All this while, moreover, Donatello had been very ill
at ease, casting awe-stricken and inquiring glances at the dead
monk; as if he could look nowhere but at that ghastly object,
merely because it shocked him. Death has probably a peculiar
horror and ugliness, when forced upon the contemplation of a
person so naturally joyous as Donatello, who lived with com-
pleteness in the present moment, and was able to form but vague
images of the future.

"What is the matter, Donatello?" whispered Miriam, soothingly. "You are quite in a tremble, my poor friend! What is it?"

"This awful chant from beneath the church," answered Donatello; "it oppresses me; the air is so heavy with it that I can scarcely draw my breath. And yonder dead monk! I feel as if he were lying right across my heart."

"Take courage!" whispered she again, "come; we will approach close to the dead monk. The only way, in such cases, is to stare the ugly horror right in the face; never a side-long glance, nor a half-look, for those are what show a frightful thing in its frightfullest aspect. Lean on me, dearest friend! My heart is very strong for both of us. Be brave; and all is well."

Donatello hung back for a moment, but then pressed close to Miriam's side, and suffered her to lead him up to the bier. The sculptor followed. A number of persons, chiefly women, with several children among them, were standing about the corpse; and as our three friends drew nigh, a mother knelt down, and caused her little boy to kneel, both kissing the beads and crucifix that hung from the monk's girdle. Possibly he had died in the odor of sanctity; or, at all events, death and his brown frock and cowl made a sacred image of this reverend father.

The dead monk was clad, as when alive, in the brown woollen frock of the Capuchins, with the hood drawn over his head, but so as to leave the features and a portion of the beard uncovered.[1] His rosary and cross hung at his side; his hands were folded over his breast; his feet (he was of a bare-footed order in his lifetime, and continued so in death) protruded from beneath his habit, stiff and stark, with a more waxen look than even his face. They were tied together at the ankles with a black ribbon.

The countenance, as we have already said, was fully displayed. It had a purplish hue upon it, unlike the paleness of an ordinary corpse, but as little resembling the flush of natural life. The eyelids were but partially drawn down, and showed the eyeballs beneath; as if the deceased friar were stealing a glimpse at the bystanders, to watch whether they were duly impressed with the solemnity of his obsequies. The shaggy eyebrows gave sternness to the look.

Miriam passed between two of the lighted candles, and stood close beside the bier.

"My God!" murmured she. "What is this?"

She grasped Donatello's hand, and, at the same instant, felt him give a convulsive shudder, which she knew to have been caused by a sudden and terrible throb of the heart. His hand, by an instantaneous change, became like ice within hers, which likewise grew so icy, that their insensible fingers might have rattled, one against the other. No wonder that their blood curdled; no wonder that their hearts leaped and paused! The dead

[1]See note 5, p. 136.

face of the monk, gazing at them beneath its half-closed eyelids, was the same visage that had glared upon their naked souls, the past midnight, as Donatello flung him over the precipice.

The sculptor was standing at the foot of the bier, and had not yet seen the monk's features.

"Those naked feet!" said he. "I know not why, but they affect me strangely. They have walked to and fro over the hard pavements of Rome, and through a hundred other rough ways of this life, where the monk went begging for his brotherhood; along the cloisters and dreary corridors of his convent, too, from his youth upward! It is a suggestive idea, to track those worn feet backward through all the paths they have trodden, ever since they were the tender and rosy-little feet of a baby, and (cold as they are now) were kept warm in his mother's hand."

As his companions, whom the sculptor supposed to be close by him, made no response to his fanciful musing, he looked up, and saw them at the head of the bier. He advanced thither himself.

"Ha!" exclaimed he.

He cast a horror-stricken and bewildered glance at Miriam, but withdrew it immediately. Not that he had any definite suspicion, or, it may be, even a remote idea, that she could be held responsible, in the least degree, for this man's sudden death. In truth, it seemed too wild a thought, to connect, in reality, Miriam's persecutor of many past months and the vagabond of the preceding night, with the dead Capuchin of to-day. It resembled one of those unaccountable changes and interminglings of identity, which so often occur among the personages of a dream. But Kenyon, as befitted the professor of an imaginative art, was endowed with an exceedingly quick sensibility, which was apt to give him intimations of the true state of matters that lay beyond his actual vision. There was a whisper in his ear; it said, "Hush!" Without asking himself wherefore, he resolved to be silent as regarded the mysterious discovery which he had made, and to leave any remark or explanation to be voluntarily

offered by Miriam. If she never spoke, then let the riddle be un-
solved.

And now occurred a circumstance that would seem too
fantastic to be told, if it had not actually happened, precisely as
we set it down. As the three friends stood by the bier, they saw
that a little stream of blood had begun to ooze from the dead
monk's nostrils; it crept slowly towards the thicket of his beard,
where, in the course of a moment or two, it hid itself.[2]

"How strange!" ejaculated Kenyon. "The monk died of
apoplexy, I suppose, or by some sudden accident, and the blood
has not yet congealed."

"Do you consider that a sufficient explanation?" asked
Miriam, with a smile from which the sculptor involuntarily
turned away his eyes. "Does it satisfy you?"

"And why not?" he inquired.

"Of course, you know the old superstition about this phenomenon of blood flowing from a dead body," she rejoined.
"How can we tell but that the murderer of this monk (or, possibly, it may be only that privileged murderer, his physician)
may have just entered the church?"

"I cannot jest about it," said Kenyon. "It is an ugly sight!"

"True, true; horrible to see, or dream of!" she replied,
with one of those long, tremulous sighs, which so often betray
a sick heart by escaping unexpectedly. "We will not look at it
any more. Come away, Donatello. Let us escape from this dismal church. The sunshine will do you good."

When had ever a woman such a trial to sustain as this! By
no possible supposition could Miriam explain the identity of the
dead Capuchin, quietly and decorously laid out in the nave of

[2]Hawthorne and Sophia witnessed such a phenomenon in the Capuchin church on Feb. 16, 1858. Sophia cut the relevant passage out of the
Italian Notebooks with the following comment: " 'The Marble Faun' takes
up this description of the church and of the dead monk, which we really
saw, just as recounted, even to the sudden stream of blood which flowed
from the nostrils, as we looked at him" (*NB*, p. 78).

his convent church, with that of her murdered persecutor, flung
heedlessly at the foot of the precipice. The effect upon her
imagination was, as if a strange and unknown corpse had miraculously, while she was gazing at it, assumed the likeness of that
face, so terrible henceforth in her remembrance. It was a symbol,
perhaps, of the deadly iteration with which she was doomed to
behold the image of her crime reflected back upon her in a
thousand ways, and converting the great, calm face of Nature, in
the whole, and in its innumerable details, into a manifold reminiscence of that one dead visage.

No sooner had Miriam turned away from the bier, and
gone a few steps, than she fancied the likeness altogether an illusion, which would vanish at a closer and colder view. She must
look at it again, therefore, and at once; or else the grave would
close over the face, and leave the awful fantasy that had connected itself therewith, fixed ineffaceably in her brain.

"Wait for me, one moment!" she said to her companions.
"Only a moment!"

So she went back, and gazed once more at the corpse. Yes;
these were the features that Miriam had known so well; this
was the visage that she remembered from a far longer date than
the most intimate of her friends suspected; this form of clay
had held the evil spirit which blasted her sweet youth, and compelled her, as it were, to stain her womanhood with crime. But,
whether it were the majesty of death, or something originally
noble and lofty in the character of the dead, which the soul had
stamped upon the features, as it left them; so it was that Miriam
now quailed and shook, not for the vulgar horror of the spectacle, but for the severe, reproachful glance that seemed to come
from between those half-closed lids. True, there had been
nothing, in his lifetime, viler than this man. She knew it; there
was no other fact within her consciousness that she felt to be so
certain; and yet, because her persecutor found himself safe and
irrefutable in death, he frowned upon his victim, and threw back
the blame on her!

"Is it thou, indeed?" she murmured, under her breath.

"Then thou hast no right to scowl upon me so! But art thou real, or a vision?"

She bent down over the dead monk, till one of her rich curls brushed against his forehead. She touched one of his folded hands with her finger.

"It is he!" said Miriam. "There is the scar, that I know so well, on his brow. And it is no vision; he is palpable to my touch! I will question the fact no longer, but deal with it as I best can."

It was wonderful to see how the crisis developed in Miriam its own proper strength, and the faculty of sustaining the demands which it made upon her fortitude. She ceased to tremble; the beautiful woman gazed sternly at her dead enemy, endeavoring to meet and quell the look of accusation that he threw from between his half-closed eyelids.

"No; thou shalt not scowl me down!" said she. "Neither now, nor when we stand together at the Judgment Seat. I fear not to meet thee there. Farewell, till that next encounter!"

Haughtily waving her hand, Miriam rejoined her friends, who were awaiting her at the door of the church. As they went out, the sacristan stopped them, and proposed to show the cemetery of the convent, where the deceased members of the fraternity are laid to rest in sacred earth, brought long ago from Jerusalem.

"And will yonder monk be buried there?" she asked.

"Brother Antonio?" exclaimed the sacristan. "Surely, our good brother will be put to bed there! His grave is already dug, and the last occupant has made room for him. Will you look at it, signorina?"

"I will!" said Miriam.

"Then excuse me," observed Kenyon; "for I shall leave you. One dead monk has more than sufficed me; and I am not bold enough to face the whole mortality of the convent."

It was easy to see, by Donatello's looks, that he, as well as the sculptor, would gladly have escaped a visit to the famous cemetery of the Cappuccini. But Miriam's nerves were strained to such a pitch, that she anticipated a certain solace and absolute relief in passing from one ghastly spectacle to another of long-accumulated ugliness; and there was, besides, a singular sense of duty which impelled her to look at the final resting-place of the being whose fate had been so disastrously involved with her own. She therefore followed the sacristan's guidance, and drew her companion along with her, whispering encouragement as they went.

The cemetery is beneath the church, but entirely above ground, and lighted by a row of iron-grated windows without glass. A corridor runs along beside these windows, and gives access to three or four vaulted recesses, or chapels, of considerable breadth and height, the floor of which consists of the consecrated earth of Jerusalem. It is smoothed decorously over the deceased brethren of the convent, and is kept quite free from grass or weeds, such as would grow even in these gloomy recesses, if pains were not bestowed to root them up. But, as the cemetery is small, and it is a precious privilege to sleep in holy ground, the brotherhood are immemorially accustomed, when one of their number dies, to take the longest-buried skeleton out of the oldest grave, and lay the new slumberer there instead. Thus, each of the good friars, in his turn, enjoys the luxury of a consecrated bed, attended with the slight drawback of being forced to get up long before daybreak, as it were, and make room for another lodger.

The arrangement of the unearthed skeletons is what makes the special interest of the cemetery. The arched and vaulted walls of the burial recesses are supported by massive pillars and pilasters made of thigh-bones and skulls; the whole material of the structure appears to be of a similar kind; and the knobs and embossed ornaments of this strange architecture are represented by the joints of the spine, and the more delicate tracery by the smaller bones of the human frame. The summits of the arches are adorned with entire skeletons, looking as if they were wrought most skilfully in bas-relief. There is no possibility of describing how ugly and grotesque is the effect, combined with a certain artistic merit, nor how much perverted ingenuity has been shown in this queer way, nor what a multitude of dead monks, through how many hundred years, must have contributed their bony framework to build up these great arches of mortality. On some of the skulls there are inscriptions, purporting that such a monk, who formerly made use of that particular headpiece, died on such a day and year; but vastly the greater number are piled up indistinguishably into the architectural design like the many deaths that make up the one glory of a victory.

In the side walls of the vaults are niches where skeleton monks sit or stand, clad in the brown habits that they wore in life, and labelled with their names and the dates of their decease. Their skulls (some quite bare, and others still covered with yellow skin, and hair that has known the earth-damps) look out from beneath their hoods, grinning hideously repulsive. One reverend father has his mouth wide open, as if he had died in the midst of a howl of terror and remorse, which perhaps is even now screeching through eternity. As a general thing, however, these frocked and hooded skeletons seem to take a more cheerful view of their position, and try with ghastly smiles to turn it into a jest. But the cemetery of the Capuchins is no place to nourish celestial hopes: the soul sinks forlorn and wretched under all this burden of dusty death; the holy earth from Jerusalem, so imbued is it with mortality, has grown as barren of the flowers of Paradise as it is of earthly weeds and grass. Thank Heaven for its blue sky; it needs a long, upward gaze to give us back our faith. Not here can we feel ourselves immortal, where the very altars in these chapels of horrible consecration are heaps of human bones.[3]

[3]In this paragraph Hawthorne expresses his dislike for the Church's graphic eschatology. He was Emersonian enough to seek the correspondence between religious feelings and the beauties of the natural world. On the whole his attitude toward the Church is more sympathetic than critical, as John Waldron shows in his unpublished doctoral dissertation, "Nathanial Hawthorne's Attitude Towards the Catholic Church" (Georgetown University, 1930).

Yet let us give the cemetery the praise that it deserves. There is no disagreeable scent, such as might have been expected from the decay of so many holy persons, in whatever odor of sanctity they may have taken their departure. The same number of living monks would not smell half so unexceptionably.

Miriam went gloomily along the corridor, from one vaulted Golgotha[4] to another, until in the farthest recess she beheld an open grave.

"Is that for him who lies yonder in the nave?" she asked.

"Yes, signorina, this is to be the resting-place of brother Antonio, who came to his death last night," answered the sacristan; "and in yonder niche, you see, sits a brother who was buried thirty years ago, and has risen to give him place."

"It is not a satisfactory idea," observed Miriam, "that you poor friars cannot call even your graves permanently your own. You must lie down in them, methinks, with a nervous anticipation of being disturbed, like weary men who know that they shall be summoned out of bed at midnight. Is it not possible (if money were to be paid for the privilege) to leave Brother Antonio—if that be his name—in the occupancy of that narrow grave till the last trumpet sounds?"

"By no means, signorina; neither is it needful or desirable," answered the sacristan. "A quarter of a century's sleep in the sweet earth of Jerusalem is better than a thousand years in any other soil. Our brethren find good rest there. No ghost was ever known to steal out of this blessed cemetery."

"That is well," responded Miriam; "may he whom you now lay to sleep prove no exception to the rule!"

As they left the cemetery she put money into the sacristan's hand to an amount that made his eyes open wide and glisten, and requested that it might be expended in masses for the repose of Father Antonio's soul.

---

[4]The hill near Jerusalem where Christ was crucified; but here Hawthorne takes the literal meaning, "place of the skull."

CHAPTER 22.   *The Medici Gardens*

"Donatello," said Miriam, anxiously, as they came through the Piazza Barberini, "what can I do for you, my beloved friend? You are shaking as with the cold fit of the Roman fever."

"Yes," said Donatello; "my heart shivers."

As soon as she could collect her thoughts, Miriam led the young man to the gardens of the Villa Medici, hoping that the quiet shade and sunshine of that delightful retreat would a little revive his spirits. The grounds are there laid out in the old fashion of straight paths, with borders of box, which form hedges of great height and density, and are shorn and trimmed to the evenness of a wall of stone, at the top and sides. There are green alleys, with long vistas, overshadowed by ilex-trees; and at each intersection of the paths, the visitor finds seats of lichen-covered stone to repose upon, and marble statues that look forlornly at him, regretful of their lost noses. In the more open portions of the garden, before the sculptured front of the villa, you see fountains and flower-beds, and, in their season, a profusion of roses, from which the genial sun of Italy distils a fragrance, to be scattered abroad by the no less genial breeze.

But Donatello drew no delight from these things. He walked onward in silent apathy, and looked at Miriam with strangely half-awakened and bewildered eyes, when she sought to bring his mind into sympathy with hers, and so relieve his heart of the burden that lay lumpishly upon it.

She made him sit down on a stone bench, where two embowered alleys crossed each other; so that they could discern the approach of any casual intruder, a long way down the path.

"My sweet friend," she said, taking one of his passive hands in both of hers, "what can I say to comfort you?"

"Nothing!" replied Donatello, with sombre reserve. "Nothing will ever comfort me."

"I accept my own misery," continued Miriam, "my own guilt, if guilt it be—and, whether guilt or misery, I shall know how to deal with it. But you, dearest friend, that were the rarest creature in all this world, and seemed a being to whom sorrow could not cling—you, whom I half fancied to belong to a race that had vanished forever, you only surviving, to show mankind how genial and how joyous life used to be, in some long-gone age —what had you to do with grief or crime?"

"They came to me as to other men," said Donatello, broodingly. "Doubtless I was born to them."

"No, no; they came with me," replied Miriam. "Mine is the responsibility! Alas! wherefore was I born? Why did we ever meet? Why did I not drive you from me, knowing—for my heart foreboded it—that the cloud in which I walked would likewise envelop you!"

Donatello stirred uneasily, with the irritable impatience that is often combined with a mood of leaden despondency. A brown lizard with two tails—a monster often engendered by the Roman sunshine—ran across his foot, and made him start. Then he sat silent awhile, and so did Miriam, trying to dissolve her whole heart into sympathy, and lavish it all upon him, were it only for a moment's cordial.

The young man lifted his hand to his breast, and, unintentionally, as Miriam's hand was within his, he lifted that along with it.

"I have a great weight here!" said he.

The fancy struck Miriam (but she drove it resolutely down) that Donatello almost imperceptibly shuddered, while, in pressing his own hand against his heart, he pressed hers there too.

"Rest your heart on me, dearest one!" she resumed. "Let me bear all its weight; I am well able to bear it; for I am a woman, and I love you! I love you, Donatello! Is there no comfort for you in this avowal? Look at me! Heretofore, you have found me pleasant to your sight. Gaze into my eyes! Gaze into my soul! Search as deeply as you may, you can never see half the tenderness and devotion that I henceforth cherish for you. All that I ask, is your acceptance of the utter self-sacrifice (but it shall be no sacrifice, to my great love) with which I seek to remedy the evil you have incurred for my sake!"

All this fervor on Miriam's part; on Donatello's, a heavy silence.

"Oh, speak to me!" she exclaimed. "Only promise me to be, by-and-by, a little happy!"

"Happy?" murmured Donatello. "Ah, never again! never again!"

"Never? Ah, that is a terrible word to say to me!" answered Miriam. "A terrible word to let fall upon a woman's heart, when she loves you, and is conscious of having caused your misery! If you love me, Donatello, speak it not again. And surely you did love me?"

"I did," replied Donatello, gloomily and absently.

Miriam released the young man's hand, but suffered one of her own to lie close to his, and waited a moment to see whether he would make any effort to retain it. There was much depending upon that simple experiment.

With a deep sigh—as when, sometimes, a slumberer turns over in a troubled dream—Donatello changed his position, and clasped both his hands over his forehead. The genial warmth of a Roman April kindling into May was in the atmosphere around them; but when Miriam saw that involuntary movement and heard that sigh of relief (for so she interpreted it), a shiver ran through her frame, as if the iciest wind of the Apennines were blowing over her.

"He has done himself a greater wrong than I dreamed of," thought she, with unutterable compassion. "Alas! it was a sad mistake! He might have had a kind of bliss in the consequences of this deed, had he been impelled to it by a love vital enough to survive the frenzy of that terrible moment—mighty enough to make its own law, and justify itself against the natural remorse. But to have perpetrated a dreadful murder (and such was his crime, unless love, annihilating moral distinctions, made it otherwise) on no better warrant than a boy's idle fantasy! I pity him from the very depths of my soul! As for myself, I am past my own or others' pity."

She arose from the young man's side, and stood before him with a sad, commiserating aspect; it was the look of a ruined soul, bewailing, in him, a grief less than what her profounder sympathies imposed upon herself.

"Donatello, we must part," she said, with melancholy firmness. "Yes; leave me! Go back to your old tower, which overlooks the green valley you have told me of, among the Apennines. Then, all that has passed will be recognized as but an ugly dream. For, in dreams, the conscience sleeps, and we often stain ourselves with guilt of which we should be incapable in our waking moments. The deed you seemed to do, last night, was no more than such a dream; there was as little substance in what you fancied yourself doing. Go; and forget it all!"

"Ah, that terrible face!" said Donatello, pressing his hands over his eyes. "Do you call that unreal?"

"Yes; for you beheld it with dreaming eyes," replied Miriam. "It was unreal; and, that you may feel it so, it is requisite that you see this face of mine no more. Once, you may have thought it beautiful; now, it has lost its charm. Yet it would still retain a miserable potency to bring back the past illusion, and, in its train, the remorse and anguish that would darken all your life. Leave me, therefore, and forget me."

"Forget you, Miriam!" said Donatello, roused somewhat from his apathy of despair. "If I could remember you, and behold you, apart from that frightful visage which stares at me over your shoulder, that were a consolation, at least, if not a joy."

"But since that visage haunts you along with mine," rejoined Miriam, glancing behind her, "we needs must part. Farewell, then! But if ever—in distress, peril, shame, poverty, or whatever anguish is most poignant, whatever burden heaviest— you should require a life to be given wholly, only to make your own a little easier, then summon me! As the case now stands between us, you have bought me dear,[1] and find me of little worth. Fling me away, therefore! May you never need me more! But, if otherwise, a wish—almost an unuttered wish— will bring me to you!"

She stood a moment, expecting a reply. But Donatello's eyes had again fallen on the ground, and he had not, in his be- wildered mind and over-burdened heart, a word to respond.

"That hour I speak of may never come," said Miriam. "So farewell—farewell forever."

"Farewell," said Donatello.

His voice hardly made its way through the environment of unaccustomed thoughts and emotions which had settled over him like a dense and dark cloud. Not improbably, he beheld Miriam through so dim a medium that she looked visionary; heard her speak only in a thin, faint echo.

She turned from the young man, and, much as her heart yearned towards him, she would not profane that heavy parting by an embrace, or even a pressure of the hand. So soon after the semblance of such mighty love, and after it had been the impulse to so terrible a deed, they parted, in all outward show, as coldly as people part whose whole mutual intercourse has been en- circled within a single hour.

And Donatello, when Miriam had departed, stretched him- self at full length on the stone bench, and drew his hat over his eyes, as the idle and light-hearted youths of dreamy Italy are accustomed to do, when they lie down in the first convenient shade, and snatch a noonday slumber. A stupor was upon him, which he mistook for such drowsiness as he had known in his innocent past life. But, by-and-by, he raised himself slowly and left the garden. Sometimes poor Donatello started, as if he heard

[1] I.e., "you have paid too much for me."

a shriek; sometimes he shrank back, as if a face, fearful to behold, were thrust close to his own. In this dismal mood, bewildered with the novelty of sin and grief, he had little left of that singular resemblance, on account of which, and for their sport, his three friends had fantastically recognized him as the veritable Faun of Praxiteles.

CHAPTER 23. *Miriam and Hilda*

On leaving the Medici Gardens, Miriam felt herself astray in the world; and having no special reason to seek one place more than another, she suffered chance to direct her steps as it would. Thus it happened, that, involving herself in the crookedness of Rome, she saw Hilda's tower rising before her, and was put in mind to climb up to the young girl's aëry, and ask why she had broken her engagement at the church of the Capuchins. People often do the idlest acts of their lifetimes in their heaviest and most anxious moments; so that it would have been no wonder had Miriam been impelled only by so slight a motive of curiosity as we have indicated. But she remembered, too, and with a quaking heart, what the sculptor had mentioned of Hilda's retracing her steps towards the courtyard of the Palazzo Caffe-relli in quest of Miriam herself. Had she been compelled to choose between infamy in the eyes of the whole world, or in Hilda's eyes alone, she would unhesitatingly have accepted the former, on condition of remaining spotless in the estimation of her white-souled friend. This possibility, therefore, that Hilda had witnessed the scene of the past night, was unquestionably the cause that drew Miriam to the tower, and made her linger and falter as she approached it.

As she drew near, there were tokens to which her disturbed mind gave a sinister interpretation. Some of her friend's airy family, the doves, with their heads imbedded disconsolately in their bosoms, were squatted in a corner of the piazza; others had alighted on the heads, wings, shoulders, and trumpets of the marble angels which adorned the façade of the neighboring church; two or three had betaken themselves to the Virgin's shrine; and as many as could find room were sitting on Hilda's window-sill. But all of them, so Miriam fancied, had a look of weary expectation and disappointment—no flights, no flutter-ings, no cooing murmur; something that ought to have made their day glad and bright, was evidently left out of this day's history. And, furthermore, Hilda's white window-curtain was closely drawn, with only that one little aperture at the side, which Miriam remembered noticing the night before.

"Be quiet," said Miriam to her own heart, pressing her hand hard upon it. 'Why shouldst thou throb now?—Hast thou not endured more terrible things than this?"

Whatever were her apprehensions, she would not turn back. It might be—and the solace would be worth a world—that Hilda, knowing nothing of the past night's calamity, would greet her friend with a sunny smile, and so restore a portion of the vital warmth, for lack of which her soul was frozen. But could Miriam, guilty as she was, permit Hilda to kiss her cheek, to clasp her hand, and thus be no longer so unspotted from the world as heretofore?

"I will never permit her sweet touch again," said Miriam, toiling up the staircase, "if I can find strength of heart to forbid it. But, oh! it would be so soothing in this wintry fever-fit of my heart. There can be no harm to my white Hilda in one parting kiss. That shall be all!"

But, on reaching the upper landing-place, Miriam paused, and stirred not again till she had brought herself to an immov-able resolve.

"My lips, my hand, shall never meet Hilda's more," said she.

Meanwhile, Hilda sat listlessly in her painting-room. Had you looked into the little adjoining chamber, you might have seen the slight imprint of her figure on the bed, but would also have detected at once that the white counterpane had not been turned down. The pillow was more disturbed; she had turned her face upon it, the poor child, and bedewed it with some of those tears (among the most chill and forlorn that gush from human sorrow) which the innocent heart pours forth at its first actual discovery that sin is in the world. The young and pure are not apt to find out that miserable truth until it is brought home to them by the guiltiness of some trusted friend. They may have heard much of the evil of the world, and seem to know it, but only as an impalpable theory. In due time, some mortal, whom they reverence too highly, is commissioned by Providence to teach them this direful lesson; he perpetrates a sin; and Adam falls anew, and Paradise, heretofore in unfaded bloom, is lost again, and closed forever, with the fiery swords gleaming at its gates.

The chair in which Hilda sat was near the portrait of Beatrice Cenci, which had not yet been taken from the easel. It is a peculiarity of this picture, that its profoundest expression eludes a straightforward glance, and can only be caught by side glimpses, or when the eye falls casually upon it; even as if the painted face had a life and consciousness of its own, and, resolving not to betray its secret of grief or guilt, permitted the true tokens to come forth only when it imagined itself unseen. No other such magical effect has ever been wrought by pencil.[1]

Now, opposite the easel hung a looking-glass, in which Beatrice's face and Hilda's were both reflected. In one of her weary, nerveless changes of position, Hilda happened to throw her eyes on the glass, and took in both these images at one unpremeditated glance. She fancied—nor was it without horror—that Beatrice's expression, seen aside and vanishing in a moment, had been depicted in her own face likewise, and flitted from it as timorously.

"Am I, too, stained with guilt?" thought the poor girl, hiding her face in her hands.

Not so, thank Heaven! But, as regards Beatrice's picture, the incident suggests a theory which may account for its unutterable grief and mysterious shadow of guilt, without detracting from the purity which we love to attribute to that ill-

[1]This paragraph is taken almost verbatim from Hawthorne's notebook entry for May 15, 1859 (*NB*, pp. 504–505).

fated girl. Who, indeed, can look at that mouth—with its lips half apart, as innocent as a baby's that has been crying—and not pronounce Beatrice sinless! It was the intimate consciousness of her father's sin that threw its shadow over her, and frightened her into a remote and inaccessible region, where no sympathy could come. It was the knowledge of Miriam's guilt, that lent the same expression to Hilda's face.

But Hilda nervously moved her chair, so that the images in the glass should be no longer visible. She now watched a speck of sunshine that came through a shuttered window, and crept from object to object, indicating each with a touch of its bright finger, and then letting them all vanish successively. In like manner, her mind, so like sunlight in its natural cheerfulness, went from thought to thought, but found nothing that it could dwell upon for comfort. Never before had this young, energetic, active spirit known what it is to be despondent. It was the unreality of the world that made her so. Her dearest friend, whose heart seemed the most solid and richest of Hilda's possessions, had no existence for her any more; and in that dreary void, out of which Miriam had disappeared, the substance, the truth, the integrity of life, the motives of effort, the joy of success, had departed along with her.

It was long past noon, when a step came up the staircase. It had passed beyond the limits where there was communication with the lower regions of the palace, and was mounting the successive flights which led only to Hilda's precincts. Faint as the tread was, she heard and recognized it. It startled her into sudden life. Her first impulse was to spring to the door of the studio, and fasten it with lock and bolt. But a second thought made her feel that this would be an unworthy cowardice, on her own part, and also that Miriam—only yesterday her closest friend— had a right to be told, face to face, that thenceforth they must be forever strangers.

She heard Miriam pause, outside of the door. We have already seen what was the latter's resolve with respect to any kiss or pressure of the hand between Hilda and herself. We

know not what became of the resolution. As Miriam was of a
highly impulsive character, it may have vanished at the first sight
of Hilda; but, at all events, she appeared to have dressed herself
up in a garb of sunshine, and was disclosed, as the door swung
open, in all the glow of her remarkable beauty. The truth was,
her heart leaped convulsively towards the only refuge that it
had, or hoped. She forgot, just one instant, all cause for holding
herself aloof. Ordinarily there was a certain reserve in Miriam's
demonstrations of affection, in consonance with the delicacy of
her friend. To-day, she opened her arms to take Hilda in.

"Dearest, darling Hilda!" she exclaimed. "It gives me new
life to see you!"

Hilda was standing in the middle of the room. When her
friend made a step or two from the door, she put forth her hands
with an involuntary repellent gesture, so expressive, that Miriam
at once felt a great chasm opening itself between them two.
They might gaze at one another from the opposite sides, but
without the possibility of ever meeting more; or, at least, since
the chasm could never be bridged over, they must tread the
whole round of Eternity to meet on the other side. There was
even a terror in the thought of their meeting again. It was as if
Hilda or Miriam were dead, and could no longer hold intercourse without violating a spiritual law.

Yet, in the wantonness of her despair, Miriam made one
more step towards the friend whom she had lost.

"Do not come nearer, Miriam!" said Hilda.

Her look and tone were those of sorrowful entreaty, and
yet they expressed a kind of confidence, as if the girl were conscious of a safeguard that could not be violated.

"What has happened between us, Hilda?" asked Miriam.
"Are we not friends?"

"No, no!" said Hilda, shuddering.

"At least we have been friends," continued Miriam. "I
loved you dearly! I love you still! You were to me as a younger
sister; yes, dearer than sisters of the same blood; for you and I
were so lonely, Hilda, that the whole world pressed us together

by its solitude and strangeness. Then, will you not touch my hand? Am I not the same as yesterday?"

"Alas! no, Miriam!" said Hilda.

"Yes, the same—the same for you, Hilda," rejoined her lost friend. "Were you to touch my hand, you would find it as warm to your grasp as ever. If you were sick or suffering, I would watch night and day for you. It is in such simple offices that true affection shows itself; and so I speak of them. Yet now, Hilda, your very look seems to put me beyond the limits of humankind!"

"It is not I, Miriam," said Hilda; "not I that have done this."

"You, and you only, Hilda," replied Miriam, stirred up to make her own cause good by the repellent force which her friend opposed to her. "I am a woman, as I was yesterday; endowed with the same truth of nature, the same warmth of heart, the same genuine and earnest love, which you have always known in me. In any regard that concerns yourself, I am not changed. And believe me, Hilda, when a human being has chosen a friend out of all the world, it is only some faithlessness between themselves, rendering true intercourse impossible, that can justify either friend in severing the bond. Have I deceived you? Then cast me off! Have I wronged you personally? Then forgive me, if you can. But, have I sinned against God and man, and deeply sinned? Then be more my friend than ever, for I need you more."

"Do not bewilder me thus, Miriam!" exclaimed Hilda, who had not forborne to express, by look and gesture, the anguish which this interview inflicted on her. "If I were one of God's angels, with a nature incapable of stain, and garments that never could be spotted, I would keep ever at your side, and try to lead you upward. But I am a poor, lonely girl, whom God has set here in an evil world, and given her only a white robe, and bid her wear it back to Him, as white as when she put it on. Your powerful magnetism would be too much for me. The pure, white atmosphere, in which I try to discern what things are good and true, would be discolored. And, therefore, Miriam, before it is too late, I mean to put faith in this awful heart-quake, which warns me henceforth to avoid you."

"Ah, this is hard! Ah, this is terrible!" murmured Miriam, dropping her forehead in her hands. In a moment or two she looked up again, as pale as death, but with a composed countenance: "I always said, Hilda, that you were merciless; for I had perception of it, even while you loved me best. You have no sin, nor any conception of what it is; and therefore you are so terribly severe! As an angel, you are not amiss; but, as a human creature, and a woman among earthly men and women, you need a sin to soften you."

"God forgive me," said Hilda, "if I have said a needlessly cruel word!"

"Let it pass," answered Miriam; "I, whose heart it has smitten upon, forgive you. And tell me, before we part forever, what have you seen or known of me, since we last met?"

"A terrible thing, Miriam," said Hilda, growing paler than before.

"Do you see it written in my face, or painted in my eyes?" inquired Miriam, her trouble seeking relief in a half-frenzied raillery. "I would fain know how it is that Providence, or fate, brings eye-witnesses to watch us, when we fancy ourselves acting in the remotest privacy. Did all Rome see it, then? Or, at least, our merry company of artists? Or is it some blood-stain on me, or death-scent in my garments? They say that monstrous deformities sprout out of fiends, who once were lovely angels. Do you perceive such in me already? Tell me, by our past friendship, Hilda, all you know."

Thus adjured, and frightened by the wild emotion which Miriam could not suppress, Hilda strove to tell what she had witnessed.

"After the rest of the party had passed on, I went back to speak to you," she said; "for there seemed to be a trouble on your mind, and I wished to share it with you, if you could permit me. The door of the little courtyard was partly shut; but I pushed it open, and saw you within, and Donatello, and a third person, whom I had before noticed in the shadow of a niche. He approached you, Miriam. You knelt to him!—I saw Donatello spring upon him! I would have shrieked, but my throat was dry. I would have rushed forward; but my limbs seemed rooted to the earth.—It was all like a flash of lightning. A look passed from your eyes to Donatello's—a look——"

"Yes, Hilda, yes!" exclaimed Miriam, with intense eagerness. "Do not pause now! That look?"

"It revealed all your heart, Miriam," continued Hilda, covering her eyes as if to shut out the recollection; "a look of hatred, triumph, vengeance, and, as it were, joy at some unhoped-for relief."

"Ah! Donatello was right, then," murmured Miriam, who shook throughout all her frame. "My eyes bade him do it! Go on, Hilda."

"It all passed so quickly—all like a glare of lightning," said Hilda, "and yet it seemed to me that Donatello had paused, while one might draw a breath. But that look!—Ah, Miriam, spare me. Need I tell more?"

"No more; there needs no more, Hilda," replied Miriam, bowing her head, as if listening to a sentence of condemnation from a supreme tribunal. "It is enough! You have satisfied my mind on a point where it was greatly disturbed. Henceforward, I shall be quiet. Thank you, Hilda."

She was on the point of departing, but turned back again from the threshold.

"This is a terrible secret to be kept in a young girl's bosom," she observed; "what will you do with it, my poor child?"

"Heaven help and guide me," answered Hilda, bursting into tears; "for the burden of it crushes me to the earth! It seems a crime to know of such a thing, and to keep it to myself. It knocks within my heart continually, threatening, imploring, insisting to be let out! Oh, my mother!—my mother! Were she yet living, I would travel over land and sea to tell her this dark secret, as I told all the little troubles of my infancy. But I am alone—alone! Miriam, you were my dearest, only friend. Advise me what to do."

This was a singular appeal, no doubt, from the stainless maiden to the guilty woman, whom she had just banished from her heart forever. But it bore striking testimony to the impression which Miriam's natural uprightness and impulsive generosity had made on the friend who knew her best; and it deeply comforted the poor criminal, by proving to her that the bond between Hilda and herself was vital yet.

As far as she was able, Miriam at once responded to the girl's cry for help.

"If I deemed it good for your peace of mind," she said, "to bear testimony against me for this deed, in the face of all the world, no consideration of myself should weigh with me an instant. But I believe that you would find no relief in such a course. What men call justice lies chiefly in outward formalities, and has never the close application and fitness that would be satisfactory to a soul like yours. I cannot be fairly tried and judged before an earthly tribunal; and of this, Hilda, you would perhaps become fatally conscious, when it was too late. Roman justice, above all things, is a byword. What have you to do with it? Leave all such thoughts aside! Yet, Hilda, I would not have you keep my secret imprisoned in your heart, if it tries to leap out, and stings you, like a wild, venomous thing, when you thrust it back again. Have you no other friend, now that you have been forced to give me up?"

"No other," answered Hilda, sadly.

"Yes; Kenyon!" rejoined Miriam.

"He cannot be my friend," said Hilda, "because—because —I have fancied that he sought to be something more."

"Fear nothing!" replied Miriam, shaking her head, with a strange smile. "This story will frighten his newborn love out of its little life, if that be what you wish. Tell him the secret, then, and take his wise and honorable counsel as to what should next be done. I know not what else to say."

"I never dreamed," said Hilda,—"how could you think it?

—of betraying you to justice. But I see how it is, Miriam. I must keep your secret, and die of it, unless God sends me some relief by methods which are now beyond my power to imagine. It is very dreadful. Ah! now I understand how the sins of generations past have created an atmosphere of sin for those that follow. While there is a single guilty person in the universe, each innocent one must feel his innocence tortured by that guilt. Your deed, Miriam, has darkened the whole sky!"

Poor Hilda turned from her unhappy friend, and, sinking on her knees in a corner of the chamber, could not be prevailed upon to utter another word. And Miriam, with a long regard from the threshold, bade farewell to this dove's nest, this one little nook of pure thoughts and innocent enthusiasms, into which she had brought such trouble. Every crime destroys more Edens than our own!

CHAPTER 24. *The Tower Among the Apennines*

It was in June, that the sculptor, Kenyon, arrived on horseback at the gate of an ancient country-house (which, from some of its features, might almost be called a castle) situated in a part of Tuscany somewhat remote from the ordinary track of tourists. Thither we must now accompany him, and endeavor to make our story flow onward, like a streamlet, past a gray tower that rises on the hill-side, overlooking a spacious valley, which is set in the grand framework of the Apennines.

The sculptor had left Rome with the retreating tide of foreign residents. For, as summer approaches, the Niobe of Nations[1] is made to bewail anew, and doubtless with sincerity, the loss of that large part of her population, which she derives from other lands, and on whom depends much of whatever remnant of prosperity she still enjoys. Rome, at this season, is pervaded and overhung with atmospheric terrors, and insulated within a charmed and deadly circle. The crowd of wandering tourists betake themselves to Switzerland, to the Rhine, or, from this central home of the world, to their native homes in England or America, which they are apt thenceforward to look upon as provincial, after once having yielded to the spell of the Eternal City. The artist, who contemplates an indefinite succession of

[1]Niobe, legendary queen of Thebes, boasted of her fourteen children to Leto, mistress of Zeus and mother of Apollo and Artemis. Leto dispatched Apollo and Artemis to kill all but two of Niobe's children. Zeus turned Niobe into a stone image of grief out of pity for her. Thus Hawthorne describes the annual exodus of tourists in the spring to avoid the Roman fever and the Roman heat.

winters in this home of art (though his first thought was merely to improve himself by a brief visit), goes forth, in the summer time, to sketch scenery and costume among the Tuscan hills, and pour, if he can, the purple air of Italy over his canvas. He studies the old schools of art in the mountain-towns where they were born, and where they are still to be seen in the faded frescoes of Giotto and Cimabue, on the walls of many a church, or in the dark chapels, in which the sacristan draws aside the veil from a treasured picture of Perugino.[2] Thence, the happy painter goes to walk the long, bright galleries of Florence, or to steal glowing colors from the miraculous works, which he finds in a score of Venetian palaces. Such summers as these, spent amid whatever is exquisite in art, or wild and picturesque in nature, may not inadequately repay him for the chill neglect and disappointment through which he has probably languished, in his Roman winter. This sunny, shadowy, breezy, wandering life, in which he seeks for beauty as his treasure, and gathers for his winter's honey what is but a passing fragrance to all other men, is worth living for, come afterwards what may. Even if he die unrecognized, the artist has had his share of enjoyment and success.

Kenyon had seen, at a distance of many miles, the old villa or castle, towards which his journey lay, looking from its height over a broad expanse of valley. As he drew nearer, however, it had been hidden among the inequalities of the hill-side, until the winding road brought him almost to the iron gateway. The sculptor found this substantial barrier fastened with lock and bolt. There was no bell, nor other instrument of sound; and, after summoning the invisible garrison with his voice, instead of a trumpet, he had leisure to take a glance at the exterior of the fortress.

About thirty yards within the gateway rose a square

[2]Giotto di Bondone (1266–1337), the first of the great Italian masters, was a pupil of Giovanni Cimabue (1240–1302), who used architectural settings in forming his figures. Pietro Perugino (1446–1523), the master of Raphael, painted several frescoes and panels in his native Perugia.

tower, lofty enough to be a very prominent object in the land-scape, and more than sufficiently massive in proportion to its height.[3] Its antiquity was evidently such, that, in a climate of more abundant moisture, the ivy would have mantled it from head to foot in a garment that might, by this time, have been centuries old, though ever new. In the dry Italian air, however, Nature had only so far adopted this old pile of stonework as to cover almost every hand's-breadth of it with close-clinging lichens and yellow moss; and the immemorial growth of these kindly productions rendered the general hue of the tower soft and venerable, and took away the aspect of nakedness which would have made its age drearier than now.

Up and down the height of the tower were scattered three or four windows, the lower ones grated with iron bars, the upper ones vacant both of window-frames and glass. Besides these larger openings, there were several loopholes and little square apertures, which might be supposed to light the staircase, that doubtless climbed the interior towards the battlemented and machicolated summit. With this last-mentioned warlike garniture upon its stern old head and brow, the tower seemed evidently a stronghold of times long past. Many a crossbowman had shot his shafts from those windows and loopholes, and from the vantage height of those gray battlements; many a flight of arrows, too, had hit all round about the embrasures above, or the apertures below, where the helmet of a defender had momen-tarily glimmered. On festal nights, moreover, a hundred lamps had often gleamed afar over the valley, suspended from the iron hooks that were ranged for the purpose beneath the battlements and every window.

Connected with the tower, and extending behind it, there seemed to be a very spacious residence, chiefly of more modern date. It perhaps owed much of its fresher appearance, however,

---

[3]The tower and landscape are drawn from the Villa Montauto, Casa del Bello, which the Hawthornes rented for August and September, 1858.

to a coat of stucco and yellow wash, which is a sort of renovation very much in vogue with the Italians. Kenyon noticed over a door-way, in the portion of the edifice immediately adjacent to the tower, a cross, which, with a bell suspended above the roof, indicated that this was a consecrated precinct, and the chapel of the mansion.

Meanwhile, the hot sun so incommoded the unsheltered traveller, that he shouted forth another impatient summons. Happening, at the same moment, to look upward, he saw a figure leaning from an embrasure of the battlements, and gazing down at him.

"Ho, Signor Count!" cried the sculptor waving his straw hat, for he recognized the face, after a moment's doubt. "This is a warm reception, truly! Pray bid your porter let me in, before the sun shrivels me quite into a cinder."

"I will come myself," responded Donatello, flinging down his voice out of the clouds, as it were; "old Tomaso and old Stella are both asleep no doubt, and the rest of the people are in the vineyard. But I have expected you, and you are welcome!"

The young count,—as perhaps we had better designate him in his ancestral tower,—vanished from the battlements; and Kenyon saw his figure appear successively at each of the windows, as he descended. On every reappearance, he turned his face towards the sculptor and gave a nod and smile; for a kindly impulse prompted him thus to assure his visitor of a welcome, after keeping him so long at an inhospitable threshold.

Kenyon, however, (naturally and professionally expert at reading the expression of the human countenance) had a vague sense that this was not the young friend whom he had known so familiarly in Rome; not the sylvan and untutored youth, whom Miriam, Hilda, and himself, had liked, laughed at, and sported with; not the Donatello whose identity they had so playfully mixed up with that of the Faun of Praxiteles.

Finally, when his host had emerged from a side-portal of the mansion, and approached the gateway, the traveller still felt that there was something lost, or something gained (he hardly knew which), that set the Donatello of to-day irreconcilably at odds with him of yesterday. His very gait showed it, in a certain gravity, a weight and measure of step, that had nothing in common with the irregular buoyancy which used to distinguish him. His face was paler and thinner, and the lips less full, and less apart.

"I have looked for you a long while," said Donatello; and, though his voice sounded differently, and cut out its words more sharply than had been its wont, still there was a smile shining on his face, that, for the moment, quite brought back the Faun. "I shall be more cheerful, perhaps, now that you have come. It is very solitary here."

"I have come slowly along, often lingering, often turning aside," replied Kenyon; "for I found a great deal to interest me in the mediæval sculpture hidden away in the churches hereabouts. An artist, whether painter or sculptor, may be pardoned for loitering through such a region. But what a fine old tower! Its tall front is like a page of black-letter, taken from the history of the Italian republics."

"I know little or nothing of its history," said the count, glancing upward at the battlements, where he had just been standing. "But I thank my forefathers for building it so high. I like the windy summit better than the world below, and spend much of my time there, now-a-days."

"It is a pity you are not a star-gazer," observed Kenyon, also looking up. "It is higher than Galileo's tower, which I saw, a week or two ago, outside of the walls of Florence."

"A star-gazer? I am one," replied Donatello. "I sleep in the tower, and often watch very late on the battlements. There is a dismal old staircase to climb, however, before reaching the top, and a succession of dismal chambers, from story to story. Some of them were prison chambers in times past, as old Tomaso will tell you."

The repugnance intimated in his tone at the idea of this gloomy staircase and these ghostly, dimly lighted rooms, reminded Kenyon of the original Donatello, much more than his present custom of midnight vigils on the battlements.

"I shall be glad to share your watch," said the guest; "especially by moonlight. The prospect of this broad valley must be very fine. But I was not aware, my friend, that these were your country habits. I have fancied you in a sort of Arcadian life, tasting rich figs, and squeezing the juice out of the sunniest grapes, and sleeping soundly, all night, after a day of simple pleasures."

"I may have known such a life, when I was younger," answered the count, gravely. "I am not a boy now. Time flies over us, but leaves its shadow behind."

The sculptor could not but smile at the triteness of the remark, which, nevertheless had a kind of originality as coming from Donatello. He had thought it out from his own experience, and perhaps considered himself as communicating a new truth to mankind.

They were now advancing up the courtyard; and the long extent of the villa, with its iron-barred lower windows and balconied upper ones, became visible, stretching back towards a grove of trees.

"At some period of your family history," observed Kenyon, "the Counts of Monte Beni must have led a patriarchal life in this vast house. A great-grandsire and all his descendants might find ample verge here, and with space, too, for each separate brood of little ones to play within its own precincts. Is your present household a large one?"

"Only myself," answered Donatello, "and Tomaso, who has been butler since my grandfather's time, and old Stella, who goes sweeping and dusting about the chambers, and Girolamo, the cook, who has but an idle life of it. He shall send you up a chicken forthwith. But, first of all, I must summon one of the contadini[4] from the farmhouse yonder, to take your horse to the stable."

[4]Peasants.

Accordingly, the young count shouted amain, and with such effect, that, after several repetitions of the outcry, an old gray woman protruded her head and a broom-handle from a chamber window; the venerable butler emerged from a recess in the side of the house, where was a well, or reservoir, in which he had been cleansing a small wine-cask; and a sunburnt contadino, in his shirt-sleeves, showed himself on the outskirts of the vine-yard, with some kind of a farming tool in his hand. Donatello found employment for all these retainers in providing accommodation for his guest and steed, and then ushered the sculptor into the vestibule of the house.

It was a square and lofty entrance room, which, by the solidity of its construction, might have been an Etruscan tomb, being paved and walled with heavy blocks of stone, and vaulted almost as massively overhead. On two sides, there were doors, opening into long suites of anterooms and saloons; on the third side, a stone staircase, of spacious breadth, ascended by dignified degrees and with wide resting-places, to another floor of similar extent. Through one of the doors, which was ajar, Kenyon beheld an almost interminable vista of apartments, opening one beyond the other, and reminding him of the hundred rooms in Blue Beard's castle, or the countless halls in some palace of the Arabian Nights.

It must have been a numerous family, indeed, that could ever have sufficed to people with human life so large an abode as this, and impart social warmth to such a wide world within doors. The sculptor confessed to himself, that Donatello could allege reason enough for growing melancholy, having only his own personality to vivify it all.

"How a woman's face would brighten it up!" he ejaculated, not intending to be overheard.

But, glancing at Donatello, he saw a stern and sorrowful look in his eyes, which altered his youthful face as much as if it had seen thirty years of trouble; and, at the same moment, old Stella showed herself through one of the door-ways, as the only representative of her sex at Monte Beni.

CHAPTER 25. *Sunshine*

"Come," said the Count, "I see you already find the old house dismal. So do I, indeed! And yet it was a cheerful place in my boyhood. But, you see, in my father's days (and the same was true of all my endless line of grandfathers, as I have heard), there used to be uncles, aunts, and all manner of kindred, dwelling together as one family. They were a merry and kindly race of people, for the most part, and kept one another's hearts warm."

"Two hearts might be enough for warmth," observed the sculptor, "even in so large a house as this. One solitary heart, it is true, may be apt to shiver a little. But, I trust, my friend, that the genial blood of your race still flows in many veins besides your own?"

"I am the last," said Donatello, gloomily. "They have all vanished from me, since my childhood. Old Tomaso will tell you that the air of Monte Beni is not so favorable to length of days as it used to be. But that is not the secret of the quick extinction of my kindred."

"Then you are aware of a more satisfactory reason?" suggested Kenyon.

"I thought of one, the other night, while I was gazing at the stars," answered Donatello; "but, pardon me, I do not mean to tell it. One cause, however, of the longer and healthier life of my forefathers, was, that they had many pleasant customs, and means of making themselves glad, and their guests and friends along with them. Now-a-days we have but one!"

"And what is that?" asked the sculptor.

"You shall see!" said his young host.

By this time, he had ushered the sculptor into one of the numberless saloons; and, calling for refreshment, old Stella placed a cold fowl upon the table, and quickly followed it with a savory omelet, which Girolamo had lost no time in preparing. She also brought some cherries, plums, and apricots, and a plate-full of particularly delicate figs, of last year's growth. The butler showing his white head at the door, his master beckoned to him.

"Tomaso, bring some Sunshine!" said he.

The readiest method of obeying this order, one might suppose, would have been, to fling wide the green window-blinds, and let the glow of the summer noon into the carefully shaded room. But, at Monte Beni, with provident caution against the wintry days, when there is little sunshine, and the rainy ones, when there is none, it was the hereditary custom to keep their Sunshine stored away in the cellar. Old Tomaso quickly produced some of it in a small, straw-covered flask, out of which he extracted the cork, and inserted a little cotton wool, to absorb the olive oil that kept the precious liquid from the air.

"This is a wine," observed the Count, "the secret of making which has been kept in our family for centuries upon centuries; nor would it avail any man to steal the secret, unless he could also steal the vineyard, in which alone the Monte Beni grape can be produced. There is little else left me, save that patch of vines. Taste some of their juice, and tell me whether it is worthy to be called Sunshine! for that is its name."

"A glorious name, too!" cried the sculptor.

"Taste it," said Donatello, filling his friend's glass and pouring likewise a little into his own. "But first smell its fragrance; for the wine is very lavish of it, and will scatter it all abroad."

"Ah, how exquisite!" said Kenyon. "No other wine has a bouquet like this. The flavor must be rare indeed, if it fulfil the promise of this fragrance, which is like the airy sweetness of youthful hopes, that no realities will ever satisfy!"

This invaluable liquor was of a pale golden hue, like other of the rarest Italian wines, and, if carelessly and irreligiously quaffed, might have been mistaken for a very fine sort of Champagne. It was not, however, an effervescing wine, although its delicate piquancy produced a somewhat similar effect upon the palate. Sipping, the guest longed to sip again; but the wine demanded so deliberate a pause, in order to detect the hidden peculiarities and subtle exquisiteness of its flavor, that to drink it was really more a moral than a physical enjoyment. There was a deliciousness in it that eluded analysis, and—like whatever else is superlatively good—was perhaps better appreciated in the memory than by present consciousness. One of its most ethereal charms lay in the transitory life of the wine's richest qualities; for, while it required a certain leisure and delay, yet, if you lingered too long upon the draught, it became disenchanted both of its fragrance and its flavor.

The lustre should not be forgotten, among the other admirable endowments of the Monte Beni wine; for, as it stood in Kenyon's glass, a little circle of light glowed on the table round about it, as if it were really so much golden sunshine.

"I feel myself a better man for that ethereal potation," observed the sculptor. "The finest Orvieto, or that famous wine, the Est Est Est of Montefiascone, is vulgar in comparison. This is surely the wine of the Golden Age, such as Bacchus himself first taught mankind to press from the choicest of his grapes. My dear Count, why is it not illustrious? The pale, liquid gold, in every such flask as that, might be solidified into golden scudi, and would quickly make you a millionaire!"

Tomaso, the old butler, who was standing by the table, and enjoying the praises of the wine quite as much as if bestowed upon himself, made answer,—

"We have a tradition, signore," said he, "that this rare wine of our vineyard would lose all its wonderful qualities, if any of it were sent to market. The Counts of Monte Beni have never parted with a single flask of it for gold. At their banquets, in the olden time, they have entertained princes, cardinals, and once an emperor, and once a pope, with this delicious wine, and always, even to this day, it has been their custom to let it flow freely, when those whom they love and honor sit at the board. But the grand duke himself could not drink that wine, except it were under this very roof!"

"What you tell me, my good friend," replied Kenyon,

"makes me venerate the Sunshine of Monte Beni even more abundantly than before. As I understand you, it is a sort of consecrated juice, and symbolizes the holy virtues of hospitality and social kindliness?"

"Why, partly so, signore," said the old butler, with a shrewd twinkle in his eye; "but, to speak out all the truth, there is another excellent reason why neither a cask nor a flask of our precious vintage should ever be sent to market. The wine, signore, is so fond of its native home, that a transportation of even a few miles, turns it quite sour. And yet it is a wine that keeps well in the cellar, underneath this floor, and gathers fragrance, flavor, and brightness in its dark dungeon. That very flask of Sunshine, now, has kept itself for you, sir guest, (as a maid reserves her sweetness till her lover comes for it,) ever since a merry vintage-time, when the Signore Count here was a boy!"

"You must not wait for Tomaso to end his discourse about the wine, before drinking off your glass," observed Donatello. "When once the flask is uncorked, its finest qualities lose little time in making their escape. I doubt whether your last sip will be quite so delicious as you found the first."[1]

And, in truth, the sculptor fancied that the Sunshine became almost imperceptibly clouded, as he approached the bottom of the flask. The effect of the wine, however, was a gentle exhilaration, which did not so speedily pass away.

Being thus refreshed, Kenyon looked round him at the antique saloon in which they sat. It was constructed in a most ponderous style, with a stone floor, on which heavy pilasters were planted against the wall, supporting arches that crossed one another in the vaulted ceiling. The upright walls, as well as

[1]Cf. Hawthorne's notebook account of the same phenomenon: "At Viterbo, however, I called for some wine of Montefiascone, and had a little straw-covered flask, which the waiter assured us was the genuine est-wine. It was of golden color, and very delicate, somewhat resembling still champagne, but finer, and requiring a calmer pause to appreciate its subtle delight. Its good qualities, however, are so evanescent, that the fine flavor became almost imperceptible before we finished the flask" (*NB*, pp. 476–477).

the compartments of the roof, were completely covered with frescoes, which doubtless had been brilliant when first executed, and perhaps for generations afterwards. The designs were of a festive and joyous character, representing Arcadian scenes, where nymphs, fauns, and satyrs, disported themselves among mortal youths and maidens; and Pan, and the god of wine, and he of sunshine and music, disdained not to brighten some sylvan merry-making with the scarcely veiled glory of their presence. A wreath of dancing figures, in admirable variety of shape and motion, was festooned quite round the cornice of the room.

In its first splendor, the saloon must have presented an aspect both gorgeous and enlivening; for it invested some of the cheerfullest ideas and emotions of which the human mind is susceptible with the external reality of beautiful form, and rich, harmonious glow and variety of color. But the frescoes were now very ancient. They had been rubbed and scrubbed by old Stella and many a predecessor, and had been defaced in one spot, and retouched in another, and had peeled from the wall in patches, and had hidden some of their brightest portions under dreary dust, till the joyousness had quite vanished out of them all. It was often difficult to puzzle out the design; and even where it was more readily intelligible, the figures showed like the ghosts of dead and buried joys—the closer their resemblance to the happy past, the gloomier now. For it is thus, that with only an inconsiderable change, the gladdest objects and existences become the saddest; hope fading into disappointment; joy darkening into grief, and festal splendor into funereal duskiness; and all evolving, as their moral, a grim identity between gay things and sorrowful ones. Only give them a little time, and they turn out to be just alike!

"There has been much festivity in this saloon, if I may judge by the character of its frescoes," remarked Kenyon, whose spirits were still upheld by the mild potency of the Monte Beni wine. "Your forefathers, my dear Count, must have been joyous fellows, keeping up the vintage merriment throughout the year. It does me good to think of them gladdening the hearts of men and women, with their wine of Sunshine, even in the Iron age, as Pan and Bacchus, whom we see yonder, did in the Golden one!"[2]

"Yes; there have been merry times in the banquet-hall of Monte Beni, even within my own remembrance," replied Donatello, looking gravely at the painted walls. "It was meant for mirth, as you see; and when I brought my own cheerfulness into the saloon, these frescoes looked cheerful too. But methinks they have all faded, since I saw them last."

"It would be a good idea," said the sculptor, falling into his companion's vein, and helping him out with an illustration which Donatello himself could not have put into shape, "to convert this saloon into a chapel; and when the priest tells his hearers of the instability of earthly joys, and would show how drearily they vanish, he may point to these pictures, that were so joyous, and are so dismal. He could not illustrate his theme so aptly in any other way."

"True, indeed," answered the Count, his former simplicity strangely mixing itself up with an experience that had changed him; "and yonder, where the minstrels used to stand, the altar shall be placed. A sinful man might do all the more effective penance in this old banquet-hall."

"But I should regret to have suggested so ungenial a transformation in your hospitable saloon," continued Kenyon, duly noting the change in Donatello's characteristics. "You startle me, my friend, by so ascetic a design! It would hardly have entered your head, when we first met. Pray do not—if I may take the freedom of a somewhat elder man to advise you," added he, smiling—"pray do not, under a notion of improvement, take upon yourself to be sombre, thoughtful, and penitential, like all the rest of us."

Donatello made no answer, but sat awhile, appearing to

[2]The Iron Age began in Greece about 1000 B.C. The contrast here is between historical and mythological time—the so-called Golden Age. For Pan, see note 4, p. 82; Bacchus was the Roman god of wine.

follow with his eyes one of the figures, which was repeated many times over in the groups upon the walls and ceiling. It formed the principal link of an allegory, by which (as is often the case in such pictorial designs) the whole series of frescoes were bound together, but which it would be impossible, or, at least, very wearisome, to unravel. The sculptor's eyes took a similar direction, and soon began to trace through the vicissitudes —once gay, now sombre—in which the old artist had involved it, the same individual figure. He fancied a resemblance in it to Donatello himself; and it put him in mind of one of the purposes with which he had come to Monte Beni.

"My dear Count," said he, "I have a proposal to make. You must let me employ a little of my leisure in modelling your bust. You remember what a striking resemblance we all of us— Hilda, Miriam, and I—found between your features and those of the Faun of Praxiteles. Then, it seemed an identity; but now that I know your face better, the likeness is far less apparent. Your head in marble would be a treasure to me. Shall I have it?"

"I have a weakness which I fear I cannot overcome," replied the Count, turning away his face, "It troubles me to be looked at steadfastly."

"I have observed it since we have been sitting here, though never before," rejoined the sculptor. "It is a kind of nervousness, I apprehend, which you caught in the Roman air, and which grows upon you, in your solitary life. It need be no hindrance to my taking your bust; for I will catch the likeness and expression by side glimpses, which (if portrait painters and bust makers did but know it) always bring home richer results than a broad stare."

"You may take me if you have the power," said Donatello; but, even as he spoke, he turned away his face; "and if you can see what makes me shrink from you, you are welcome to put it in the bust. It is not my will, but my necessity, to avoid men's eyes. Only," he added, with a smile which made Kenyon doubt whether he might not as well copy the Faun as model a new bust, "only, you know, you must not insist on my uncovering these ears of mine!"

"Nay; I never should dream of such a thing," answered the sculptor, laughing as the young count shook his clustering curls. "I could not hope to persuade you, remembering how Miriam once failed!"

Nothing is more unaccountable than the spell that often lurks in a spoken word. A thought may be present to the mind, so distinctly that no utterance could make it more so; and two minds may be conscious of the same thought, in which one or both take the profoundest interest; but as long as it remains unspoken, their familiar talk flows quietly over the hidden idea, as a rivulet may sparkle and dimple over something sunken in its bed. But, speak the word; and it is like bringing up a drowned body out of the deepest pool of the rivulet, which has been aware of the horrible secret all along, in spite of its smiling surface.[3]

And even so, when Kenyon chanced to make a distinct reference to Donatello's relations with Miriam (though the subject was already in both their minds), a ghastly emotion rose up out of the depths of the young count's heart. He trembled either with anger or terror, and glared at the sculptor with wild eyes, like a wolf that meets you in the forest, and hesitates whether to flee or turn to bay. But, as Kenyon still looked calmly at him, his aspect gradually became less disturbed, though far from resuming its former quietude.

"You have spoken her name," said he, at last, in an altered and tremulous tone; "tell me, now, all that you know of her."

"I scarcely think that I have any later intelligence than yourself," answered Kenyon; "Miriam left Rome at about the time of your own departure. Within a day or two after our last meeting at the Church of the Capuchins, I called at her studio and found it vacant. Whither she has gone, I cannot tell."

Donatello asked no further questions.

They rose from table, and strolled together about the premises, whiling away the afternoon with brief intervals of

[3]This is exactly what Hawthorne did at the end of *The Blithedale Romance*, when Miles Coverdale, Hollingsworth, and Silas spear the body of the suicide Zenobia and drag it from a pool at midnight.

unsatisfactory conversation, and many shadowy silences. The
sculptor had a perception of change in his companion,—possibly of growth and development, but certainly of change,—
which saddened him, because it took away much of the simple
grace that was the best of Donatello's peculiarities.

Kenyon betook himself to repose that night in a grim, old,
vaulted apartment, which, in the lapse of five or six centuries,
had probably been the birth, bridal, and death chamber of a
great many generations of the Monte Beni family. He was
aroused, soon after daylight, by the clamor of a tribe of beggars
who had taken their stand in a little rustic lane that crept beside
that portion of the villa, and were addressing their petitions to
the open windows. By-and-by, they appeared to have received
alms, and took their departure.

"Some charitable Christian has sent those vagabonds
away," thought the sculptor, as he resumed his interrupted nap;
"who could it be? Donatello has his own rooms in the tower;
Stella, Tomaso, and the cook are a world's width off; and I
fancied myself the only inhabitant in this part of the house."

In the breadth and space which so delightfully characterize
an Italian villa, a dozen guests might have had each his suite of
apartments without infringing upon one another's ample precincts.[4] But, so far as Kenyon knew, he was the only visitor
beneath Donatello's widely extended roof.

[4]Hawthorne was much impressed by the size of his rented villa:
"The rest of the day was spent mostly in exploring the premises. The house
itself is of almost bewildering extent, insomuch that we might each of us
have a suite of rooms individually. I have established myself on the ground
floor, where I have a dressing-room, a large vaulted saloon, hung with
yellow damask, and a square writing-study, the walls and ceilings of the
two latter apartments being ornamented with angels and cherubs aloft in
fresco, and with temples, statues, vases, broken columns, peacocks, parrots,
vines, and sunflowers below. I know not how many more saloons, anterooms, and sleeping-chambers there are on this same basement story, besides an equal number over them, and a great subterranean establishment"
(NB, p. 380).

CHAPTER 26. *The Pedigree of Monte Beni*[1]

From the old butler, whom he found to be a very gracious and affable personage, Kenyon soon learned many curious particulars about the family history and hereditary peculiarities of the Counts of Monte Beni. There was a pedigree, the later portion of which—(that is to say, for a little more than a thousand years)—a genealogist would have found delight in tracing out, link by link, and authenticating by records and documentary evidences. It would have been as difficult, however, to follow up the stream of Donatello's ancestry to its dim source, as travellers have found it to reach the mysterious fountains of the Nile. And, far beyond the region of definite and demonstrable fact, a romancer might have strayed into a region of old poetry, where the rich soil, so long uncultivated and untrodden, had lapsed into nearly its primeval state of wilderness. Among those antique paths, now overgrown with tangled and riotous vegetation, the wanderer must needs follow his own guidance, and probably arrive nowhither at last.

The race of Monte Beni, beyond a doubt, was one of the oldest in Italy, where families appear to survive at least, if not to flourish, on their half-decayed roots, oftener than in England or France. It came down in a broad track from the Middle Ages; but, at epochs anterior to those, it was distinctly visible in the gloom of the period before chivalry put forth its flower; and farther still, we are almost afraid to say, it was seen, though with

[1]Here begins volume two of the first American edition (the English edition was published in three volumes as was the custom with Victorian novels).

a fainter and wavering course, in the early morn of Christendom, when the Roman Empire had hardly begun to show symptoms of decline. At that venerable distance, the heralds gave up the lineage in despair.

But where written record left the genealogy of Monte Beni, tradition took it up, and carried it without dread or shame beyond the Imperial ages into the times of the Roman republic; beyond those, again, into the epoch of kingly rule. Nor even so remotely among the mossy centuries did it pause, but strayed onward into that gray antiquity of which there is no token left, save its cavernous tombs, and a few bronzes, and some quaintly wrought ornaments of gold, and gems with mystic figures and inscriptions. There, or thereabouts, the line was supposed to have had its origin in the sylvan life of Etruria,[2] while Italy was yet guiltless of Rome.

Of course, as we regret to say, the earlier and very much the larger portion of this respectable descent—and the same is true of many briefer pedigrees—must be looked upon as altogether mythical. Still, it threw a romantic interest around the unquestionable antiquity of the Monte Beni family, and over that tract of their own vines and fig-trees, beneath the shade of which they had unquestionably dwelt for immemorial ages. And there they had laid the foundations of their tower, so long ago that one half of its height was said to be sunken under the surface and to hide subterranean chambers which once were cheerful with the olden sunshine.

One story, or myth, that had mixed itself up with their mouldy genealogy, interested the sculptor by its wild, and perhaps grotesque, yet not unfascinating peculiarity. He caught at it the more eagerly, as it afforded a shadowy and whimsical semblance of explanation for the likeness which he, with Miriam

---

[2]The pre-Roman area of Tuscany and West Umbria; its inhabitants were known as Etruscans (*fl.* 500 B.C.). Skilled in metalworking, pottery-making, and agriculture, the Etruscans were finally defeated by the Romans in 396 B.C. and absorbed into the Roman state.

and Hilda, had seen or fancied, between Donatello and the Faun of Praxiteles.

The Monte Beni family, as this legend averred, drew their origin from the Pelasgic race,[3] who peopled Italy in times that may be called pre-historic. It was the same noble breed of men, of Asiatic birth, that settled in Greece; the same happy and poetic kindred who dwelt in Arcadia, and—whether they ever lived such life or not—enriched the world with dreams, at least, and fables, lovely, if unsubstantial, of a Golden Age. In those delicious times, when deities and demigods appeared familiarly on earth, mingling with its inhabitants as friend with friend; when nymphs, satyrs, and the whole train of classic faith or fable, hardly took pains to hide themselves in the primeval woods;—at that auspicious period the lineage of Monte Beni had its rise. Its progenitor was a being not altogether human, yet partaking so largely of the gentlest human qualities, as to be neither awful nor shocking to the imagination. A sylvan creature, native among the woods, had loved a mortal maiden, and—perhaps by kindness, and the subtle courtesies which love might teach to his simplicity, or possibly by a ruder wooing—had won her to his haunts. In due time, he gained her womanly affection; and, making their bridal bower, for aught we know, in the hollow of a great tree, the pair spent a happy wedded life in that ancient neighborhood where now stood Donatello's tower.

From this union sprung a vigorous progeny that took its place unquestioned among human families. In that age, however, and long afterwards, it showed the ineffaceable lineaments of its wild paternity: it was a pleasant and kindly race of men, but capable of savage fierceness, and never quite restrainable within the trammels of social law. They were strong, active, genial, cheerful as the sunshine, passionate as the tornado. Their lives were rendered blissful by an unsought harmony with nature.

But, as centuries passed away, the Faun's wild blood had necessarily been attempered with constant intermixtures from

[3]Aboriginal, non-Greek inhabitants of Greece.

the more ordinary streams of human life. It lost many of its original qualities, and served, for the most part, only to bestow an unconquerable vigor which kept the family from extinction, and enabled them to make their own part good throughout the perils and rude emergencies of their interminable descent. In the constant wars with which Italy was plagued, by the dissensions of her petty states and republics, there was a demand for native hardihood.

The successive members of the Monte Beni family showed valor and policy enough, at all events, to keep their hereditary possessions out of the clutch of grasping neighbors, and probably differed very little from the other feudal barons with whom they fought and feasted. Such a degree of conformity with the manners of the generations, through which it survived, must have been essential to the prolonged continuance of the race.

It is well known, however, that any hereditary peculiarity —as a supernumerary finger, or an anomalous shape of feature, like the Austrian lip[4]—is wont to show itself in a family after a very wayward fashion. It skips at its own pleasure along the line, and, latent for half a century or so, crops out again in a great-grandson. And thus, it was said, from a period beyond memory or record, there had ever and anon been a descendant of the Monte Benis bearing nearly all the characteristics that were attributed to the original founder of the race. Some traditions even went so far as to enumerate the ears, covered with a delicate fur, and shaped like a pointed leaf, among the proofs of authentic descent which were seen in these favored individuals. We appreciate the beauty of such tokens of a nearer kindred to

[4]A prominent and haughty lower lip characteristic of dictators, most obvious in our own time in the caricatures of Benito Mussolini. Note Sophia Hawthorne's description of the Grand Duke of Florence: " 'he looked like a monkey with an evil disposition, and had that frightful, coarse, protruding under-lip, peculiar to the Imperial race of Austria. It is worth while,' adds Mrs. Hawthorne, 'to extinguish the race for the sake of expunging that lip, and all that it signifies.' " Quoted in Julian Hawthorne, *Hawthorne and His Wife*, Vol. II (New York: Archon, 1968), p. 197.

the great family of nature than other mortals bear; but it would
be idle to ask credit for a statement which might be deemed to
partake so largely of the grotesque.

But it was indisputable that, once in a century, or oftener,
a son of Monte Beni gathered into himself the scattered qualities
of his race, and reproduced the character that had been assigned
to it from immemorial times. Beautiful, strong, brave, kindly,
sincere, of honest impulses, and endowed with simple tastes and
the love of homely pleasures, he was believed to possess gifts by
which he could associate himself with the wild things of the
forests, and with the fowls of the air, and could feel a sympathy
even with the trees, among which it was his joy to dwell. On the
other hand, there were deficiencies both of intellect and heart,
and especially, as it seemed, in the development of the higher
portion of man's nature. These defects were less perceptible in
early youth, but showed themselves more strongly with advancing age, when, as the animal spirits settled down upon a lower
level, the representative of the Monte Benis was apt to become
sensual, addicted to gross pleasures, heavy, unsympathizing, and
insulated within the narrow limits of a surly selfishness.

A similar change, indeed, is no more than what we constantly observe to take place in persons who are not careful to
substitute other graces for those which they inevitably lose
along with the quick sensibility and joyous vivacity of youth. At
worst, the reigning Count of Monte Beni, as his hair grew white,
was still a jolly old fellow over his flask of wine—the wine that
Bacchus himself was fabled to have taught his sylvan ancestor
how to express, and from what choicest grapes, which would
ripen only in a certain divinely favored portion of the Monte
Beni vineyard.

The family, be it observed, were both proud and ashamed
of these legends; but whatever part of them they might consent
to incorporate into their ancestral history, they steadily repudiated all that referred to their one distinctive feature, the pointed
and furry ears. In a great many years past, no sober credence had
been yielded to the mythical portion of the pedigree. It might,

however, be considered as typifying some such assemblage of qualities—in this case, chiefly remarkable for their simplicity and naturalness—as, when they reappear in successive generations, constitute what we call family character. The sculptor found, moreover, on the evidence of some old portraits, that the physical features of the race had long been similar to what he now saw them in Donatello. With accumulating years, it is true, the Monte Beni face had a tendency to look grim and savage; and, in two or three instances, the family pictures glared at the spectator in the eyes like some surly animal, that had lost its good-humor when it outlived its playfulness.

The young count accorded his guest full liberty to investigate the personal annals of these pictured worthies, as well as all the rest of his progenitors; and ample materials were at hand in many chests of worm-eaten papers and yellow parchments, that had been gathering into larger and dustier piles ever since the dark ages. But, to confess the truth, the information afforded by these musty documents was so much more prosaic than what Kenyon acquired from Tomaso's legends, that even the superior authenticity of the former could not reconcile him to its dulness.

What especially delighted the sculptor, was the analogy between Donatello's character, as he himself knew it, and those peculiar traits which the old butler's narrative assumed to have been long hereditary in the race. He was amused at finding, too, that not only Tomaso but the peasantry of the estate and neighboring village recognized his friend as a genuine Monte Beni, of the original type. They seemed to cherish a great affection for the young count, and were full of stories about his sportive childhood; how he had played among the little rustics, and been at once the wildest and the sweetest of them all; and how, in his very infancy, he had plunged into the deep pools of the streamlets and never been drowned, and had clambered to the topmost branches of tall trees without ever breaking his neck. No such mischance could happen to the sylvan child, because, handling all the elements of nature so fearlessly and freely, nothing had either the power or the will to do him harm.

He grew up, said these humble friends, the playmate not only of all mortal kind, but of creatures of the woods; although, when Kenyon pressed them for some particulars of this latter mode of companionship, they could remember little more than a few anecdotes of a pet fox, which used to growl and snap at everybody save Donatello himself.

But they enlarged—and never were weary of the theme—upon the blithesome effects of Donatello's presence in his rosy childhood and budding youth. Their hovels had always glowed like sunshine when he entered them; so that, as the peasants expressed it, their young master had never darkened a door-way in his life. He was the soul of vintage festivals. While he was a mere infant, scarcely able to run alone, it had been the custom to make him tread the wine-press with his tender little feet, if it were only to crush one cluster of the grapes. And the grape-juice that gushed beneath his childish tread, be it ever so small in quantity, sufficed to impart a pleasant flavor to a whole cask of wine. The race of Monte Beni—so these rustic chroniclers assured the sculptor—had possessed the gift from the oldest of old times of expressing good wine from ordinary grapes, and a ravishing liquor from the choice growth of their vineyard.

In a word, as he listened to such tales as these, Kenyon could have imagined that the valleys and hill-sides about him were a veritable Arcadia, and that Donatello was not merely a sylvan faun, but the genial wine-god in his very person. Making many allowances for the poetic fancies of Italian peasants, he set it down for fact, that his friend, in a simple way, and among rustic folks, had been an exceedingly delightful fellow in his younger days.

But the contadini sometimes added, shaking their heads and sighing, that the young count was sadly changed since he went to Rome. The village girls now missed the merry smile with which he used to greet them.

The sculptor inquired of his good friend Tomaso, whether he, too, had noticed the shadow which was said to have recently fallen over Donatello's life.

"Ah, yes, signor!" answered the old butler, "it is even so, since he came back from that wicked and miserable city. The world has grown either too evil, or else too wise and sad, for such men as the old Counts of Monte Beni used to be. His very first taste of it, as you see, has changed and spoilt my poor young lord. There had not been a single count in the family these hundred years and more, who was so true a Monte Beni, of the antique stamp, as this poor signorino; and now it brings the tears into my eyes to hear him sighing over a cup of Sunshine! Ah, it is a sad world now!"

"Then you think there was a merrier world once?" asked Kenyon.

"Surely, signor," said Tomaso; "a merrier world, and merrier Counts of Monte Beni to live in it! Such tales of them as I have heard, when I was a child on my grandfather's knee! The good old man remembered a lord of Monte Beni—at least, he had heard of such a one, though I will not make oath upon the holy crucifix that my grandsire lived in his time—who used to go into the woods and call pretty damsels out of the fountains, and out of the trunks of the old trees. That merry lord was known to dance with them a whole long summer afternoon! When shall we see such frolics in our days?"

"Not soon, I am afraid," acquiesced the sculptor. "You are right, excellent Tomaso; the world is sadder now!"

And, in truth, while our friend smiled at these wild fables, he sighed in the same breath to think how the once genial earth produces, in every successive generation, fewer flowers than used to gladden the preceding ones. Not that the modes and seeming possibilities of human enjoyment are rarer in our refined and softened era,—(on the contrary, they never before were nearly so abundant,)—but that mankind are getting so far beyond the childhood of their race that they scorn to be happy any longer. A simple and joyous character can find no place for itself among the sage and sombre figures that would put his unsophisticated cheerfulness to shame. The entire system of man's affairs, as at present established, is built up purposely to exclude the careless and happy soul. The very children would upbraid the wretched individual who should endeavor to take life and the world as—what we might naturally suppose them meant for—a place and opportunity for enjoyment.

It is the iron rule in our days to require an object and a purpose in life. It makes us all parts of a complicated scheme of progress, which can only result in our arrival at a colder and drearier region than we were born in. It insists upon everybody's adding somewhat—a mite, perhaps, but earned by incessant ef-fort—to an accumulated pile of usefulness, of which the only use will be, to burden our posterity with even heavier thoughts and more inordinate labor than our own. No life now wanders like an unfettered stream; there is a mill-wheel for the tiniest rivulet to turn. We go all wrong, by too strenuous a resolution to go all right.

Therefore it was—so, at least, the sculptor thought, al-though partly suspicious of Donatello's darker misfortune—that the young count found it impossible now-a-days to be what his forefathers had been. He could not live their healthy life of animal spirits, in their sympathy with nature, and brotherhood with all that breathed around them. Nature, in beast, fowl, and tree, and earth, flood, and sky, is what it was of old; but sin, care, and self-consciousness have set the human portion of the world askew; and thus the simplest character is ever the surest to go astray.

"At any rate, Tomaso," said Kenyon, doing his best to comfort the old man, "let us hope that your young lord will still enjoy himself at vintage-time. By the aspect of the vineyard, I judge that this will be a famous year for the golden wine of Monte Beni. As long as your grapes produce that admirable liquor, sad as you think the world, neither the count nor his guests will quite forget to smile."

"Ah, signor," rejoined the butler with a sigh, "but he scarcely wets his lips with the sunny juice."

"There is yet another hope," observed Kenyon; "the young count may fall in love, and bring home a fair and laugh-ing wife to chase the gloom out of yonder old, frescoed saloon. Do you think he could do a better thing, my good Tomaso?"

"Maybe not, signor," said the sage butler, looking earnestly at him; "and, maybe, not a worse!"

The sculptor fancied that the good old man had it partly in his mind to make some remark, or communicate some fact, which, on second thoughts, he resolved to keep concealed in his own breast. He now took his departure cellarward, shaking his white head and muttering to himself, and did not reappear till dinner-time, when he favored Kenyon, whom he had taken far into his good graces, with a choicer flask of Sunshine than had yet blessed his palate.

To say the truth, this golden wine was no unnecessary ingredient towards making the life of Monte Beni palatable. It seemed a pity that Donatello did not drink a little more of it, and go jollily to bed at least, even if he should awake with an accession of darker melancholy the next morning.

Nevertheless, there was no lack of outward means for leading an agreeable life in the old villa. Wandering musicians haunted the precincts of Monte Beni, where they seemed to claim a prescriptive right; they made the lawn and shrubbery tuneful with the sound of fiddle, harp, and flute, and now and then with the tangled squeaking of a bagpipe. Improvvisatori[5] likewise came and told tales or recited verses to the contadini— among whom Kenyon often was an auditor—after their day's work in the vineyard. Jugglers, too, obtained permission to do feats of magic in the hall, where they set even the sage Tomaso, and Stella, Girolamo, and the peasant girls from the farmhouse, all of a broad grin, between merriment and wonder. These good people got food and lodging for their pleasant pains, and some of the small wine[6] of Tuscany, and a reasonable handful of the Grand Duke's copper coin, to keep up the hospitable renown of Monte Beni. But, very seldom had they the young count as a listener or spectator. There were sometimes dances by moon-

[5] Wandering story-tellers and bards.
[6] Table wine or *vin ordinaire*, as opposed to choice vintage, or *grand cru*.

light on the lawn, but never since he came from Rome did Donatello's presence deepen the blushes of the pretty contadinas, or
his footstep weary out the most agile partner or competitor as
once it was sure to do.

Paupers—for this kind of vermin infested the house of
Monte Beni worse than any other spot in beggar-haunted Italy
—stood beneath all the windows, making loud supplication, or
even established themselves on the marble steps of the grand
entrance. They ate and drank, and filled their bags, and pocketed
the little money that was given them, and went forth on their
devious ways, showering blessings innumerable on the mansion
and its lord, and on the souls of his deceased forefathers, who
had always been just such simpletons as to be compassionate to
beggary. But, in spite of their favorable prayers—by which
Italian philanthropists set great store—a cloud seemed to hang
over these once Arcadian precincts, and to be darkest around
the summit of the tower where Donatello was wont to sit and
brood.

CHAPTER 27. *Myths*

After the sculptor's arrival, however, the young count sometimes came down from his forlorn elevation, and rambled with him among the neighboring woods and hills. He led his friend to many enchanting nooks, with which he himself had been familiar in his childhood. But of late, as he remarked to Kenyon, a sort of strangeness had overgrown them, like clusters of dark shrubbery, so that he hardly recognized the places which he had known and loved so well.

To the sculptor's eye, nevertheless, they were still rich with beauty. They were picturesque in that sweetly impressive way, where wildness, in a long lapse of years, has crept over scenes that have been once adorned with the careful art and toil of man; and when man could do no more for them, time and nature came, and wrought hand in hand to bring them to a soft and venerable perfection. There grew the fig-tree that had run wild and taken to wife the vine, which likewise had gone rampant out of all human control; so that the two wild things had tangled and knotted themselves into a wild marriage-bond, and hung their various progeny—the luscious figs, the grapes, oozy with the southern juice, and both endowed with a wild flavor that added the final charm—on the same bough together.

In Kenyon's opinion, never was any other nook so lovely as a certain little dell which he and Donatello visited. It was hollowed in among the hills, and open to a glimpse of the broad, fertile valley. A fountain had its birth here, and fell into a marble basin, which was all covered with moss and shaggy with water-weeds. Over the gush of the small stream, with an urn in her arms, stood a marble nymph, whose nakedness the moss had kindly clothed as with a garment; and the long trails and tresses of the maidenhair had done what they could in the poor thing's behalf, by hanging themselves about her waist. In former days—it might be a remote antiquity—this lady of the fountain had first received the infant tide into her urn and poured it thence into the marble basin. But now the sculptured urn had a great crack from top to bottom; and the discontented nymph was compelled to see the basin fill itself through a channel which she could not control, although with water long ago consecrated to her.[1]

For this reason, or some other, she looked terribly forlorn; and you might have fancied that the whole fountain was but the overflow of her lonely tears.

"This was a place that I used greatly to delight in," remarked Donatello, sighing. "As a child, and as a boy, I have been very happy here."

"And, as a man, I should ask no fitter place to be happy in," answered Kenyon. "But you, my friend, are of such a social nature, that I should hardly have thought these lonely haunts would take your fancy. It is a place for a poet to dream in, and people it with the beings of his imagination."

"I am no poet, that I know of," said Donatello, "but yet, as I tell you, I have been very happy here, in the company of this fountain and this nymph. It is said that a Faun, my eldest forefather, brought home hither to this very spot a human maiden, whom he loved and wedded. This spring of delicious water was their household well."

"It is a most enchanting fable!" exclaimed Kenyon; "that is, if it be not a fact."

"And why not a fact?" said the simple Donatello. "There is likewise another sweet old story connected with this spot. But, now that I remember it, it seems to me more sad than sweet, though formerly the sorrow, in which it closes, did not

[1]This fountain is entirely Hawthorne's invention, added for the mood of the scene. He noted several times in his notebooks that the plain around the Villa Montauto was dry.

so much impress me. If I had the gift of tale-telling, this one would be sure to interest you mightily."

"Pray tell it," said Kenyon; "no matter whether well or ill. These wild legends have often the most powerful charm when least artfully told."

So the young count narrated a myth of one of his progenitors,—he might have lived a century ago, or a thousand years, or before the Christian epoch, for anything that Donatello knew to the contrary,—who had made acquaintance with a fair creature belonging to this fountain. Whether woman or sprite was a mystery, as was all else about her, except that her life and soul were somehow interfused throughout the gushing water. She was a fresh, cool, dewy thing, sunny and shadowy, full of pleasant little mischiefs, fitful and changeable with the whim of the moment, but yet as constant as her native stream, which kept the same gush and flow forever, while marble crumbled over and around it. The fountain woman loved the youth,—a knight, as Donatello called him,—for, according to the legend, his race was akin to hers. At least, whether kin or no, there had been friendship and sympathy of old betwixt an ancestor of his, with furry ears, and the long-lived lady of the fountain. And, after all those ages, she was still as young as a May morning, and as frolicsome as a bird upon a tree, or a breeze that makes merry with the leaves.

She taught him how to call her from her pebbly source, and they spent many a happy hour together, more especially in the fervor of the summer days. For often as he sat waiting for her by the margin of the spring, she would suddenly fall down around him in a shower of sunny raindrops, with a rainbow glowing through them, and forthwith gather herself up into the likeness of a beautiful girl, laughing—or was it the warble of the rill over the pebbles?—to see the youth's amazement.

Thus, kind maiden that she was, the hot atmosphere became deliciously cool and fragrant for this favored knight; and, furthermore, when he knelt down to drink out of the spring, nothing was more common than for a pair of rosy lips to come up out of its little depths, and touch his mouth with the thrill of a sweet, cool, dewy kiss!

"It is a delightful story for the hot noon of your Tuscan summer," observed the sculptor, at this point. "But the deportment of the watery lady must have had a most chilling influence in midwinter. Her lover would find it, very literally, a cold reception!"

"I suppose," said Donatello, rather sulkily, "you are making fun of the story. But I see nothing laughable in the thing itself, nor in what you say about it."

He went on to relate, that for a long while, the knight found infinite pleasure and comfort in the friendship of the fountain nymph. In his merriest hours, she gladdened him with her sportive humor. If ever he was annoyed with earthly trouble, she laid her moist hand upon his brow, and charmed the fret and fever quite away.

But one day—one fatal noontide—the young knight came rushing with hasty and irregular steps to the accustomed fountain. He called the nymph; but—no doubt because there was something unusual and frightful in his tone—she did not appear, nor answer him. He flung himself down, and washed his hands and bathed his feverish brow in the cool, pure water. And then, there was a sound of woe; it might have been a woman's voice; it might have been only the sighing of the brook over the pebbles. The water shrank away from the youth's hands, and left his brow as dry and feverish as before.—

Donatello here came to a dead pause.

"Why did the water shrink from this unhappy knight?" inquired the sculptor.

"Because he had tried to wash off a blood-stain!" said the young count, in a horror-stricken whisper. "The guilty man had polluted the pure water. The nymph might have comforted him in sorrow, but could not cleanse his conscience of a crime."

"And did he never behold her more?" asked Kenyon.

"Never, but once," replied his friend. "He never beheld

her blessed face but once again, and then there was a blood-stain on the poor nymph's brow; it was the stain his guilt had left in the fountain where he tried to wash it off. He mourned for her his whole life long, and employed the best sculptor of the time to carve this statue of the nymph from his description of her aspect. But, though my ancestor would fain have had the image wear her happiest look, the artist, unlike yourself, was so impressed with the mournfulness of the story, that, in spite of his best efforts, he made her forlorn, and forever weeping, as you see!"

Kenyon found a certain charm in this simple legend. Whether so intended or not, he understood it as an apologue, typifying the soothing and genial effects of an habitual inter-course with nature, in all ordinary cares and griefs; while, on the other hand, her mild influences fall short in their effect upon the ruder passions, and are altogether powerless in the dread fever-fit or deadly chill of guilt.

"Do you say," he asked, "that the nymph's face has never since been shown to any mortal? Methinks, you, by your native qualities, are as well entitled to her favor as ever your progeni-tor could have been. Why have you not summoned her?"

"I called her often when I was a silly child," answered Donatello; and he added, in an inward voice,—"Thank Heaven, she did not come!"

"Then you never saw her?" said the sculptor.

"Never in my life!" rejoined the count. "No, my dear friend, I have not seen the nymph; although here, by her foun-tain, I used to make many strange acquaintances; for, from my earliest childhood, I was familiar with whatever creatures haunt the woods. You would have laughed to see the friends I had among them; yes, among the wild, nimble things, that reckon man their deadliest enemy! How it was first taught me, I cannot tell; but there was a charm—a voice, a murmur, a kind of chant —by which I called the woodland inhabitants, the furry people, and the feathered people, in a language that they seemed to understand."

"I have heard of such a gift," responded the sculptor gravely, "but never before met with a person endowed with it. Pray, try the charm; and lest I should frighten your friends away, I will withdraw into this thicket, and merely peep at them."

"I doubt," said Donatello, "whether they will remember my voice now. It changes, you know, as the boy grows towards manhood."

Nevertheless, as the young count's good-nature and easy persuadability were among his best characteristics, he set about complying with Kenyon's request. The latter, in his concealment among the shrubbery, heard him send forth a sort of modulated breath, wild, rude, yet harmonious. It struck the auditor as at once the strangest and the most natural utterance that had ever reached his ears. Any idle boy, it should seem, singing to himself, and setting his wordless song to no other or more definite tune than the play of his own pulses, might produce a sound almost identical with this; and yet, it was as individual as a murmur of the breeze. Donatello tried it, over and over again, with many breaks, at first, and pauses of uncertainty; then with more confidence, and a fuller swell, like a wayfarer groping out of obscurity into the light, and moving with freer footsteps as it brightens around him.

Anon, his voice appeared to fill the air, yet not with an obtrusive clangor. The sound was of a murmurous character, soft, attractive, persuasive, friendly. The sculptor fancied that such might have been the original voice and utterance of the natural man, before the sophistication of the human intellect formed what we now call language. In this broad dialect—broad as the sympathies of nature—the human brother might have spoken to his inarticulate brotherhood that prowl the woods, or soar upon the wing, and have been intelligible, to such extent as to win their confidence.

The sound had its pathos too. At some of its simple cadences, the tears came quietly into Kenyon's eyes. They welled up slowly from his heart, which was thrilling with an emotion more delightful than he had often felt before, but which he forebore to analyze, lest, if he seized it, it should at once perish in his grasp.

Donatello paused two or three times, and seemed to listen; then, recommencing, he poured his spirit and life more earnestly into the strain. And, finally,—or else the sculptor's hope and imagination deceived him,—soft treads were audible upon the fallen leaves. There was a rustling among the shrubbery; a whirr of wings, moreover, that hovered in the air. It may have been all an illusion; but Kenyon fancied that he could distinguish the stealthy, cat-like movement of some small forest citizen, and that he could even see its doubtful shadow, if not really its substance. But, all at once, whatever might be the reason, there ensued a hurried rush and scamper of little feet; and then the sculptor heard a wild, sorrowful cry, and through the crevices of the thicket beheld Donatello fling himself on the ground.

Emerging from his hiding-place, he saw no living thing, save a brown lizard (it was of the tarantula species) rustling away through the sunshine. To all present appearance, this venomous reptile was the only creature that had responded to the young count's efforts to renew his intercourse with the lower orders of nature.

"What has happened to you?" exclaimed Kenyon, stooping down over his friend, and wondering at the anguish which he betrayed.

"Death, death!" sobbed Donatello. "They know it!"

He grovelled beside the fountain, in a fit of such passionate sobbing and weeping, that it seemed as if his heart had broken, and spilt its wild sorrows upon the ground. His unrestrained grief and childish tears made Kenyon sensible in how small a degree the customs and restraints of society had really acted upon this young man, in spite of the quietude of his ordinary deportment. In response to his friend's efforts to console him, he murmured words hardly more articulate than the strange chant, which he had so recently been breathing into the air.

"They know it!" was all that Kenyon could yet distinguish. "They know it!"

"Who know it?" asked the sculptor. "And what is it they know?"

"They know it!" repeated Donatello, trembling. "They shun me! All nature shrinks from me, and shudders at me! I live in the midst of a curse, that hems me round with a circle of fire! No innocent thing can come near me."

"Be comforted, my dear friend," said Kenyon, kneeling beside him. "You labor under some illusion, but no curse. As for this strange, natural spell, which you have been exercising, and of which I have heard before, though I never believed in, nor expected to witness it, I am satisfied that you still possess it. It was my own half-concealed presence, no doubt, and some involuntary little movement of mine, that scared away your forest friends."

"They are friends of mine no longer," answered Donatello.

"We all of us, as we grow older," rejoined Kenyon, "lose somewhat of our proximity to nature. It is the price we pay for experience."

"A heavy price, then!" said Donatello, rising from the ground. "But we will speak no more of it. Forget this scene, my dear friend. In your eyes, it must look very absurd. It is a grief, I presume, to all men, to find the pleasant privileges and properties of early life departing from them. That grief has now befallen me. Well; I shall waste no more tears for such a cause!"

Nothing else made Kenyon so sensible of a change in Donatello, as his newly acquired power of dealing with his own emotions, and, after a struggle more or less fierce, thrusting them down into the prison-cells where he usually kept them confined. The restraint which he now put upon himself, and the mask of dull composure which he succeeded in clasping over his still beautiful, and once faun-like face, affected the sensitive sculptor more sadly than even the unrestrained passion of the preceding scene. It is a very miserable epoch, when the evil necessities of life, in our tortuous world, first get the better of us so far, as to compel us to attempt throwing a cloud over our transparency. Simplicity increases in value the longer we can keep it, and the further we carry it onward into life; the loss of a child's simplicity, in the inevitable lapse of years, causes but a natural sigh or two, because even his mother feared that he could not keep it always. But after a young man has brought it through his childhood, and has still worn it in his bosom, not as an early dew-drop, but as a diamond of pure, white lustre,— it is a pity to lose it, then. And thus, when Kenyon saw how much his friend had now to hide, and how well he hid it, he could have wept, although his tears would have been even idler than those which Donatello had just shed.

They parted on the lawn before the house, the count to climb his tower, and the sculptor to read an antique edition of Dante, which he had found among some old volumes of Catholic devotion, in a seldom-visited room. Tomaso met him in the entrance hall, and showed a desire to speak.

"Our poor signorino looks very sad to-day!" he said.

"Even so, good Tomaso," replied the sculptor. "Would that we could raise his spirits a little!"

"There might be means, signor," answered the old butler, "if one might but be sure that they were the right ones. We men are but rough nurses for a sick body or a sick spirit."

"Women, you would say, my good friend, are better," said the sculptor, struck by an intelligence in the butler's face. "That is possible! But it depends."

"Ah! we will wait a little longer," said Tomaso, with the customary shake of his head.

CHAPTER 28. *The Owl Tower*

"Will you not show me your tower?" said the sculptor one day to his friend.

"It is plainly enough to be seen, methinks," answered the count, with a kind of sulkiness that often appeared in him, as one of the little symptoms of inward trouble.

"Yes; its exterior is visible far and wide," said Kenyon. "But such a gray, moss-grown tower as this, however valuable as an object of scenery, will certainly be quite as interesting inside as out. It cannot be less than six hundred years old; the foundations and lower story are much older than that, I should judge; and traditions probably cling to the walls within quite as plentifully as the gray and yellow lichens cluster on its face without."

"No doubt," replied Donatello; "but I know little of such things, and never could comprehend the interest which some of you Forestieri take in them. A year or two ago an English signor with a venerable white beard—they say he was a magician, too —came hither from as far off as Florence, just to see my tower."

"Ah, I have seen him at Florence," observed Kenyon. "He is a necromancer, as you say, and dwells in an old mansion of the Knights Templars, close by the Ponte Vecchio, with a great many ghostly books, pictures, and antiquities, to make the house gloomy, and one bright-eyed little girl to keep it cheerful!"[1]

[1]Hawthorne is referring to an English artist and antiquarian named Seymour Kirkup (1788–1880), who specialized in the occult and claimed to have conversed with Dante through his medium, a beautiful Italian peasant girl named Regina Ronti. She was in love with a young peasant; she died giving birth to a little girl whom the ingenuous Kirkup claimed as his own, named Imogen, and reared as his daughter. See Julian Hawthorne, *Hawthorne and His Circle* (New York: Harper, 1903), pp. 345–348.

"I know him only by his white beard," said Donatello; "but he could have told you a great deal about the tower, and the sieges which it has stood, and the prisoners who have been confined in it. And he gathered up all the traditions of the Monte Beni family, and, among the rest, the sad one which I told you at the fountain the other day. He had known mighty poets, he said, in his earlier life;[2] and the most illustrious of them would have rejoiced to preserve such a legend in immortal rhyme—especially if he could have had some of our wine of Sunshine to help out his inspiration!"

"Any man might be a poet, as well as Byron, with such wine and such a theme," rejoined the sculptor. "But, shall we climb your tower? The thunderstorm gathering yonder among the hills will be a spectacle worth witnessing."

"Come, then," said the Count, adding, with a sigh, "it has a weary staircase, and dismal chambers, and it is very lonesome at the summit!"

"Like a man's life, when he has climbed to eminence," remarked the sculptor; "or, let us rather say, with its difficult steps, and the dark prison-cells you speak of, your tower resembles the spiritual experience of many a sinful soul, which, nevertheless, may struggle upward into the pure air and light of Heaven at last!"

Donatello sighed again, and led the way up into the tower.

Mounting the broad staircase that ascended from the entrance hall, they traversed the great wilderness of a house, through some obscure passages, and came to a low, ancient doorway. It admitted them to a narrow turret-stair which zigzagged upward, lighted in its progress by loopholes and iron-barred windows. Reaching the top of the first flight, the Count threw open a door of worm-eaten oak, and disclosed a chamber that occupied the whole area of the tower. It was most pitiably forlorn of aspect, with a brick-paved floor, bare holes through the

[2]Kirkup knew Byron, Shelley, Leigh Hunt, and Edward Trelawney in his youth.

massive walls, grated with iron, instead of windows, and for furniture an old stool, which increased the dreariness of the place tenfold, by suggesting an idea of its having once been tenanted.

"This was a prisoner's cell in the old days," said Donatello; "the white-bearded necromancer, of whom I told you, found out that a certain famous monk was confined here, about five hundred years ago. He was a very holy man, and was afterwards burned at the stake in the Grand-ducal Square at Firenze.[3] There have always been stories, Tomaso says, of a hooded monk creeping up and down these stairs, or standing in the door-way of this chamber. It must needs be the ghost of the ancient prisoner. Do you believe in ghosts?"

"I can hardly tell," replied Kenyon; "on the whole, I think not."

"Neither do I," responded the Count; "for, if spirits ever came back, I should surely have met one within these two months past. Ghosts never rise! So much I know, and am glad to know it!"

Following the narrow staircase still higher, they came to another room of similar size and equally forlorn, but inhabited by two personages of a race which from time immemorial have held proprietorship and occupancy in ruined towers. These were a pair of owls, who, being doubtless acquainted with Donatello, showed little sign of alarm at the entrance of visitors. They gave a dismal croak or two, and hopped aside into the darkest corner; since it was not yet their hour to flap duskily abroad.

"They do not desert me, like my other feather acquaint-

[3]Possibly an allusion to Girolamo Savonarola (1452–1498), a zealous Dominican reformer who opposed the corrupt Borgia Pope, Alexander VI. Savonarola became the virtual ruler of Florence when the Medici were expelled in 1494. He was excommunicated by Alexander VI in 1497 but continued to denounce papal corruption until arrested, tortured, and hanged as a false prophet by city authorities in 1498. In the novel the hooded monk is analogous to the dead Model and reminds Donatello of his sin.

ances," observed the young count, with a sad smile, alluding to
the scene which Kenyon had witnessed at the fountain side.
"When I was a wild, playful boy, the owls did not love me half
so well."

He made no further pause here, but led his friend up
another flight of steps; while, at every stage, the windows and
narrow loopholes afforded Kenyon more extensive eyeshots
over hill and valley, and allowed him to taste the cool purity of
mid-atmosphere. At length they reached the topmost chamber,
directly beneath the roof of the tower.

"This is my own abode," said Donatello; "my own owl's
nest."

In fact, the room was fitted up as a bedchamber, though
in a style of the utmost simplicity. It likewise served as an
oratory; there being a crucifix in one corner, and a multitude of
holy emblems, such as Catholics judge it necessary to help their
devotion withal. Several ugly little prints, representing the suf-
ferings of the Saviour, and the martyrdoms of saints, hung on
the wall; and, behind the crucifix, there was a good copy of
Titian's Magdalen of the Pitti Palace, clad only in the flow of
her golden ringlets. She had a confident look, (but it was Titian's
fault, not the penitent woman's,) as if expecting to win heaven
by the free display of her earthly charms.[4] Inside of a glass case,
appeared an image of the sacred Bambino, in the guise of a little
waxen boy, very prettily made, reclining among flowers, like a

---

[4]Titian (1477–1576), whose real name was Tiziano Vecellio, was a
sensuous, highly coloristic Renaissance painter. The Pitti Palace, in Florence, was begun in 1435 by the architect Filippo Brunelleschi, but never
completed. It is famous for its stonework facade and its art collection.

Cf. Hawthorne's judgment on the original painting by Titian: "This
Magdalen is very coarse and sensual, with only an impudent assumption of
penitence and religious sentiment, scarcely so deep as the eyelids; but it is
a splendid picture, nevertheless, with those naked, lifelike arms, and the
hands that press the rich locks about her, and so carefully permit those
voluptuous breasts to be seen. She a penitent! She would shake off all pretence to it as easily as she would shake aside that clustering hair. . . . Titian
must have been a very good-for-nothing old man" (NB, pp. 330–331).

Cupid, and holding up a heart that resembled a bit of red sealing-wax. A small vase of precious marble was full of holy water.

Beneath the crucifix, on a table, lay a human skull, which looked as if it might have been dug up out of some old grave. But, examining it more closely, Kenyon saw that it was carved in gray alabaster, most skilfully done to the death, with accurate imitation of the teeth, the sutures, the empty eye-caverns, and the fragile little bones of the nose. This hideous emblem rested on a cushion of white marble, so nicely wrought that you seemed to see the impression of the heavy skull in a silken and downy substance.

Donatello dipped his fingers into the holy-water vase, and crossed himself. After doing so, he trembled.

"I have no right to make the sacred symbol on a sinful breast!" he said.

"On what mortal breast can it be made then?" asked the sculptor. "Is there one that hides no sin?"

"But these blessed emblems make you smile, I fear," resumed the Count, looking askance at his friend. "You heretics, I know, attempt to pray without even a crucifix to kneel at."

"I, at least, whom you call a heretic, reverence that holy symbol," answered Kenyon. "What I am most inclined to murmur at, is this death's head. I could laugh, moreover, in its ugly face! It is absurdly monstrous, my dear friend, thus to fling the dead weight of our mortality upon our immortal hopes. While we live on earth, 'tis true, we must needs carry our skeletons about with us; but, for heaven's sake, do not let us burden our spirits with them, in our feeble efforts to soar upward! Believe me, it will change the whole aspect of death, if you can once disconnect it, in your idea, with that corruption from which it disengages our higher part."

"I do not well understand you," said Donatello; and he took up the alabaster skull, shuddering, and evidently feeling it a kind of penance to touch it. "I only know that this skull has been in my family for centuries. Old Tomaso has a story that it was copied by a famous sculptor from the skull of that same unhappy knight who loved the fountain-lady, and lost her by a blood-stain. He lived and died with a deep sense of sin upon him, and, on his death-bed, he ordained that this token of him should go down to his posterity. And my forefathers, being a cheerful race of men in their natural disposition, found it needful to have the skull often before their eyes, because they dearly loved life and its enjoyments, and hated the very thought of death."

"I am afraid," said Kenyon, "they liked it none the better, for seeing its face under this abominable mask."

Without further discussion, the Count led the way up one more flight of stairs, at the end of which they emerged upon the summit of the tower. The sculptor felt as if his being were suddenly magnified a hundredfold; so wide was the Umbrian valley that suddenly opened before him, set in its grand frame-work of nearer and more distant hills. It seemed as if all Italy lay under his eyes in that one picture. For there was the broad, sunny smile of God, which we fancy to be spread over that favored land more abundantly than on other regions, and, beneath it, glowed a most rich and varied fertility. The trim vineyards were there, and the fig-trees, and the mulberries, and the smoky-hued tracts of the olive-orchards; there, too, were fields of every kind of grain, among which waved the Indian corn, putting Kenyon in mind of the fondly-remembered acres of his father's homestead. White villas, gray convents, church-spires, villages, towns, each with its battlemented walls and towered gateway, were scattered upon this spacious map; a river gleamed across it; and lakes opened their blue eyes in its face, reflecting heaven, lest mortals should forget that better land, when they beheld the earth so beautiful.

What made the valley look still wider, was the two or three varieties of weather that were visible on its surface, all at the same instant of time. Here lay the quiet sunshine; there fell the great black patches of ominous shadow from the clouds; and behind them, like a giant of league-long strides, came hurrying the thunderstorm, which had already swept midway across the plain. In the rear of the approaching tempest, brightened forth again the sunny splendor, which its progress had darkened with so terrible a frown.

All round this majestic landscape, the bald-peaked or forest-crowned mountains descended boldly upon the plain. On many of their spurs and midway declivities, and even on their summits, stood cities, some of them famous of old; for these had been the seats and nurseries of early art, where the flower of beauty sprang out of a rocky soil, and in a high, keen atmosphere, when the richest and most sheltered gardens failed to nourish it.

"Thank God for letting me again behold this scene!" said the sculptor, a devout man in his way, reverently taking off his hat. "I have viewed it from many points, and never without as full a sensation of gratitude as my heart seems capable of feeling. How it strengthens the poor human spirit in its reliance on His providence, to ascend but this little way above the common level, and so attain a somewhat wider glimpse of His dealings with mankind. He doeth all things right! His will be done!"

"You discern something that is hidden from me," observed Donatello, gloomily, yet striving with unwonted grasp to catch the analogies which so cheered his friend. "I see sunshine on one spot, and cloud in another, and no reason for it in either case. The sun on you; the cloud on me! What comfort can I draw from this?"

"Nay, I cannot preach," said Kenyon, "with a page of heaven and a page of earth spread wide open before us! Only begin to read it, and you will find it interpreting itself without the aid of words. It is a great mistake to try to put our best thoughts into human language. When we ascend into the higher regions of emotion and spiritual enjoyment, they are only expressible by such grand hieroglyphics as these around us."

They stood awhile, contemplating the scene; but, as inevitably happens after a spiritual flight, it was not long before the sculptor felt his wings flagging in the rarity of the upper atmosphere. He was glad to let himself quietly downward out of mid-sky, as it were, and alight on the solid platform of the battlemented tower. He looked about him, and beheld growing out of the stone pavement, which formed the roof, a little shrub, with green and glossy leaves. It was the only green thing there; and heaven knows how its seeds had ever been planted, at that airy height, or how it had found nourishment for its small life, in the chinks of the stones; for it had no earth, and nothing more like soil than the crumbling mortar, which had been crammed into the crevices in a long-past age.

Yet the plant seemed fond of its native site; and Donatello said it had always grown there, from his earliest remembrance, and never, he believed, any smaller or any larger than they saw it now.

"I wonder if the shrub teaches you any good lesson," said he, observing the interest with which Kenyon examined it. "If the wide valley has a great meaning, this plant ought to have at least a little one; and it has been growing on our tower long enough to have learned how to speak it."

"Oh, certainly!" answered the sculptor; "the shrub has its moral, or it would have perished long ago. And, no doubt, it is for your use and edification, since you have had it before your eyes all your lifetime, and now are moved to ask what may be its lesson."

"It teaches me nothing," said the simple Donatello, stooping over the plant, and perplexing himself with a minute scrutiny. "But here was a worm that would have killed it; an ugly creature, which I will fling over the battlements."

CHAPTER 29. *On the Battlements*

The sculptor now looked through an embrasure, and threw down a bit of lime, watching its fall, till it struck upon a stone bench at the rocky foundation of the tower, and flew into many fragments.

"Pray pardon me for helping Time to crumble away your ancestral walls," said he. "But I am one of those persons who have a natural tendency to climb heights, and to stand on the verge of them, measuring the depth below. If I were to do just as I like, at this moment, I should fling myself down after that bit of lime. It is a very singular temptation, and all but irresistible; partly, I believe, because it might be so easily done, and partly because such momentous consequences would ensue, without my being compelled to wait a moment for them. Have you never felt this strange impulse of an evil spirit at your back, shoving you towards a precipice?"

"Ah, no!" cried Donatello, shrinking from the battle-mented wall with a face of horror. "I cling to life in a way which you cannot conceive; it has been so rich, so warm, so sunny!—and beyond its verge, nothing but the chilly dark! And then a fall from a precipice is such an awful death!"

"Nay; if it be a great height," said Kenyon, "a man would leave his life in the air, and never feel the hard shock at the bottom."

"That is not the way with this kind of death!" exclaimed Donatello, in a low, horror-stricken voice, which grew higher and more full of emotion as he proceeded. "Imagine a fellow-creature,—breathing, now, and looking you in the face,—and now tumbling down, down, down, with a long shriek wavering after him, all the way! He does not leave his life in the air! No;

but it keeps in him till he thumps against the stones, a horribly long while; then, he lies there frightfully quiet, a dead heap of bruised flesh and broken bones! A quiver runs through the crushed mass; and no more movement after that! No; not if you would give your soul to make him stir a finger! Ah, terrible! Yes, yes; I would fain fling myself down for the very dread of it, that I might endure it once for all, and dream of it no more!"

"How forcibly—how frightfully you conceive this!" said the sculptor, aghast at the passionate horror which was betrayed in the count's words, and still more in his wild gestures and ghastly look. "Nay, if the height of your tower affects your imagination thus, you do wrong to trust yourself here in solitude, and in the night-time, and at all unguarded hours. You are not safe in your chamber. It is but a step or two; and what if a vivid dream should lead you up hither, at midnight, and act itself out as a reality!"

Donatello had hidden his face in his hands, and was leaning against the parapet.

"No fear of that!" said he. "Whatever the dream may be, I am too genuine a coward to act out my own death in it."

The paroxysm passed away, and the two friends continued their desultory talk, very much as if no such interruption had occurred. Nevertheless, it affected the sculptor with infinite pity to see this young man, who had been born to gladness as an assured heritage, now involved in a misty bewilderment of grievous thoughts, amid which he seemed to go staggering blindfold. Kenyon, not without an unshaped suspicion of the definite fact, knew that his condition must have resulted from the weight and gloom of life, now first, through the agency of a secret trouble, making themselves felt on a character that had heretofore breathed only an atmosphere of joy. The effect of this hard lesson, upon Donatello's intellect and disposition, was very striking. It was perceptible that he had already had glimpses of strange and subtle matters in those dark caverns, into which all men must descend, if they would know anything beneath the surface and illusive pleasures of existence. And when they emerge, though dazzled and blinded by the first glare of daylight, they take truer and sadder views of life forever afterwards.

From some mysterious source, as the sculptor felt assured, a soul had been inspired into the young count's simplicity, since their intercourse in Rome. He now showed a far deeper sense, and an intelligence that began to deal with high subjects, though in a feeble and childish way. He evinced, too, a more definite and a nobler individuality, but developed out of grief and pain, and fearfully conscious of the pangs that had given it birth. Every human life, if it ascends to truth or delves down to reality, must undergo a similar change; but sometimes, perhaps, the instruction comes without the sorrow; and oftener the sorrow teaches no lesson that abides with us. In Donatello's case, it was pitiful, and almost ludicrous, to observe the confused struggle that he made; how completely he was taken by surprise; how ill-prepared he stood, on this old battle-field of the world, to fight with such an inevitable foe as mortal calamity, and sin for its stronger ally.

"And yet," thought Kenyon, "the poor fellow bears himself like a hero, too! If he would only tell me his trouble, or give me an opening to speak frankly about it, I might help him; but he finds it too horrible to be uttered, and fancies himself the only mortal that ever felt the anguish of remorse. Yes; he believes that nobody ever endured his agony before; so that— sharp enough in itself—it has all the additional zest of a torture just invented to plague him individually."

The sculptor endeavored to dismiss the painful subject from his mind; and, leaning against the battlements, he turned his face southward and westward, and gazed across the breadth of the valley. His thoughts flew far beyond even those wide boundaries, taking an air-line from Donatello's tower to another turret that ascended into the sky of the summer afternoon, invisibly to him, above the roofs of distant Rome. Then rose tumultuously into his consciousness that strong love for Hilda, which it was his habit to confine in one of the heart's inner chambers, because he had found no encouragement to bring it forward. But now, he felt a strange pull at his heartstrings. It could not have been more perceptible, if all the way between these battlements and Hilda's dove-cote, had stretched an exquisitely sensitive cord, which, at the hither end, was knotted with his aforesaid heartstrings, and, at the remoter one, was grasped by a gentle hand. His breath grew tremulous. He put his hand to his breast; so distinctly did he seem to feel that cord drawn once—and again, and again, as if—though still it was bashfully intimated—there were an importunate demand for his presence. Oh! for the white wings of Hilda's doves, that he might have flown thither, and alighted at the virgin's shrine!

But lovers, and Kenyon knew it well, project so lifelike a copy of their mistresses out of their own imaginations, that it can pull at the heartstrings almost as perceptibly as the genuine original. No airy intimations are to be trusted; no evidences of responsive affection less positive than whispered and broken words, or tender pressures of the hand, allowed and half-returned; or glances, that distil many passionate avowals into one gleam of richly-colored light. Even these should be weighed rigorously, at the instant; for, in another instant, the imagination seizes on them as its property, and stamps them with its own arbitrary value. But Hilda's maidenly reserve had given her lover no such tokens, to be interpreted either by his hopes or fears.

"Yonder, over mountain and valley, lies Rome," said the sculptor; "shall you return thither in the autumn?"

"Never! I hate Rome," answered Donatello; "and have good cause."

"And yet it was a pleasant winter that we spent there," observed Kenyon, "and with pleasant friends about us. You would meet them again there—all of them."

"All?" asked Donatello.

"All, to the best of my belief," said the sculptor; "but you need not go to Rome to seek them. If there were one of those friends, whose life-line was twisted with your own, I am enough of a fatalist to feel assured that you will meet that one again,

wander whither you may. Neither can we escape the companions whom Providence assigns for us, by climbing an old tower
like this."

"Yet the stairs are steep and dark," rejoined the Count;
"none but yourself would seek me here, or find me, if they
sought."

As Donatello did not take advantage of this opening which
his friend had kindly afforded him, to pour out his hidden
troubles, the latter again threw aside the subject, and returned
to the enjoyment of the scene before him. The thunderstorm,
which he had beheld striding across the valley, had passed to the
left of Monte Beni, and was continuing its march towards the
hills that formed the boundary on the eastward. Above the
whole valley, indeed, the sky was heavy with tumbling vapors
interspersed with which were tracts of blue, vividly brightened
by the sun; but, in the east, where the tempest was yet trailing its
ragged skirts, lay a dusky region of cloud and sullen mist, in
which some of the hills appeared of a dark-purple hue. Others
became so indistinct, that the spectator could not tell rocky
height from impalpable cloud. Far into this misty cloud-region,
however,—within the domain of chaos, as it were,—hill-tops
were seen brightening in the sunshine; they looked like fragments of the world, broken adrift and based on nothingness, or
like portions of a sphere destined to exist, but not yet finally
compacted.

The sculptor, habitually drawing many of the images and
illustrations of his thoughts from the plastic art, fancied that the
scene represented the process of the Creator, when He held the
new, imperfect earth in His hand, and modelled it.

"What a magic is in mist and vapor among the mountains!"
he exclaimed. "With their help, one single scene becomes a
thousand. The cloud-scenery gives such variety to a hilly landscape that it would be worth while to journalize its aspect from
hour to hour. A cloud, however,—as I have myself experienced,
—is apt to grow solid and as heavy as a stone the instant that
you take in hand to describe it. But, in my own art, I have

found great use in clouds. Such silvery ones as those to the northward, for example, have often suggested sculpturesque groups, figures, and attitudes; they are especially rich in attitudes of living repose, which a sculptor only hits upon by the rarest good fortune. When I go back to my dear native land, the clouds along the horizon will be my only gallery of art!"

"I can see cloud-shapes too," said Donatello; "yonder is one that shifts strangely; it has been like people whom I knew. And now, if I watch it a little longer it will take the figure of a monk reclining, with his cowl about his head and drawn partly over his face, and—well! did I not tell you so?"

"I think," remarked Kenyon, "we can hardly be gazing at the same cloud. What I behold is a reclining figure, to be sure, but feminine, and with a despondent air, wonderfully well expressed in the wavering outline from head to foot. It moves my very heart by something indefinable that it suggests."

"I see the figure, and almost the face," said the Count, adding, in a lower voice, "It is Miriam's!"

"No, not Miriam's," answered the sculptor.

While the two gazers thus found their own reminiscences and presentiments floating among the clouds, the day drew to its close, and now showed them the fair spectacle of an Italian sunset. The sky was soft and bright, but not so gorgeous as Kenyon had seen it, a thousand times, in America; for there the western sky is wont to be set aflame with breadths and depths of color, with which poets seek in vain to dye their verses, and which painters never dare to copy. As beheld from the tower of Monte Beni, the scene was tenderly magnificent, with mild gradations of hue, and a lavish outpouring of gold, but rather such gold as we see on the leaf of a bright flower than the burnished glow of metal from the mine. Or, if metallic, it looked airy and unsubstantial, like the glorified dreams of an alchemist. And speedily—more speedily than in our own clime—came the twilight and, brightening through its gray transparency, the stars.

A swarm of minute insects that had been hovering all day

round the battlements were now swept away by the freshness of a rising breeze. The two owls in the chamber beneath Donatello's uttered their soft, melancholy cry,—which, with national avoidance of harsh sounds, Italian owls substitute for the hoot of their kindred in other countries,—and flew darkling forth among the shrubbery. A convent-bell rang out, near at hand, and was not only echoed among the hills, but answered by another bell, and still another, which doubtless had further and further responses, at various distances along the valley; for, like the English drum-beat around the globe, there is a chain of convent-bells from end to end, and cross-wise, and in all possible directions over priest-ridden Italy.

"Come," said the sculptor, "the evening air grows cool. It is time to descend."

"Time for you, my friend," replied the Count, and he hesitated a little before adding, "I must keep a vigil here for some hours longer. It is my frequent custom to keep vigils; and sometimes the thought occurs to me whether it were not better to keep them in yonder convent the bell of which just now seemed to summon me. Would I do wisely do you think, to exchange this old tower for a cell?"

"What! Turn monk?" exclaimed his friend. "A horrible idea!"

"True," said Donatello sighing. "Therefore, if at all, I purpose doing it."

"Then think of it no more, for Heaven's sake!" cried the sculptor. "There are a thousand better and more poignant methods of being miserable than that, if to be miserable is what you wish. Nay; I question whether a monk keeps himself up to the intellectual and spiritual height which misery implies. A monk—I judge from their sensual physiognomies, which meet me at every turn—is inevitably a beast! Their souls, if they have any to begin with, perish out of them, before their sluggish, swinish existence is half done. Better, a million times, to stand star-gazing on these airy battlements, than to smother your new germ of a higher life in a monkish cell!"

"You make me tremble," said Donatello, "by your bold aspersion of men who have devoted themselves to God's service!"

"They serve neither God nor man, and themselves least of all, though their motives be utterly selfish," replied Kenyon. "Avoid the convent, my dear friend, as you would shun the death of the soul! But, for my own part, if I had an insupportable burden,—if, for any cause, I were bent upon sacrificing every earthly hope as a peace-offering towards heaven, —I would make the wide world my cell, and good deeds to mankind my prayer. Many penitent men have done this, and found peace in it."

"Ah! but you are a heretic!" said the Count.

Yet his face brightened beneath the stars; and, looking at it through the twilight, the sculptor's remembrance went back to that scene in the Capitol, where, both in features and expression, Donatello had seemed identical with the Faun. And still there was a resemblance; for now, when first the idea was suggested of living for the welfare of his fellow-creatures, the original beauty, which sorrow had partly effaced, came back elevated and spiritualized. In the black depths, the Faun had found a soul, and was struggling with it towards the light of heaven.

The illumination, it is true, soon faded out of Donatello's face. The idea of life-long and unselfish effort was too high to be received by him with more than a momentary comprehension. An Italian, indeed, seldom dreams of being philanthropic, except in bestowing alms among the paupers, who appeal to his beneficence at every step; nor does it occur to him that there are fitter modes of propitiating Heaven than by penances, pilgrimages, and offerings at shrines. Perhaps, too, their system has its share of moral advantages; they, at all events, cannot well pride themselves, as our own more energetic benevolence is apt to do, upon sharing in the counsels of Providence and kindly helping out its otherwise impracticable designs.

And now the broad valley twinkled with lights, that glimmered through its duskiness, like the fire-flies in the garden of a Florentine palace. A gleam of lightning from the rear of the tempest showed the circumference of hills, and the great space between, as the last cannon-flash of a retreating army reddens across the field where it has fought. The sculptor was on the point of descending the turret-stair, when, somewhere in the darkness that lay beneath them, a woman's voice was heard, singing a low, sad strain.

"Hark!" said he, laying his hand on Donatello's arm.

And Donatello had said "Hark!" at the same instant.

The song (if song it could be called, that had only a wild rhythm, and flowed forth in the fitful measure of a wind-harp) did not clothe itself in the sharp brilliancy of the Italian tongue. The words, so far as they could be distinguished, were German, and therefore unintelligible to the count, and hardly less so to the sculptor; being softened and molten, as it were, into the melancholy richness of the voice that sang them. It was as the murmur of a soul bewildered amid the sinful gloom of earth, and retaining only enough memory of a better state to make sad music of the wail, which would else have been a despairing shriek. Never was there profounder pathos than breathed through that mysterious voice; it brought the tears into the sculptor's eyes, with remembrances and forebodings of whatever sorrow he had felt or apprehended; it made Donatello sob, as chiming in with the anguish that he found unutterable, and giving it the expression which he vaguely sought.

But, when the emotion was at its profoundest depth, the voice rose out of it, yet so gradually that a gloom seemed to pervade it, far upward from the abyss, and not entirely to fall away as it ascended into a higher and purer region. At last, the auditors could have fancied that the melody, with its rich sweetness all there, and much of its sorrow gone, was floating around the very summit of the tower.

"Donatello," said the sculptor, when there was silence again; "had that voice no message for your ear?"

"I dare not receive it," said Donatello; "the anguish of which it spoke abides with me: the hope dies away with the breath that brought it hither. It is not good for me to hear that voice."

The sculptor sighed, and left the poor penitent keeping his vigil on the tower.

Kenyon, it will be remembered, had asked Donatello's permission to model his bust. The work had now made considerable progress, and necessarily kept the sculptor's thoughts brooding much and often upon his host's personal characteristics. These it was his difficult office to bring out from their depths, and interpret them to all men, showing them what they could not discern for themselves, yet must be compelled to recognize at a glance, on the surface of a block of marble.

He had never undertaken a portrait-bust which gave him so much trouble as Donatello's; not that there was any special difficulty in hitting the likeness, though even in this respect the grace and harmony of the features seemed inconsistent with a prominent expression of individuality; but he was chiefly perplexed how to make this genial and kindly type of countenance the index of the mind within. His acuteness and his sympathies, indeed, were both somewhat at fault in their efforts to enlighten him as to the moral phase through which the count was now passing. If at one sitting he caught a glimpse of what appeared to be a genuine and permanent trait, it would probably be less perceptible on a second occasion, and perhaps have vanished entirely at a third. So evanescent a show of character threw the sculptor into despair; not marble or clay, but cloud and vapor was the material in which it ought to be represented. Even the ponderous depression which constantly weighed upon Donatello's heart could not compel him into the kind of repose which the plastic art requires.

Hopeless of a good result, Kenyon gave up all preconceptions about the character of his subject, and let his hands work uncontrolled with the clay, somewhat as a spiritual medium, while holding a pen, yields it to an unseen guidance other than that of her own will. Now and then he fancied that this plan was destined to be the successful one. A skill and insight beyond his consciousness seemed occasionally to take up the task. The mystery, the miracle, of imbuing an inanimate substance with thought, feeling, and all the intangible attributes of the soul, appeared on the verge of being wrought. And now, as he flattered himself, the true image of his friend was about to emerge from the facile material, bringing with it more of Donatello's character than the keenest observer could detect at any one moment in the face of the original. Vain expectation! some touch, whereby the artist thought to improve or hasten the result, interfered with the design of his unseen spiritual assistant, and spoilt the whole. There was still the moist, brown clay, indeed, and the features of Donatello, but without any semblance of intelligent and sympathetic life.

"The difficulty will drive me mad, I verily believe!" cried the sculptor, nervously. "Look at the wretched piece of work yourself, my dear friend, and tell me whether you recognize any manner of likeness to your inner man?"

"None," replied Donatello, speaking the simple truth. "It is like looking a stranger in the face."

This frankly unfavorable testimony so wrought with the sensitive artist, that he fell into a passion with the stubborn image, and cared not what might happen to it thenceforward. Wielding that wonderful power which sculptors possess over moist clay, however refractory it may show itself in certain respects, he compressed, elongated, widened, and otherwise altered the features of the bust in mere recklessness, and at every change inquired of the Count whether the expression became anywise more satisfactory.

"Stop!" cried Donatello, at last, catching the sculptor's hand. "Let it remain so!"

By some accidental handling of the clay, entirely independent of his own will, Kenyon had given the countenance a distorted and violent look combining animal fierceness with intelligent hatred. Had Hilda, or had Miriam seen the bust, with the expression which it had now assumed, they might have recognized Donatello's face as they beheld it at that terrible moment when he held his victim over the edge of the precipice.

"What have I done?" said the sculptor, shocked at his own casual production. "It were a sin to let the clay which bears your features harden into a look like that. Cain never wore an uglier one."

"For that very reason, let it remain!" answered the Count, who had grown pale as ashes at the aspect of his crime, thus strangely presented to him in another of the many guises under which guilt stares the criminal in the face. "Do not alter it! Chisel it, rather, in eternal marble! I will set it up in my oratory and keep it continually before my eyes. Sadder and more horrible is a face like this, alive with my own crime, than the dead skull which my forefathers handed down to me!"

But, without in the least heeding Donatello's remonstrances, the sculptor again applied his artful fingers to the clay, and compelled the bust to dismiss the expression that had so startled them both.

"Believe me," said he, turning his eyes upon his friend, full of grave and tender sympathy, "you know not what is requisite for your spiritual growth, seeking, as you do, to keep your soul perpetually in the unwholesome region of remorse. It was needful for you to pass through that dark valley, but it is infinitely dangerous to linger there too long; there is poison in the atmosphere, when we sit down and brood in it, instead of girding up our loins to press onward. Not despondency, not slothful anguish, is what you now require—but effort! Has there been an unutterable evil in your young life? Then crowd it out with good, or it will lie corrupting there forever, and cause your capacity for better things to partake its noisome corruption!"

"You stir up many thoughts," said Donatello, pressing his
hand upon his brow, "but the multitude and the whirl of them
make me dizzy."

They now left the sculptor's temporary studio, without
observing that his last accidental touches, with which he hurriedly effaced the look of deadly rage, had given the bust a
higher and sweeter expression than it had hitherto worn. It is
to be regretted that Kenyon had not seen it; for only an artist,
perhaps, can conceive the irksomeness, the irritation of brain,
the depression of spirits, that resulted from his failure to satisfy
himself, after so much toil and thought as he had bestowed on
Donatello's bust. In case of success, indeed, all this thoughtful
toil would have been reckoned, not only as well bestowed, but
as among the happiest hours of his life; whereas, deeming himself to have failed, it was just so much of life that had better
never have been lived; for thus does the good or ill result of his
labor throw back sunshine or gloom upon the artist's mind.
The sculptor, therefore, would have done well to glance again
at his work; for here were still the features of the antique
Faun, but now illuminated with a higher meaning, such as
the old marble never bore.

Donatello having quitted him, Kenyon spent the rest of the
day strolling about the pleasant precincts of Monte Beni,
where the summer was now so far advanced that it began,
indeed, to partake of the ripe wealth of autumn. Apricots had
long been abundant, and had passed away, and plums and
cherries along with them. But now came great, juicy pears,
melting and delicious, and peaches of goodly size and tempting
aspect, though cold and watery to the palate, compared with
the sculptor's rich reminiscences of that fruit in America. The
purple figs had already enjoyed their day, and the white ones
were luscious now. The contadini (who, by this time, knew
Kenyon well) found many clusters of ripe grapes for him, in
every little globe of which was included a fragrant draught
of the sunny Monte Beni wine.

Unexpectedly, in a nook, close by the farm-house, he hap-

pened upon a spot where the vintage had actually commenced.
A great heap of early-ripened grapes had been gathered, and
thrown into a mighty tub. In the middle of it stood a lusty and
jolly contadino, nor stood, merely, but stamped with all his
might, and danced amain; while the red juice bathed his feet,
and threw its foam midway up his brown and shaggy legs.
Here, then, was the very process that shows so picturesquely
in Scripture and in poetry, of treading out the wine-press and
dyeing the feet and garments with the crimson effusion as with
the blood of a battle-field. The memory of the process does
not make the Tuscan wine taste more deliciously. The contadini hospitably offered Kenyon a sample of the new liquor,
that had already stood fermenting for a day or two. He had
tried a similar draught, however, in years past, and was little
inclined to make proof of it again; for he knew that it would
be a sour and bitter juice, a wine of woe and tribulation, and
that, the more a man drinks of such liquor, the sorrier he is
likely to be.[1]

   The scene reminded the sculptor of our New England vin-
tages, where the big piles of golden and rosy apples lie under
the orchard trees, in the mild, autumnal sunshine; and the
creaking cider-mill, set in motion by a circumgyratory horse,
is all a-gush with the luscious juice. To speak frankly, the
cider-making is the more picturesque sight of the two, and
the new, sweet cider an infinitely better drink than the ordinary, unripe Tuscan wine. Such as it is, however, the latter
fills thousands upon thousands of small, flat barrels, and, still
growing thinner and sharper, loses the little life it had, as wine,
and becomes apotheosized as a more praiseworthy vinegar.

   Yet all these vineyard scenes, and the processes connected
with the culture of the grape, had a flavor of poetry about
them. The toil that produces those kindly gifts of nature which

[1]Hawthorne witnessed the wine-pressing at Monte Beni in the late
September of 1858. This passage is taken almost verbatim from his notebook entry for September 23, 1858. See *NB*, pp. 420–421.

are not the substance of life, but its luxury, is unlike other toil. We are inclined to fancy that it does not bend the sturdy frame and stiffen the overwrought muscles, like the labor that is devoted in sad, hard earnest to raise grain for sour bread. Certainly, the sunburnt young men and dark-cheeked laughing girls, who weeded the rich acres of Monte Beni, might well enough have passed for inhabitants of an unsophisticated Arcadia. Later in the season, when the true vintage-time should come, and the wine of Sunshine gush into the vats, it was hardly too wild a dream that Bacchus himself might revisit the haunts which he loved of old. But, alas, where now would he find the Faun with whom we see him consorting in so many an antique group?

Donatello's remorseful anguish saddened this primitive and delightful life. Kenyon had a pain of his own, moreover, although not all a pain, in the never quiet, never satisfied yearning of his heart towards Hilda. He was authorized to use little freedom towards that shy maiden, even in his visions; so that he almost reproached himself when sometimes his imagination pictured in detail, the sweet years that they might spend together, in a retreat like this. It had just that rarest quality of remoteness from the actual and ordinary world—a remoteness through which all delights might visit them freely, sifted from all troubles—which lovers so reasonably insist upon, in their ideal arrangements for a happy union. It is possible, indeed, that even Donatello's grief and Kenyon's pale, sunless affection, lent a charm to Monte Beni, which it could not have retained amid a more redundant joyousness. The sculptor strayed amid its vineyards and orchards, its dells and tangled shrubberies, with somewhat the sensations of an adventurer who should find his way to the site of ancient Eden, and behold its loveliness through the transparency of that gloom which has been brooding over those haunts of innocence ever since the fall. Adam saw it in a brighter sunshine, but never knew the shade of pensive beauty which Eden won from his expulsion.

It was in the decline of the afternoon that Kenyon returned from his long, musing ramble. Old Tomaso—between whom and himself for some time past there had been a mysterious understanding—met him in the entrance hall, and drew him a little aside.

"The signorina would speak with you," he whispered.

"In the chapel?" asked the sculptor.

"No; in the saloon beyond it," answered the butler; "the entrance—you once saw the signorina appear through it—is near the altar, hidden behind the tapestry."

Kenyon lost no time in obeying the summons.

In an old Tuscan villa, a chapel ordinarily makes one among the numerous apartments; though it often happens that the door is permanently closed, the key lost, and the place left to itself, in dusty sanctity, like that chamber in man's heart where he hides his religious awe. This was very much the case with the chapel of Monte Beni. One rainy day, however, in his wanderings through the great, intricate house, Kenyon had unexpectedly found his way into it, and been impressed by its solemn aspect. The arched windows, high upward in the wall, and darkened with dust and cobweb, threw down a dim light that showed the altar, with a picture of a martyrdom above, and some tall tapers ranged before it. They had apparently been lighted, and burned an hour or two, and been extinguished perhaps half a century before. The marble vase at the entrance held some hardened mud at the bottom, accruing from the dust that had settled into it during the gradual evaporation of the holy water; and a spider (being an insect that delights in pointing the moral of desolation and neglect) had taken pains to weave a prodigiously thick tissue across the circular brim. An old family banner, tattered by the moths, drooped from the vaulted roof. In niches, there were some mediaeval busts of Donatello's forgotten ancestry; and among them, it might be, the forlorn visage of that hapless knight between whom and the fountain-nymph had occurred such tender love passages.

Throughout all the jovial prosperity of Monte Beni, this one spot within the domestic walls had kept itself silent, stern and sad. When the individual or the family retired from song and mirth, they here sought those realities which men do not invite their festive associates to share. And here, on the occasion above referred to, the sculptor had discovered—accidentally, so far as he was concerned, though with a purpose on her part—that there was a guest under Donatello's roof, whose presence the Count himself did not suspect. An interview had since taken place, and he was now summoned to another.

He crossed the chapel, in compliance with Tomaso's instructions, and passing through the side entrance, found himself in a saloon, of no great size, but more magnificent than he had supposed the villa to contain. As it was vacant, Kenyon had leisure to pace it once or twice, and examine it with a careless sort of scrutiny, before any person appeared.

This beautiful hall was floored with rich marbles, in artistically arranged figures and compartments. The walls, likewise, were almost entirely cased in marble of various kinds, the prevalent variety being giallo antico,[1] intermixed with verd-antique,[2] and others equally precious. The splendor of the giallo antico, however, was what gave character to the saloon; and the large and deep niches, apparently intended for full-length statues, along the walls, were lined with the same costly material. Without visiting Italy, one can have no idea of the beauty and magnificence that are produced by these fittings-up of polished marble. Without such experience, indeed, we do not even know what marble means, in any sense, save as the white limestone of which we carve our mantel-pieces. This rich hall of Monte Beni, moreover, was adorned, at its upper end, with two pillars that seemed to consist of oriental alabaster; and wherever there was a space vacant of precious and variegated marble, it was frescoed with ornaments in arabesque. Above, there was a coved and vaulted ceiling, glowing with pictured scenes, which affected Kenyon with a vague

[1]Literally, "antique yellow." A rich yellow marble found among ruins in Italy and employed as a decoration.
[2]Literally, "antique green." An ornamental variety of marble, composed chiefly of serpentine mixed with calcite and dolomite.

sense of splendor, without his twisting his neck to gaze at them.

It is one of the special excellencies of such a saloon of polished and richly-colored marble, that decay can never tarnish it.
Until the house crumbles down upon it, it shines indestructibly,
and with a little dusting looks just as brilliant in its three
hundredth year as the day after the final slab of giallo antico
was fitted into the wall. To the sculptor, at this first view of it,
it seemed a hall where the sun was magically imprisoned, and
must always shine. He anticipated Miriam's entrance, arrayed
in queenly robes, and beaming with even more than the singular beauty that had heretofore distinguished her.

While this thought was passing through his mind, the pillared door, at the upper end of the saloon, was partly opened,
and Miriam appeared. She was very pale, and dressed in deep
mourning. As she advanced towards the sculptor, the feebleness
of her step was so apparent that he made haste to meet her,
apprehending that she might sink down on the marble floor,
without the instant support of his arm.

But, with a gleam of her natural self-reliance, she declined
his aid, and, after touching her cold hand to his, went and sat
down on one of the cushioned divans that were ranged against
the wall.

"You are very ill, Miriam!" said Kenyon, much shocked at
her appearance. "I had not thought of this."

"No; not so ill as I seem to you," she answered, adding de-
spondently, "yet I am ill enough, I believe, to die, unless some
change speedily occurs."

"What, then, is your disorder?" asked the sculptor; "and
what the remedy?"

"The disorder!" repeated Miriam. "There is none that I
know of, save too much life and strength, without a purpose
for one or the other. It is my too redundant energy that is
slowly—or perhaps rapidly—wearing me away, because I can
apply it to no use. The object, which I am bound to consider
my only one on earth, fails me utterly. The sacrifice which

I yearn to make of myself, my hopes, my everything, is coldly put aside. Nothing is left for me but to brood, brood, brood, all day, all night in unprofitable longings and repinings."

"This is very sad, Miriam," said Kenyon.

"Ay, indeed; I fancy so," she replied, with a short, unnatural laugh.

"With all your activity of mind," resumed he—"so fertile in plans as I have known you—can you imagine no method of bringing your resources into play?"

"My mind is not active any longer," answered Miriam, in a cold, indifferent tone. "It deals with one thought and no more. One recollection paralyzes it. It is not remorse; do not think it! I put myself out of the question, and feel neither regret nor penitence on my own behalf. But what benumbs me—what robs me of all power—it is no secret for a woman to tell a man, yet I care not though you know it—is the certainty that I am, and must ever be, an object of horror in Donatello's sight."

The sculptor—a young man, and cherishing a love which insulated him from the wild experiences which some men gather—was startled to perceive how Miriam's rich, ill-regulated nature impelled her to fling herself, conscience and all, on one passion, the object of which intellectually seemed far beneath her.

"How have you obtained the certainty of which you speak?" asked he, after a pause.

"Oh, by a sure token," said Miriam; "a gesture, merely; a shudder, a cold shiver that ran through him one sunny morning when his hand happened to touch mine! But it was enough."

"I firmly believe, Miriam," said the sculptor, "that he loves you still."

She started, and a flush of color came tremulously over the paleness of her cheek.

"Yes," repeated Kenyon, "if my interest in Donatello—and in yourself, Miriam—endows me with any true insight, he not only loves you still, but with a force and depth proportioned to the stronger grasp of his faculties, in their new development."

"Do not deceive me," said Miriam, growing pale again.

"Not for the world!" replied Kenyon. "Here is what I take to be the truth. There was an interval, no doubt, when the horror of some calamity, which I need not shape out in my conjectures, threw Donatello into a stupor of misery. Connected with the first shock there was an intolerable pain and shuddering repugnance attaching themselves to all the circumstances and surroundings of the event that so terribly affected him. Was his dearest friend involved within the horror of that moment, he would shrink from her as he shrank most of all from himself. But as his mind roused itself,—as it rose to a higher life than he had hitherto experienced,—whatever had been true and permanent within him revived by the selfsame impulse. So has it been with his love."

"But, surely," said Miriam, "he knows that I am here! Why, then, except that I am odious to him, does he not bid me welcome?"

"He is, I believe, aware of your presence here," answered the sculptor. "Your song, a night or two ago, must have revealed it to him, and, in truth, I had fancied that there was already a consciousness of it in his mind. But, the more passionately he longs for your society, the more religiously he deems himself bound to avoid it. The idea of a life-long penance has taken strong possession of Donatello. He gropes blindly about him for some method of sharp self-torture, and finds, of course, no other so efficacious as this."

"But, he loves me," repeated Miriam, in a low voice, to herself. "Yes; he loves me!"

It was strange to observe the womanly softness that came over her, as she admitted that comfort into her bosom. The cold, unnatural indifference of her manner, a kind of frozen passionateness, which had shocked and chilled the sculptor, disappeared. She blushed, and turned away her eyes, knowing that there was more surprise and joy in their dewy glances, than any man save one ought to detect there.

"In other respects," she inquired at length, "is he much changed?"

"A wonderful process is going forward in Donatello's mind," answered the sculptor. "The germs of faculties that have heretofore slept are fast springing into activity. The world of thought is disclosing itself to his inward sight. He startles me, at times, with his perception of deep truths; and, quite as often, it must be owned he compels me to smile by the intermixture of his former simplicity with a new intelligence. But, he is bewildered with the revelations that each day brings. Out of his bitter agony, a soul and intellect, I could almost say, have been inspired into him."

"Ah, I could help him here!" cried Miriam, clasping her hands. "And how sweet a toil to bend and adapt my whole nature to do him good! To instruct, to elevate, to enrich his mind with the wealth that would flow in upon me, had I such a motive for acquiring it! who else can perform the task? Who else has the tender sympathy which he requires? Who else, save only me,—a woman, a sharer in the same dread secret, a partaker in one identical guilt,—could meet him on such terms of intimate equality as the case demands? With this object before me, I might feel a right to live! Without it, it is a shame for me to have lived so long."

"I fully agree with you," said Kenyon, "that your true place is by his side."

"Surely it is," replied Miriam. "If Donatello is entitled to aught on earth, it is to my complete self-sacrifice for his sake. It does not weaken his claim, methinks, that my only prospect of happiness—a fearful word, however—lies in the good that may accrue to him from our intercourse. But he rejects me! He will not listen to the whisper of his heart, telling him that she, most wretched, who beguiled him into evil, might guide him to a higher innocence than that from which he fell. How is this first, great difficulty to be obviated?"

"It lies at your own option, Miriam, to do away the obstacle, at any moment," remarked the sculptor. "It is but to ascend Donatello's tower, and you will meet him there, under the eye of God."

"I dare not," answered Miriam. "No; I dare not!"

"Do you fear," asked the sculptor, "the dread eyewitness whom I have named?"

"No; for, as far as I can see into that cloudy and inscrutable thing, my heart, it has none but pure motives," replied Miriam. "But, my friend, you little know what a weak or what a strong creature, a woman is! I fear not Heaven, in this case, at least, but—shall I confess it? I am greatly in dread of Donatello. Once, he shuddered at my touch. If he shudder once again, or frown, I die!"

Kenyon could not but marvel at the subjection into which this proud and self-dependent woman had wilfully flung herself, hanging her life upon the chance of an angry or favorable regard from a person who, a little while before, had seemed the plaything of a moment. But, in Miriam's eyes, Donatello was always, thenceforth, invested with the tragic dignity of their hour of crime; and, furthermore, the keen and deep insight, with which her love endowed her, enabled her to know him far better than he could be known by ordinary observation. Beyond all question, since she loved him so, there was a force in Donatello worthy of her respect and love.

"You see my weakness," said Miriam, flinging out her hands, as a person does when a defect is acknowledged, and beyond remedy. "What I need, now, is an opportunity to show my strength."

"It has occurred to me," Kenyon remarked, "that the time is come, when it may be desirable to remove Donatello from the complete seclusion in which he buries himself. He has struggled long enough with one idea. He now needs a variety of thought, which cannot be otherwise so readily supplied to him, as through the medium of a variety of scenes. His mind is awakened, now; his heart, though full of pain, is no longer benumbed. They should have food and solace. If he linger here much longer, I fear that he may sink back into a lethargy. The extreme excitability, which circumstances have imparted to his moral system, has its dangers and its advantages; it being one of the dangers, that an obdurate scar may supervene upon its very tenderness. Solitude has done what it could for him; now, for a while, let him be enticed into the outer world."

"What is your plan, then?" asked Miriam.

"Simply," replied Kenyon, "to persuade Donatello to be my companion in a ramble among these hills and valleys. The little adventures and vicissitudes of travel will do him infinite good. After his recent profound experience, he will re-create the world by the new eyes with which he will regard it. He will escape, I hope, out of a morbid life, and find his way into a healthy one."

"And what is to be my part in this process?" inquired Miriam sadly, and not without jealousy. "You are taking him from me, and putting yourself, and all manner of living interests, into the place which I ought to fill!"

"It would rejoice me, Miriam, to yield the entire responsibility of this office to yourself," answered the sculptor. "I do not pretend to be the guide and counsellor whom Donatello needs; for, to mention no other obstacle, I am a man, and between man and man there is always an insuperable gulf. They can never quite grasp each other's hands; and therefore man never derives any intimate help, any heart-sustenance, from his brother man, but from woman,—his mother, his sister, or his wife. Be Donatello's friend at need, therefore, and most gladly will I resign him!"

"It is not kind to taunt me thus," said Miriam. "I have told you that I cannot do what you suggest, because I dare not."

"Well, then," rejoined the sculptor, "see if there is any

possibility of adapting yourself to my scheme. The incidents
of a journey often fling people together in the oddest, and
therefore the most natural way. Supposing you were to find
yourself on the same route, a reunion with Donatello might
ensue, and Providence have a larger hand in it than either of
us."

"It is not a hopeful plan," said Miriam, shaking her head,
after a moment's thought; "yet I will not reject it without a
trial. Only, in case it fail, here is a resolution to which I bind
myself, come what come may! You know the bronze statue
of Pope Julius in the great square of Perugia?[3] I remember
standing in the shadow of that statue one sunny noontime and
being impressed by its paternal aspect, and fancying that a
blessing fell upon me from its outstretched hand. Ever since, I
have had a superstition,—you will call it foolish, but sad and
ill-fated persons always dream such things,—that, if I waited
long enough in that same spot, some good event would come
to pass. Well, my friend, precisely a fortnight after you begin
your tour,—unless we sooner meet,—bring Donatello, at
noon, to the base of the statue. You will find me there!"

Kenyon assented to the proposed arrangement, and, after
some conversation respecting his contemplated line of travel,
prepared to take his leave. As he met Miriam's eyes, in bidding
farewell, he was surprised at the new, tender gladness that
beamed out of them, and at the appearance of health and
bloom, which, in this little while, had overspread her face.

"May I tell you, Miriam," said he, smiling, "that you are
still as beautiful as ever?"

"You have a right to notice it," she replied, "for, if it be
so, my faded bloom has been revived by the hopes you give
me. Do you, then, think me beautiful? I rejoice, most truly.

[3]Pope Julius III reigned from Feb. 7, 1550, to March 23, 1555. A
patron of the arts, his last years were marked by extensive nepotism in
dispensing ecclesiastical offices. Here he is the artistic and symbolic confessor
rather than the historical Julius, however. See the illustration, p. 313.

Beauty—if I possess it—shall be one of the instruments by which I will try to educate and elevate him, to whose good I solely dedicate myself."

The sculptor had nearly reached the door, when, hearing her call him, he turned back, and beheld Miriam still standing where he had left her, in the magnificent hall which seemed only a fit setting for her beauty. She beckoned him to return.

"You are a man of refined taste," said she; "more than that, —a man of delicate sensibility. Now tell me frankly, and on your honor! Have I not shocked you many times during this interview by my betrayal of woman's cause, my lack of feminine modesty, my reckless, passionate, most indecorous avowal, that I live only in the life of one who perhaps scorns and shudders at me?"

Thus adjured, however difficult the point to which she brought him, the sculptor was not a man to swerve aside from the simple truth.

"Miriam," replied he, "you exaggerate the impression made upon my mind; but it has been painful, and somewhat of the character which you suppose."

"I knew it," said Miriam, mournfully, but with no resentment. "What remains of my finer nature would have told me so, even if it had not been perceptible in all your manner. Well, my dear friend, when you go back to Rome, tell Hilda what her severity has done! She was all womanhood to me; and when she cast me off, I had no longer any terms to keep with the reserves and decorums of my sex. Hilda has set me free! Pray tell her so, from Miriam, and thank her!"

"I shall tell Hilda nothing that will give her pain," answered Kenyon. "But, Miriam,—though I know not what passed between her and yourself,—I feel—and let the noble frankness of your disposition forgive me, if I say so—I feel that she was right. You have a thousand admirable qualities. Whatever mass of evil may have fallen into your life,—pardon me, but your own words suggest it,—you are still as capable as ever

of many high and heroic virtues. But the white, shining purity
of Hilda's nature is a thing apart; and she is bound, by the
undefiled material of which God moulded her, to keep that
severity which I, as well as you, have recognized."

"Oh, you are right!" said Miriam; "I never questioned it;
though, as I told you, when she cast me off, it severed some
few remaining bonds between me and decorous womanhood.
But were there anything to forgive, I do forgive her. May
you win her virgin heart; for methinks there can be few men in
this evil world who are not more unworthy of her than yourself."

CHAPTER 32. *Scenes by the Way*

When it came to the point of quitting the reposeful life of Monte Beni, the sculptor was not without regrets, and would willingly have dreamed a little longer of the sweet paradise on earth that Hilda's presence there might make. Nevertheless, amid all its repose, he had begun to be sensible of a restless melancholy, to which the cultivators of the ideal arts are more liable than sturdier men. On his own part, therefore, and leaving Donatello out of the case, he would have judged it well to go. He made parting visits to the legendary dell, and to other delightful spots with which he had grown familiar; he climbed the tower again, and saw a sunset and a moonrise over the great valley; he drank, on the eve of his departure, one flask, and then another, of the Monte Beni Sunshine, and stored up its flavor in his memory, as the standard of what is exquisite in wine. These things accomplished, Kenyon was ready for the journey.

Donatello had not very easily been stirred out of the peculiar sluggishness, which inthralls and bewitches melancholy people. He had offered merely a passive resistance, however, not an active one, to his friend's schemes; and when the appointed hour came, he yielded to the impulse which Kenyon failed not to apply; and was started upon the journey before he had made up his mind to undertake it. They wandered forth at large, like two knights-errant among the valleys, and the mountains, and the old mountain-towns of that picturesque and lovely region. Save to keep the appointment with Miriam, a fortnight thereafter, in the great square of Perugia, there was nothing more definite in the sculptor's plan, than that they should let themselves be blown hither and thither like

279

winged seeds, that mount upon each wandering breeze. Yet there was an idea of fatality implied in the simile of the winged seeds which did not altogether suit Kenyon's fancy; for, if you look closely into the matter it will be seen that whatever appears most vagrant, and utterly purposeless, turns out, in the end, to have been impelled the most surely on a preordained and unswerving track. Chance and change love to deal with men's settled plans, not with their idle vagaries. If we desire unexpected and unimaginable events, we should contrive an iron framework, such as we fancy may compel the future to take one inevitable shape; then comes in the unexpected, and shatters our design in fragments.

The travellers set forth on horseback, and purposed to perform much of their aimless journeyings, under the moon, and in the cool of the morning or evening twilight; the mid-day sun, while summer had hardly begun to trail its departing skirts over Tuscany, being still too fervid to allow of noontide exposure.

For a while, they wandered in that same broad valley which Kenyon had viewed with such delight from the Monte Beni tower. The sculptor soon began to enjoy the idle activity of their new life, which the lapse of a day or two sufficed to establish as a kind of system; it is so natural for mankind to be nomadic, that a very little taste of that primitive mode of existence subverts the settled habits of many preceding years. Kenyon's cares, and whatever gloomy ideas before possessed him, seemed to be left at Monte Beni, and were scarcely remembered by the time that its gray tower grew indistinguishable on the brown hill-side. His perceptive faculties, which had found little exercise of late, amid so thoughtful a way of life, became keen, and kept his eyes busy with a hundred agreeable scenes.

He delighted in the picturesque bits of rustic character and manners, so little of which ever comes upon the surface of our life at home. There for example, were the old women, tending pigs or sheep by the wayside. As they followed the vagrant steps of their charge, these venerable ladies kept spinning yarn with that elsewhere forgotten contrivance, the distaff; and so wrinkled and stern-looking were they, that you might have taken them for the Parcæ,[1] spinning the threads of human destiny. In contrast with their great grandmothers were the children, leading goats of shaggy beard, tied by the horns, and letting them browse on branch and shrub. It is the fashion of Italy to add the petty industry of age and childhood to the sum of human toil. To the eyes of an observer from the western world, it was a strange spectacle to see sturdy, sunburnt creatures, in petticoats, but otherwise manlike, toiling side by side with male laborers, in the rudest work of the fields. These sturdy women (if as such we must recognize them) wore the high-crowned, broad-brimmed hat of Tuscan straw, the customary female head-apparel; and, as every breeze blew back its breadth of brim, the sunshine constantly added depth to the brown glow of their cheeks. The elder sisterhood, however, set off their witch-like ugliness to the worst advantage with black felt hats, bequeathed them, one would fancy, by their long-buried husbands.

Another ordinary sight, as sylvan as the above, and more agreeable, was a girl, bearing on her back a huge bundle of green twigs and shrubs, or grass, intermixed with scarlet poppies and blue flowers; the verdant burden being sometimes of such size as to hide the bearer's figure, and seem a self-moving mass of fragrant bloom and verdure. Oftener, however, the bundle reached only half-way down the back of the rustic nymph, leaving in sight her well-developed lower limbs, and the crooked knife, hanging behind her, with which she had been reaping this strange harvest sheaf. A pre-Raphaelite artist (he, for instance, who painted so marvellously a wind-swept heap of autumnal leaves)[2] might find an admirable subject in

[1] The Fates.
[2] Hawthorne is probably alluding to Sir John Millais (1829–1896) and his greatest painting, *Autumn Leaves*, painted in 1856 and exhibited at

one of these Tuscan girls stepping with a free, erect, and graceful carriage. The miscellaneous herbage and tangled twigs and
blossoms of her bundle, crowning her head (while her ruddy,
comely face looks out between the hanging side festoons like
a larger flower), would give the painter boundless scope for
the minute delineation which he loves.

Though mixed up with what was rude and earthlike,
there was still a remote, dreamlike, Arcadian charm, which
is scarcely to be found in the daily toil of other lands. Among
the pleasant features of the wayside were always the vines,
clambering on fig-trees, or other sturdy trunks; they wreathed
themselves, in huge and rich festoons, from one tree to another,
suspending clusters of ripening grapes in the interval between.
Under such careless mode of culture, the luxuriant vine is a
lovelier spectacle than where it produces a more precious
liquor, and is therefore more artificially restrained and trimmed.
Nothing can be more picturesque than an old grape-vine,
with almost a trunk of its own, clinging fast around its
supporting tree. Nor does the picture lack its moral. You
might twist it to more than one grave purpose, as you saw
how the knotted, serpentine growth imprisoned within its
strong embrace the friend that had supported its tender infancy; and how (as seemingly flexible natures are prone to
do) it converted the sturdier tree entirely to its own selfish
ends, extending its innumerable arms on every bough, and
permitting hardly a leaf to sprout except its own. It occurred
to Kenyon, that the enemies of the vine, in his native land,

---

the Royal Academy Exhibition in London in that year. The painting hangs
in the Manchester City Gallery, where Hawthorne saw it before leaving
for France and Italy in January, 1858.

The Pre-Raphaelite Movement, led by Dante Gabriel Rossetti, Millais, and W. Holman Hunt, together with William Morris and John
Ruskin (to whom Millais was closest), was an artistic and poetic protest
against the industrialism and materialism of Victorian England. These
artists and others, poets and painters alike, attempted to emulate the simplicity and piety of Cimabue, Giotto, and Fra Angelico.

might here have seen an emblem of the remorseless gripe, which the habit of vinous enjoyment lays upon its victim, possessing him wholly, and letting him live no life but such as it bestows.

The scene was not less characteristic when their path led the two wanderers through some small, ancient town. There, besides the peculiarities of present life, they saw tokens of the life that had long ago been lived and flung aside. The little town, such as we see in our mind's eye, would have its gate and surrounding walls, so ancient and massive that ages had not sufficed to crumble them away; but in the lofty upper portion of the gateway, (still standing over the empty arch where there was no longer a gate to shut), there would be a dove-cote, and peaceful doves for the only warders. Pumpkins lay ripening in the open chambers of the structure. Then, as for the town-wall, on the outside an orchard extends peacefully along its base, full, not of apple-trees, but of those old humorists with gnarled trunks and twisted boughs, the olives. Houses have been built upon the ramparts, or burrowed out of their ponderous foundation. Even the gray, martial towers crowned with ruined turrets, have been converted into rustic habitations, from the windows of which hang ears of Indian corn. At a door, that has been broken through the massive stonework, where it was meant to be strongest, some contadini are winnowing grain. Small windows, too, are pierced through the whole line of ancient wall, so that it seems a row of dwellings with one continuous front, built in a strange style of needless strength; but remnants of the old battlements and machicolations are interspersed with the homely chambers and earthen-tiled house-tops; and all along its extent both grape-vines and running flower-shrubs are encouraged to clamber and sport over the roughnesses of its decay.

Finally the long grass intermixed with weeds and wild flowers, waves on the uppermost height of the shattered rampart; and it is exceedingly pleasant in the golden sunshine of the afternoon to behold the warlike precinct so friendly in its old days, and so overgrown with rural peace. In its guard-rooms, its prison-chambers, and scooped out of its ponderous breadth, there are dwellings now-a-days where happy human lives are spent. Human parents and broods of children nestle in them, even as the swallows nestle in the little crevices along the broken summit of the wall.

Passing through the gateway of this same little town, challenged only by those watchful sentinels, the pigeons, we find ourselves in a long, narrow street, paved from side to side with flagstones, in the old Roman fashion. Nothing can exceed the grim ugliness of the houses, most of which are three or four stories high, stone built, gray, dilapidated, or half-covered with plaster in patches, and contiguous all along from end to end of the town. Nature, in the shape of tree, shrub, or grassy side-walk, is as much shut out from the one street of the rustic village as from the heart of any swarming city. The dark and half-ruinous habitations, with their small windows, many of which are drearily closed with wooden shutters, are but magnified hovels, piled story upon story, and squalid with the grime that successive ages have left behind them. It would be a hideous scene to contemplate in a rainy day, or when no human life pervaded it. In the summer-noon, however, it possesses vivacity enough to keep itself cheerful; for all the within-doors of the village then bubbles over upon the flagstones, or looks out from the small windows, and from here and there a balcony. Some of the populace are at the butcher's shop; others are at the fountain, which gushes into a marble basin that resembles an antique sarcophagus. A tailor is sewing before his door, with a young priest seated sociably beside him; a burly friar goes by with an empty wine-barrel on his head; children are at play; women at their own doorsteps mend clothes, embroider, weave hats of Tuscan straw, or twirl the distaff. Many idlers, meanwhile, strolling from one group to another, let the warm day slide by in the sweet, interminable task of doing nothing.

From all these people there comes a babblement that

seems quite disproportioned to the number of tongues that make it. So many words are not uttered in a New England village throughout the year (except it be at a political caucus or town-meeting) as are spoken here, with no especial purpose, in a single day. Neither so many words, nor so much laughter; for people talk about nothing as if they were terribly in earnest, and make merry at nothing, as if it were the best of all possible jokes. In so long a time as they have existed, and within such narrow precincts, these little walled towns are brought into a closeness of society that makes them but a larger household. All the inhabitants are akin to each, and each to all; they assemble in the street as their common saloon, and thus live and die in a familiarity of intercourse, such as never can be known where a village is open at either end, and all round-about, and has ample room within itself.

Stuck up beside the door of one house, in this village street, is a withered bough; and on a stone seat, just under the shadow of the bough, sits a party of jolly drinkers, making proof of the new wine, or quaffing the old, as their often-tried and comfortable friend. Kenyon draws bridle here (for the bough, or bush, is a symbol of the wine-shop at this day in Italy, as it was three hundred years ago in England), and calls for a goblet of the deep-hued purple juice, well diluted with water from the fountain. The Sunshine of Monte Beni would be welcome now. Meanwhile, Donatello has ridden onward, but alights where a shrine, with a burning lamp before it, is built into the wall of an inn-stable. He kneels, and crosses himself, and mutters a brief prayer, without attracting notice from the passers-by, many of whom are parenthetically devout, in a similar fashion. By this time the sculptor has drunk off his wine-and-water, and our two travellers resume their way, emerging from the opposite gate of the village.

Before them, again, lies the broad valley, with a mist so thinly scattered over it as to be perceptible only in the distance, and most so in the nooks of the hills. Now that we have called it mist, it seems a mistake not rather to have called it sunshine;

the glory of so much light being mingled with so little gloom, in the airy material of that vapor. Be it mist or sunshine, it adds a touch of ideal beauty to the scene, almost persuading the spectator that this valley and those hills are visionary, because their visible atmosphere is so like the substance of a dream.

Immediately about them, however, there were abundant tokens that the country was not really the paradise it looked to be, at a casual glance. Neither the wretched cottages nor the dreary farm-houses seemed to partake of the prosperity, with which so kindly a climate, and so fertile a portion of Mother Earth's bosom, should have filled them, one and all. But, possibly, the peasant inhabitants do not exist in so grimy a poverty; and in homes so comfortless, as a stranger, with his native ideas of those matters, would be likely to imagine. The Italians appear to possess none of that emulative pride which we see in our New England villages, where every householder, according to his taste and means, endeavors to make his homestead an ornament to the grassy and elm-shadowed wayside. In Italy there are no neat doorsteps and thresholds; no pleasant, vine-sheltered porches; none of those grass-plots or smoothly-shorn lawns, which hospitably invite the imagination into the sweet domestic interiors of English life. Everything, however sunny and luxuriant may be the scene around, is especially disheartening in the immediate neighborhood of an Italian home.

An artist, it is true, might often thank his stars for those old houses, so picturesquely time-stained, and with the plaster falling in blotches from the ancient brickwork. The prison-like, iron-barred windows, and the wide-arched, dismal entrance, admitting on one hand to the stable, on the other to the kitchen, might impress him as far better worth his pencil than the newly-painted pine boxes, in which—if he be an American—his countrymen live and thrive. But there is reason to suspect that a people are waning to decay and ruin the moment that their life becomes fascinating either in the poet's imagination or the painter's eye.

As usual, on Italian waysides, the wanderers passed great, black crosses, hung with all the instruments of the sacred agony and passion; there was the crown of thorns, the hammer and nails, the pincers, the spear, the sponge; and perched over the whole, the cock that crowed to Saint Peter's remorseful conscience. Thus, while the fertile scene showed the neverfailing beneficence of the Creator towards man in his transitory state, these symbols reminded each wayfarer of the Saviour's infinitely greater love for him as an immortal spirit. Beholding these consecrated stations, the idea seemed to strike Donatello of converting the otherwise aimless journey into a penitential pilgrimage. At each of them he alighted to kneel and kiss the cross, and humbly press his forehead against its foot; and this so invariably, that the sculptor soon learned to draw bridle of his own accord. It may be, too, heretic as he was, that Kenyon likewise put up a prayer, rendered more fervent by the symbols before his eyes, for the peace of his friend's conscience, and the pardon of the sin that so oppressed him.

Not only at the crosses did Donatello kneel, but at each of the many shrines, where the blessed Virgin in fresco—faded with sunshine and half washed out with showers—looked benignly at her worshipper; or where she was represented in a wooden image, or a bas-relief of plaster or marble, as accorded with the means of the devout person who built, or restored from a mediæval antiquity, these places of wayside worship. They were everywhere; under arched niches, or in little penthouses with a brick tiled roof, just large enough to shelter them; or perhaps in some bit of old Roman masonry, the founders of which had died before the Advent;[3] or in the wall of a country inn or farm-house, or at the midway point of a bridge, or in the shallow cavity of a natural rock, or high upward in the deep cuts of the road. It appeared to the sculptor that Donatello prayed the more earnestly and the more hopefully at

[3] I.e., before the coming of Christ.

these shrines, because the mild face of the Madonna promised him to intercede as a tender mother betwixt the poor culprit and the awfulness of judgment.

It was beautiful to observe, indeed, how tender was the soul of man and woman towards the Virgin mother, in recognition of the tenderness which, as their faith taught them, she immortally cherishes towards all human souls. In the wire-work screen, before each shrine, hung offerings of roses, or whatever flower was sweetest and most seasonable; some already wilted and withered, some fresh with that very morning's dew-drops. Flowers there were, too, that, being artificial, never bloomed on earth, nor would ever fade. The thought occurred to Kenyon, that flower-pots with living plants, might be set within the niches, or even that rose-trees, and all kinds of flowering shrubs, might be reared under the shrines and taught to twine and wreathe themselves around; so that the Virgin should dwell within a bower of verdure, bloom, and fragrant freshness, symbolizing a homage perpetually new. There are many things in the religious customs of these people that seem good; many things, at least, that might be both good and beautiful, if the soul of goodness and the sense of beauty were as much alive in the Italians now as they must have been when those customs were first imagined and adopted. But, instead of blossoms on the shrub, or freshly gathered, with the dew-drops on their leaves, their worship, now-a-days, is best symbolized by the artificial flower.

The sculptor fancied, moreover, (but perhaps it was his heresy that suggested the idea,) that it would be of happy influence to place a comfortable and shady seat beneath every wayside shrine. Then, the weary and sun-scorched traveller, while resting himself under her protecting shadow, might thank the Virgin for her hospitality. Nor perchance, were he to regale himself, even in such a consecrated spot, with the fragrance of a pipe, would it rise to heaven more offensively than the smoke of priestly incense. We do ourselves wrong, and too meanly estimate the Holiness above us, when we deem that any act or enjoyment, good in itself, is not good to do religiously.

Whatever may be the iniquities of the papal system, it was a wise and lovely sentiment, that set up the frequent shrine and cross along the roadside. No wayfarer, bent on whatever worldly errand, can fail to be reminded, at every mile or two, that this is not the business which most concerns him. The pleasure-seeker is silently admonished to look heavenward for a joy infinitely greater than he now pursues. The wretch in temptation beholds the cross, and is warned, that if he yield, the Saviour's agony for his sake will have been endured in vain. The stubborn criminal, whose heart has long been like a stone, feels it throb anew with dread and hope, and our poor Donatello, as he went kneeling from shrine to cross, and from cross to shrine, doubtless found an efficacy in these symbols that helped him towards a higher penitence.

Whether the young Count of Monte Beni noticed the fact, or no, there was more than one incident of their journey that led Kenyon to believe, that they were attended, or closely followed, or preceded, near at hand, by some one who took an interest in their motions. As it were, the step, the sweeping garment, the faintly-heard breath, of an invisible companion, was beside them, as they went on their way. It was like a dream that had strayed out of their slumber and was haunting them in the daytime, when its shadowy substance could have neither density nor outline, in the too obtrusive light. After sunset, it grew a little more distinct.

"On the left of that last shrine," asked the sculptor, as they rode, under the moon, "did you observe the figure of a woman kneeling, with her face hidden in her hands?"

"I never looked that way," replied Donatello. "I was saying my own prayer. It was some penitent, perchance. May the Blessed Virgin be the more gracious to the poor soul, because she is a woman."

CHAPTER 33. *Pictured Windows*

After wide wanderings through the valley, the two travellers directed their course towards its boundary of hills. Here, the natural scenery and men's modifications of it immediately took a different aspect from that of the fertile and smiling plain. Not unfrequently there was a convent on the hill-side; or, on some insulated promontory, a ruined castle, once the den of a robber chieftain, who was accustomed to dash down from his commanding height upon the road that wound below. For ages back, the old fortress had been flinging down its crumbling ramparts, stone by stone, towards the grimy village at its foot.

Their road wound onward among the hills, which rose steep and lofty from the scanty level space that lay between them. They continually thrust their great bulks before the wayfarers, as if grimly resolute to forbid their passage, or closed abruptly behind them, when they still dared to proceed. A gigantic hill would set its foot right down before them, and only at the last moment, would grudgingly withdraw it, just far enough to let them creep towards another obstacle. Adown these rough heights were visible the dry tracks of many a mountain-torrent that had lived a life too fierce and passionate to be a long one. Or, perhaps a stream was yet hurrying shyly along the edge of a far wider bed of pebbles and shelving rock than it seemed to need, though not too wide for the swollen rage of which this shy rivulet was capable. A stone bridge bestrode it, the ponderous arches of which were upheld and rendered indestructible by the weight of the very stones that threatened to crush them down. Old Roman toil was perceptible in the foundations of that massive bridge; the first weight that it ever bore was that of an army of the Republic.

Threading these defiles, they would arrive at some immemorial city, crowning the high summit of a hill with its cathedral, its many churches, and public edifices, all of Gothic architecture. With no more level ground than a single piazza, in the midst, the ancient town tumbled its crooked and narrow streets down the mountainside, through arched passages and by steps of stone. The aspect of everything was awfully old; older, indeed, in its effect on the imagination, than Rome itself, because history does not lay its finger on these forgotten edifices and tell us all about their origin. Etruscan princes may have dwelt in them. A thousand years, at all events, would seem but a middle age for these structures. They are built of such huge, square stones, that their appearance of ponderous durability distresses the beholder with the idea that they can never fall—never crumble away—never be less fit than now for human habitation. Many of them may once have been palaces, and still retain a squalid grandeur. But, gazing at them, we recognize how undesirable it is to build the tabernacle of our brief lifetime out of permanent materials, and with a view to their being occupied by future generations.

All towns should be made capable of purification by fire, or of decay within each half-century. Otherwise, they become the hereditary haunts of vermin and noisomeness, besides standing apart from the possibility of such improvements as are constantly introduced into the rest of man's contrivances and accommodations. It is beautiful, no doubt, and exceedingly satisfactory to some of our natural instincts, to imagine our far posterity dwelling under the same roof-tree as ourselves. Still, when people insist on building indestructible houses, they incur, or their children do, a misfortune analogous to that of the Sibyl, when she obtained the grievous boon of immortality.[1] So, we may build almost immortal habitations, it is true;

---

[1] The Cumaean Sibyl sought the gift of eternal life but neglected to ask for eternal youth as well; unfortunately, her wish was granted.

but we cannot keep them from growing old, musty, unwhole-some, dreary, full of death-scents, ghosts, and murder-stains; in short, habitations such as one sees everywhere in Italy, be they hovels or palaces.

"You should go with me to my native country," observed the sculptor, to Donatello. "In that fortunate land, each gen-eration has only its own sins and sorrows to bear. Here, it seems as if all the weary and dreary Past were piled upon the back of the Present. If I were to lose my spirits in this country —if I were to suffer any heavy misfortune here—methinks it would be impossible to stand up against it, under such adverse influences."

"The sky itself is an old roof, now," answered the Count; "and, no doubt, the sins of mankind have made it gloomier than it used to be."

"Oh, my poor Faun," thought Kenyon to himself, "how art thou changed!"

A city, like this of which we speak, seems a sort of stony growth out of the hill-side, or a fossilized town; so ancient and strange it looks, without enough of life and juiciness in it to be any longer susceptible of decay. An earthquake would afford it the only chance of being ruined, beyond its present ruin.

Yet, though dead to all the purposes for which we live to-day, the place has its glorious recollections, and not merely rude and warlike ones, but those of brighter and milder triumphs, the fruits of which we still enjoy. Italy can count several of these lifeless towns which, four or five hundred years ago, were each the birthplace of its own school of art; nor have they yet forgotten to be proud of the dark, old pictures, and the faded frescoes, the pristine beauty of which was a light and gladness to the world. But now, unless one happens to be a painter, these famous works make us miserably desperate. They are poor, dim ghosts of what, when Giotto or Cimabue first created them, threw a splendor along the stately aisles; so far gone towards nothingness, in our day, that scarcely a hint of design or expression can glimmer through the dusk. Those

early artists did well to paint their frescoes. Glowing on the
church walls, they might be looked upon as symbols of the
living spirit that made Catholicism a true religion, and that
glorified it as long as it retained a genuine life; they filled the
transepts with a radiant throng of saints and angels, and threw
around the high altar a faint reflection—as much as mortals
could see, or bear—of a Diviner Presence. But now that the
colors are so wretchedly bedimmed—now that blotches of
plastered wall dot the frescoes all over, like a mean reality
thrusting itself through life's brightest illusions,—the next best
artist to Cimabue or Giotto or Ghirlandaio or Pinturicchio,[2]
will be he that shall reverently cover their ruined masterpieces
with whitewash![3]

Kenyon, however, being an earnest student and critic of
Art, lingered long before these pathetic relics; and Donatello, in
his present phase of penitence, thought no time spent amiss
while he could be kneeling before an altar. Whenever they
found a cathedral, therefore, or a Gothic church, the two
travellers were of one mind to enter it. In some of these holy
edifices they saw pictures that time had not dimmed nor injured in the least, though they perhaps belonged to as old a
school of Art as any that were perishing around them. These

[2]For Giotto and Cimabue, see note 2, p. 208. Domenico Ghirlandaio
(1449–1494) taught Michelangelo and painted magnificent frescoes of his
contemporaries in Florence. Pinturicchio, "little painter," whose real name
was Bernardino di Betto, is known for his frescoes depicting the life of
Pope Pius II (fl. 1458–1464).

[3]Hawthorne is thinking here especially of the Cathedral in Assisi,
which did not impress him: "The ecclesiastics of old time did an excellent
thing in covering the interiors of their churches with brilliant frescos, thus
filling the holy places with saints and angels, and almost with the presence
of the Divinity. The modern ecclesiastics do the next best thing in ob-
literating the wretched remnants of what has had its day and done its
office. These frescos might be looked upon as the symbol of the living
spirit that made Catholicism a true religion, and glorified it as long as it
did live; now the glory and beauty have departed from one and the other"
(NB, pp. 242–243).

were the painted windows; and as often as he gazed at them the sculptor blessed the mediæval time, and its gorgeous contrivances of splendor; for surely the skill of man has never accomplished, nor his mind imagined, any other beauty or glory worthy to be compared with these.[4]

It is the special excellence of pictured glass, that the light, which falls merely on the outside of other pictures, is here interfused throughout the work; it illuminates the design, and invests it with a living radiance; and in requital the unfading colors transmute the common daylight into a miracle of richness and glory in its passage through the heavenly substance of the blessed and angelic shapes which throng the high-arched window.

"It is a woful thing," cried Kenyon, while one of these frail, yet enduring and fadeless pictures threw its hues on his face, and on the pavement of the church around him,—"a sad necessity that any Christian soul should pass from earth without once seeing an antique painted window, with the bright Italian sunshine glowing through it! There is no other such true symbol of the glories of the better world, where a celestial radiance will be inherent in all things and persons, and render each continually transparent to the sight of all."

"But what a horror it would be," said Donatello, sadly, "if there were a soul among them through which the light could not be transfused."

"Yes; and perhaps this is to be the punishment of sin," replied the sculptor; "not that it shall be made evident to the

---

[4]Cf. Hawthorne's comment on the painted windows of the Cathedral in Perugia: "We found the Cathedral very stately with its great arches, and darkly magnificent with the dim rich light coming through its painted windows, some of which are reckoned the most beautiful that the whole world has to show. The hues are far more brilliant than those of any painted glass I saw in England, and a great wheel window looks like a constellation of many-colored gems. The old English glass gets so smoky and dull with dust, that its pristine beauty cannot any longer be even imagined; nor did I imagine it till I saw these Italian windows" (*NB*, pp. 261–262).

universe, which can profit nothing by such knowledge, but that it shall insulate the sinner from all sweet society by rendering him impermeable to light, and, therefore, unrecognizable in the abode of heavenly simplicity and truth. Then, what remains for him, but the dreariness of infinite and eternal solitude."

"That would be a horrible destiny, indeed!" said Donatello.

His voice as he spoke the words had a hollow and dreary cadence, as if he anticipated some such frozen solitude for himself. A figure in a dark robe was lurking in the obscurity of a side-chapel close by, and made an impulsive movement forward, but hesitated as Donatello spoke again.

"But there might be a more miserable torture than to be solitary forever," said he. "Think of having a single companion in eternity, and instead of finding any consolation, or at all events variety of torture, to see your own weary, weary sin repeated in that inseparable soul."

"I think, my dear Count, you have never read Dante," observed Kenyon. "That idea is somewhat in his style, but I cannot help regretting that it came into your mind just then."

The dark-robed figure had shrunk back, and was quite lost to sight among the shadows of the chapel.

"There was an English poet," resumed Kenyon, turning again towards the window; "who speaks of the 'dim, religious light,'[5] transmitted through painted glass. I always admired this richly descriptive phrase; but, though he was once in Italy, I question whether Milton ever saw any but the dingy pictures in the dusty windows of English cathedrals, imperfectly shown by the gray English daylight. He would else have illuminated that word, 'dim,' with some epithet that should not chase away the dimness, yet should make it glow like a million

---

[5]And storied windows richly dight,
     Casting a dim religious light.
                    MILTON, *Il Penseroso*, ll. 159–160.

of rubies, sapphires, emeralds, and topazes. Is it not so with yonder window? The pictures are most brilliant in themselves, yet dim with tenderness and reverence, because God himself is shining through them."

"The pictures fill me with emotion, but not such as you seem to experience," said Donatello. "I tremble at those awful saints; and, most of all, at the figure above them. He glows with Divine wrath!"

"My dear friend," exclaimed Kenyon, "how strangely your eyes have transmuted the expression of the figure! It is divine love, not wrath."

"To my eyes," said Donatello, stubbornly, "it is wrath, not love! Each must interpret for himself."

The friends left the church, and, looking up from the exterior, at the window which they had just been contemplating within, nothing was visible but the merest outline of dusky shapes. Neither the individual likeness of saint, angel, nor Saviour, and far less the combined scheme and purport of the picture, could anywise be made out. That miracle of radiant art, thus viewed, was nothing better than an incomprehensible obscurity, without a gleam of beauty to induce the beholder to attempt unravelling it.

"And this," thought the sculptor, "is a most forcible emblem of the different aspect of religious truth and sacred story, as viewed from the warm interior of Belief, or from its cold and dreary outside. Christian Faith is a grand Cathedral, with divinely pictured windows. Standing without, you see no glory, nor can possibly imagine any; standing within, every ray of light reveals a harmony of unspeakable splendors."

After Kenyon and Donatello emerged from the church, however, they had better opportunity for acts of charity and mercy than for religious contemplation; being immediately surrounded by a swarm of beggars, who are the present possessors of Italy, and share the spoil of the stranger with the fleas and mosquitos, their formidable allies. These pests—the human ones—had hunted the two travellers at every stage of their journey. From village to village, ragged boys and girls kept almost under the horses' feet; hoary grandsires and grandams caught glimpses of their approach, and hobbled to intercept them at some point of vantage; blind men stared them out of countenance with their sightless orbs; women held up their unwashed babies; cripples displayed their wooden legs, their grievous scars, their dangling, boneless arms, their broken backs, their burden of a hump, or whatever infirmity or deformity Providence had assigned them for an inheritance. On the highest mountain summit—in the most shadowy ravine— there was a beggar waiting for them. In one small village, Kenyon had the curiosity to count merely how many children were crying, whining, and bellowing all at once for alms. They proved to be more than forty of as ragged and dirty little imps as any in the world; besides whom, all the wrinkled matrons, and most of the village maids, and not a few stalwart men, held out their hands grimly, piteously, or smilingly, in the forlorn hope of whatever trifle of coin might remain in pockets already so fearfully taxed. Had they been permitted, they would gladly have knelt down and worshipped the travellers, and have cursed them, without rising from their knees, if the expected boon failed to be awarded.

Yet they were not so miserably poor but that the grown people kept houses over their heads. In the way of food, they had, at least, vegetables in their little gardens, pigs and chickens to kill, eggs to fry into omelets with oil, wine to drink, and many other things to make life comfortable. As for the children, when no more small coin appeared to be forthcoming, they began to laugh and play, and turn heels over head, showing themselves jolly and vivacious brats, and evidently as well fed as need be. The truth is, the Italian peasantry look upon strangers as the almoners of Providence, and therefore feel no more shame in asking and receiving alms, than in availing themselves of providential bounties in whatever other form.

In accordance with his nature, Donatello was always exceedingly charitable to these ragged battalions, and appeared to derive a certain consolation from the prayers which many of them put up in his behalf. In Italy a copper coin of minute value will often make all the difference between a vindictive curse, (death by apoplexy being the favorite one,) mumbled in an old witch's toothless jaws, and a prayer from the same lips, so earnest that it would seem to reward the charitable soul with at least a puff of grateful breath to help him heavenward. Good wishes being so cheap, though possibly not very efficacious, and anathemas so exceedingly bitter, (even if the greater portion of their poison remain in the mouth that utters them,) it may be wise to expend some reasonable amount in the purchase of the former. Donatello invariably did so; and as he distributed his alms under the pictured window, of which we have been speaking, no less than seven ancient women lifted their hands and besought blessings on his head.

"Come," said the sculptor, rejoicing at the happier expression which he saw in his friend's face, "I think your steed will not stumble with you to-day. Each of these old dames looks as much like Horace's Atra Cura[6] as can well be conceived; but, though there are seven of them, they will make your burden on horseback lighter instead of heavier."[7]

"Are we to ride far?" asked the Count.

"A tolerable journey betwixt now and to-morrow noon," Kenyon replied; "for, at that hour, I purpose to be standing by the Pope's statue in the great square of Perugia."

[6]A schoolboy's tag from Horace:

> sed Timor et Minae
> scandunt eodem quo dominus, neque
> decedit aerata triremi et
> post equitem sedet atra Cura.

"But Fear and Threats climb to the selfsame spot the owner does, nor does black Care quit the brass-bound galley and even takes her seat behind the horseman." *Odes* III. i. Loeb Library translation, tr. C. E. Bennett (Cambridge, Mass.: Harvard University Press). Horace is extolling the simple life here and satirizing the material concerns of the wealthy.

[7]I.e., they will lighten Donatello's heavy purse.

CHAPTER 34. *Market-Day in Perugia*

Perugia, on its lofty hill-top, was reached by the two travellers before the sun had quite kissed away the early freshness of the morning. Since midnight, there had been a heavy rain, bringing infinite refreshment to the scene of verdure and fertility amid which this ancient civilization stands; insomuch that Kenyon loitered, when they came to the gray city-wall, and was loth to give up the prospect of the sunny wilderness that lay below. It was as green as England, and bright as Italy alone. There was the wide valley, sweeping down and spreading away on all sides from the weed-grown ramparts, and bounded afar by mountains, which lay asleep in the sun, with thin mists and silvery clouds floating about their heads by way of morning dreams.

"It lacks still two hours of noon," said the sculptor to his friend, as they stood under the arch of the gateway, waiting for their passports to be examined; "will you come with me to see some admirable frescoes by Perugino?[1] There is a hall in the Exchange, of no great magnitude, but covered with what must have been (at the time it was painted) such magnificence and beauty as the world had not elsewhere to show."

"It depresses me to look at old frescoes," responded the Count; "it is a pain, yet not enough of a pain to answer as a penance."

[1]Literally, "he of Perugia," Umbrian painter (*ca.* 1445–1523) whose real name was Pietro di Christoforo Vannucci. He painted frescoes for the Sistine Chapel in Rome, decorated the Exchange in Perugia, and taught Raphael, who far surpassed him in fresco painting.

"Will you look at some pictures by Fra Angelico[2] in the Church of San Domenico?" asked Kenyon; "they are full of religious sincerity. When one studies them faithfully, it is like holding a conversation about heavenly things with a tender and devout-minded man."

"You have shown me some of Fra Angelico's pictures, I remember," answered Donatello; "his angels look as if they had never taken a flight out of heaven; and his saints seem to have been born saints, and always to have lived so. Young maidens, and all innocent persons, I doubt not, may find great delight and profit in looking at such holy pictures. But they are not for me."

"Your criticism, I fancy, has great moral depth," replied Kenyon; "and I see in it the reason why Hilda so highly appreciates Fra Angelico's pictures. Well; we will let all such matters pass for to-day, and stroll about this fine old city till noon."

They wandered to and fro, accordingly, and lost themselves among the strange, precipitate passages, which, in Perugia, are called streets. Some of them are like caverns, being arched all over, and plunging down abruptly towards an unknown darkness; which, when you have fathomed its depths, admits you to a daylight that you scarcely hoped to behold again. Here they met shabby men, and the careworn wives and mothers of the people, some of whom guided children in leading-strings through those dim and antique thoroughfares, where a hundred generations had passed before the little feet of to-day began to tread them. Thence they climbed upward again, and came to the level plateau, on the summit of the hill, where are situated the grand piazza and the principal public edifices.

[2]Dominican brother (1387–1455), the greatest of the early Italian painters. He painted religious subjects at the Dominican friary in Fiesole, outside Florence. His best-known work is probably *The Adoration of the Magi*, on which he collaborated with Fra Lippo Lippi (*ca.* 1406–1469). The painting hangs in the National Gallery, Washington, D.C.

It happened to be market-day in Perugia. The great square, therefore, presented a far more vivacious spectacle than would have been witnessed in it at any other time of the week, though not so lively as to overcome the gray solemnity of the architectural portion of the scene. In the shadow of the cathedral and other old Gothic structures (seeking shelter from the sunshine that fell across the rest of the piazza) was a crowd of people, engaged as buyers or sellers in the petty traffic of a country-fair. Dealers had erected booths and stalls on the pavement, and overspread them with scanty awnings, beneath which they stood, vociferously crying their merchandise; such as shoes, hats and caps, yarn stockings, cheap jewelry and cutlery, books, chiefly little volumes of a religious character, and a few French novels; toys, tin-ware, old iron, cloth, rosaries of beads, crucifixes, cakes, biscuits, sugar-plums, and innumerable little odds and ends, which we see no object in advertising. Baskets of grapes, figs, and pears, stood on the ground. Donkeys, bearing panniers stuffed out with kitchen vegetables, and requiring an ample road-way, roughly shouldered aside the throng.

Crowded as the square was, a juggler found room to spread out a white cloth upon the pavement, and cover it with cups, plates, balls, cards,—the whole material of his magic, in short, —wherewith he proceeded to work miracles under the noonday sun. An organ-grinder at one point, and a clarion and a flute at another, accomplished what they could towards filling the wide space with tuneful noise. Their small uproar, however, was nearly drowned by the multitudinous voices of the people, bargaining, quarrelling, laughing, and babbling copiously at random; for the briskness of the mountain atmosphere, or some other cause, made everybody so loquacious that more words were wasted in Perugia on this one market-day, than the noisiest piazza of Rome would utter in a month.

Through all this petty tumult, which kept beguiling one's eyes and upper strata of thought, it was delightful to catch glimpses of the grand old architecture that stood around the square. The life of the flitting moment, existing in the antique shell of an age gone by, has a fascination which we do not find in either the past or present, taken by themselves. It might seem irreverent to make the gray cathedral and the tall, time-worn palaces echo back the exuberant vociferation of the market; but they did so, and caused the sound to assume a kind of poetic rhythm, and themselves looked only the more majestic for their condescension.

On one side, there was an immense edifice devoted to public purposes, with an antique gallery, and a range of arched and stone-mullioned windows, running along its front; and by way of entrance it had a central Gothic arch, elaborately wreathed around with sculptured semicircles, within which the spectator was aware of a stately and impressive gloom. Though merely the municipal council house and exchange of a decayed country town, this structure was worthy to have held in one portion of it the parliament-hall of a nation, and in the other, the state apartments of its ruler. On another side of the square rose the mediæval front of the cathedral, where the imagination of a Gothic architect had long ago flowered out indestructibly, achieving, in the first place, a grand design, and then covering it with such abundant detail of ornament, that the magnitude of the work seemed less a miracle than its minuteness. You would suppose that he must have softened the stone into wax, until his most delicate fancies were modelled in the pliant material, and then had hardened it to stone again. The whole was a vast, black-letter page of the richest and quaintest poetry. In fit keeping with all this old magnificence, was a great marble fountain, where again the Gothic imagination showed its overflow and gratuity of device in the manifold sculptures which it lavished as freely as the water did its shifting shapes.

Besides the two venerable structures which we have described there were lofty palaces, perhaps of as old a date, rising story above story, and adorned with balconies, whence, hundreds of years ago, the princely occupants had been accustomed to gaze down at the sports, business, and popular assemblages of the piazza. And, beyond all question, they thus witnessed the erection of a bronze statue, which, three centuries since, was placed on the pedestal that it still occupies.

"I never come to Perugia," said Kenyon, "without spending as much time as I can spare in studying yonder statue of Pope Julius the Third.[3] Those sculptors of the middle age have fitter lessons for the professors of my art than we can find in the Grecian masterpieces. They belong to our Christian civilization; and, being earnest works, they always express something which we do not get from the antique. Will you look at it?"

"Willingly," replied the Count, "for I see, even so far off, that the statue is bestowing a benediction, and there is a feeling in my heart that I may be permitted to share it."

Remembering the similar idea which Miriam a short time before had expressed, the sculptor smiled hopefully at the coincidence. They made their way through the throng of the market-place, and approached close to the iron railing that protected the pedestal of the statue.

It was the figure of a pope, arrayed in his pontifical robes, and crowned with the tiara. He sat in a bronze chair, elevated high above the pavement, and seemed to take kindly yet authoritative cognizance of the busy scene which was at that moment passing before his eyes. His right hand was raised and spread abroad, as if in the act of shedding forth a benediction, which every man—so broad, so wise, and so serenely affectionate was the bronze pope's regard—might hope to feel quietly descending upon the need, or the distress, that he had closest at his heart. The statue had life and observation in it, as well as patriarchal majesty. An imaginative spectator could not but be impressed with the idea that this benignly awful representative of divine and human authority might rise from his brazen chair, should any great public exigency demand

[3]See illustration, p. 313, and note 3, p. 276.

his interposition, and encourage or restrain the people by his gesture, or even by prophetic utterances worthy of so grand a presence.

And, in the long, calm intervals, amid the quiet lapse of ages, the pontiff watched the daily turmoil around his seat, listening with majestic patience to the market cries, and all the petty uproar that awoke the echoes of the stately old piazza. He was the enduring friend of these men, and of their forefathers and children,—the familiar face of generations.

"The pope's blessing, methinks, has fallen upon you," observed the sculptor, looking at his friend.

In truth, Donatello's countenance indicated a healthier spirit than while he was brooding in his melancholy tower. The change of scene, the breaking up of custom, the fresh flow of incidents, the sense of being homeless, and therefore free, had done something for our poor Faun; these circumstances had at least promoted a reaction, which might else have been slower in its progress. Then, no doubt, the bright day, the gay spectacle of the market-place, and the sympathetic exhilaration of so many people's cheerfulness, had each their suitable effect on a temper naturally prone to be glad. Perhaps, too, he was magnetically conscious of a presence that formerly sufficed to make him happy. Be the cause what it might, Donatello's eyes shone with a serene and hopeful expression, while looking upward at the bronze pope, to whose widely diffused blessing, it may be, he attributed all this good influence.

"Yes, my dear friend," said he, in reply to the sculptor's remark, "I feel the blessing upon my spirit."

"It is wonderful," said Kenyon, with a smile, "wonderful and delightful to think how long a good man's beneficence may be potent, even after his death. How great, then, must have been the efficacy of this excellent pontiff's blessing while he was alive!"

"I have heard," remarked the Count, "that there was a brazen image set up in the Wilderness, the sight of which

healed the Israelites of their poisonous and rankling wounds.[4]
If it be the blessed Virgin's pleasure, why should not this
holy image before us do me equal good? A wound has long
been rankling in my soul, and filling it with poison."

"I did wrong to smile," answered Kenyon. "It is not for
me to limit Providence in its operations on man's spirit."

While they stood talking, the clock of the neighboring
cathedral told the hour, with twelve reverberating strokes,
which it flung down upon the crowded market-place, as if
warning one and all to take advantage of the bronze pontiff's
benediction, or of Heaven's blessing, however proffered, before
the opportunity were lost.

"High noon," said the sculptor. "It is Miriam's hour!"

[4]The Israelites murmured against God and were stung by poisonous
snakes. Repenting of their sin, they besought Moses to heal them. The
Lord had him fashion a serpent of bronze, attached to a rod; whosoever
was touched by the rod was healed of his snake-bite. See Numbers 21:4–9.

CHAPTER 35. *The Bronze Pontiff's Benediction*

When the last of the twelve strokes had fallen from the cathedral clock, Kenyon threw his eyes over the busy scene of the market-place, expecting to discern Miriam somewhere in the crowd. He looked next towards the cathedral itself, where it was reasonable to imagine that she might have taken shelter, while awaiting her appointed time. Seeing no trace of her in either direction, his eyes came back from their quest somewhat disappointed, and rested on a figure which was leaning, like Donatello and himself, on the iron balustrade that surrounded the statue. Only a moment before, they two had been alone.

It was the figure of a woman, with her head bowed on her hands, as if she deeply felt—what we have been endeavoring to convey into our feeble description—the benign and awe-inspiring influence which the pontiff's statue exercises upon a sensitive spectator. No matter though it were modelled for a Catholic chief priest, the desolate heart, whatever be its religion, recognizes in that image the likeness of a father.

"Miriam," said the sculptor, with a tremor in his voice, "is it yourself?"

"It is I," she replied; "I am faithful to my engagement, though with many fears."

She lifted her head, and revealed to Kenyon—revealed to Donatello likewise—the well-remembered features of Miriam. They were pale and worn, but distinguished even now, though less gorgeously, by a beauty that might be imagined bright enough to glimmer with its own light in a dim cathedral aisle, and had no need to shrink from the severer test of the mid-day sun. But she seemed tremulous, and hardly able to go through with a scene which at a distance she had found courage to undertake.

"You are most welcome, Miriam!" said the sculptor, seeking to afford her the encouragement which he saw she so greatly required. "I have a hopeful trust that the result of this interview will be propitious. Come; let me lead you to Donatello."

"No, Kenyon, no!" whispered Miriam, shrinking back; "unless of his own accord he speaks my name—unless he bids me stay—no word shall ever pass between him and me. It is not that I take upon me to be proud at this late hour. Among other feminine qualities, I threw away my pride when Hilda cast me off."

"If not pride, what else restrains you?" Kenyon asked, a little angry at her unseasonable scruples, and also at this half-complaining reference to Hilda's just severity. "After daring so much, it is no time for fear! If we let him part from you without a word, your opportunity of doing him inestimable good is lost forever."

"True; it will be lost forever!" repeated Miriam, sadly. "But, dear friend, will it be my fault? I willingly fling my woman's pride at his feet. But—do you not see?—his heart must be left freely to its own decision whether to recognize me, because on his voluntary choice depends the whole question whether my devotion will do him good or harm. Except he feel an infinite need of me, I am a burden and fatal obstruction to him!"

"Take your own course, then, Miriam," said Kenyon; "and doubtless, the crisis being what it is, your spirit is better instructed for its emergencies than mine."

While the foregoing words passed between them they had withdrawn a little from the immediate vicinity of the statue, so as to be out of Donatello's hearing. Still, however, they were beneath the pontiff's outstretched hand; and Miriam, with her beauty and her sorrow, looked up into his benignant face, as if she had come thither for his pardon and paternal affection, and despaired of so vast a boon.

Meanwhile, she had not stood thus long in the public square of Perugia, without attracting the observation of many eyes. With their quick sense of beauty, these Italians had recognized her loveliness, and spared not to take their fill of gazing at it; though their native gentleness and courtesy made their homage far less obtrusive than that of Germans, French, or Anglo-Saxons might have been. It is not improbable that Miriam had planned this momentous interview, on so public a spot and at high noon, with an eye to the sort of protection that would be thrown over it by a multitude of eye-witnesses. In circumstances of profound feeling and passion, there is often a sense that too great a seclusion cannot be endured; there is an indefinite dread of being quite alone with the object of our deepest interest. The species of solitude that a crowd harbors within itself, is felt to be preferable, in certain conditions of the heart, to the remoteness of a desert or the depths of an untrodden wood. Hatred, love, or whatever kind of too intense emotion, or even indifference, where emotion has once been, instinctively seeks to interpose some barrier between itself and the corresponding passion in another breast. This, we suspect, was what Miriam had thought of, in coming to the thronged piazza; partly this, and partly, as she said, her superstition that the benign statue held good influences in store.

But Donatello remained leaning against the balustrade. She dared not glance towards him, to see whether he were pale and agitated, or calm as ice. Only, she knew that the moments were fleetly lapsing away, and that his heart must call her soon, or the voice would never reach her. She turned quite away from him and spoke again to the sculptor.

"I have wished to meet you," said she, "for more than one reason. News have come to me respecting a dear friend of ours. Nay, not of mine! I dare not call her a friend of mine, though once the dearest."

"Do you speak of Hilda?" exclaimed Kenyon, with quick alarm. "Has anything befallen her? When I last heard of her, she was still in Rome, and well."

"Hilda remains in Rome," replied Miriam, "nor is she

ill as regards physical health, though much depressed in spirits. She lives quite alone in her dove-cote; not a friend near her, not one in Rome, which, you know, is deserted by all but its native inhabitants. I fear for her health, if she continue long in such solitude, with despondency preying on her mind. I tell you this, knowing the interest which the rare beauty of her character has awakened in you."

"I will go to Rome!" said the sculptor, in great emotion. "Hilda has never allowed me to manifest more than a friendly regard; but, at least, she cannot prevent my watching over her at a humble distance. I will set out this very hour."

"Do not leave us now!" whispered Miriam, imploringly, and laying her hand on his arm. "One moment more! Ah; he has no word for me!"

"Miriam!" said Donatello.

Though but a single word, and the first that he had spoken, its tone was a warrant of the sad and tender depth from which it came. It told Miriam things of infinite importance, and, first of all, that he still loved her. The sense of their mutual crime had stunned, but not destroyed the vitality of his affection; it was therefore indestructible. That tone, too, bespoke an altered and deepened character; it told of a vivified intellect, and of spiritual instruction that had come through sorrow and remorse; so that instead of the wild boy, the thing of sportive, animal nature, the sylvan Faun—here was now the man of feeling and intelligence.

She turned towards him, while his voice still reverberated in the depths of her soul.

"You have called me!" said she.

"Because my deepest heart has need of you!" he replied. "Forgive, Miriam, the coldness, the hardness with which I parted from you! I was bewildered with strange horror and gloom."

"Alas! and it was I that brought it on you," said she. "What repentance, what self-sacrifice, can atone for that infinite wrong? There was something so sacred in the innocent and joyous life which you were leading! A happy person is such an unaccustomed and holy creature, in this sad world! And, encountering so rare a being, and gifted with the power of sympathy with his sunny life, it was my doom, mine, to bring him within the limits of sinful, sorrowful mortality! Bid me depart, Donatello! Fling me off! No good, through my agency, can follow upon such a mighty evil!"

"Miriam," said he, "our lot lies together. Is it not so? Tell me, in Heaven's name, if it be otherwise?"

Donatello's conscience was evidently perplexed with doubt, whether the communion of a crime, such as they two were jointly stained with, ought not to stifle all the instinctive motions of their hearts, impelling them one towards the other. Miriam, on the other hand, remorsefully questioned with herself, whether the misery, already accruing from her influence, should not warn her to withdraw from his path. In this momentous interview therefore, two souls were groping for each other in the darkness of guilt and sorrow, and hardly were bold enough to grasp the cold hands that they found.

The sculptor stood watching the scene with earnest sympathy.

"It seems irreverent," said he, at length; "intrusive, if not irreverent, for a third person to thrust himself between the two solely concerned in a crisis like the present. Yet, possibly as a bystander, though a deeply interested one, I may discern somewhat of truth that is hidden from you both—may, at least, interpret or suggest some ideas which you might not so readily convey to each other."

"Speak!" said Miriam; "we confide in you."

"Speak!" said Donatello. "You are true and upright."

"I well know," rejoined Kenyon, "that I shall not succeed in uttering the few, deep words which, in this matter, as in all others, include the absolute truth. But, here, Miriam, is one whom a terrible misfortune has begun to educate; it has taken him, and through your agency, out of a wild and happy state, which, within circumscribed limits, gave him joys that he cannot elsewhere find on earth. On his behalf, you have incurred a responsibility which you cannot fling aside.

And here, Donatello, is one whom Providence marks out as intimately connected with your destiny. The mysterious process, by which our earthly life instructs us for another state of being, was begun for you by her. She has rich gifts of heart and mind, a suggestive power, a magnetic influence, a sympathetic knowledge, which, wisely and religiously exercised, are what your condition needs. She possesses what you require, and, with utter self-devotion, will use it for your good. The bond betwixt you, therefore, is a true one, and never—except by Heaven's own act—should be rent asunder."

"Ah; he has spoken the truth!" cried Donatello, grasping Miriam's hand.

"The very truth, dear friend," cried Miriam.

"But take heed," resumed the sculptor, anxious not to violate the integrity of his own conscience. "Take heed; for you love one another, and yet your bond is twined with such black threads, that you must never look upon it as identical with the ties that unite other loving souls. It is for mutual support; it is for one another's final good; it is for effort, for sacrifice, but not for earthly happiness. If such be your motive, believe me, friends, it were better to relinquish each other's hands at this sad moment. There would be no holy sanction on your wedded life."

"None," said Donatello, shuddering. "We know it well."

"None," repeated Miriam, also shuddering. "United—miserably entangled with me, rather—by a bond of guilt, our union might be for eternity, indeed, and most intimate; but, through all that endless duration, I should be conscious of his horror."

"Not for earthly bliss, therefore," said Kenyon, "but for mutual elevation, and encouragement towards a severe and painful life, you take each other's hands. And if, out of toil, sacrifice, prayer, penitence, and earnest effort towards right things, there comes, at length, a sombre and thoughtful happiness, taste it, and thank Heaven! So that you live not for it—so that it be a wayside flower, springing along a path that leads to higher ends—it will be Heaven's gracious gift, and a token that it recognizes your union here below."

"Have you no more to say?" asked Miriam, earnestly. "There is matter of sorrow and lofty consolation strangely mingled in your words."

"Only this, dear Miriam," said the sculptor; "If ever, in your lives, the highest duty should require from either of you the sacrifice of the other, meet the occasion without shrinking. This is all."[1]

While Kenyon spoke, Donatello had evidently taken in the ideas which he propounded, and had ennobled them by the sincerity of his reception. His aspect unconsciously assumed a dignity, which, elevating his former beauty, accorded with the change that had long been taking place in his interior self. He was a man, revolving grave and deep thoughts in his breast. He still held Miriam's hand; and there they stood, the beautiful man, the beautiful woman, united forever, as they felt, in the presence of these thousand eye-witnesses, who gazed so curiously at the unintelligible scene. Doubtless, the crowd recognized them as lovers, and fancied this a betrothal that was destined to result in life-long happiness. And, possibly, it might be so. Who can tell where happiness may come; or where, though an expected guest, it may never show its face? Perhaps—shy, subtle thing—it had crept into this sad marriage-bond, when the partners would have trembled at its presence as a crime.

"Farewell!" said Kenyon, "I go to Rome."

"Farewell, true friend!" said Miriam.

"Farewell!" said Donatello too. "May you be happy. You have no guilt to make you shrink from happiness."

At this moment it so chanced that all the three friends by one impulse glanced upward at the statue of Pope Julius; and there was the majestic figure stretching out the hand of

[1]Hawthorne is drawing a parallel between Kenyon and the Bronze Pontiff; his words here echo the words of the marriage ceremony.

Alinari-Art Reference Bureau

Pope Julius III (V. Danti, 1555)
THE MARKETPLACE, PERUGIA

benediction over them, and bending down upon this guilty and repentant pair its visage of grand benignity. There is a singular effect oftentimes when, out of the midst of engrossing thought and deep absorption, we suddenly look up, and catch a glimpse of external objects. We seem at such moments to look farther and deeper into them, than by any premeditated observation; it is as if they met our eyes alive, and with all their hidden meaning on the surface, but grew again inanimate and inscrutable the instant that they become aware of our glances. So now at that unexpected glimpse, Miriam, Donatello, and the sculptor, all three imagined that they beheld the bronze pontiff endowed with spiritual life. A blessing was felt descending upon them from his outstretched hand; he approved by look and gesture the pledge of a deep union that had passed under his auspices.

CHAPTER 36. *Hilda's Tower*

When we have once known Rome, and left her where she lies, like a long decaying corpse, retaining a trace of the noble shape it was, but with accumulated dust and a fungous growth overspreading all its more admirable features—left her in utter weariness, no doubt, of her narrow, crooked, intricate streets, so uncomfortably paved with little squares of lava that to tread over them is a penitential pilgrimage, so indescribably ugly, moreover, so cold, so alley-like, into which the sun never falls, and where a chill wind forces its deadly breath into our lungs—left her, tired of the sight of those immense seven-storied, yellow-washed hovels, or call them palaces, where all that is dreary in domestic life seems magnified and multiplied, and weary of climbing those staircases, which ascend from a ground-floor of cook-shops, cobblers' stalls, stables, and regiments of cavalry, to a middle region of princes, cardinals, and ambassadors, and an upper tier of artists, just beneath the unattainable sky—left her, worn out with shivering at the cheerless and smoky fireside by day, and feasting with our own substance the ravenous little populace of a Roman bed at night—left her, sick at heart of Italian trickery, which has uprooted whatever faith in man's integrity had endured till now, and sick at stomach of sour bread, sour wine, rancid butter, and bad cookery, needlessly bestowed on evil meats—left her, disgusted with the pretence of holiness and the reality of nastiness, each equally omnipresent—left her, half lifeless from the languid atmosphere, the vital principle of which has been used up long ago, or corrupted by myriads of slaughters—left her, crushed down in spirit with the desolation of her ruin, and the hopelessness of her future

—left her, in short, hating her with all our might, and adding our individual curse to the infinite anathema which her old crimes have unmistakably brought down,—when we have left Rome in such mood as this, we are astonished by the discovery, by-and-by, that our heartstrings have mysteriously attached themselves to the Eternal City, and are drawing us thitherward again, as if it were more familiar, more intimately our home, than even the spot where we were born.[1]

It is with a kindred sentiment, that we now follow the course of our story back through the Flaminian Gate, and, threading our way to the Via Portoghese, climb the staircase to the upper chamber of the tower, where we last saw Hilda.

Hilda all along intended to pass the summer in Rome; for she had laid out many high and delightful tasks, which she could the better complete while her favorite haunts were deserted by the multitude that thronged them, throughout the winter and early spring. Nor did she dread the summer atmosphere, although generally held to be so pestilential. She had already made trial of it, two years before, and found no worse effect than a kind of dreamy languor, which was dissipated by the first cool breezes that came with autumn. The thickly populated centre of the city, indeed, is never affected by the feverish influence that lies in wait in the Campagna, like a besieging foe, and nightly haunts those beautiful lawns and woodlands, around the suburban villas, just at the season when they most resemble Paradise. What the flaming sword was to the first Eden, such is the malaria to these sweet gardens and groves. We may wander through them, of an afternoon, it is true, but they cannot be made a home and a reality, and to sleep among them is death. They are but illusions, therefore, like the show of gleaming waters and shadowy foliage in a desert.

[1]This remarkable opening sentence summarizes Hawthorne's ambivalent attitude towards Rome and the Church and reveals the deep fascination which Rome held for him.

But Rome, within the walls, at this dreaded season, enjoys its festal days, and makes itself merry with characteristic and hereditary pastimes, for which its broad piazzas afford abundant room. It leads its own life with a freer spirit, now that the artists and foreign visitors are scattered abroad. No bloom, perhaps, would be visible in a cheek that should be unvisited, throughout the summer, by more invigorating winds than any within fifty miles of the city; no bloom, but yet, if the mind kept its healthy energy, a subdued and colorless well-being. There was consequently little risk in Hilda's purpose to pass the summer days in the galleries of Roman palaces, and her nights in that aërial chamber, whither the heavy breath of the city and its suburbs could not aspire. It would probably harm her no more than it did the white doves, who sought the same high atmosphere at sunset, and, when morning came, flew down into the narrow streets, about their daily business, as Hilda likewise did.

With the Virgin's aid and blessing, which might be hoped for even by a heretic, who so religiously lit the lamp before her shrine, the New England girl would sleep securely in her old Roman tower, and go forth on her pictorial pilgrimages without dread or peril. In view of such a summer, Hilda had anticipated many months of lonely, but unalloyed enjoyment. Not that she had a churlish disinclination to society, or needed to be told that we taste one intellectual pleasure twice, and with double the result, when we taste it with a friend. But, keeping a maiden heart within her bosom, she rejoiced in the freedom that enabled her still to choose her own sphere, and dwell in it, if she pleased, without another inmate.

Her expectation, however, of a delightful summer was wofully disappointed. Even had she formed no previous plan of remaining there, it is improbable that Hilda would have gathered energy to stir from Rome. A torpor, heretofore unknown to her vivacious though quiet temperament, had possessed itself of the poor girl, like a half-dead serpent knotting its cold, inextricable wreaths about her limbs. It was that peculiar despair, that chill and heavy misery, which only the innocent can experience, although it possesses many of the gloomy characteristics that mark a sense of guilt. It was that heart-sickness, which, it is to be hoped, we may all of us have been pure enough to feel, once in our lives, but the capacity for which is usually exhausted early, and perhaps with a single agony. It was that dismal certainty of the existence of evil in the world, which, though we may fancy ourselves fully assured of the sad mystery long before, never becomes a portion of our practical belief until it takes substance and reality from the sin of some guide, whom we have deeply trusted and revered, or some friend whom we have dearly loved.

When that knowledge comes, it is as if a cloud had suddenly gathered over the morning light; so dark a cloud, that there seems to be no longer any sunshine behind it or above it. The character of our individual beloved one having invested itself with all the attributes of right,—that one friend being to us the symbol and representative of whatever is good and true,—when he falls, the effect is almost as if the sky fell with him, bringing down in chaotic ruin the columns that upheld our faith. We struggle forth again, no doubt, bruised and bewildered. We stare wildly about us, and discover—or, it may be, we never make the discovery—that it was not actually the sky that has tumbled down, but merely a frail structure of our own rearing, which never rose higher than the house-tops, and has fallen because we founded it on nothing. But the crash, and the affright and trouble, are as overwhelming, for the time, as if the catastrophe involved the whole moral world. Remembering these things, let them suggest one generous motive for walking heedfully amid the defilement of earthly ways! Let us reflect, that the highest path is pointed out by the pure Ideal of those who look up to us, and who, if we tread less loftily, may never look so high again.

Hilda's situation was made infinitely more wretched by

the necessity of confining all her trouble within her own consciousness. To this innocent girl, holding the knowledge of Miriam's crime within her tender and delicate soul, the effect was almost the same as if she herself had participated in the guilt. Indeed, partaking the human nature of those who could perpetrate such deeds, she felt her own spotlessness impugned.

Had there been but a single friend—or, not a friend, since friends were no longer to be confided in, after Miriam had betrayed her trust—but, had there been any calm, wise mind, any sympathizing intelligence; or, if not these, any dull, half-listening ear into which she might have flung the dreadful secret, as into an echoless cavern—what a relief would have ensued! But this awful loneliness! It enveloped her whithersoever she went. It was a shadow in the sunshine of festal days; a mist between her eyes and the pictures at which she strove to look; a chill dungeon, which kept her in its gray twilight and fed her with its unwholesome air, fit only for a criminal to breathe and pine in! She could not escape from it. In the effort to do so, straying farther into the intricate passages of our nature, she stumbled, ever and again, over this deadly idea of mortal guilt.

Poor sufferer for another's sin! Poor wellspring of a virgin's heart, into which a murdered corpse had casually fallen, and whence it could not be drawn forth again, but lay there, day after day, night after night, tainting its sweet atmosphere with the scent of crime and ugly death!

The strange sorrow that had befallen Hilda did not fail to impress its mysterious seal upon her face, and to make itself perceptible to sensitive observers in her manner and carriage. A young Italian artist, who frequented the same galleries which Hilda haunted, grew deeply interested in her expression. One day, while she stood before Leonardo da Vinci's picture of Joanna of Arragon,[2] but evidently without seeing it,—for,

[2]Joanna of Arragon is Joan of Arc. The painting hangs in the Sciarra Palace, where Hawthorne saw it in March of 1858.

though it had attracted her eyes, a fancied resemblance to Miriam had immediately drawn away her thoughts,—this artist drew a hasty sketch which he afterwards elaborated into a finished portrait. It represented Hilda as gazing with sad and earnest horror at a blood-spot which she seemed just then to have discovered on her white robe. The picture attracted considerable notice. Copies of an engraving from it may still be found in the print-shops along the Corso. By many connoisseurs, the idea of the face was supposed to have been suggested by the portrait of Beatrice Cenci;[3] and, in fact, there was a look somewhat similar to poor Beatrice's forlorn gaze out of the dreary isolation and remoteness, in which a terrible doom had involved a tender soul. But the modern artist strenuously upheld the originality of his own picture, as well as the stainless purity of its subject, and chose to call it—and was laughed at for his pains—"Innocence, dying of a blood-stain!"

"Your picture, Signor Panini, does you credit," remarked the picture-dealer, who had bought it of the young man for fifteen scudi, and afterwards sold it for ten times the sum; "but it would be worth a better price if you had given it a more intelligible title. Looking at the face and expression of this fair signorina, we seem to comprehend readily enough, that she is undergoing one or another of those troubles of the heart to which young ladies are but too liable. But what is this blood-stain? And what has innocence to do with it? Has she stabbed her perfidious lover with a bodkin?"[4]

"She! she commit a crime!" cried the young artist. "Can you look at the innocent anguish in her face, and ask that question? No; but, as I read the mystery, a man has been slain in her presence, and the blood, spirting accidentally on her white robe, has made a stain which eats into her life."

"Then, in the name of her patron saint," exclaimed the picture-dealer, "why don't she get the robe made white again

[3]See note 1, p. 64.
[4]A dagger. 15 scudi would have been the equivalent of $4.00 in 1860.

at the expense of a few baiocchi[5] to her washer-woman? No, no, my dear Panini. The picture being now my property, I shall call it 'The Signorina's Vengeance.' She has stabbed her lover overnight, and is repenting it betimes the next morning. So interpreted, the picture becomes an intelligible and very natural representation of a not uncommon fact."

Thus coarsely does the world translate all finer griefs that meet its eye. It is more a coarse world than an unkind one.

But Hilda sought nothing either from the world's delicacy or its pity, and never dreamed of its misinterpretations. Her doves often flew in through the windows of the tower, winged messengers, bringing her what sympathy they could, and uttering soft, tender, and complaining sounds, deep in their bosoms, which soothed the girl more than a distincter utterance might. And sometimes Hilda moaned quietly among the doves, teaching her voice to accord with theirs, and thus finding a temporary relief from the burden of her incommunicable sorrow, as if a little portion of it, at least, had been told to these innocent friends, and understood, and pitied.

When she trimmed the lamp before the Virgin's shrine, Hilda gazed at the sacred image, and, rude as was the workmanship, beheld, or fancied, expressed with the quaint, powerful simplicty which sculptors sometimes had five hundred years ago, a woman's tenderness responding to her gaze. If she knelt, if she prayed, if her oppressed heart besought the sympathy of divine womanhood afar in bliss, but not remote, because forever humanized by the memory of mortal griefs, was Hilda to be blamed? It was not a Catholic kneeling at an idolatrous shrine, but a child lifting its tear-stained face to seek comfort from a mother.

[5]Small Roman coins worth a half-penny each.

CHAPTER 37. *The Emptiness of Picture-Galleries*

Hilda descended, day by day, from her dove-cote, and went to one or another of the great, old palaces,—the Pamfili Doria, the Corsini, the Sciarra, the Borghese, the Colonna,—where the door-keepers knew her well, and offered her a kindly greeting. But they shook their heads and sighed, on observing the languid step with which the poor girl toiled up the grand marble staircases. There was no more of that cheery alacrity with which she used to flit upward, as if her doves had lent her their wings, nor of that glow of happy spirits which had been wont to set the tarnished gilding of the picture-frames and the shabby splendor of the furniture all a-glimmer, as she hastened to her congenial and delightful toil.

An old German artist, whom she often met in the galleries, once laid a paternal hand on Hilda's head, and bade her go back to her own country.

"Go back soon," he said, with kindly freedom and directness, "or you will go never more. And, if you go not, why, at least, do you spend the whole summer-time in Rome? The air has been breathed too often, in so many thousand years, and is not wholesome for a little foreign flower like you, my child, a delicate wood-anemone from the western forest-land."

"I have no task nor duty anywhere but here," replied Hilda. "The old masters will not set me free!"

"Ah, those old masters!" cried the veteran artist, shaking his head. "They are a tyrannous race! You will find them of too mighty a spirit to be dealt with, for long together, by the slender hand, the fragile mind, and the delicate heart, of a young girl. Remember that Raphael's genius wore out that divinest painter before half his life was lived. Since you feel his influence powerfully enough to reproduce his miracles so well, it will assuredly consume you like a flame."

"That might have been my peril once," answered Hilda. "It is not so now."

"Yes, fair maiden, you stand in that peril now!" insisted the kind old man; and he added, smiling, yet in a melancholy vein, and with a German grotesqueness of idea, "Some fine morning, I shall come to the Pinacotheca of the Vatican, with my palette and my brushes, and shall look for my little American artist that sees into the very heart of the grand pictures! And what shall I behold? A heap of white ashes on the marble floor, just in front of the divine Raphael's picture of the Madonna di Foligno! Nothing more, upon my word! The fire, which the poor child feels so fervently, will have gone into her innermost, and burnt her quite up!"

"It would be a happy martyrdom!" said Hilda, faintly smiling. "But I am far from being worthy of it. What troubles me much, among other troubles, is quite the reverse of what you think. The old masters hold me here, it is true, but they no longer warm me with their influence. It is not flame consuming, but torpor chilling me, that helps to make me wretched."

"Perchance, then," said the German, looking keenly at her, "Raphael has a rival in your heart? He was your first-love; but young maidens are not always constant, and one flame is sometimes extinguished by another!"

Hilda shook her head, and turned away.

She had spoken the truth, however, in alleging that torpor, rather than fire, was what she had now to dread. In these gloomy days that had befallen her, it was a great additional calamity that she felt conscious of the present dimness of an insight, which she once possessed in more than ordinary measure. She had lost—and she trembled lest it should have departed forever—the faculty of appreciating those great works of art, which heretofore had made so large a portion of her happiness. It was no wonder.

A picture, however admirable the painter's art, and wonderful his power, requires of the spectator a surrender of himself, in due proportion with the miracle which has been wrought. Let the canvas glow as it may, you must look with the eye of faith, or its highest excellence escapes you. There is always the necessity of helping out the painter's art with your own resources of sensibility and imagination. Not that these qualities shall really add anything to what the master has effected; but they must be put so entirely under his control, and work along with him to such an extent, that, in a different mood, when you are cold and critical, instead of sympathetic, you will be apt to fancy that the loftier merits of the picture were of your own dreaming, not of his creating.

Like all revelations of the better life, the adequate perception of a great work of art demands a gifted simplicity of vision. In this, and in her self-surrender, and the depth and tenderness of her sympathy, had lain Hilda's remarkable power as a copyist of the old masters. And now that her capacity of emotion was choked up with a horrible experience, it inevitably followed that she should seek in vain, among those friends so venerated and beloved, for the marvels which they had heretofore shown her. In spite of a reverence that lingered longer than her recognition, their poor worshipper became almost an infidel, and sometimes doubted whether the pictorial art be not altogether a delusion.

For the first time in her life, Hilda now grew acquainted with that icy demon of weariness, who haunts great picture-galleries. He is a plausible Mephistopheles,[1] and possesses the

[1] The devil who bargains for the soul of Faust by granting him any wish; here Hawthorne suggests that the exclusive veneration of old painters destroys the human emotions to which they appeal. The Dutch and Flemish painters alluded to here are all of the Domestic School: David Teniers (1582–1649) painted scenes of everyday peasant life; Gerard Douw (1613–1675) headed the School of Leyden and painted landscapes with an

magic that is the destruction of all other magic. He annihilates color, warmth, and, more especially, sentiment and passion, at a touch. If he spare anything, it will be some such matter as an earthen pipkin, or a bunch of herrings by Teniers; a brass kettle, in which you can see your face, by Gerard Douw; a furred robe, or the silken texture of a mantle, or a straw hat, by Van Mieris; or a long-stalked wineglass, transparent and full of shifting reflections, or a bit of bread and cheese, or an over-ripe peach, with a fly upon it, truer than reality itself, by the school of Dutch Conjurers. These men, and a few Flemings, whispers the wicked demon, were the only painters. The mighty Italian masters, as you deem them, were not human, nor addressed their works to human sympathies, but to a false intellectual taste, which they themselves were the first to create. Well might they call their doings "art," for they substituted art instead of nature. Their fashion is past, and ought, indeed, to have died and been buried along with them.

Then there is such a terrible lack of variety in their subjects. The churchmen, their great patrons, suggested most of their themes, and a dead mythology the rest. A quarter-part, probably, of any large collection of pictures, consists of Virgins and infant Christs, repeated over and over again in pretty much an identical spirit, and generally with no more mixture of the Divine than just enough to spoil them as representations

---

enamel-like surface; his most characteristic device is the frame within a frame. Frans Van Mieris (1635–1681) was chiefly interested in capturing physical textures on his canvases. Hawthorne acknowledges the appeal of surfaces here. He seems to have preferred such domestic art to that of the great Italian masters. He says of the Uffizi's collection: "Landscapes by Rembrandt; fat Graces and other plump nudities by Rubens; brass pans and earthen pots and herrings by Teniers and other Dutchmen; none by Gerard Dow, I think, but several by Mieris; all of which were like bread and beef and ale, after having been fed too long on main dishes. This is really a wonderful collection of pictures; and from first to last—from Giotto to the men of yesterday—they are in admirable condition, and may be appreciated for all the merit that they ever possessed" (NB, p. 290).

of maternity and childhood, with which everybody's heart might have something to do. Half of the other pictures are Magdalens, Flights into Egypt, Crucifixions, Depositions from the Cross, Pietas, Noli-me-tangeres, or the Sacrifice of Abraham,[2] or martyrdoms of saints, originally painted as altarpieces, or for the shrines of chapels, and wofully lacking the accompaniments which the artist had in view.

The remainder of the gallery comprises mythological subjects, such as nude Venuses, Ledas, Graces,[3] and, in short, a general apotheosis of nudity, once fresh and rosy perhaps, but yellow and dingy in our day, and retaining only a traditionary charm. These impure pictures are from the same illustrious and impious hands that adventured to call before us the august forms of Apostles and Saints, the Blessed Mother of the Redeemer, and her Son, at his death, and in his glory, and even the awfulness of Him to whom the martyrs, dead a thousand years ago, have not yet dared to raise their eyes. They seem to take up one task or the other—the disrobed woman whom they call Venus, or the type of highest and tenderest womanhood in the mother of their Saviour—with equal readiness, but to achieve the former with far more satisfactory success. If an artist sometimes produced a picture of

[2]Mary Magdalen, a repentant prostitute, was the first to see Jesus after the Resurrection; the Flight into Egypt refers to the escape of Mary, Joseph, and the Child Jesus from Herod; a Pieta is a picture or sculpture of the dead Jesus in the arms of his mother; Noli-me-tangeres, literally, "Don't touch me," from John 20:17, were paintings of Jesus and Mary Magdalen after the Resurrection and before his ascent to the Father. Noli-me-tangeres were favorite subjects of the Renaissance painters. Abraham was told to sacrifice his son Isaac to please the Lord; at the last moment the Lord reprieved Isaac and rewarded Abraham for his fidelity. See Genesis 22:1-19.

[3]Venus was the Roman goddess of love; Leda was raped by Zeus in the form of a swan. The three Graces—Aglaia, Thalia, and Euphrosyne—were daughters of Zeus and portrayed beauty and charm. Once again Hawthorne voices his disapproval of nude paintings here; he believed that clothes were natural to man and ought to be painted as such.

the Virgin, possessing warmth enough to excite devotional feeling, it was probably the object of his earthly love to whom he thus paid the stupendous and fearful homage of setting up her portrait to be worshipped, not figuratively as a mortal, but by religious souls in their earnest aspirations towards Divinity. And who can trust the religious sentiment of Raphael, or receive any of his Virgins as heaven-descended likenesses, after seeing, for example, the Fornarina of the Barberini palace, and feeling how sensual the artist must have been to paint such a brazen trollop of his own accord, and lovingly? Would the Blessed Mary reveal herself to his spiritual vision, and favor him with sittings alternately with that type of glowing earthliness, the Fornarina?[4]

But no sooner have we given expression to this irreverent criticism, than a throng of spiritual faces look reproachfully upon us. We see cherubs by Raphael, whose baby-innocence could only have been nursed in paradise; angels by Raphael as innocent as they, but whose serene intelligence embraces both earthly and celestial things; madonnas by Raphael, on whose lips he has impressed a holy and delicate reserve, implying sanctity on earth, and into whose soft eyes he has thrown a light which he never could have imagined except by raising his own eyes with a pure aspiration heavenward. We remember, too, that divinest countenance in the Transfiguration, and withdraw all that we have said.

Poor Hilda, however, in her gloomiest moments, was never guilty of the high treason suggested in the above remarks against her beloved and honored Raphael. She had a faculty (which, fortunately for themselves, pure women often have) of ignoring all moral blotches in a character that won her ad-

[4]At the same time, Hawthorne admired nudes in spite of his principles. Ernest Earnest calls this ambivalence regarding nudes, typical among the American artists in Rome at that time, "puritan prurience." Raphael painted *The Fornarina* (a girl baker) seated, wearing a turban, and holding a diaphanous wrap below her left breast.

miration. She purified the objects of her regard by the mere act
of turning such spotless eyes upon them.

Hilda's despondency, nevertheless, while it dulled her
perceptions in one respect, had deepened them in another; she
saw beauty less vividly, but felt truth, or the lack of it, more
profoundly. She began to suspect that some, at least, of her
venerated painters, had left an inevitable hollowness in their
works, because, in the most renowned of them, they essayed
to express to the world what they had not in their own souls.
They deified their light and wandering affections, and were
continually playing off the tremendous jest, alluded to above,
of offering the features of some venal beauty to be enshrined
in the holiest places. A deficiency of earnestness and absolute
truth is generally discoverable in Italian pictures, after the art
had become consummate. When you demand what is deepest,
these painters have not wherewithal to respond. They substituted a keen intellectual perception, and a marvellous knack of
external arrangement, instead of the live sympathy and sentiment which should have been their inspiration. And hence it
happens, that shallow and worldly men are among the best
critics of their works; a taste for pictorial art is often no more
than a polish upon the hard enamel of an artificial character.
Hilda had lavished her whole heart upon it, and found (just as
if she had lavished it upon a human idol) that the greater part
was thrown away.

For some of the earlier painters, however, she still retained much of her former reverence. Fra Angelico, she felt,
must have breathed a humble aspiration between every two
touches of his brush, in order to have made the finished picture
such a visible prayer as we behold it, in the guise of a prim
angel, or a saint without the human nature. Through all these
dusky centuries, his works may still help a struggling heart to
pray. Perugino was evidently a devout man; and the Virgin
therefore revealed herself to him in loftier and sweeter faces of
celestial womanhood, and yet wih a kind of homeliness in their
human mould, than even the genius of Raphael could imagine.

Sodoma, beyond a question, both prayed and wept, while painting his fresco, at Siena, of Christ bound to a pillar.[5]

In her present need and hunger for a spiritual revelation,
Hilda felt a vast and weary longing to see this last-mentioned
picture once again. It is inexpressibly touching. So weary is
the Saviour, and utterly worn out with agony, that his lips have
fallen apart from mere exhaustion; his eyes seem to be set; he
tries to lean his head against the pillar, but is kept from sinking
down upon the ground only by the cords that bind him. One
of the most striking effects produced, is the sense of loneliness.
You behold Christ deserted both in heaven and earth; that
despair is in him which wrung forth the saddest utterance man
ever made, "Why hast Thou forsaken me?" Even in this extremity, however, he is still divine. The great and reverent
painter has not suffered the Son of God to be merely an object
of pity, though depicting him in a state so profoundly pitiful.
He is rescued from it, we know not how,—by nothing less
than miracle,—by a celestial majesty and beauty, and some
quality of which these are the outward garniture. He is as
much, and as visibly, our Redeemer, there bound, there faint-
ing, and bleeding from the scourge, with the cross in view, as
if he sat on his throne of glory in the heavens! Sodoma, in this
matchless picture, has done more towards reconciling the in-
congruity of Divine Omnipotence and outraged, suffering Humanity, combined in one person, than the theologians ever did.
This hallowed work of genius shows what pictorial art,

[5]The chronological sequence here of Fra Angelico (*ca.* 1400–1455),
Perugino (*ca.* 1445–1523), and Sodoma (*ca.* 1477–1549) demonstrates the
increasingly emotional content of Italian Renaissance art and prepares us
for Hilda's confession in Chapter 39.

Hawthorne was particularly moved by Sodoma's fresco of Christ
bound to the pillar: "I do believe that painting has never done anything
better, so far as expression is concerned, than this figure. In all these generations since it was painted it must have softened thousands of hearts,
drawn down rivers of tears, been more effectual than a million of sermons.
Really, it is a thing to stand and weep at. No other painter has done anything that can deserve to be compared to this" (*NB*, pp. 446–447).

devoutly exercised, might effect in behalf of religious truth; involving, as it does, deeper mysteries of revelation, and bringing them closer to man's heart, and making him tenderer to be impressed by them, than the most eloquent words of preacher or prophet.

It is not of pictures like the above, that galleries, in Rome or elsewhere, are made up, but of productions immeasurably below them, and requiring to be appreciated by a very different frame of mind. Few amateurs are endowed with a tender susceptibility to the sentiment of a picture; they are not won from an evil life, nor anywise morally improved by it. The love of art, therefore, differs widely in its influence from the love of nature; whereas, if art had not strayed away from its legitimate paths and aims, it ought to soften and sweeten the lives of its worshippers, in even a more exquisite degree than the contemplation of natural objects. But, of its own potency it has no such effect; and it fails, likewise, in that other test of its moral value which poor Hilda was now involuntarily trying upon it. It cannot comfort the heart in affliction; it grows dim when the shadow is upon us.

So the melancholy girl wandered through those long galleries, and over the mosaic pavements of vast, solitary saloons, wondering what had become of the splendor that used to beam upon her from the walls. She grew sadly critical, and condemned almost everything that she was wont to admire. Heretofore, her sympathy went deeply into a picture, yet seemed to leave a depth which it was inadequate to sound; now, on the contrary, her perceptive faculty penetrated the canvas like a steel probe, and found but a crust of paint over an emptiness. Not that she gave up all art as worthless; only it had lost its consecration. One picture in ten thousand, perhaps, ought to live in the applause of mankind, from generation to generation, until the colors fade and blacken out of sight, or the canvas rot entirely away. For the rest, let them be piled in garrets, just as the tolerable poets are shelved, when their little day is over. Is a painter more sacred than a poet?

And as for these galleries of Roman palaces, they were to Hilda—though she still trod them with the forlorn hope of getting back her sympathies—they were drearier than the whitewashed walls of a prison corridor. If a magnificent palace were founded, as was generally the case, on hardened guilt and a stony conscience—if the prince or cardinal who stole the marble of his vast mansion from the Coliseum, or some Roman temple, had perpetrated still deadlier crimes, as probably he did —there could be no fitter punishment for his ghost than to wander perpetually through these long suites of rooms, over the cold marble or mosaic of the floors, growing chillier at every eternal footstep. Fancy the progenitor of the Dorias[6] thus haunting those heavy halls where his posterity reside! Nor would it assuage his monotonous misery, but increase it manifold, to be compelled to scrutinize those masterpieces of art, which he collected with so much cost and care, and gazing at them unintelligently, still leave a further portion of his vital warmth at every one.

Such, or of a similar kind, is the torment of those who seek to enjoy pictures in an uncongenial mood. Every haunter of picture-galleries, we should imagine, must have experienced it, in greater or less degree; Hilda never till now, but now most bitterly.

And now, for the first time in her lengthened absence, comprising so many years of her young life, she began to be acquainted with the exile's pain. Her pictorial imagination brought up vivid scenes of her native village, with its great, old elm-trees; and the neat, comfortable houses, scattered along the wide, grassy margin of its street, and the white meeting-house, and her mother's very door, and the stream of gold-brown water, which her taste for color had kept flowing, all this while, through her remembrance. Oh, dreary streets, pal-

---

[6]The Dorias were a wealthy and powerful Genoese family; their splendid palace on the Corso, the Pamfili Doria, houses a large collection of paintings, frescoes, and sculpture.

aces, churches, and imperial sepulchres of hot and dusty Rome, with the muddy Tiber eddying through the midst, instead of the gold-brown rivulet! How she pined under this crumbly magnificence, as if it were piled all upon her human heart! How she yearned for that native homeliness, those familiar sights, those faces which she had known always, those days that never brought any strange event; that life of sober week-days; and a solemn sabbath at the close! The peculiar fragrance of a flower-bed, which Hilda used to cultivate, came freshly to her memory, across the windy sea, and through the long years since the flowers had withered. Her heart grew faint at the hundred reminiscences that were awakened by that re-membered smell of dead blossoms; it was like opening a drawer, where many things were laid away, and every one of them scented with lavender and dried rose-leaves.

We ought not to betray Hilda's secret; but it is the truth, that being so sad, and so utterly alone, and in such great need of sympathy, her thoughts sometimes recurred to the sculptor. Had she met him now, her heart, indeed, might not have been won, but her confidence would have flown to him like a bird to its nest. One summer afternoon, especially, Hilda leaned over the battlements of her tower, and looked over Rome towards the distant mountains, whither Kenyon had told her that he was going.

"Oh, that he were here," she sighed; "I perish under this terrible secret; and he might help me to endure it. Oh, that he were here!"

That very afternoon, as the reader may remember, Ken-yon felt Hilda's hand pulling at the silken cord that was con-nected with his heartstrings, as he stood looking towards Rome from the battlements of Monte Beni.

CHAPTER 38. *Altars and Incense*

Rome has a certain species of consolation readier at hand, for all the necessitous, than any other spot under the sky; and Hilda's despondent state made her peculiarly liable to the peril, if peril it can justly be termed, of seeking, or consenting, to be thus consoled.

Had the Jesuits[1] known the situation of this troubled heart, her inheritance of New England Puritanism would hardly have protected the poor girl from the pious strategy of those good fathers. Knowing, as they do, how to work each proper engine, it would have been ultimately impossible for Hilda to resist the attractions of a faith, which so marvellously adapts itself to every human need. Not, indeed, that it can satisfy the soul's cravings, but, at least, it can sometimes help the soul towards a higher satisfaction than the faith contains within itself. It supplies a multitude of external forms, in which the spiritual may be clothed and manifested; it has many painted windows, as it were, through which the celestial sunshine, else disregarded, may make itself gloriously perceptible in visions of beauty and splendor. There is no one want or weakness of human nature, for which Catholicism will own itself without a remedy; cordials, certainly, it possesses in abun-

[1]Famous religious order founded in 1539 by Ignatius Loyola (1491–1556), a Spaniard. Because of their numbers and their influence in Rome, the Father General is sometimes called "The Black Pope." Hawthorne takes the conventional Protestant attitude toward the Jesuits, imputing to them subtle craft, sophistry, and casuistry, e.g., the term "jesuitical." Note his remarkably well-balanced attitude toward the Jesuits and the Church in the next two paragraphs, however.

dance, and sedatives in inexhaustible variety, and what may once have been genuine medicaments, though a little the worse for long keeping.

To do it justice, Catholicism is such a miracle of fitness for its own ends, many of which might seem to be admirable ones, that it is difficult to imagine it a contrivance of mere man. Its mighty machinery was forged and put together, not on middle earth, but either above or below. If there were but angels to work it, instead of the very different class of engineers who now manage its cranks and safety-valves, the system would soon vindicate the dignity and holiness of its origin.

Hilda had heretofore made many pilgrimages among the churches of Rome, for the sake of wondering at their gorgeousness. Without a glimpse at these palaces of worship, it is impossible to imagine the magnificence of the religion that reared them. Many of them shine with burnished gold. They glow with pictures. Their walls, columns, and arches, seem a quarry of precious stones, so beautiful and costly are the marbles with which they are inlaid. Their pavements are often a mosaic, of rare workmanship. Around their lofty cornices, hover flights of sculptured angels; and within the vault of the ceiling and the swelling interior of the dome, there are frescoes of such brilliancy, and wrought with so artful a perspective, that the sky, peopled with sainted forms, appears to be opened, only a little way above the spectator. Then there are chapels, opening from the side-aisles and transepts, decorated by princes for their own burial-places, and as shrines for their especial saints. In these, the splendor of the entire edifice is intensified and gathered to a focus. Unless words were gems, that would flame with many-colored light upon the page, and throw thence a tremulous glimmer into the reader's eyes, it were vain to attempt a description of a princely chapel.

Restless with her trouble, Hilda now entered upon another pilgrimage among these altars and shrines. She climbed the hundred steps of the Ara Cœli; she trod the broad, silent nave of St. John Lateran; she stood in the Pantheon,[2] under the round opening in the dome, through which the blue, sunny sky still gazes down, as it used to gaze when there were Roman deities in the antique niches. She went into every church that rose before her, but not now to wonder at its magnificence, which she hardly noticed more than if it had been the pine-built interior of a New England meeting-house.

She went (and it was a dangerous errand) to observe how closely and comfortingly the Popish faith applied itself to all human occasions. It was impossible to doubt that multitudes of people found their spiritual advantage in it, who would find none at all in our own formless mode of worship; which, besides, so far as the sympathy of prayerful souls is concerned, can be enjoyed only at stated and too infrequent periods. But here, whenever the hunger for divine nutriment came upon the soul, it could on the instant be appeased. At one or another altar, the incense was forever ascending; the mass always being performed, and carrying upward with it the devotion of such as had not words for their own prayer. And yet, if the worshipper had his individual petition to offer, his own heart-secret to whisper below his breath, there were divine auditors ever ready to receive it from his lips; and what encouraged him still more, these auditors had not always been divine, but kept, within their heavenly memories, the tender humility of a human experience. Now a saint in heaven, but once a man on earth.

Hilda saw peasants, citizens, soldiers, nobles, women with bare heads, ladies in their silks, entering the churches individually, kneeling for moments, or for hours, and directing their inaudible devotions to the shrine of some saint of their own

[2]Santa Maria D'Aracoeli, a church rising from the highest point on Capitoline Hill, was once the national church of the Roman people and the nobility. St. John Lateran is one of the four principal basilicas in Rome. The Pantheon is a grandiose monument built to the gods by Agrippa (*ca.* 63 B.C.–12 B.C.), the Roman general who defeated Pompey and Antony.

choice. In his hallowed person, they felt themselves possessed of an own friend in heaven. They were too humble to approach the Deity directly. Conscious of their unworthiness, they asked the mediation of their sympathizing patron, who, on the score of his ancient martyrdom, and after many ages of celestial life, might venture to talk with the Divine Presence, almost as friend with friend. Though dumb before its Judge, even despair could speak, and pour out the misery of its soul like water, to an advocate so wise to comprehend the case, and eloquent to plead it, and powerful to win pardon, whatever were the guilt. Hilda witnessed what she deemed to be an example of this species of confidence between a young man and his saint. He stood before a shrine, writhing, wringing his hands, contorting his whole frame in an agony of remorseful recollection, but finally knelt down to weep and pray. If this youth had been a Protestant, he would have kept all that torture pent up in his heart, and let it burn there till it seared him into indifference.

Often, and long, Hilda lingered before the shrines and chapels of the Virgin, and departed from them with reluctant steps. Here, perhaps, strange as it may seem, her delicate appreciation of art stood her in good stead, and lost Catholicism a convert. If the painter had represented Mary with a heavenly face, poor Hilda was now in the very mood to worship her, and adopt the faith in which she held so elevated a position. But she saw that it was merely the flattered portrait of an earthly beauty; the wife, at best, of the artist; or, it might be, a peasant girl of the Campagna, or some Roman princess, to whom he desired to pay his court. For love, or some even less justifiable motive, the old painter had apotheosized these women; he thus gained for them, as far as his skill would go, not only the meed of immortality, but the privilege of presiding over Christian altars, and of being worshipped with far holier fervors than while they dwelt on earth. Hilda's fine sense of the fit and decorous could not be betrayed into kneeling at such a shrine.

She never found just the virgin mother whom she needed.
Here, it was an earthly mother, worshipping the earthly baby
in her lap, as any and every mother does, from Eve's time
downward. In another picture, there was a dim sense, shown
in the mother's face, of some divine quality in the child. In a
third, the artist seemed to have had a higher perception, and had
striven hard to shadow out the Virgin's joy at bringing the
Saviour into the world, and her awe and love, inextricably
mingled, of the little form which she pressed against her bosom.
So far was good. But still, Hilda looked for something more; a
face of celestial beauty, but human as well as heavenly, and
with the shadow of past grief upon it; bright with immortal
youth, yet matronly and motherly; and endowed with a
queenly dignity, but infinitely tender, as the highest and deepest attribute of her divinity.

"Ah," thought Hilda to herself, "why should not there
be a woman to listen to the prayers of women? a mother in
heaven for all motherless girls like me? In all God's thought
and care for us, can He have withheld this boon, which our
weakness so much needs?"

Oftener than to the other churches, she wandered into
Saint Peter's. Within its vast limits, she thought, and beneath
the sweep of its great dome, there should be space for all
forms of Christian truth; room both for the faithful and the
heretic to kneel; due help for every creature's spiritual want.

Hilda had not always been adequately impressed by the
grandeur of this mighty cathedral. When she first lifted the
heavy leathern curtain, at one of the doors, a shadowy edifice
in her imagination had been dazzled out of sight by the reality.
Her preconception of Saint Peter's was a structure of no
definite outline, misty in its architecture, dim and gray and
huge, stretching into an interminable perspective, and over-
arched by a dome like the cloudy firmament. Beneath that
vast breadth and height, as she had fancied them, the personal
man might feel his littleness, and the soul triumph in its immensity. So, in her earlier visits, when the compassed splendor

of the actual interior glowed before her eyes, she had profanely called it a great prettiness; a gay piece of cabinet-work, on a Titanic scale; a jewel casket, marvellously magnified.

This latter image best pleased her fancy; a casket, all inlaid, in the inside, with precious stones of various hue, so that there should not be a hair's-breadth of the small interior unadorned with its resplendent gem. Then, conceive this minute wonder of a mosaic box, increased to the magnitude of a cathedral, without losing the intense lustre of its littleness, but all its petty glory striving to be sublime. The magic transformation from the minute to the vast has not been so cunningly effected but that the rich adornment still counteracts the impression of space and loftiness. The spectator is more sensible of its limits than of its extent.

Until after many visits, Hilda continued to mourn for that dim, illimitable interior, which with her eyes shut she had seen from childhood, but which vanished at her first glimpse through the actual door. Her childish vision seemed preferable to the cathedral, which Michael Angelo, and all the great architects, had built; because, of the dream edifice, she had said, "How vast it is!" while of the real Saint Peter's she could only say, "After all, it is not so immense!" Besides, such as the church is, it can nowhere be made visible at one glance. It stands in its own way. You see an aisle or a transept; you see the nave, or the tribune; but, on account of its ponderous piers and other obstructions, it is only by this fragmentary process that you get an idea of the cathedral.

There is no answering such objections. The great church smiles calmly upon its critics, and, for all response, says, "Look at me!" and if you still murmur for the loss of your shadowy perspective, there comes no reply, save, "Look at me!" in endless repetition, as the one thing to be said. And, after looking many times, with long intervals between, you discover that the cathedral has gradually extended itself over the whole compass of your idea; it covers all the site of your visionary temple, and has room for its cloudy pinnacles beneath the dome.

One afternoon, as Hilda entered Saint Peter's in sombre mood, its interior beamed upon her with all the effect of a new creation. It seemed an embodiment of whatever the imagination could conceive, or the heart desire, as a magnificent, comprehensive, majestic symbol of religious faith. All splendor was included within its verge, and there was space for all. She gazed with delight even at the multiplicity of ornament. She was glad of the cherubim that fluttered upon the pilasters, and of the marble doves, hovering, unexpectedly, with green olive-branches of precious stones. She could spare nothing, now, of the manifold magnificence that had been lavished, in a hundred places, richly enough to have made world-famous shrines in any other church, but which here melted away into the vast, sunny breadth, and were of no separate account. Yet each contributed its little all towards the grandeur of the whole.

She would not have banished one of those grim popes, who sit each over his own tomb, scattering cold benedictions out of their marble hands; nor a single frozen sister of the Allegoric family, to whom—as, like hired mourners at an English funeral, it costs them no wear and tear of heart—is assigned the office of weeping for the dead.[3] If you choose to see these things, they present themselves; if you deem them unsuitable and out of place, they vanish, individually, but leave their life upon the walls.

The pavement! it stretched out illimitably, a plain of many-colored marble, where thousands of worshippers might kneel together, and shadowless angels tread among them without brushing their heavenly garments against those earthly ones. The roof! the dome! Rich, gorgeous, filled with sunshine, cheerfully sublime, and fadeless after centuries, those lofty depths seemed to translate the heavens to mortal comprehension, and help the spirit upward to a yet higher and wider sphere. Must not the faith, that built this matchless edifice, and

[3]The Muses; see Edmund Spenser's poem, "The Tears of the Muses."

warmed, illuminated, and overflowed from it, include whatever can satisfy human aspirations at the loftiest, or minister to human necessity at the sorest? If Religion had a material home, was it not here?

As the scene which we but faintly suggest shone calmly before the New England maiden at her entrance, she moved, as if by very instinct, to one of the vases of holy water, upborne against a column by two mighty cherubs. Hilda dipped her fingers, and had almost signed the cross upon her breast, but forbore, and trembled, while shaking the water from her finger-tips. She felt as if her mother's spirit, somewhere within the dome, were looking down upon her child, the daughter of Puritan forefathers, and weeping to behold her ensnared by these gaudy superstitions. So she strayed sadly onward, up the nave, and towards the hundred golden lights that swarm before the high altar. Seeing a woman, a priest, and a soldier, kneel to kiss the toe of the brazen St. Peter, who protrudes it beyond his pedestal, for the purpose, polished bright with former salutations, while a child stood on tiptoe to do the same, the glory of the church was darkened before Hilda's eyes. But again she went onward into remoter regions. She turned into the right transept, and thence found her way to a shrine, in the extreme corner of the edifice, which is adorned with a mosaic copy of Guido's beautiful Archangel, treading on the prostrate fiend.

This was one of the few pictures, which, in these dreary days, had not faded nor deteriorated in Hilda's estimation; not that it was better than many in which she no longer took an interest; but the subtle delicacy of the painter's genius was peculiarly adapted to her character. She felt, while gazing at it, that the artist had done a great thing, not merely for the Church of Rome, but for the cause of Good. The moral of the picture, the immortal youth and loveliness of Virtue, and its irresistible might against ugly Evil, appealed as much to Puritans as Catholics.

Suddenly, and as if it were done in a dream, Hilda

found herself kneeling before the shrine, under the ever-burning lamp that throws its ray upon the Archangel's face. She laid her forehead on the marble steps before the altar, and sobbed out a prayer; she hardly knew to whom, whether Michael, the Virgin, or the Father; she hardly knew for what, save only a vague longing, that thus the burden of her spirit might be lightened a little.

In an instant she snatched herself up, as it were, from her knees, all a-throb with the emotions which were struggling to force their way out of her heart by the avenue that had so nearly been opened for them. Yet there was a strange sense of relief won by that momentary, passionate prayer; a strange joy, moreover, whether for what she had done, or for what she had escaped doing, Hilda could not tell. But she felt as one half stifled, who has stolen a breath of air.

Next to the shrine where she had knelt, there is another, adorned with a picture by Guercino, representing a maiden's body in the jaws of the sepulchre, and her lover weeping over it; while her beatified spirit looks down upon the scene, in the society of the Saviour and a throng of saints. Hilda wondered if it were not possible, by some miracle of faith, so to rise above her present despondency that she might look down upon what she was, just as Petronilla in the picture looked at her own corpse.[4] A hope, born of hysteric trouble, fluttered in her heart. A presentiment, or what she fancied such, whispered her, that, before she had finished the circuit of the cathedral, relief would come.

The unhappy are continually tantalized by similar delusions of succor near at hand; at least, the despair is very dark that has no such will-o'-the-wisp to glimmer in it.

[4]Guercino was an Italian eclectic painter (*ca.* 1591–1666) influenced by Guido. Petronilla was probably a 3rd-century martyr. A basilica was erected over her tomb in the 4th century by Pope Siricius. She is depicted as a little girl holding a palm and a book. Hawthorne alludes to the late 4th-century fresco of Veneranda and St. Petronilla in the Cemetery of Domitilla.

CHAPTER 39. *The World's Cathedral*

Still gliding onward, Hilda now looked up into the dome, where the sunshine came through the western windows, and threw across long shafts of light. They rested upon the mosaic figures of two evangelists above the cornice. These great beams of radiance, traversing what seemed the empty space, were made visible in misty glory, by the holy cloud of incense, else unseen, which had risen into the middle dome. It was to Hilda as if she beheld the worship of the priest and people ascending heavenward, purified from its alloy of earth, and acquiring celestial substance in the golden atmosphere to which it aspired. She wondered if angels did not sometimes hover within the dome, and show themselves, in brief glimpses, floating amid the sunshine and the glorified vapor, to those who devoutly worshipped on the pavement.

She had now come into the southern transept. Around this portion of the church are ranged a number of confessionals. They are small tabernacles of carved wood, with a closet for the priest in the centre; and, on either side, a space for a penitent to kneel, and breathe his confession through a perforated auricle into the good father's ear. Observing this arrangement, though already familiar to her, our poor Hilda was anew impressed with the infinite convenience—if we may use so poor a phrase—of the Catholic religion to its devout believers.

Who, in truth, that considers the matter, can resist a similar impression! In the hottest fever-fit of life, they can

342

always find, ready for their need, a cool, quiet, beautiful place
of worship. They may enter its sacred precincts at any hour,
leaving the fret and trouble of the world behind them, and
purifying themselves with a touch of holy water at the threshold. In the calm interior, fragrant of rich and soothing incense, they may hold converse with some saint, their awful,
kindly friend. And most precious privilege of all, whatever
perplexity, sorrow, guilt, may weigh upon their souls, they can
fling down the dark burden at the foot of the cross, and go
forth—to sin no more, nor be any longer disquieted; but to
live again in the freshness and elasticity of innocence.

"Do not these inestimable advantages," thought Hilda,
"or some of them, at least, belong to Christianity itself? Are
they not a part of the blessings which the system was meant
to bestow upon mankind? Can the faith in which I was born
and bred be perfect, if it leave a weak girl like me to wander,
desolate, with this great trouble crushing me down?"

A poignant anguish thrilled within her breast; it was
like a thing that had life, and was struggling to get out.

"Oh, help! Oh, help!" cried Hilda; "I cannot, cannot
bear it!"

Only by the reverberations that followed—arch echoing
the sound to arch, and a pope of bronze repeating it to a pope
of marble, as each sat enthroned over his tomb—did Hilda
become aware that she had really spoken above her breath.
But, in that great space, there is no need to hush up the heart
within one's own bosom, so carefully as elsewhere; and, if
the cry reached any distant auditor, it came broken into many
fragments, and from various quarters of the church.

Approaching one of the confessionals, she saw a woman
kneeling within. Just as Hilda drew near, the penitent rose,
came forth, and kissed the hand of the priest, who regarded
her with a look of paternal benignity, and appeared to be
giving her some spiritual counsel, in a low voice. She then
knelt to receive his blessing, which was fervently bestowed.
Hilda was so struck with the peace and joy in the woman's

face, that, as the latter retired, she could not help speaking to her.

"You look very happy!" said she. "Is it so sweet, then, to go to the confessional?"

"Oh, very sweet, my dear signorina!" answered the woman, with moistened eyes and an affectionate smile; for she was so thoroughly softened with what she had been doing, that she felt as if Hilda were her younger sister. "My heart is at rest now. Thanks be to the Saviour, and the blessed Virgin and the saints, and this good father, there is no more trouble for poor Teresa!"

"I am glad for your sake," said Hilda, sighing for her own. "I am a poor heretic, but a human sister; and I rejoice for you!"

She went from one to another of the confessionals, and, looking at each, perceived that they were inscribed with gilt letters: on one, Pro Italica Lingua; on another, Pro Flandrica Lingua; on a third, Pro Polonica Lingua; on a fourth, Pro Illyrica Lingua; on a fifth, Pro Hispanica Lingua.[1] In this vast and hospitable cathedral, worthy to be the religious heart of the whole world, there was room for all nations; there was access to the Divine Grace for every Christian soul; there was an ear for what the overburdened heart might have to murmur, speak in what native tongue it would.

When Hilda had almost completed the circuit of the transept, she came to a confessional—the central part was closed, but a mystic rod protruded from it, indicating the presence of a priest within—on which was inscribed, Pro Anglica Lingua.[2]

It was the word in season! If she had heard her mother's voice from within the tabernacle, calling her, in her own mother-tongue, to come and lay her poor head in her lap, and sob out all her troubles, Hilda could not have responded with

[1] In these stalls confessions are heard in Italian, Flemish, Polish, Croatian, and Spanish.
[2] I.e., "for the English language."

a more inevitable obedience. She did not think; she only felt. Within her heart was a great need. Close at hand, within the veil of the confessional, was the relief. She flung herself down in the penitent's place; and, tremulously, passionately, with sobs, tears, and the turbulent overflow of emotion too long repressed, she poured out the dark story which had infused its poison into her innocent life.

Hilda had not seen, nor could she now see, the visage of the priest. But, at intervals, in the pauses of that strange confession, half choked by the struggle of her feelings towards an outlet, she heard a mild, calm voice, somewhat mellowed by age. It spoke soothingly; it encouraged her; it led her on by apposite questions that seemed to be suggested by a great and tender interest, and acted like magnetism in attracting the girl's confidence to this unseen friend. The priest's share in the interview, indeed, resembled that of one who removes the stones, clustered branches, or whatever entanglements impede the current of a swollen stream. Hilda could have imagined— so much to the purpose were his inquiries—that he was already acquainted with some outline of what she strove to tell him.

Thus assisted, she revealed the whole of her terrible se- cret! The whole, except that no name escaped her lips.

And, ah, what a relief! When the hysteric gasp, the strife between words and sobs, had subsided, what a torture had passed away from her soul! It was all gone; her bosom was as pure now as in her childhood. She was a girl again; she was Hilda of the dove-cote; not that doubtful creature whom her own doves had hardly recognized as their mistress and play- mate, by reason of the death-scent that clung to her garments!

After she had ceased to speak, Hilda heard the priest bestir himself with an old man's reluctant movement. He stepped out of the confessional; and as the girl was still kneeling in the penitential corner, he summoned her forth.

"Stand up, my daughter," said the mild voice of the confessor; "what we have further to say must be spoken face to face."

Hilda did his bidding, and stood before him with a down-cast visage, which flushed and grew pale again. But it had the wonderful beauty which we may often observe in those who have recently gone through a great struggle, and won the peace that lies just on the other side. We see it in a new mother's face; we see it in the faces of the dead; and in Hilda's countenance—which had always a rare natural charm for her friends—this glory of peace made her as lovely as an angel.

On her part, Hilda beheld a venerable figure with hair as white as snow, and a face strikingly characterized by benevolence. It bore marks of thought, however, and penetrative insight; although the keen glances of the eyes were now somewhat bedimmed with tears, which the aged shed, or almost shed, on lighter stress of emotion than would elicit them from younger men.

"It has not escaped my observation, daughter," said the priest, "that this is your first acquaintance with the confessional. How is this?"

"Father," replied Hilda, raising her eyes, and again letting them fall, "I am of New England birth, and was bred as what you call a heretic."

"From New England!" exclaimed the priest. "It was my own birthplace, likewise; nor have fifty years of absence made me cease to love it. But, a heretic! And are you reconciled to the Church?"

"Never, father," said Hilda.

"And, that being the case," demanded the old man, "on what ground, my daughter, have you sought to avail yourself of these blessed privileges, confined exclusively to members of the one true Church, of confession and absolution?"

"Absolution, father?" exclaimed Hilda, shrinking back. "Oh, no, no! I never dreamed of that! Only our Heavenly Father can forgive my sins; and it is only by sincere repentance of whatever wrong I may have done, and by my own best efforts towards a higher life, that I can hope for His forgiveness! God forbid that I should ask absolution from mortal man!"

"Then, wherefore," rejoined the priest, with somewhat less mildness in his tone, "wherefore, I ask again, have you taken possession, as I may term it, of this holy ordinance; being a heretic, and neither seeking to share, nor having faith in, the unspeakable advantages which the Church offers to its penitents?"

"Father," answered Hilda, trying to tell the old man the simple truth, "I am a motherless girl, and a stranger here in Italy. I had only God to take care of me, and be my closest friend; and the terrible, terrible crime, which I have revealed to you, thrust itself between Him and me; so that I groped for Him in the darkness, as it were, and found Him not—found nothing but a dreadful solitude, and this crime in the midst of it! I could not bear it. It seemed as if I made the awful guilt my own, by keeping it hidden in my heart. I grew a fearful thing to myself. I was going mad!"

"It was a grievous trial, my poor child!" observed the confessor. "Your relief, I trust, will prove to be greater than you yet know!"

"I feel already how immense it is!" said Hilda, looking gratefully in his face. "Surely, father, it was the hand of Providence that led me hither, and made me feel that this vast temple of Christianity, this great home of religion, must needs contain some cure, some ease, at least, for my unutterable anguish. And it has proved so. I have told the hideous secret; told it under the sacred seal of the Confessional; and now it will burthen my poor heart no more!"

"But, daughter," answered the venerable priest, not unmoved by what Hilda said, "you forget! you mistake!—you claim a privilege to which you have not entitled yourself! The seal of the confessional, do you say? God forbid that it should ever be broken, where it has been fairly impressed; but it applies only to matters that have been confided to its keeping in a certain prescribed method, and by persons, moreover, who have faith in the sanctity of the ordinance. I hold myself, and any learned casuist[3] of the Church would hold me, as free to disclose all the particulars of what you term your confession, as if they had come to my knowledge in a secular way."

"This is not right, father!" said Hilda, fixing her eyes on the old man's.

"Do not you see, child," he rejoined, with some little heat—"with all your nicety of conscience, cannot you recognize it as my duty to make the story known to the proper authorities; a great crime against public justice being involved, and further evil consequences likely to ensue?"

"No, father, no!" answered Hilda, courageously, her cheeks flushing and her eyes brightening as she spoke. "Trust a girl's simple heart sooner than any casuist of your Church, however learned he may be. Trust your own heart, too! I came to your confessional, father, as I devoutly believe, by the direct impulse of Heaven, which also brought you hither to-day, in its mercy and love, to relieve me of a torture that I could no longer bear. I trusted in the pledge which your Church has always held sacred between the priest and the human soul, which, through his medium, is struggling towards its Father above. What I have confided to you lies sacredly between God and yourself. Let it rest there, father; for this is right, and if you do otherwise, you will perpetrate a great wrong, both as a priest and a man! And, believe me, no question, no torture, shall ever force my lips to utter what would be necessary, in order to make my confession available towards the punishment of the guilty ones. Leave Providence to deal with them!"

[3]A casuist uses the "case method" for educing moral principles from hypothetical situations; more often the term signifies one "who makes the worse appear the better reason." Jesuits used the case method and were often called casuists in both senses of the word. The priest's self-identification perfectly fits Hawthorne's ambivalence toward him, the practice of confession, and the Church in general.

"My quiet little countrywoman," said the priest, with half a smile on his kindly old face, "you can pluck up a spirit, I perceive, when you fancy an occasion for one."

"I have spirit only to do what I think right," replied Hilda, simply. "In other respects, I am timorous."

"But you confuse yourself between right feelings and very foolish inferences," continued the priest, "as is the wont of women—so much I have learnt by long experience in the confessional—be they young or old. However, to set your heart at rest, there is no probable need for me to reveal the matter. What you have told, if I mistake not, and perhaps more, is already known in the quarter which it most concerns."

"Known!" exclaimed Hilda. "Known to the authorities of Rome! And what will be the consequence?"

"Hush," answered the confessor, laying his finger on his lips. "I tell you my supposition—mind, it is no assertion of the fact—in order that you may go the more cheerfully on your way, not deeming yourself burdened with any responsibility as concerns this dark deed. And now, daughter, what have you to give in return for an old man's kindness and sympathy?"

"My grateful remembrance," said Hilda, fervently, "as long as I live!"

"And nothing more?" the priest inquired, with a persuasive smile. "Will you not reward him with a great joy; one of the last joys that he may know on earth, and a fit one to take with him into the better world? In a word, will you not allow him to bring you, as a stray lamb, into the true fold? You have experienced some little taste of the relief and comfort which the Church keeps abundantly in store for all its faithful children. Come home, dear child,—poor wanderer, who hast caught a glimpse of the heavenly light,—come home, and be at rest."

"Father," said Hilda, much moved by his kindly earnestness; in which, however, genuine as it was, there might still be a leaven of professional craft. "I dare not come a step

farther than Providence shall guide me. Do not let it grieve
you, therefore, if I never return to the confessional; never dip
my fingers in holy water; never sign my bosom with the
cross. I am a daughter of the Puritans. But, in spite of my
heresy," she added, with a sweet, tearful smile, "you may one
day see the poor girl, to whom you have done this great
Christian kindness, coming to remind you of it, and thank
you for it, in the Better Land."

The old priest shook his head. But, as he stretched out
his hands at the same moment, in the act of benediction, Hilda
knelt down and received the blessing with as devout a simplicity as any Catholic of them all.

CHAPTER 40.   *Hilda and a Friend*

When Hilda knelt to receive the priest's benediction, the act was witnessed by a person who stood leaning against the marble balustrade that surrounds the hundred golden lights, before the high altar. He had stood there, indeed, from the moment of the girl's entrance into the confessional. His start of surprise, at first beholding her, and the anxious gloom that afterwards settled on his face, sufficiently betokened that he felt a deep and sad interest in what was going forward.

After Hilda had bidden the priest farewell, she came slowly towards the high altar. The individual, to whom we have alluded, seemed irresolute whether to advance or retire. His hesitation lasted so long, that the maiden, straying through a happy reverie, had crossed the wide extent of the pavement between the confessional and the altar, before he had decided whether to meet her. At last, when within a pace or two, she raised her eyes and recognized Kenyon.

"It is you!" she exclaimed, with joyful surprise. "I am so happy."

In truth, the sculptor had never before seen, nor hardly imagined, such a figure of peaceful beatitude as Hilda now presented. While coming towards him in the solemn radiance which, at that period of the day, is diffused through the transept, and showered down beneath the dome, she seemed of the same substance as the atmosphere that enveloped her. He could scarcely tell whether she was imbued with sunshine, or whether it was a glow of happiness that shone out of her.

At all events, it was a marvellous change from the sad girl, who had entered the confessional bewildered with anguish, to this bright, yet softened image of religious consolation that emerged from it. It was as if one of the throng of angelic people, who might be hovering in the sunny depths of the dome, had alighted on the pavement. Indeed, this capability of transfiguration, which we often see wrought by inward delight on persons far less capable of it than Hilda, suggests how angels come by their beauty. It grows out of their happiness, and lasts forever only because that is immortal.

She held out her hand, and Kenyon was glad to take it in his own, if only to assure himself that she was made of earthly material.

"Yes, Hilda, I see that you are very happy," he replied, gloomily, and withdrawing his hand after a single pressure. "For me, I never was less so than at this moment."

"Has any misfortune befallen you?" asked Hilda, with earnestness. "Pray tell me; and you shall have my sympathy, though I must still be very happy. Now, I know how it is, that the saints above are touched by the sorrows of distressed people on earth, and yet are never made wretched by them. Not that I profess to be a saint, you know," she added, smiling radiantly. "But the heart grows so large, and so rich, and so variously endowed, when it has a great sense of bliss, that it can give smiles to some, and tears to others, with equal sincerity, and enjoy its own peace throughout all."

"Do not say you are no saint!" answered Kenyon, with a smile, though he felt that the tears stood in his eyes. "You will still be Saint Hilda, whatever Church may canonize you."

"Ah! you would not have said so, had you seen me but an hour ago!" murmured she. "I was so wretched, that there seemed a grievous sin in it."

"And what has made you so suddenly happy?" inquired the sculptor. "But first, Hilda, will you not tell me why you were so wretched?"

"Had I met you yesterday, I might have told you that," she replied. "To-day, there is no need."

"Your happiness, then?" said the sculptor, as sadly as before. "Whence comes it?"

"A great burden has been lifted from my heart,—from

my conscience, I had almost said," answered Hilda, without shunning the glance that he fixed upon her. "I am a new creature, since this morning, Heaven be praised for it! It was a blessed hour—a blessed impulse—that brought me to this beautiful and glorious cathedral. I shall hold it in loving remembrance while I live, as the spot where I found infinite peace after infinite trouble."

Her heart seemed so full, that it spilt its new gush of happiness, as it were, like rich and sunny wine out of an overbrimming goblet. Kenyon saw that she was in one of those moods of elevated feeling, when the soul is upheld by a strange tranquillity, which is really more passionate, and less controllable, than emotions far exceeding it in violence. He felt that there would be indelicacy, if he ought not rather to call it impiety, in his stealing upon Hilda, while she was thus beyond her own guardianship, and surprising her out of secrets which she might afterwards bitterly regret betraying to him. Therefore, though yearning to know what had happened, he resolved to forbear further question.

Simple and earnest people, however, being accustomed to speak from their genuine impulses, cannot easily, as craftier men do, avoid the subject which they have at heart. As often as the sculptor unclosed his lips, such words as these were ready to burst out:—

"Hilda, have you flung your angelic purity into that mass of unspeakable corruption, the Roman Church?"

"What were you saying?" she asked, as Kenyon forced back an almost uttered exclamation of this kind.

"I was thinking of what you have just remarked about the cathedral," said he, looking up into the mighty hollow of the dome. "It is indeed a magnificent structure, and an adequate expression of the Faith which built it. When I behold it in a proper mood,—that is to say, when I bring my mind into a fair relation with the minds and purposes of its spiritual and material architects,—I see but one or two criticisms to make. One is, that it needs painted windows."

"Oh, no!" said Hilda. "They would be quite inconsistent

with so much richness of color in the interior of the church. Besides, it is a Gothic ornament, and only suited to that style of architecture, which requires a gorgeous dimness."

"Nevertheless," continued the sculptor, "yonder square apertures, filled with ordinary panes of glass, are quite out of keeping with the superabundant splendor of everything about them. They remind me of that portion of Aladdin's palace which he left unfinished, in order that his royal father-in-law might put the finishing touch.[1] Daylight, in its natural state, ought not to be admitted here. It should stream through a brilliant illusion of saints and hierarchies, and old scriptural images, and symbolized dogmas, purple, blue, golden, and a broad flame of scarlet. Then, it would be just such an illumination as the Catholic faith allows to its believers. But, give me—to live and die in—the pure, white light of heaven!"

"Why do you look so sorrowfully at me?" asked Hilda, quietly meeting his disturbed gaze. "What would you say to me? I love the white light too!"

"I fancied so," answered Kenyon. "Forgive me Hilda; but I must needs speak. You seemed to me a rare mixture of impressibility, sympathy, sensitiveness to many influences, with a certain quality of common sense;—no, not that, but a higher and finer attribute, for which I find no better word. However tremulously you might vibrate, this quality, I supposed, would always bring you back to the equipoise. You were a creature of imagination, and yet as truly a New England

[1]Cf. Hawthorne's preference for painted windows: "a window with only the white sunshine coming through it, or even with a glimpse of the blue Italian sky, looks like a portion left unfinished, and therefore a blotch in the rich wall. It is like the one spot in Aladdin's palace which he left for the king, his father-in-law, to finish, after his fairy architects had exhausted their magnificence on the rest; and the sun, like the king, fails in the effort" (*NB*, p. 74). In *The Thousand and One Nights* Aladdin built a palace with a salon at the top, having 24 windows, all but one enriched with diamonds, rubies, and emeralds. The jewelers of the king could not make a window to match the others, so Aladdin commanded the slave of the lamp to finish the window; he did so.

girl as any with whom you grew up in your native village. If there were one person in the world, whose native rectitude of thought, and something deeper, more reliable, than thought, I would have trusted against all the arts of a priesthood,— whose taste alone, so exquisite and sincere that it rose to be a moral virtue, I would have rested upon as a sufficient safeguard—it was yourself!"

"I am conscious of no such high and delicate qualities as you allow me," answered Hilda. "But what have I done that a girl of New England birth and culture, with the right sense that her mother taught her, and the conscience that she developed in her, should not do?"

"Hilda, I saw you at the confessional!" said Kenyon.

"Ah, well, my dear friend," replied Hilda, casting down her eyes, and looking somewhat confused, yet not ashamed, "you must try to forgive me for that,—if you deem it wrong, —because it has saved my reason, and made me very happy. Had you been here yesterday, I would have confessed to you."

"Would to Heaven I had!" ejaculated Kenyon.

"I think," Hilda resumed, "I shall never go to the confessional again; for there can scarcely come such a sore trial twice in my life. If I had been a wiser girl, a stronger, and a more sensible, very likely I might not have gone to the confessional at all. It was the sin of others that drove me thither; not my own, though it almost seemed so. Being what I am, I must either have done what you saw me doing, or have gone mad. Would that have been better?"

"Then you are not a Catholic?" asked the sculptor, earnestly.

"Really, I do not quite know what I am," replied Hilda, encountering his eyes with a frank and simple gaze. "I have a great deal of faith, and Catholicism seems to have a great deal of good. Why should not I be a Catholic, if I find there what I need, and what I cannot find elsewhere? The more I see of this worship, the more I wonder at the exuberance with which it adapts itself to all the demands of human infirmity. If its ministers were but a little more than human, above all error, pure from all iniquity, what a religion would it be!"

"I need not fear your perversion to the Catholic faith," remarked Kenyon, "if you are at all aware of the bitter sarcasm implied in your last observation. It is very just. Only, the exceeding ingenuity of the system stamps it as the contrivance of man, or some worse author; not an emanation of the broad and simple wisdom from on high."

"It may be so," said Hilda; "but I meant no sarcasm."

Thus conversing, the two friends went together down the grand extent of the nave. Before leaving the church, they turned to admire again its mighty breadth, the remoteness of the glory behind the altar, and the effect of visionary splendor and magnificence imparted by the long bars of smoky sunshine, which travelled so far before arriving at a place of rest.

"Thank Heaven for having brought me hither!" said Hilda, fervently.

Kenyon's mind was deeply disturbed by his idea of her Catholic propensities; and now what he deemed her disproportionate and misapplied veneration for the sublime edifice, stung him into irreverence.

"The best thing I know of St. Peter's," observed he, "is its equable temperature. We are now enjoying the coolness of last winter, which, a few months hence, will be the warmth of the present summer. It has no cure, I suspect, in all its length and breadth, for a sick soul, but it would make an admirable atmospheric hospital for sick bodies. What a delightful shelter would it be for the invalids who throng to Rome, where the sirocco steals away their strength, and the tramontana[2] stabs them through and through, like cold steel with a poisoned point! But, within these walls, the thermometer never varies. Winter and summer are married at the high altar, and dwell together in perfect harmony."

[2]The sirocco is the oppressive south wind from Africa; the tramontana, "across the mountains," is the north wind.

"Yes," said Hilda; "and I have always felt this soft, unchanging climate of Saint Peter's to be another manifestation of its sanctity."

"That is not precisely my idea," replied Kenyon. "But what a delicious life it would be, if a colony of people with delicate lungs—or merely with delicate fancies—could take up their abode in this ever-mild and tranquil air. These architectural tombs of the popes might serve for dwellings, and each brazen sepulchral doorway would become a domestic threshold. Then the lover, if he dared, might say to his mistress, 'Will you share my tomb with me?' and, winning her soft consent, he would lead her to the altar, and thence to yonder sepulchre of Pope Gregory,[3] which should be their nuptial home. What a life would be theirs, Hilda, in their marble Eden!"

"It is not kind, nor like yourself," said Hilda, gently, "to throw ridicule on emotions which are genuine. I revere this glorious church for itself and its purposes; and love it, moreover, because here I have found sweet peace, after a great anguish."

"Forgive me," answered the sculptor, "and I will do so no more. My heart is not so irreverent as my words."

They went through the piazza of Saint Peter's and the adjacent streets, silently at first; but, before reaching the bridge of St. Angelo, Hilda's flow of spirits began to bubble forth, like the gush of a streamlet that has been shut up by frost, or by a heavy stone over its source. Kenyon had never found her so delightful as now; so softened out of the chillness of her virgin pride; so full of fresh thoughts, at which he was often moved to smile, although, on turning them over a little more, he sometimes discovered that they looked fanciful only because so absolutely true.

[3]Gregory V (*fl.* 996–999), chaplain to the Holy Roman Emperor Otto III, was appointed Pope at the age of 24. A reformer, he died suddenly at 27, the first Pope to cooperate harmoniously with the Emperor. He is buried in the grotto of St. Peter's.

But, indeed, she was not quite in a normal state. Emerging from gloom into sudden cheerfulness, the effect upon Hilda was as if she were just now created. After long torpor, receiving back her intellectual activity, she derived an exquisite pleasure from the use of her faculties, which were set in motion by causes that seemed inadequate. She continually brought to Kenyon's mind the image of a child, making its plaything of every object, but sporting in good faith, and with a kind of seriousness. Looking up, for example, at the statue of St. Michael, on the top of Hadrian's castellated tomb, Hilda fancied an interview between the Archangel and the old emperor's ghost, who was naturally displeased at finding his mausoleum, which he had ordained for the stately and solemn repose of his ashes, converted to its present purposes.

"But St. Michael, no doubt," she thoughtfully remarked, "would finally convince the Emperor Hadrian, that where a warlike despot is sown as the seed, a fortress and a prison are the only possible crop."[4]

They stopped on the bridge to look into the swift eddying flow of the yellow Tiber, a mud-puddle in strenuous motion; and Hilda wondered whether the seven-branched golden candlestick, the holy candlestick of the Jews—which was lost at the Ponte Molle,[5] in Constantine's time—had yet been swept as far down the river as this.

"It probably stuck where it fell," said the sculptor; "and, by this time, is imbedded thirty feet deep in the mud of the Tiber. Nothing will ever bring it to light again."

"I fancy you are mistaken," replied Hilda, smiling.

[4]The tomb of Emperor Hadrian (*fl.* A.D. 117–138) was a massive stone structure on the banks of the Tiber; at this time it was used as a prison.

[5]Hilda refers to the menorah; see note 5, p. 156. The Milvian Bridge, or Ponte Molle, connected the Flaminian Way and the city gate. Over this bridge Roman triumphs entered the city, and here too Constantine saw the angel with the cross and the banner emblazoned with the motto "In this sign conquer."

"There was a meaning and purpose in each of its seven branches, and such a candlestick cannot be lost forever. When it is found again, and seven lights are kindled and burning in it, the whole world will gain the illumination which it needs. Would not this be an admirable idea for a mystic story or parable, or seven-branched allegory, full of poetry, art, philosophy, and religion? It shall be called 'The Recovery of the Sacred Candlestick.' As each branch is lighted, it shall have a differently colored lustre from the other six; and when all the seven are kindled, their radiance shall combine into the intense white light of truth."

"Positively, Hilda, this is a magnificent conception," cried Kenyon. "The more I look at it, the brighter it burns."

"I think so too," said Hilda, enjoying a childlike pleasure in her own idea. "The theme is better suited for verse than prose; and when I go home to America, I will suggest it to one of our poets. Or, seven poets might write the poem together, each lighting a separate branch of the Sacred Candlestick."

"Then you think of going home?" Kenyon asked.

"Only yesterday," she replied, "I longed to flee away. Now, all is changed, and, being happy again, I should feel deep regret at leaving the Pictorial Land.[6] But, I cannot tell. In Rome, there is something dreary and awful, which we can never quite escape. At least, I thought so yesterday."

When they reached the Via Portoghese, and approached Hilda's tower, the doves, who were waiting aloft, flung themselves upon the air, and came floating down about her head. The girl caressed them, and responded to their cooings with similar sounds from her own lips, and with words of endearment; and their joyful flutterings and airy little flights, evidently impelled by pure exuberance of spirits, seemed to show that the doves had a real sympathy with their mistress's state of mind. For peace had descended upon her like a dove.

[6]Note that Hilda, like Hawthorne, saw Italy in artistic terms.

Bidding the sculptor farewell, Hilda climbed her tower, and came forth upon its summit to trim the Virgin's lamp. The doves, well knowing her custom, had flown up thither to meet her, and again hovered about her head; and very lovely was her aspect, in the evening sunlight, which had little further to do with the world, just then, save to fling a golden glory on Hilda's hair, and vanish.

Turning her eyes down into the dusky street which she had just quitted, Hilda saw the sculptor still there, and waved her hand to him.

"How sad and dim he looks, down there in that dreary street!" she said to herself. "Something weighs upon his spirits. Would I could comfort him."

"How like a spirit she looks, aloft there, with the evening glory round her head, and those winged creatures claiming her as akin to them!" thought Kenyon, on his part. "How far above me! how unattainable! Ah, if I could lift myself to her region! Or—if it be not a sin to wish it—would that I might draw her down to an earthly fireside!"

What a sweet reverence is that, when a young man deems his mistress a little more than mortal, and almost chides himself for longing to bring her close to his heart! A trifling circumstance, but such as lovers make much of, gave him hope. One of the doves, which had been resting on Hilda's shoulder, suddenly flew downward, as if recognizing him as its mistress's dear friend; and perhaps commissioned with an errand of regard, brushed his upturned face with its wings, and again soared aloft.

The sculptor watched the bird's return, and saw Hilda greet it with a smile.

CHAPTER 41. *Snowdrops and Maidenly Delights*

It being still considerably earlier than the period at which artists and tourists are accustomed to assemble in Rome, the sculptor and Hilda found themselves comparatively alone there. The dense mass of native Roman life in the midst of which they were, served to press them nearer to one another. It was as if they had been thrown together on a desert island. Or, they seemed to have wandered, by some strange chance, out of the common world, and encountered each other in a depopulated city, where there were streets of lonely palaces, and unreckonable treasures of beautiful and admirable things, of which they two became the sole inheritors.

In such circumstances, Hilda's gentle reserve must have been stronger than her kindly disposition permitted, if the friendship between Kenyon and herself had not grown as warm as a maiden's friendship can ever be, without absolutely and avowedly blooming into love. On the sculptor's side, the amaranthine flower was already in full blow. But it is very beautiful, though the lover's heart may grow chill at the perception, to see how the snow will sometimes linger in a virgin's breast, even after the spring is well advanced. In such alpine soils, the summer will not be anticipated; we seek vainly for passionate flowers, and blossoms of fervid hue and spicy fragrance, finding only snowdrops and sunless violets, when it is almost the full season for the crimson rose.

With so much tenderness as Hilda had in her nature, it was strange that she so reluctantly admitted the idea of love; especially as, in the sculptor, she found both congeniality and variety of taste, and likenesses and differences of character;

these being as essential as those to any poignancy of mutual emotion.

So Hilda, as far as Kenyon could discern, still did not love him, though she admitted him within the quiet circle of her affections as a dear friend and trusty counsellor. If we knew what is best for us, or could be content with what is reasonably good, the sculptor might well have been satisfied, for a season, with this calm intimacy, which so sweetly kept him a stranger in her heart, and a ceremonious guest; and yet allowed him the free enjoyment of all but its deeper recesses. The flowers that grow outside of those inner sanctities have a wild, hasty charm, which it is well to prove; there may be sweeter ones within the sacred precinct, but none that will die while you are handling them, and bequeathe you a delicious legacy, as these do, in the perception of their evanescence and unreality.

And this may be the reason, after all, why Hilda, like so many other maidens, lingered on the hither side of passion; her finer instinct and keener sensibility made her enjoy those pale delights in a degree of which men are incapable. She hesitated to grasp a richer happiness, as possessing already such measure of it as her heart could hold, and of a quality most agreeable to her virgin tastes.

Certainly, they both were very happy. Kenyon's genius, unconsciously wrought upon by Hilda's influence, took a more delicate character than heretofore. He modelled, among other things, a beautiful little statue of maidenhood gathering a snowdrop. It was never put into marble, however, because the sculptor soon recognized it as one of those fragile creations which are true only to the moment that produces them, and are wronged if we try to imprison their airy excellence in a permanent material.

On her part, Hilda returned to her customary occupations with a fresh love for them, and yet with a deeper look into the heart of things; such as those necessarily acquire, who have passed from picture-galleries into dungeon gloom, and thence come back to the picture-gallery again. It is questionable whether she was ever so perfect a copyist thenceforth. She could not yield herself up to the painter so unreservedly as in times past; her character had developed a sturdier quality, which made her less pliable to the influence of other minds. She saw into the picture as profoundly as ever, and perhaps more so, but not with the devout sympathy that had formerly given her entire possession of the old master's idea. She had known such a reality, that it taught her to distinguish inevitably the large portion that is unreal, in every work of art. Instructed by sorrow, she felt that there is something beyond almost all which pictorial genius has produced; and she never forgot those sad wanderings from gallery to gallery, and from church to church, when she had vainly sought a type of the virgin mother, or the Saviour, or saint, or martyr, which a soul in extreme need might recognize as the adequate one.

How, indeed, should she have found such! How could Holiness be revealed to the artists of an age when the greatest of them put genius and imagination in the place of spiritual insight, and when, from the pope downward, all Christendom was corrupt?

Meanwhile, months wore away, and Rome received back that large portion of its lifeblood which runs in the veins of its foreign and temporary population. English visitors established themselves in the hotels, and in all the sunny suites of apartments, in the streets convenient to the Piazza di Spagna; the English tongue was heard familiarly along the Corso, and English children sported in the Pincian Gardens.

The native Romans, on the other hand, like the butterflies and grasshoppers, resigned themselves to the short, sharp misery which winter brings to a people whose arrangements are made almost exclusively with a view to summer. Keeping no fire within-doors, except possibly a spark or two in the kitchen, they crept out of their cheerless houses into the narrow, sunless, sepulchral streets, bringing their firesides along with them, in the shape of little earthern pots, vases, or pipkins, full of lighted charcoal and warm ashes, over which they held

their tingling finger-ends. Even in this half-torpid wretchedness, they still seemed to dread a pestilence in the sunshine,
and kept on the shady side of the piazzas, as scrupulously as
in summer. Through the open door-ways—no need to shut
them when the weather within was bleaker than without—a
glimpse into the interior of their dwellings showed the un-
carpeted brick-floors, as dismal as the pavement of a tomb.

They drew their old cloaks about them, nevertheless, and
threw the corners over their shoulders, with the dignity of attitude and action that have come down to these modern citizens,
as their sole inheritance from the togaed nation. Somehow or
other, they managed to keep up their poor, frostbitten hearts
against the pitiless atmosphere with a quiet and uncomplaining
endurance that really seems the most respectable point in the
present Roman character. For, in New England, or in Russia, or
scarcely in a hut of the Esquimaux, there is no such discomfort
to be borne as by Romans in wintry weather, when the orange-
trees bear icy fruit in the gardens; and when the rims of all the
fountains are shaggy with icicles, and the fountain of Trevi
skimmed almost across with a glassy surface; and when there is
a slide in the piazza of St. Peter's, and a fringe of brown, frozen
foam along the eastern shore of the Tiber, and sometimes a fall
of great snow-flakes into the dreary lanes and alleys of the
miserable city. Cold blasts, that bring death with them, now
blow upon the shivering invalids, who came hither in the hope
of breathing balmy airs.

Wherever we pass our summers, may all our inclement
months, from November to April, henceforth be spent in some
country that recognizes winter as an integral portion of its
year![1]

Now, too, there was especial discomfort in the stately
picture-galleries, where nobody indeed,—not the princely or

[1]We can see Hawthorne's psychological preparation for his return
to Concord at this point, toward the end of his writing stint in England.
Note, by contrast, his earlier aversion to New England winters in his notebook entry for May 22, 1858: "[Miss Bremer] talked, among other things,
of the winters in Sweden, and said that she liked them, long and severe as

priestly founders, nor any who have inherited their cheerless magnificence,—ever dreamed of such an impossibility as
fireside warmth, since those great palaces were built. Hilda,
therefore, finding her fingers so much benumbed that the
spiritual influence could not be transmitted to them, was persuaded to leave her easel before a picture, on one of these
wintry days, and pay a visit to Kenyon's studio. But neither
was the studio anything better than a dismal den, with its
marble shapes shivering around the walls, cold as the snow-
images which the sculptor used to model, in his boyhood, and
sadly behold them weep themselves away at the first thaw.

Kenyon's Roman artisans, all this while, had been at work
on the Cleopatra. The fierce Egyptian queen had now struggled
almost out of the imprisoning stone; or, rather, the workmen
had found her within the mass of marble, imprisoned there by
magic, but still fervid to the touch with fiery life, the fossil
woman of an age that produced statelier, stronger, and more
passionate creatures than our own. You already felt her compressed heat, and were aware of a tiger-like character even in
her repose. If Octavius should make his appearance, though the
marble still held her within its embrace, it was evident that she
would tear herself forth in a twinkling, either to spring en-
raged at his throat, or, sinking into his arms, to make one more
proof of her rich blandishments, or falling lowly at his feet,
to try the efficacy of a woman's tears.

"I am ashamed to tell you how much I admire this statue,"
said Hilda. "No other sculptor could have done it."

"This is very sweet for me to hear," replied Kenyon;
"and since your reserve keeps you from saying more, I shall
imagine you expressing everything that an artist would wish to
hear said about his work."

"You will not easily go beyond my genuine opinion,"
answered Hilda, with a smile.

---

they are; and this made me feel ashamed of dreading the winters of New
England, as I did before coming from home, and do now still more, after
five or six mild English winters" (*NB*, p. 214).

"Ah, your kind word makes me very happy," said the sculptor, "and I need it, just now, on behalf of my Cleopatra. That inevitable period has come—for I have found it inevitable, in regard to all my works—when I look at what I fancied to be a statue, lacking only breath to make it live, and find it a mere lump of senseless stone, into which I have not really succeeded in moulding the spiritual part of my idea. I should like, now— only it would be such shameful treatment for a discrowned queen, and my own offspring, too—I should like to hit poor Cleopatra a bitter blow on her Egyptian nose with this mallet."

"That is a blow which all statues seem doomed to receive, sooner or later, though seldom from the hand that sculptured them," said Hilda, laughing. "But you must not let yourself be too much disheartened by the decay of your faith in what you produce. I have heard a poet express similar distaste for his own most exquisite poems, and I am afraid that this final despair, and sense of shortcoming, must always be the reward and punishment of those who try to grapple with a great or beautiful idea. It only proves that you have been able to imagine things too high for mortal faculties to execute. The idea leaves you an imperfect image of itself, which you at first mistake for the ethereal reality, but soon find that the latter has escaped out of your closest embrace."

"And the only consolation is," remarked Kenyon, "that the blurred and imperfect image may still make a very respectable appearance in the eyes of those who have not seen the original."

"More than that," rejoined Hilda; "for there is a class of spectators whose sympathy will help them to see the perfect through a mist of imperfection. Nobody, I think, ought to read poetry, or look at pictures or statues, who cannot find a great deal more in them than the poet or artist has actually expressed. Their highest merit is suggestiveness."

"You, Hilda, are yourself the only critic in whom I have much faith," said Kenyon. "Had you condemned Cleopatra, nothing should have saved her."

"You invest me with such an awful responsibility," she replied, "that I shall not dare to say a single word about your other works."

"At least," said the sculptor, "tell me whether you recognize this bust."

He pointed to a bust of Donatello. It was not the one which Kenyon had begun to model at Monte Beni, but a reminiscence of the Count's face, wrought under the influence of all the sculptor's knowledge of his history, and of his personal and hereditary character. It stood on a wooden pedestal, not nearly finished, but with fine, white dust and small chips of marble scattered about it, and itself incrusted all round with the white, shapeless substance of the block. In the midst appeared the features, lacking sharpness, and very much resembling a fossil countenance—but we have already used this simile, in reference to Cleopatra—with the accumulations of long-past ages clinging to it.

And yet, strange to say, the face had an expression, and a more recognizable one than Kenyon had succeeded in putting into the clay model at Monte Beni. The reader is probably acquainted with Thorwaldsen's[2] three-fold analogy,—the clay model, the Life; the plaster cast, the Death; and the sculptured marble, the Resurrection,—and it seemed to be made good by the spirit that was kindling up these imperfect features, like a lambent flame.

"I was not quite sure, at first glance, that I knew the face," observed Hilda; "the likeness surely is not a striking one. There is a good deal of external resemblance, still, to the features of the Faun of Praxiteles, between whom and Donatello, you know, we once insisted that there was a perfect twin-brotherhood. But the expression is now so very different!"

"What do you take it to be?" asked the sculptor.

"I hardly know how to define it," she answered. "But it

[2]Bertel Thorwaldsen (1770–1844), a Danish scupltor who spent much of his working life in Rome; mentor of the American sculptor Horatio Greenough.

has an effect as if I could see this countenance gradually brightening while I look at it. It gives the impression of a growing intellectual power and moral sense. Donatello's face used to evince little more than a genial, pleasurable sort of vivacity, and capability of enjoyment. But, here, a soul is being breathed into him; it is the Faun, but advancing towards a state of higher development."

"Hilda, do you see all this?" exclaimed Kenyon, in considerable surprise. "I may have had such an idea in my mind, but was quite unaware that I had succeeded in conveying it into the marble."

"Forgive me," said Hilda, "but I question whether this striking effect has been brought about by any skill or purpose on the sculptor's part. Is it not, perhaps, the chance result of the bust being just so far shaped out, in the marble, as the process of moral growth had advanced in the original? A few more strokes of the chisel might change the whole expression, and so spoil it for what it is now worth."

"I believe you are right," answered Kenyon, thoughtfully examining his work; "and, strangely enough, it was the very expression that I tried unsuccessfully to produce in the clay model. Well; not another chip shall be struck from the marble."

And, accordingly, Donatello's bust (like that rude, rough mass of the head of Brutus, by Michael Angelo, at Florence) has ever since remained in an unfinished state. Most spectators mistake it for an unsuccessful attempt towards copying the features of the Faun of Praxiteles. One observer in a thousand is conscious of something more, and lingers long over this mysterious face, departing from it reluctantly, and with many a glance thrown backward. What perplexes him is the riddle that he sees propounded there; the riddle of the soul's growth, taking its first impulse amid remorse and pain, and struggling through the incrustations of the senses. It was the contemplation of this imperfect portrait of Donatello that originally interested us in his history, and impelled us to elicit from Kenyon what he knew of his friend's adventures.

CHAPTER 42. *Reminiscences of Miriam*

When Hilda and himself turned away from the unfinished bust, the sculptor's mind still dwelt upon the reminiscences which it suggested.

"You have not seen Donatello recently," he remarked, "and therefore cannot be aware how sadly he is changed."

"No wonder!" exclaimed Hilda, growing pale.

The terrible scene which she had witnessed, when Donatello's face gleamed out in so fierce a light, came back upon her memory, almost for the first time since she knelt at the confessional. Hilda, as is sometimes the case with persons whose delicate organization requires a peculiar safeguard, had an elastic faculty of throwing off such recollections as would be too painful for endurance. The first shock of Donatello's and Miriam's crime had, indeed, broken through the frail defence of this voluntary forgetfulness; but, once enabled to relieve herself of the ponderous anguish over which she had so long brooded, she had practised a subtle watchfulness in preventing its return.

"No wonder, do you say?" repeated the sculptor, looking at her with interest, but not exactly with surprise; for he had long suspected that Hilda had a painful knowledge of events which he himself little more than surmised. "Then you know!— you have heard! But what can you possibly have heard, and through what channel?"

"Nothing!" replied Hilda, faintly. "Not one word has reached my ears from the lips of any human being. Let us never speak of it again! No, no! never again!"

"And Miriam!" said Kenyon, with irrepressible interest. "Is it also forbidden to speak of her?"

"Hush! do not even utter her name! Try not to think of it!" Hilda whispered. "It may bring terrible consequences!"

"My dear Hilda!" exclaimed Kenyon, regarding her with wonder and deep sympathy. "My sweet friend, have you had this secret hidden in your delicate, maidenly heart, through all these many months! No wonder that your life was withering out of you."

"It was so, indeed!" said Hilda, shuddering. "Even now, I sicken at the recollection."

"And how could it have come to your knowledge?" continued the sculptor. "But, no matter! Do not torture yourself with referring to the subject. Only, if at any time it should be a relief to you, remember that we can speak freely together, for Miriam has herself suggested a confidence between us."

"Miriam has suggested this!" exclaimed Hilda. "Yes, I remember, now, her advising that the secret should be shared with you. But I have survived the death-struggle that it cost me, and need make no further revelations. And Miriam has spoken to you! What manner of woman can she be, who, after sharing in such a deed, can make it a topic of conversation with her friends?"

"Ah, Hilda," replied Kenyon, "you do not know, for you could never learn it from your own heart, which is all purity and rectitude, what a mixture of good there may be in things evil; and how the greatest criminal, if you look at his conduct from his own point of view, or from any side-point, may seem not so unquestionably guilty, after all. So with Miriam; so with Donatello. They are, perhaps, partners in what we must call awful guilt; and yet, I will own to you,—when I think of the original cause, the motives, the feelings, the sudden concurrence of circumstances thrusting them onward, the urgency of the moment, and the sublime unselfishness on either part,—I know not well how to distinguish it from much that the world calls heroism. Might we not render some such verdict as this?—'Worthy of Death, but not unworthy of Love!'"[1]

"Never!" answered Hilda, looking at the matter through the clear crystal medium of her own integrity. "This thing, as regards its causes, is all a mystery to me, and must remain so. But there is, I believe, only one right and one wrong; and I do not understand, and may God keep me from ever understanding, how two things so totally unlike can be mistaken for one another; nor how two mortal foes, as Right and Wrong surely are, can work together in the same deed. This is my faith; and I should be led astray, if you could persuade me to give it up."

"Alas for poor human nature, then!" said Kenyon, sadly, and yet half smiling at Hilda's unworldly and impracticable theory. "I always felt you, my dear friend, a terribly severe judge, and have been perplexed to conceive how such tender sympathy could coexist with the remorselessness of a steel blade. You need no mercy, and therefore know not how to show any."

"That sounds like a bitter gibe," said Hilda, with the tears springing into her eyes. "But I cannot help it. It does not alter my perception of the truth. If there be any such dreadful mixture of good and evil as you affirm,—and which appears to me almost more shocking than pure evil,—then the good is turned to poison, not the evil to wholesomeness."

The sculptor seemed disposed to say something more, but yielded to the gentle steadfastness with which Hilda declined to listen. She grew very sad; for a reference to this one dismal topic had set, as it were, a prison-door ajar, and allowed a throng of torturing recollections to escape from their dungeons into the pure air and white radiance of her soul. She bade Kenyon a briefer farewell than ordinary, and went homeward to her tower.

In spite of her efforts to withdraw them to other subjects, her thoughts dwelt upon Miriam; and, as had not heretofore happened, they brought with them a painful doubt whether a

---

[1]This aphorism is probably invented for the occasion.

wrong had not been committed, on Hilda's part, towards the friend once so beloved. Something that Miriam had said, in their final conversation, recurred to her memory, and seemed now to deserve more weight than Hilda had assigned to it, in her horror at the crime just perpetrated. It was not that the deed looked less wicked and terrible in the retrospect; but she asked herself whether there were not other questions to be considered, aside from that single one of Miriam's guilt or innocence; as, for example, whether a close bond of friendship, in which we once voluntarily engage, ought to be severed on account of any unworthiness, which we subsequently detect in our friend. For, in these unions of hearts,—call them marriage, or whatever else,—we take each other for better, for worse. Availing ourselves of our friend's intimate affection, we pledge our own, as to be relied upon in every emergency. And what sadder, more desperate emergency could there be, than had befallen Miriam? Who more need the tender succor of the innocent, than wretches stained with guilt? And must a selfish care for the spotlessness of our own garments keep us from pressing the guilty ones close to our hearts, wherein, for the very reason that we are innocent, lies their securest refuge from further ill?

It was a sad thing for Hilda to find this moral enigma propounded to her conscience; and to feel that, whichever way she might settle it, there would be a cry of wrong on the other side. Still the idea stubbornly came back, that the tie between Miriam and herself had been real, the affection true, and that therefore the implied compact was not to be shaken off.

"Miriam loved me well," thought Hilda, remorsefully, "and I failed her at her sorest need."

Miriam loved her well; and not less ardent had been the affection which Miriam's warm, tender, and generous characteristics had excited in Hilda's more reserved and quiet nature. It had never been extinguished; for, in part, the wretchedness which Hilda had since endured was but the struggle and writhing of her sensibility, still yearning towards her friend. And now, at the earliest encouragement, it awoke again, and cried out piteously, complaining of the violence that had been done it.

Recurring to the delinquencies of which she fancied (we say "fancied," because we do not unhesitatingly adopt Hilda's present view, but rather suppose her misled by her feelings)— of which she fancied herself guilty towards her friend, she suddenly remembered a sealed packet that Miriam had confided to her. It had been put into her hands with earnest injunctions of secrecy and care, and if unclaimed after a certain period, was to be delivered according to its address. Hilda had forgotten it; or, rather, she had kept the thought of this commission in the background of her consciousness, with all other thoughts referring to Miriam.

But now, the recollection of this packet, and the evident stress which Miriam laid upon its delivery at the specified time, impelled Hilda to hurry up the staircase of her tower, dreading lest the period should already have elapsed.

No; the hour had not gone by, but was on the very point of passing. Hilda read the brief note of instruction, on a corner of the envelope, and discovered, that, in case of Miriam's absence from Rome, the packet was to be taken to its destination that very day.

"How nearly I had violated my promise!" said Hilda. "And, since we are separated forever, it has the sacredness of an injunction from a dead friend. There is no time to be lost."

So Hilda set forth in the decline of the afternoon, and pursued her way towards the quarter of the city in which stands the Palazzo Cenci. Her habit of self-reliance was so simply strong, so natural, and now so well established by long use, that the idea of peril seldom or never occurred to Hilda, in her lonely life.

She differed, in this particular, from the generality of her sex; although the customs and character of her native land often produce women who meet the world with gentle fearlessness, and discover that its terrors have been absurdly exaggerated by the tradition of mankind. In ninety-nine cases out

of a hundred, the apprehensiveness of women is quite gratuitous. Even as matters now stand, they are really safer in perilous
situations and emergencies, than men; and might be still more
so, if they trusted themselves more confidingly to the chivalry
of manhood. In all her wanderings about Rome, Hilda had gone
and returned as securely as she had been accustomed to tread
the familiar street of her New England village, where every
face wore a look of recognition. With respect to whatever was
evil, foul, and ugly, in this populous and corrupt city, she trod
as if invisible, and not only so, but blind. She was altogether
unconscious of anything wicked that went along the same pathway, but without jostling or impeding her, any more than gross
substance hinders the wanderings of a spirit. Thus it is, that,
bad as the world is said to have grown, innocence continues to
make a paradise around itself, and keep it still unfallen.

Hilda's present expedition led her into what was—physically, at least—the foulest and ugliest part of Rome. In that
vicinity lies the Ghetto,[2] where thousands of Jews are crowded
within a narrow compass, and lead a close, unclean, and multitudinous life, resembling that of maggots when they over-
populate a decaying cheese.

Hilda passed on the borders of this region, but had no
occasion to step within it. Its neighborhood, however, naturally
partook of characteristics like its own. There was a confusion
of black and hideous houses, piled massively out of the ruins of
former ages; rude and destitute of plan, as a pauper would build
his hovel, and yet displaying here and there an arched gateway,
a cornice, a pillar, or a broken arcade, that might have adorned
a palace. Many of the houses, indeed, as they stood, might once

---

[2]The Ghetto is located behind the present synagogue, built in 1904
near the Ponte Fabricio and the Theater of Marcellus; see map. For centuries all Jews were restricted to the low-lying area, flooded in every rising
of the Tiber; poor Jews live there today. Bernard Malamud has used the
Ghetto for the setting of some stories in *Idiots First*.

The Palazzo Cenci stands on the Via Arenula, in the Ghetto on the
Tiber; see map.

have been palaces, and possessed still a squalid kind of grandeur. Dirt was everywhere, strewing the narrow streets, and incrusting the tall shabbiness of the edifices, from the foundations to the roofs; it lay upon the thresholds, and looked out of the windows, and assumed the guise of human life in the children, that seemed to be engendered out of it. Their father was the sun, and their mother—a heap of Roman mud.

It is a question of speculative interest, whether the ancient Romans were as unclean a people as we everywhere find those who have succeeded them. There appears to be a kind of malignant spell in the spots that have been inhabited by these masters of the world, or made famous in their history; an inherited and inalienable curse, impelling their successors to fling dirt and defilement upon whatever temple, column, ruined palace, or triumphal arch, may be nearest at hand; and on every monument that the old Romans built. It is most probably a classic trait, regularly transmitted downward, and perhaps a little modified by the better civilization of Christianity; so that Cæsar may have trod narrower and filthier ways in his path to the Capitol, than even those of modern Rome.

As the paternal abode of Beatrice, the gloomy old palace of the Cencis had an interest for Hilda, although not sufficiently strong, hitherto, to overcome the disheartening effect of the exterior, and draw her over its threshold. The adjacent piazza, of poor aspect, contained only an old woman selling roasted chestnuts and baked squash-seeds; she looked sharply at Hilda, and inquired whether she had lost her way.

"No," said Hilda; "I seek the Palazzo Cenci."

"Yonder it is, fair signorina," replied the Roman matron. "If you wish that packet delivered, which I see in your hand, my grandson Pietro shall run with it for a baiocco.[3] The Cenci palace is a spot of ill-omen for young maidens."

Hilda thanked the old dame, but alleged the necessity of doing her errand in person. She approached the front of the

[3] A small Roman coin worth half a penny.

palace, which, with all its immensity, had but a mean appearance, and seemed an abode which the lovely shade of Beatrice would not be apt to haunt, unless her doom made it inevitable. Some soldiers stood about the portal, and gazed at the brown-haired, fair-cheeked Anglo-Saxon girl, with approving glances, but not indecorously. Hilda began to ascend the staircase, three lofty flights of which were to be surmounted, before reaching the door whither she was bound.

CHAPTER 43. *The Extinction of a Lamp*

Between Hilda and the sculptor there had been a kind of half-expressed understanding, that both were to visit the galleries of the Vatican the day subsequent to their meeting at the studio. Kenyon, accordingly, failed not to be there, and wandered through the vast ranges of apartments, but saw nothing of his expected friend. The marble faces, which stand innumerable along the walls, and have kept themselves so calm through the vicissitudes of twenty centuries, had no sympathy for his disappointment; and he, on the other hand, strode past these treasures and marvels of antique art, with the indifference which any pre-occupation of the feelings is apt to produce, in reference to objects of sculpture. Being of so cold and pure a substance, and mostly deriving their vitality more from thought than passion, they require to be seen through a perfectly transparent medium.

And, moreover, Kenyon had counted so much upon Hilda's delicate perceptions in enabling him to look at two or three of the statues, about which they had talked together, that the entire purpose of his visit was defeated by her absence. It is a delicious sort of mutual aid, when the united power of two sympathetic, yet dissimilar intelligences, is brought to bear upon a poem by reading it aloud, or upon a picture or statue, by viewing it in each other's company. Even if not a word of criticism be uttered, the insight of either party is wonderfully deepened, and the comprehension broadened; so that the inner mystery of a work of genius, hidden from one, will often reveal itself to two. Missing such help, Kenyon saw nothing at the Vatican which he had not seen a thousand times before, and more perfectly than now.

In the chill of his disappointment, he suspected that it was a very cold art to which he had devoted himself. He questioned, at that moment, whether sculpture really ever softens and warms the materials which it handles; whether carved marble is anything but limestone, after all; and whether the Apollo Belvedere itself possesses any merit above its physical beauty, or is beyond criticism even in that generally acknowledged excellence. In flitting glances, heretofore, he had seemed to behold this statue as something ethereal and godlike, but not now.

Nothing pleased him, unless it were the group of the Laocoön,[1] which, in its immortal agony, impressed Kenyon as a type of the long, fierce struggle of man, involved in the knotted entanglements of Errour and Evil, those two snakes, which, if no divine help intervene, will be sure to strangle him and his children in the end. What he most admired was the strange calmness diffused through this bitter strife; so that it resembled the rage of the sea, made calm by its immensity, or the tumult of Niagara which ceases to be tumult because it lasts forever. Thus, in the Laocoön, the horror of a moment grew to be the fate of interminable ages. Kenyon looked upon

[1]This marble statue, depicting two sea serpents enwrapping the Trojan priest and his two sons who warned the Trojans against the Greek horse, was carved by three Greek sculptors—Agesander, Athenodorus, and Polydorus (1st century B.C.) Laocoön had angered Apollo by marrying and begetting children; Poseidon sent the two serpents to punish Laocoön for the betrayal of his office.

The Apollo mentioned above is a marble copy of the original in Athens; Apollo was the god of the sun.

Cf. Hawthorne's comment on the two statues: "I saw the Apollo Belvidere as something ethereal and godlike; only for a flitting moment, however, and as if he had alighted from heaven, or shone suddenly out of the sunlight, and then had withdrawn himself again. I felt that Laocoön very powerfully, though very quietly; an immortal agony, with a strange calmness diffused through it, so that it resembles the vast rage of the sea, calm on account of its intensity; or the tumult of Niagara, which does not seem to be tumult, because it keeps pouring on forever and ever" (NB, p. 121).

the group as the one triumph of sculpture, creating the repose, which is essential to it, in the very acme of turbulent effort; but, in truth, it was his mood of unwonted despondency that made him so sensitive to the terrible magnificence, as well as to the sad moral of this work. Hilda herself could not have helped him to see it with nearly such intelligence.

A good deal more depressed than the nature of the disappointment warranted, Kenyon went to his studio, and took in hand a great lump of clay. He soon found, however, that his plastic cunning had departed from him for the time. So he wandered forth again into the uneasy streets of Rome, and walked up and down the Corso, where, at that period of the day, a throng of passers-by and loiterers choked up the narrow sidewalk. A penitent was thus brought in contact with the sculptor.

It was a figure in a white robe, with a kind of featureless mask over the face, through the apertures of which the eyes threw an unintelligible light. Such odd, questionable shapes are often seen gliding through the streets of Italian cities, and are understood to be usually persons of rank, who quit their palaces, their gayeties, their pomp and pride, and assume the penitential garb for a season, with a view of thus expiating some crime, or atoning for the aggregate of petty sins that make up a worldly life. It is their custom to ask alms, and perhaps to measure the duration of their penance by the time requisite to accumulate a sum of money out of the little droppings of individual charity. The avails[2] are devoted to some beneficent or religious purpose; so that the benefit accruing to their own souls is, in a manner, linked with a good done, or intended, to their fellow-men. These figures have a ghastly and startling effect, not so much from any very impressive peculiarity in the garb, as from the mystery which they bear about with them, and the sense that there is an acknowledged sinfulness as the nucleus of it.

[2]Alms.

In the present instance, however, the penitent asked no
alms of Kenyon; although, for the space of a minute or two,
they stood face to face, the hollow eyes of the mask encountering the sculptor's face. But, just as the crowd was about to
separate them, the former spoke, in a voice not unfamiliar to
Kenyon, though rendered remote and strange by the guilty veil
through which it penetrated.

"Is all well with you, signor?" inquired the penitent, out
of the cloud in which he walked.

"All is well," answered Kenyon. "And with you?"

But the masked penitent returned no answer, being
borne away by the pressure of the throng.

The sculptor stood watching the figure, and was almost
of a mind to hurry after him and follow up the conversation
that had been begun; but it occurred to him that there is a
sanctity (or as we might rather term it, an inviolable eti-
quette) which prohibits the recognition of persons who choose
to walk under the veil of penitence.

"How strange!" thought Kenyon to himself. "It was
surely Donatello! What can bring him to Rome, where his
recollections must be so painful, and his presence not without
peril? And Miriam! Can she have accompanied him?"

He walked on, thinking of the vast change in Donatello,
since those days of gayety and innocence, when the young
Italian was new in Rome, and was just beginning to be sensible
of a more poignant felicity than he had yet experienced, in
the sunny warmth of Miriam's smile. The growth of a soul,
which the sculptor half imagined that he had witnessed in his
friend, seemed hardly worth the heavy price that it had cost,
in the sacrifice of those simple enjoyments that were gone
forever. A creature of antique healthfulness had vanished from
the earth; and, in his stead, there was only one other morbid
and remorseful man, among millions that were cast in the
same indistinguishable mould.

The accident of thus meeting Donatello—the glad Faun
of his imagination and memory, now transformed into a
gloomy penitent—contributed to deepen the cloud that had

fallen over Kenyon's spirits. It caused him to fancy, as we generally do, in the petty troubles which extend not a hand's breadth beyond our own sphere, that the whole world was saddening around him. It took the sinister aspect of an omen, although he could not distinctly see what trouble it might forebode.

If it had not been for a peculiar sort of pique, with which lovers are much conversant, a preposterous kind of resentment which endeavors to wreak itself on the beloved object, and on one's own heart, in requital of mishaps for which neither are in fault, Kenyon might at once have betaken himself to Hilda's studio, and asked why the appointment was not kept. But the interview of today was to have been so rich in present joy, and its results so important to his future life, that the bleak failure was too much for his equanimity. He was angry with poor Hilda, and censured her without a hearing; angry with himself, too, and therefore inflicted on this latter criminal the severest penalty in his power; angry with the day that was passing over him, and would not permit its latter hours to redeem the disappointment of the morning.

To confess the truth, it had been the sculptor's purpose to stake all his hopes on that interview in the galleries of the Vatican. Straying with Hilda through those long vistas of ideal beauty, he meant, at last, to utter himself upon that theme which lovers are fain to discuss in village-lanes, in wood-paths, on seaside sands, in crowded streets; it little matters where, indeed, since roses are sure to blush along the way, and daisies and violets to spring beneath the feet, if the spoken word be graciously received. He was resolved to make proof whether the kindness, that Hilda evinced for him, was the precious token of an individual preference, or merely the sweet fragrance of her disposition, which other friends might share as largely as himself. He would try if it were possible to take this shy, yet frank, and innocently fearless creature, captive, and imprison her in his heart, and make her sensible of a wider freedom there, than in all the world besides.

It was hard, we must allow, to see the shadow of a wintry

sunset falling upon a day that was to have been so bright, and to find himself just where yesterday had left him, only with a sense of being drearily balked, and defeated without an opportunity for struggle. So much had been anticipated from these now vanished hours, that it seemed as if no other day could bring back the same golden hopes.

In a case like this, it is doubtful whether Kenyon could have done a much better thing than he actually did, by going to dine at the Café Nuovo, and drinking a flask of Montefiascone; longing, the while, for a beaker or two of Donatello's Sunshine. It would have been just the wine to cure a lover's melancholy, by illuminating his heart with tender light and warmth, and suggestions of undefined hopes, too ethereal for his morbid humor to examine and reject them.

No decided improvement resulting from the draught of Montefiascone, he went to the Teatro Argentino,[3] and sat gloomily to see an Italian comedy, which ought to have cheered him somewhat, being full of glancing merriment, and effective over everybody's risibilities except his own. The sculptor came out, however, before the close of the performance, as disconsolate as he went in.

As he made his way through the complication of narrow streets, which perplex that portion of the city, a carriage passed him. It was driven rapidly, but not too fast for the light of a gas-lamp to flare upon a face within; especially as it was bent forward, appearing to recognize him, while a beckoning hand was protruded from the window. On his part, Kenyon at once knew the face, and hastened to the carriage, which had now stopped.

"Miriam! you in Rome?" he exclaimed. "And your friends know nothing of it?"

"Is all well with you?" she asked.

[3]An 18th-century opera house; Rossini's *The Barber of Seville* opened here in 1816.

For the wine of Montefiascone, see note 1, p. 217.

This inquiry, in the identical words which Donatello had so recently addressed to him, from beneath the penitent's mask, startled the sculptor. Either the previous disquietude of his mind, or some tone in Miriam's voice, or the unaccountableness of beholding her there at all, made it seem ominous.

"All is well, I believe," answered he, doubtfully. "I am aware of no misfortune. Have you any to announce?"

He looked still more earnestly at Miriam, and felt a dreamy uncertainty whether it was really herself to whom he spoke. True; there were those beautiful features, the contour of which he had studied too often, and with a sculptor's accuracy of perception, to be in any doubt that it was Miriam's identical face. But he was conscious of a change, the nature of which he could not satisfactorily define; it might be merely her dress, which, imperfect as the light was, he saw to be richer than the simple garb that she had usually worn. The effect, he fancied, was partly owing to a gem which she had on her bosom; not a diamond, but something that glimmered with a clear, red lustre, like the stars in a southern sky. Somehow or other, this colored light seemed an emanation of herself, as if all that was passionate and glowing, in her native disposition, had crystallized upon her breast, and were just now scintillating more brilliantly than ever, in sympathy with some emotion of her heart.

Of course there could be no real doubt that it was Miriam, his artist friend, with whom and Hilda he had spent so many pleasant and familiar hours, and whom he had last seen at Perugia, bending with Donatello beneath the bronze pope's benediction. It must be that selfsame Miriam; but the sensitive sculptor felt a difference of manner, which impressed him more than he conceived it possible to be affected by so external a thing. He remembered the gossip so prevalent in Rome on Miriam's first appearance; how that she was no real artist, but the daughter of an illustrious or golden lineage, who was merely playing at necessity; mingling with human struggle for her pastime; stepping out of her native sphere only for an interlude, just as a princess might alight from her gilded equipage to go on foot through a rustic lane. And now, after a mask in which love and death had performed their several parts, she had resumed her proper character.

"Have you anything to tell me?" cried he, impatiently; for nothing causes a more disagreeable vibration of the nerves than this perception of ambiguousness in familiar persons or affairs. "Speak; for my spirits and patience have been much tried to-day."

Miriam put her finger on her lips, and seemed desirous that Kenyon should know of the presence of a third person. He now saw, indeed, that there was some one beside her in the carriage, hitherto concealed by her attitude; a man, it appeared, with a sallow Italian face, which the sculptor distinguished but imperfectly, and did not recognize.

"I can tell you nothing," she replied; and leaning towards him, she whispered—appearing then more like the Miriam whom he knew, than in what had before passed—"Only, when the lamp goes out do not despair."

The carriage drove on, leaving Kenyon to muse over this unsatisfactory interview, which seemed to have served no better purpose than to fill his mind with more ominous forebodings than before. Why were Donatello and Miriam in Rome, where both, in all likelihood, might have much to dread? And why had one and the other addressed him with a question that seemed prompted by a knowledge of some calamity, either already fallen on his unconscious head, or impending closely over him?

"I am sluggish," muttered Kenyon, to himself; "a weak, nerveless fool, devoid of energy and promptitude; or neither Donatello nor Miriam could have escaped me thus! They are aware of some misfortune that concerns me deeply. How soon am I to know it too?"

There seemed but a single calamity possible to happen within so narrow a sphere as that with which the sculptor was connected; and even to that one mode of evil he could assign no definite shape, but only felt that it must have some reference to Hilda.

Flinging aside the morbid hesitation, and the dallyings with his own wishes, which he had permitted to influence his mind throughout the day, he now hastened to the Via Portoghese. Soon the old palace stood before him, with its massive tower rising into the clouded night; obscured from view at its mid-most elevation, but revealed again, higher upward, by the Virgin's lamp that twinkled on the summit. Feeble as it was, in the broad, surrounding gloom, that little ray made no in-considerable illumination among Kenyon's sombre thoughts; for, remembering Miriam's last words, a fantasy had seized him that he should find the sacred lamp extinguished.

And, even while he stood gazing, as a mariner at the star in which he puts his trust, the light quivered, sank, gleamed up again, and finally went out, leaving the battlements of Hilda's tower in utter darkness. For the first time in centuries, the consecrated and legendary flame, before the loftiest shrine in Rome, had ceased to burn.

Kenyon knew the sanctity which Hilda (faithful Protestant, and daughter of the Puritans, as the girl was) imputed to this shrine. He was aware of the profound feeling of responsibility, as well earthly as religious, with which her conscience had been impressed, when she became the occupant of her aërial chamber, and undertook the task of keeping the consecrated lamp alight. There was an accuracy and a certainty about Hilda's movements, as regarded all matters that lay deep enough to have their roots in right or wrong, which made it as possible and safe to rely upon the timely and careful trimming of this lamp (if she were in life, and able to creep up the steps), as upon the rising of to-morrow's sun, with lustre undiminished from to-day.

The sculptor could scarcely believe his eyes, therefore, when he saw the flame flicker and expire. His sight had surely deceived him. And now, since the light did not reappear, there must be some smoke-wreath or inpenetrable mist brooding about the tower's gray old head, and obscuring it from the lower world. But no! For right over the dim battlements, as the wind chased away a mass of clouds, he beheld a star, and, moreover, by an earnest concentration of his sight, was soon able to discern even the darkened shrine itself. There was no obscurity around the tower; no infirmity of his own vision. The flame had exhausted its supply of oil, and become extinct. But where was Hilda?

A man in a cloak happened to be passing; and Kenyon —anxious to distrust the testimony of his senses, if he could get more acceptable evidence on the other side—appealed to him.

"Do me the favor, signor," said he, "to look at the top of yonder tower, and tell me whether you see the lamp burning at the Virgin's shrine."

"The lamp, signor?" answered the man, without at first troubling himself to look up. "The lamp that has burned these four hundred years! how is it possible, signor, that it should not be burning now?"

"But look!" said the sculptor, impatiently.

With good-natured indulgence for what he seemed to consider as the whim of an eccentric Forestiero, the Italian carelessly threw his eyes upward; but, as soon as he perceived that there was really no light, he lifted his hands with a vivid expression of wonder and alarm.

"The lamp is extinguished!" cried he. "The lamp that has been burning these four hundred years! This surely must portend some great misfortune; and, by my advice, signor, you will hasten hence, lest the tower tumble on our heads. A priest once told me, that, if the Virgin withdrew her blessing, and the light went out, the old Palazzo del Torre would sink into the earth, with all that dwell in it. There will be a terrible crash before morning!"

The stranger made the best of his way from the doomed premises; while Kenyon,—who would willingly have seen the tower crumble down before his eyes, on condition of Hilda's safety,—determined, late as it was, to attempt ascertaining if she were in her dove-cote.

Passing through the arched entrance,—which, as is often the case with Roman entrances, was as accessible at midnight as at noon,—he groped his way to the broad staircase, and, lighting his wax taper, went glimmering up the multitude of steps that led to Hilda's door. The hour being so unseasonable, he intended merely to knock, and, as soon as her voice from within should reassure him, to retire, keeping his explanations and apologies for a fitter time. Accordingly, reaching the lofty height where the maiden, as he trusted, lay asleep, with angels watching over her, though the Virgin seemed to have suspended her care, he tapped lightly at the door-panels—then knocked more forcibly—then thundered an impatient summons. No answer came; Hilda evidently was not there.

After assuring himself that this must be the fact, Kenyon descended the stairs, but made a pause at every successive stage, and knocked at the door of its apartment, regardless whose slumbers he might disturb, in his anxiety to learn when the girl had last been seen. But, at each closed entrance, there came those hollow echoes, which a chamber, or any dwelling, great or small, never sends out, in response to human knuckles or iron hammer, as long as there is life within to keep its heart from getting dreary.

Once, indeed, on the lower landing-place, the sculptor fancied that there was a momentary stir, inside the door, as if somebody were listening at the threshold. He hoped, at least, that the small, iron-barred aperture would be unclosed, through which Roman housekeepers are wont to take careful cognizance of applicants for admission, from a traditionary dread, perhaps, of letting in a robber or assassin. But it remained shut; neither was the sound repeated; and Kenyon concluded that his excited nerves had played a trick upon his senses, as they are apt to do when we most wish for the clear evidence of the latter.

There was nothing to be done, save to go heavily away, and await whatever good or ill to-morrow's daylight might disclose.

Betimes in the morning, therefore, Kenyon went back to the Via Portoghese, before the slant rays of the sun had descended half-way down the gray front of Hilda's tower. As he drew near its base, he saw the doves perched in full session, on the sunny height of the battlements, and a pair of them—who were probably their mistress's especial pets, and the confidants of her bosom-secrets, if Hilda had any—came shooting down, and made a feint of alighting on his shoulder. But, though they evidently recognized him, their shyness would not yet allow so decided a demonstration.

Kenyon's eyes followed them as they flew upward, hoping that they might have come as joyful messengers of the girl's safety, and that he should discern her slender form, half-hidden by the parapet, trimming the extinguished lamp at the Virgin's shrine, just as other maidens set about the little duties of a household. Or perhaps he might see her gentle and sweet face smiling down upon him, midway towards heaven, as if she had flown thither for a day or two, just to visit her kindred, but had been drawn earthward again by the spell of unacknowledged love.

But his eyes were blessed by no such fair vision or reality; nor, in truth, were the eager, unquiet flutterings of the doves indicative of any joyful intelligence, which they longed to share with Hilda's friend, but of anxious inquiries that they knew not how to utter. They could not tell, any more than he, whither their lost companion had withdrawn herself, but were in the same void despondency with him, feeling their sunny and airy lives darkened and grown imperfect, now that her sweet society was taken out of it.

In the brisk morning air, Kenyon found it much easier to pursue his researches than at the preceding midnight, when, if any slumberers heard the clamor that he made, they had responded only with sullen and drowsy maledictions, and turned to sleep again. It must be a very dear and intimate reality for which people will be content to give up a dream. When the sun was fairly up, however, it was quite another thing. The heterogeneous population, inhabiting the lower floor of the old tower, and the other extensive regions of the palace, were now willing to tell all they knew, and imagine a great deal more. The amiability of these Italians, assisted by their sharp and nimble wits, caused them to overflow with plausible suggestions, and to be very bounteous in their avowals of interest for the lost Hilda. In a less demonstrative people, such expressions would have implied an eagerness to search land and sea, and never rest till she were found. In the mouths that uttered them, they meant good wishes, and were, so far, better than indifference. There was little doubt that many of them felt a genuine kindness for the shy, brown-haired, delicate young foreign maiden, who had flown from some distant land to alight upon their tower, where she consorted only with the doves. But their energy expended itself in exclamation, and they were content to leave all more active measures to Kenyon, and to the Virgin, whose affair it was, to see that the faithful votary of her lamp received no harm.

In a great Parisian domicile, multifarious as its inhabitants might be, the concierge under the archway would be cognizant of all their incomings and issuings forth. But, except in rare cases, the general entrance and main staircase of a Roman house are left as free as the street, of which they form a sort of by-lane. The sculptor, therefore, could hope to find information about Hilda's movements only from casual observers.

On probing the knowledge of these people to the bottom, there was various testimony as to the period when the girl had last been seen. Some said that it was four days since there had been a trace of her; but an English lady, in the second piano[1] of the palace, was rather of opinion that she had met her, the morning before, with a drawing-book in her hand. Having no acquaintance with the young person, she had taken little notice, and might have been mistaken. A Count, on the piano next above, was very certain that he had lifted his hat to Hilda, under the archway, two afternoons ago. An old woman, who had formerly tended the shrine, threw some light upon the matter, by testifying that the lamp required to be replenished once, at least, in three days, though its reservoir of oil was exceedingly capacious.

On the whole, though there was other evidence enough to create some perplexity, Kenyon could not satisfy himself that she had been visible since the afternoon of the third preceding day, when a fruit-seller remembered her coming out

[1]I.e., on the second floor.

of the arched passage, with a sealed packet in her hand. As nearly as he could ascertain, this was within an hour after Hilda had taken leave of the sculptor, at his own studio, with the understanding that they were to meet at the Vatican the next day. Two nights, therefore, had intervened, during which the lost maiden was unaccounted for.

The door of Hilda's apartments was still locked, as on the preceding night; but Kenyon sought out the wife of the person who sublet them, and prevailed on her to give him admittance by means of the duplicate key, which the good woman had in her possession. On entering, the maidenly neatness and simple grace, recognizable in all the arrangements, made him visibly sensible that this was the daily haunt of a pure soul, in whom religion and the love of beauty were at one.

Thence, the sturdy Roman matron led the sculptor across a narrow passage, and threw open the door of a small chamber, on the threshold of which he reverently paused. Within, there was a bed, covered with white drapery, enclosed within snowy curtains, like a tent, and of barely width enough for a slender figure to repose upon it. The sight of this cool, airy, and secluded bower, caused the lover's heart to stir, as if enough of Hilda's gentle dreams were lingering there to make him happy for a single instant. But then came the closer consciousness of her loss, bringing along with it a sharp sting of anguish.

"Behold, signor," said the matron; "here is the little staircase by which the signorina used to ascend and trim the blessed Virgin's lamp. She was worthy to be a Catholic, such pains the good child bestowed to keep it burning; and doubtless the blessed Mary will intercede for her, in consideration of her pious offices, heretic though she was. What will become of the old palazzo, now that the lamp is extinguished, the saints above us only know! Will you mount, signor, to the battlements, and see if she have left any trace of herself there?"

The sculptor stepped across the chamber and ascended

the little staircase, which gave him access to the breezy summit of the tower. It affected him inexpressibly to see a bouquet of beautiful flowers beneath the shrine, and to recognize in them an offering of his own to Hilda, who had put them in a vase of water and dedicated them to the Virgin, in a spirit partly fanciful, perhaps, but still partaking of the religious sentiment which so profoundly influenced her character. One rose-bud, indeed, she had selected for herself from the rich mass of flowers; for Kenyon well remembered recognizing it in her bosom, when he last saw her at his studio.

"That little part of my great love she took," said he to himself. "The remainder she would have devoted to heaven; but has left it withering in the sun and wind. Ah! Hilda, Hilda, had you given me a right to watch over you, this evil had not come!"

"Be not downcast, signorino mio," said the Roman matron, in response to the deep sigh which struggled out of Kenyon's breast. "The dear little maiden, as we see, has decked yonder blessed shrine as devoutly as I myself, or any other good Catholic woman, could have done. It is a religious act, and has more than the efficacy of a prayer. The signorina will as surely come back as the sun will fall through the window to-morrow no less than to-day. Her own doves have often been missing for a day or two, but they were sure to come fluttering about her head again, when she least expected them. So will it be with this dovelike child."

"It might be so," thought Kenyon, with yearning anxiety, "if a pure maiden were as safe as a dove, in this evil world of ours."

As they returned through the studio, with the furniture and arrangements of which the sculptor was familiar, he missed a small, ebony writing-desk that he remembered as having always been placed on a table there. He knew that it was Hilda's custom to deposit her letters in this desk, as well as other little objects of which she wished to be specially careful.

"What has become of it?" he suddenly inquired, laying his hand on the table.

"Become of what, pray?" exclaimed the woman, a little disturbed. "Does the signor suspect a robbery then?"

"The signorina's writing-desk is gone," replied Kenyon; "it always stood on this table, and I myself saw it there only a few days ago."

"Ah, well!" said the woman, recovering her composure, which she seemed partly to have lost. "The signorina has doubtless taken it away with her. The fact is of good omen; for it proves that she did not go unexpectedly, and is likely to return when it may best suit her convenience."

"This is very singular," observed Kenyon. "Have the rooms been entered by yourself, or any other person, since the signorina's disappearance?"

"Not by me, signor, so help me Heaven and the saints!" said the matron. "And I question whether there are more than two keys in Rome, that will suit this strange, old lock. Here is one; and as for the other, the signorina carries it in her pocket."

The sculptor had no reason to doubt the word of this respectable dame. She appeared to be well-meaning and kind-hearted, as Roman matrons generally are; except when a fit of passion incites them to shower horrible curses on an obnoxious individual, or perhaps to stab him with the steel stiletto that serves them for a hair-pin. But Italian asseverations of any questionable fact, however true they may chance to be, have no witness of their truth in the faces of those who utter them. Their words are spoken with strange earnestness, and yet do not vouch for themselves as coming from any depth, like roots drawn out of the substance of the soul, with some of the soil clinging to them. There is always a something inscrutable, instead of frankness, in their eyes. In short, they lie so much like truth, and speak truth so much as if they were telling a lie, that their auditor suspects himself in the wrong, whether he believes or disbelieves them; it being the one thing certain, that falsehood is seldom an intolerable burden to the tenderest of Italian consciences.

"It is very strange what can have become of the desk!" repeated Kenyon, looking the woman in the face.

"Very strange, indeed, signor," she replied, meekly, without turning away her eyes in the least, but checking his insight of them at about half-an-inch below the surface. "I think the signorina must have taken it with her."

It seemed idle to linger here any longer. Kenyon therefore departed, after making an arrangement with the woman, by the terms of which she was to allow the apartments to remain in their present state, on his assuming the responsibility for the rent.

He spent the day in making such further search and investigation as he found practicable; and, though at first trammelled by an unwillingness to draw public attention to Hilda's affairs, the urgency of the circumstances soon compelled him to be thoroughly in earnest. In the course of a week, he tried all conceivable modes of fathoming the mystery, not merely by his personal efforts and those of his brother-artists and friends, but through the police who readily undertook the task, and expressed strong confidence of success. But the Roman police has very little efficacy, except in the interest of the despotism of which it is a tool. With their cocked hats, shoulder-belts, and swords, they wear a sufficiently imposing aspect, and doubtless keep their eyes open wide enough to track a political offender, but are too often blind to private outrage, be it murder or any lesser crime. Kenyon counted little upon their assistance, and profited by it not at all.

Remembering the mystic words which Miriam had addressed to him, he was anxious to meet her, but knew not whither she had gone, nor how to obtain an interview either with herself or Donatello. The days wore away, and still there were no tidings of the lost one; no lamp rekindled before the Virgin's shrine; no light shining into the lover's heart; no star of Hope—he was ready to say, as he turned his eyes almost reproachfully upward—in heaven itself!

CHAPTER 45. *The Flight of Hilda's Doves*

Along with the lamp on Hilda's tower, the sculptor now felt that a light had gone out, or, at least, was ominously obscured, to which he owed whatever cheerfulness had heretofore illuminated his cold, artistic life. The idea of this girl had been like a taper of virgin wax, burning with a pure and steady flame, and chasing away the evil spirits out of the magic circle of its beams. It had darted its rays afar, and modified the whole sphere in which Kenyon had his being. Beholding it no more, he at once found himself in darkness and astray.

This was the time, perhaps, when Kenyon first became sensible what a dreary city is Rome, and what a terrible weight is there imposed on human life, when any gloom within the heart corresponds to the spell of ruin, that has been thrown over the site of ancient empire. He wandered, as it were, and stumbled over the fallen columns, and among the tombs, and groped his way into the sepulchral darkness of the catacombs, and found no path emerging from them. The happy may well enough continue to be such, beneath the brilliant sky of Rome. But, if you go thither in melancholy mood—if you go with a ruin in your heart, or with a vacant site there, where once stood the airy fabric of happiness, now vanished —all the ponderous gloom of the Roman Past will pile itself upon that spot, and crush you down as with the heaped-up marble and granite, the earth-mounds, and multitudinous bricks, of its material decay.

It might be supposed that a melancholy man would here make acquaintance with a grim philosophy. He should learn to bear patiently his individual griefs, that endure only

for one little lifetime, when here are the tokens of such infinite misfortune on an imperial scale, and when so many far
landmarks of time, all around him, are bringing the remoteness of a thousand years ago into the sphere of yesterday.
But it is in vain that you seek this shrub of bitter sweetness
among the plants that root themselves on the roughnesses
of massive walls, or trail downward from the capitals of pillars,
or spring out of the green turf in the palace of the Cæsars. It
does not grow in Rome; not even among the five hundred
various weeds which deck the grassy arches of the Coliseum.
You look through a vista of century beyond century—
through much shadow, and a little sunshine—through barbarism and civilization, alternating with one another, like
actors that have pre-arranged their parts—through a broad
pathway of progressive generations bordered by palaces and
temples, and bestridden by old, triumphal arches, until, in the
distance, you behold the obelisks, with their unintelligible
inscriptions, hinting at a past infinitely more remote than
history can define. Your own life is as nothing, when compared
with that immeasurable distance; but still you demand, none
the less earnestly, a gleam of sunshine, instead of a speck of
shadow, on the step or two that will bring you to your quiet
rest.

How exceedingly absurd! All men, from the date of the
earliest obelisk—and of the whole world, moreover, since
that far epoch, and before—have made a similar demand, and
seldom had their wish. If they had it, what are they the better,
now? But, even while you taunt yourself with this sad lesson,
your heart cries out obstreperously for its small share of
earthly happiness, and will not be appeased by the myriads of
dead hopes that lie crushed into the soil of Rome. How wonderful that this our narrow foothold of the Present should
hold its own so constantly, and, while every moment changing,
should still be like a rock betwixt the encountering tides of
the long Past, and the infinite To-come!

Man of marble though he was, the sculptor grieved for

the Irrevocable. Looking back upon Hilda's way of life, he marvelled at his own blind stupidity, which had kept him from remonstrating—as a friend, if with no stronger right—against the risks that she continually encountered. Being so innocent, she had no means of estimating those risks, nor even a possibility of suspecting their existence. But he—who had spent years in Rome, with a man's far wider scope of observation and experience—knew things that made him shudder. It seemed to Kenyon, looking through the darkly-colored medium of his fears, that all modes of crime were crowded into the close intricacy of Roman streets, and that there was no redeeming element, such as exists in other dissolute and wicked cities.

For here was a priesthood, pampered, sensual, with red and bloated cheeks, and carnal eyes. With apparently a grosser development of animal life than most men, they were placed in an unnatural relation with woman, and thereby lost the healthy, human conscience that pertains to other human beings, who own the sweet household ties connecting them with wife and daughter. And here was an indolent nobility, with no high aims or opportunities, but cultivating a vicious way of life, as if it were an art, and the only one which they cared to learn. Here was a population, high and low, that had no genuine belief in virtue; and if they recognized any act as criminal, they might throw off all care, remorse, and memory of it, by kneeling a little while at the confesssional, and rising unburdened, active, elastic, and incited by fresh appetite for the next ensuing sin. Here was a soldiery, who felt Rome to be their conquered city, and doubtless considered themselves the legal inheritors of the foul license which Gaul, Goth, and Vandal have here exercised in days gone by.[1]

[1]The French Army, under Napoleon III, occupied the Papal States until 1870, making them a virtual protectorate of the Second Empire.

Alaric I led the Visigoths in the First Sack of Rome, A.D. 410; Gaiseric led the Vandals in the Second Sack of Rome, A.D. 455; Odoacer, chieftain of the Heruli, deposed the last emperor, Romulus Augustulus, A.D. 476.

And what localities for new crime existed in those guilty sites, where the crime of departed ages used to be at home, and had its long, hereditary haunt! what street in Rome, what ancient ruin, what one place where man had standing-room, what fallen stone was there, unstained with one or another kind of guilt! In some of the vicissitudes of the city's pride, or its calamity, the dark tide of human evil had swelled over it, far higher than the Tiber ever rose against the acclivities of the seven hills.[2] To Kenyon's morbid view, there appeared to be a contagious element, rising fog-like from the ancient depravity of Rome, and brooding over the dead and half-rotten city, as nowhere else on earth. It prolonged the tendency to crime, and developed an instantaneous growth of it, whenever an opportunity was found. And where could it be found so readily as here! In those vast palaces, there were a hundred remote nooks where Innocence might shriek in vain. Beneath meaner houses there were unsuspected dungeons that had once been princely chambers, and open to the daylight; but, on account of some wickedness there perpetrated, each passing age had thrown its handful of dust upon the spot, and buried it from sight. Only ruffians knew of its existence, and kept it for murder, and worse crime.

Such was the city through which Hilda, for three years past, had been wandering without a protector or a guide. She had trodden lightly over the crumble of old crimes; she had taken her way amid the grime and corruption which Paganism had left there, and a perverted Christianity had made more noisome; walking saint-like through it all, with white, innocent feet; until, in some dark pitfall that lay right across her path, she had vanished out of sight. It was terrible to imagine what hideous outrage might have thrust her into that abyss!

Then the lover tried to comfort himself with the idea that Hilda's sanctity was a sufficient safeguard. Ah, yes; she was so pure! The angels, that were of the same sisterhood,

[2]Ancient Rome was built on seven hills.

would never let Hilda come to harm. A miracle would be wrought on her behalf, as naturally as a father would stretch out his hand to save a best-beloved child. Providence would keep a little area and atmosphere about her, as safe and wholesome as heaven itself, although the flood of perilous iniquity might hem her round, and its black waves hang curling above her head! But these reflections were of slight avail. No doubt they were the religious truth. Yet the ways of Providence are utterly inscrutable; and many a murder has been done, and many an innocent virgin has lifted her white arms, beseeching its aid in her extremity, and all in vain, so that, though Providence is infinitely good and wise,—and perhaps for that very reason,—it may be half an eternity before the great circle of its scheme shall bring us the superabundant recompense for all these sorrows! But what the lover asked was such prompt consolation as might consist with the brief span of mortal life; the assurance of Hilda's present safety, and her restoration within that very hour.

An imaginative man, he suffered the penalty of his endowment in the hundred-fold variety of gloomily tinted scenes that it presented to him, in which Hilda was always a central figure. The sculptor forgot his marble. Rome ceased to be anything, for him, but a labyrinth of dismal streets, in one or another of which the lost girl had disappeared. He was haunted with the idea, that some circumstance, most important to be known, and perhaps, easily discoverable, had hitherto been overlooked, and that, if he could lay hold of this one clue, it would guide him directly in the track of Hilda's footsteps. With this purpose in view, he went, every morning, to the Via Portoghese, and made it the starting point of fresh investigations. After nightfall, too, he invariably returned thither, with a faint hope fluttering at his heart, that the lamp might again be shining on the summit of the tower, and would dispel this ugly mystery out of the circle consecrated by its rays. There being no point of which he could take firm hold, his mind was filled with unsubstantial hopes and fears. Once, Kenyon had seemed to cut his life in marble; now he vaguely clutched at it, and found it vapor.

In his unstrung and despondent mood, one trifling circumstance affected him with an idle pang. The doves had at first been faithful to their lost mistress. They failed not to sit in a row upon her window-sill, or to alight on the shrine, on the church-angels, and on the roofs and portals of the neighboring houses, in evident expectation of her reappearance. After the second week, however, they began to take flight, and dropping off by pairs, betook themselves to other dovecotes. Only a single dove remained, and brooded drearily beneath the shrine. The flock, that had departed, were like the many hopes that had vanished from Kenyon's heart; the one that still lingered, and looked so wretched—was it a Hope, or already a Despair?

In the street, one day, the sculptor met a priest of mild and venerable aspect; and as his mind dwelt continually upon Hilda, and was especially active in bringing up all incidents that had ever been connected with her, it immediately struck him that this was the very father with whom he had seen her at the confessional. Such trust did Hilda inspire in him, that Kenyon had never asked what was the subject of the communication between herself and this old priest. He had no reason for imagining that it could have any relation with her disappearance, so long subsequently; but, being thus brought face to face with a personage, mysteriously associated, as he now remembered, with her whom he had lost, an impulse ran before his thoughts and led the sculptor to address him.

It might be that the reverend kindliness of the old man's expression took Kenyon's heart by surprise; at all events, he spoke as if there were a recognized acquaintanceship, and an object of mutual interest between them.

"She has gone from me, father," said he.

"Of whom do you speak, my son?" inquired the priest.

"Of that sweet girl," answered Kenyon, "who knelt to you at the confessional. Surely, you must remember her, among all the mortals to whose confessions you have listened! For she alone could have had no sins to reveal."

"Yes; I remember," said the priest, with a gleam of recollection in his eyes. "She was made to bear a miraculous testimony to the efficacy of the divine ordinances of the Church, by seizing forcibly upon one of them, and finding immediate relief from it, heretic though she was. It is my purpose to publish a brief narrative of this miracle, for the edification of mankind, in Latin, Italian, and English, from the printing-press of the Propaganda. Poor child! Setting apart her heresy, she was spotless, as you say. And is she dead?"

"Heaven forbid, father!" exclaimed Kenyon, shrinking back. "But she has gone from me, I know not whither. It may be—yes, the idea seizes upon my mind—that what she revealed to you will suggest some clue to the mystery of her disappearance."

"None, my son, none," answered the priest, shaking his head; "nevertheless, I bid you be of good cheer. That young maiden is not doomed to die a heretic. Who knows what the blessed Virgin may at this moment be doing for her soul! Perhaps, when you next behold her, she will be clad in the shining white robe of the true faith."

This latter suggestion did not convey all the comfort which the old priest possibly intended by it; but he imparted it to the sculptor, along with his blessing, as the two best things that he could bestow, and said nothing further, except to bid him farewell.

When they had parted, however, the idea of Hilda's conversion to Catholicism recurred to her lover's mind, bringing with it certain reflections, that gave a new turn to his surmises about the mystery into which she had vanished. Not that he seriously apprehended—although the superabundance of her religious sentiment might mislead her for a moment—that the New England girl would permanently succumb to the scarlet superstitions which surrounded her in Italy. But the incident of the confessional—if known, as probably it was, to the eager propagandists who prowl about for souls, as cats to catch a mouse—would surely inspire the most confident expectations of bringing her over to the faith. With so pious an end in view, would Jesuitical morality be shocked at the thought of kidnapping the mortal body, for the sake of the immortal spirit that might otherwise be lost forever? Would not the kind old priest, himself, deem this to be infinitely the kindest service that he could perform for the stray lamb, who had so strangely sought his aid?

If these suppositions were well founded, Hilda was most likely a prisoner in one of the religious establishments that are so numerous in Rome. The idea, according to the aspect in which it was viewed, brought now a degree of comfort, and now an additional perplexity. On the one hand, Hilda was safe from any but spiritual assaults; on the other, where was the possibility of breaking through all those barred portals, and searching a thousand convent-cells, to set her free?

Kenyon, however, as it happened, was prevented from endeavoring to follow out this surmise, which only the state of hopeless uncertainty, that almost bewildered his reason, could have led him for a moment to entertain. A communication reached him by an unknown hand, in consequence of which, and within an hour after receiving it, he took his way through one of the gates of Rome.

It was a bright forenoon of February; a month in which the brief severity of a Roman winter is already past, and when violets and daisies begin to show themselves in spots favored by the sun. The sculptor came out of the city by the gate of San Sebastiano, and walked briskly along the Appian Way.

For the space of a mile or two beyond the gate, this ancient and famous road is as desolate and disagreeable as most of the other Roman avenues. It extends over small, uncomfortable paving-stones, between brick and plastered walls, which are very solidly constructed, and so high as almost to exclude a view of the surrounding country. The houses are of most uninviting aspect, neither picturesque, nor homelike and social; they have seldom or never a door opening on the wayside, but are accessible only from the rear, and frown inhospitably upon the traveller through iron-grated windows. Here and there appears a dreary inn, or a wine-shop, designated by the withered bush beside the entrance, within which you discern a stone-built and sepulchral interior, where guests refresh themselves with sour bread and goat's milk cheese, washed down with wine of dolorous acerbity.

At frequent intervals along the roadside, uprises the ruin of an ancient tomb. As they stand now, these structures are immensely high and broken mounds of conglomerated brick, stone, pebbles, and earth, all molten by time into a mass as solid and indestructible as if each tomb were composed of a single boulder of granite. When first erected, they were cased externally, no doubt, with slabs of polished marble, artfully wrought bas-reliefs, and all such suitable adornments, and were rendered majestically beautiful by grand architectural

403

designs. This antique splendor has long since been stolen from the dead, to decorate the palaces and churches of the living. Nothing remains to the dishonored sepulchres, except their massiveness.

Even the pyramids form hardly a stranger spectacle, or are more alien from human sympathies, than the tombs of the Appian Way, with their gigantic height, breadth, and solidity, defying time and the elements, and far too mighty to be demolished by an ordinary earthquake. Here you may see a modern dwelling, and a garden with its vines and olive-trees, perched on the lofty dilapidation of a tomb, which forms a precipice of fifty feet in depth on each of the four sides. There is a home on that funereal mound, where generations of children have been born, and successive lives been spent, undisturbed by the ghost of the stern Roman whose ashes were so preposterously burdened. Other sepulchres wear a crown of grass, shrubbery, and forest-trees, which throw out a broad sweep of branches, having had time, twice over, to be a thousand years of age. On one of them stands a tower, which, though immemorially more modern than the tomb, was itself built by immemorial hands, and is now rifted quite from top to bottom by a vast fissure of decay; the tomb-hillock, its foundation, being still as firm as ever, and likely to endure until the last trump shall rend it wide asunder, and summon forth its unknown dead.

Yes; its unknown dead! For, except in one or two doubtful instances, these mountainous sepulchral edifices have not availed to keep so much as the bare name of an individual or a family from oblivion. Ambitious of everlasting remembrance, as they were, the slumberers might just as well have gone quietly to rest, each in his pigeon-hole of a columbarium,[1] or under his little green hillock, in a graveyard, without a headstone to mark the spot. It is rather satisfactory than otherwise, to think that all these idle pains have turned out so utterly abortive.

[1]Dove-cote.

About two miles, or more, from the city-gate, and right upon the roadside, Kenyon passed an immense round pile, sepulchral in its original purposes, like those already mentioned. It was built of great blocks of hewn stone, on a vast, square foundation of rough, agglomerated material, such as composes the mass of all the other ruinous tombs. But whatever might be the cause, it was in a far better state of preservation than they. On its broad summit rose the battlements of a mediæval fortress, out of the midst of which (so long since had time begun to crumble the supplemental structure, and cover it with soil, by means of wayside dust) grew trees, bushes, and thick festoons of ivy. This tomb of a woman had become the citadel and donjon-keep of a castle; and all the care that Cecilia Metella's husband could bestow, to secure endless peace for her beloved relics, had only sufficed to make that handful of precious ashes the nucleus of battles, long ages after her death.[2]

A little beyond this point, the sculptor turned aside from the Appian Way, and directed his course across the Campagna, guided by tokens that were obvious only to himself. On one side of him, but at a distance, the Claudian aqueduct[3] was striding over fields and watercourses. Before him, many miles away, with a blue atmosphere between, rose the Alban hills, brilliantly silvered with snow and sunshine.

He was not without a companion. A buffalo-calf, that seemed shy and sociable by the selfsame impulse, had begun

[2]Cecilia Metella was the wife of Crassus, the rich man in the First Triumvirate (60 B.C.). Her tomb, built in the 1st century B.C. on the Appian Way, is a prominent landmark.

[3]A magnificent architectural feat designed and built by the Emperor Claudius A.D. 52. Hawthorne notes on October 23, 1858: "I walked onward a good distance beyond the gate [the Porta Maggiore] alongside the arches of the Claudian aqueduct, which, in this portion of it, seems to have had little repair, and to have needed little, since it was built. It looks like a long procession, striding across the Campagna toward the city, and entering the gate over one of its arches; within the gate, I saw two or three slender jets of water spurting from the crevices; this aqueduct being still in use to bring the Acqua Felice into Rome" (NB, p. 484).

to make acquaintance with him, from the moment when he left the road.[4] This frolicsome creature gambolled along, now before, now behind; standing a moment to gaze at him, with wild, curious eyes, he leaped aside and shook his shaggy head, as Kenyon advanced too nigh; then, after loitering in the rear, he came galloping up, like a charge of cavalry, but halted, all of a sudden, when the sculptor turned to look, and bolted across the Campagna, at the slightest signal of nearer approach. The young, sportive thing, Kenyon half fancied, was serving him as a guide, like the heifer that led Cadmus to the site of his destined city;[5] for, in spite of a hundred vagaries, his general course was in the right direction, and along by several objects which the sculptor had noted as landmarks of his way.

In this natural intercourse with a rude and healthy form of animal life, there was something that wonderfully revived Kenyon's spirits. The warm rays of the sun, too, were wholesome for him in body and soul; and so was a breeze that bestirred itself occasionally, as if for the sole purpose of breathing upon his cheek, and dying softly away, when he would fain have felt a little more decided kiss. This shy, but loving breeze reminded him strangely of what Hilda's deportment had sometimes been towards himself.

The weather had very much to do, no doubt, with these genial and delightful sensations, that made the sculptor so happy with mere life, in spite of a head and heart full of doleful thoughts, anxieties, and fears, which ought in all reason to have depressed him. It was like no weather that exists anywhere, save in Paradise and in Italy; certainly not in America,

[4]Hawthorne took a similar walk on the Campagna on February 24, 1858, and saw a buffalo calf in the road. Sophia excised the passage from the notebooks on the grounds that it had already appeared in *The Marble Faun* (*NB*, p. 104).

[5]In Greek mythology, the Oracle at Delphi told Cadmus to follow a cow wherever she went and to found a city on the spot where she sank with weariness. Cadmus bought a cow from some herdsmen and drove her east through Boeotia until she collapsed on the site of Thebes.

where it is always too strenuous on the side either of heat or cold. Young as the season was, and wintry as it would have been under a more rigid sky, it resembled summer rather than what we New Englanders recognize in our idea of spring. But there was an indescribable something, sweet, fresh, and remotely affectionate, which the matronly summer loses, and which thrilled, and, as it were, tickled Kenyon's heart with a feeling partly of the senses, yet far more a spiritual delight. In a word, it was as if Hilda's delicate breath were on his cheek.

After walking at a brisk pace for about half an hour, he reached a spot where an excavation appeared to have been begun, at some not very distant period. There was a hollow space in the earth, looking exceedingly like a deserted cellar, being enclosed within old subterranean walls, constructed of thin Roman bricks, and made accessible by a narrow flight of stone steps. A suburban villa had probably stood over this site, in the imperial days of Rome, and these might have been the ruins of a bathroom, or some other apartment that was required to be wholly or partly under ground. A spade can scarcely be put into that soil, so rich in lost and forgotten things, without hitting upon some discovery which would attract all eyes, in any other land. If you dig but a little way, you gather bits of precious marble, coins, rings, and engraved gems; if you go deeper, you break into columbaria, or into sculptured and richly frescoed apartments that look like festive halls, but were only sepulchres.

The sculptor descended into the cellar-like cavity, and sat down on a block of stone. His eagerness had brought him thither sooner than the appointed hour. The sunshine fell slantwise into the hollow, and happened to be resting on what Kenyon at first took to be a shapeless fragment of stone, possibly marble, which was partly concealed by the crumbling down of earth.

But his practised eye was soon aware of something artistic in this rude object. To relieve the anxious tedium of his situation, he cleared away some of the soil, which seemed to have fallen very recently, and discovered a headless figure of marble.[6] It was earth-stained, as well it might be, and had a slightly corroded surface, but at once impressed the sculptor as a Greek production, and wonderfully delicate and beautiful. The head was gone; both arms were broken off at the elbows. Protruding from the loose earth, however, Kenyon beheld the fingers of a marble hand; it was still appended to its arm, and a little further search enabled him to find the other. Placing these limbs in what the nice adjustment of the fractures proved to be their true position, the poor, fragmentary woman forthwith showed that she retained her modest instincts to the last. She had perished with them, and snatched them back at the moment of revival. For these long-buried hands immediately disposed themselves in the manner that nature prompts, as the antique artist knew, and as all the world has seen, in the Venus de' Medici.[7]

[6]On April 14, 1858, Hawthorne drove out onto the Campagna with the Storys and Henry Wilde, an American painter from Boston, to see such a statue, recently excavated. He notes: "Within this hollow space the statue had been found, and it was now standing against one of the walls, covered with a coarse cloth, or a canvas bag. This being removed, there appeared a headless marble figure, earth-stained, of course, and with a slightly corroded surface, but wonderfully delicate and beautiful, the shape, size, and attitude, apparently, of the Venus di Medici, but, as we all thought, more beautiful than that. It is supposed to be the original from which the Venus di Medici was copied. Both arms were broken off, but the greater part of both, and nearly the whole of one hand, had been found, and these being adjusted to the figure, they took the well-known position before the bosom and the middle, as if the fragmentary woman retained her instinct of modesty to the last. There were the marks on the bosom and thighs where the fingers had touched; whereas in the Venus di Medici, if I remember rightly, the fingers are sculptured quite free of the person. The man who showed the statue now lifted from a corner a round block of marble, which had been lying there among other fragments, and this he placed upon the shattered neck of the Venus; and behold, it was her head and face, perfect, all but the nose!" (*NB*, pp. 500–501).

[7]Famous statue of Venus in the Uffizi Gallery, Florence.

"What a discovery is here!" thought Kenyon to himself. "I seek for Hilda, and find a marble woman! Is the omen good or ill?"

In a corner of the excavation, lay a small round block of stone, much incrusted with earth that had dried and hardened upon it. So, at least, you would have described this object, until the sculptor lifted it, turned it hither and thither in his hands, brushed off the clinging soil, and finally placed it on the slender neck of the newly discovered statue. The effect was magical. It immediately lighted up and vivified the whole figure, endowing it with personality, soul, and intelligence. The beautiful Idea at once asserted its immortality, and converted that heap of forlorn fragments into a whole, as perfect to the mind, if not to the eye, as when the new marble gleamed with snowy lustre; nor was the impression marred by the earth that still hung upon the exquisitely graceful limbs, and even filled the lovely crevice of the lips. Kenyon cleared it away from between them, and almost deemed himself rewarded with a living smile.

It was either the prototype or a better repetition of the Venus of the Tribune.[8] But those who have been dissatisfied with the small head, the narrow, soulless face, the buttonhole eyelids, of that famous statue, and its mouth such as nature never moulded, should see the genial breadth of this far nobler and sweeter countenance. It is one of the few works of antique sculpture in which we recognize womanhood, and that, moreover, without prejudice to its divinity.

Here, then, was a treasure for the sculptor to have found! How happened it to be lying there, beside its grave of twenty centuries? Why were not the tidings of its discovery already noised abroad? The world was richer than yesterday, by something far more precious than gold. Forgotten beauty had

[8]Another Venus, inferior to the Medici Venus, in the Capitoline Museum.

come back, as beautiful as ever; a goddess had risen from her long slumber, and was a goddess still. Another cabinet in the Vatican was destined to shine as lustrously as that of the Apollo Belvedere; or, if the aged pope should resign his claim, an emperor would woo this tender marble, and win her as proudly as an imperial bride![9]

Such were the thoughts, with which Kenyon exaggerated to himself the importance of the newly-discovered statue, and strove to feel at least a portion of the interest which this event would have inspired in him, a little while before. But, in reality, he found it difficult to fix his mind upon the subject. He could hardly, we fear, be reckoned a consummate artist, because there was something dearer to him than his art; and, by the greater strength of a human affection, the divine statue seemed to fall asunder again, and become only a heap of worthless fragments.

While the sculptor sat listlessly gazing at it, there was a sound of small hoofs, clumsily galloping on the Campagna; and, soon, his frisky acquaintance, the buffalo-calf, came and peeped over the edge of the excavation. Almost at the same moment, he heard voices, which approached nearer and nearer; a man's voice, and a feminine one, talking the musical tongue of Italy. Besides the hairy visage of his four-footed friend, Kenyon now saw the figures of a peasant and a contadina, making gestures of salutation to him, on the opposite verge of the hollow space.

[9]As temporal ruler of the Papal States, the Pope had first claim on all ancient works of art discovered on his lands.

CHAPTER 47

The Peasant and Contadina

They descended into the excavation; a young peasant, in the short blue jacket, the smallclothes buttoned at the knee, and buckled shoes, that compose one of the ugliest dresses ever worn by man, except the wearer's form have a grace which any garb, or the nudity of an antique statue, would equally set off; and, hand in hand with him, a village girl, in one of those brilliant costumes largely kindled up with scarlet, and decorated with gold embroidery, in which the contadinas array themselves on feast-days. But Kenyon was not deceived; he had recognized the voices of his friends, indeed, even before their disguised figures came between him and the sunlight. Donatello was the peasant; the contadina, with the airy smile, half mirthful, though it shone out of melancholy eyes,—was Miriam.

They both greeted the sculptor with a familiar kindness which reminded him of the days when Hilda and they and he had lived so happily together, before the mysterious adventure of the catacomb. What a succession of sinister events had followed one spectral figure out of that gloomy labyrinth!

"It is carnival time, you know," said Miriam, as if in explanation of Donatello's and her own costume. "Do you remember how merrily we spent the carnival, last year?"

"It seems many years ago," replied Kenyon. "We are all so changed!"

When individuals approach one another with deep purposes on both sides, they seldom come at once to the matter which they have most at heart. They dread the electric shock of a too sudden contact with it. A natural impulse leads them to steal gradually onward, hiding themselves, as it were, behind a closer, and still a closer topic, until they stand face to face with the true point of interest. Miriam was conscious of this impulse, and partially obeyed it.

"So, your instincts as a sculptor have brought you into the presence of our newly discovered statue," she observed. "Is it not beautiful? A far truer image of immortal woman-hood than the poor little damsel at Florence, world-famous though she be."

"Most beautiful," said Kenyon, casting an indifferent glace at the Venus. "The time has been when the sight of this statue would have been enough to make the day memorable."

"And will it not do so, now?" Miriam asked. "I fancied so, indeed, when we discovered it two days ago. It is Don-atello's prize. We were sitting here together, planning an interview with you, when his keen eyes detected the fallen goddess, almost entirely buried under that heap of earth, which the clumsy excavators showered down upon her, I suppose. We congratulated ourselves, chiefly for your sake. The eyes of us three are the only ones to which she has yet revealed herself. Does it not frighten you a little, like the apparition of a lovely woman that lived of old, and has long lain in the grave?"

"Ah, Miriam! I cannot respond to you," said the sculptor, with irrepressible impatience. "Imagination and the love of art have both died out of me."

"Miriam," interposed Donatello, with gentle gravity, "why should we keep our friend in suspense? We know what anxiety he feels. Let us give him what intelligence we can."

"You are so direct and immediate, my beloved friend!" answered Miriam with an unquiet smile. "There are several reasons why I should like to play round this matter a little while, and cover it with fanciful thoughts, as we strew a grave with flowers."

"A grave!" exclaimed the sculptor.

"No grave in which your heart need be buried," she replied; "you have no such calamity to dread. But I linger and hesitate, because every word I speak brings me nearer to a crisis from which I shrink. Ah, Donatello! let us live a little longer the life of these last few days! It is so bright, so airy, so childlike, so without either past or future! Here, on the wild Campagna, you seem to have found, both for yourself and me, the life that belonged to you in early youth; the sweet, irresponsible life which you inherited from your mythic ancestry, the Fauns of Monte Beni. Our stern and black reality will come upon us speedily enough. But, first, a brief time more of this strange happiness."

"I dare not linger upon it," answered Donatello, with an expression that reminded the sculptor of the gloomiest days of his remorse at Monte Beni. "I dare to be so happy as you have seen me, only because I have felt the time to be so brief."

"One day, then!" pleaded Miriam. "One more day in the wild freedom of this sweet-scented air."

"Well, one more day," said Donatello, smiling; and his smile touched Kenyon with a pathos beyond words, there being gayety and sadness both melted into it; 'but here is Hilda's friend, and our own. Comfort him, at least, and set his heart at rest, since you have it partly in your power."

"Ah, surely he might endure his pangs a little longer!" cried Miriam, turning to Kenyon with a tricksy, fitful kind of mirth, that served to hide some solemn necessity, too sad and serious to be looked at in its naked aspect. "You love us both, I think, and will be content to suffer for our sakes, one other day. Do I ask too much?"

"Tell me of Hilda," replied the sculptor; "tell me only that she is safe, and keep back what else you will."

"Hilda is safe," said Miriam. "There is a Providence purposely for Hilda, as I remember to have told you long ago. But a great trouble—an evil deed, let us acknowledge it— has spread out its dark branches so widely, that the shadow falls on innocence as well as guilt. There was one slight link that connected your sweet Hilda with a crime which it was her unhappy fortune to witness, but of which, I need not say, she was as guiltless as the angels that looked out of heaven, and saw it too. No matter, now, what the consequence has been. You shall have your lost Hilda back, and—who knows—perhaps tenderer than she was."

"But when will she return?" persisted the sculptor, "Tell me the when, and where, and how!"

"A little patience. Do not press me so," said Miriam; and again Kenyon was struck by the spritelike, fitful characteristic of her manner, and a sort of hysteric gayety, which seemed to be a will-o'-the-wisp from a sorrow stagnant at her heart. "You have more time to spare than I. First, listen to something that I have to tell. We will talk of Hilda by-and-by."

Then Miriam spoke of her own life, and told facts that threw a gleam of light over many things which had perplexed the sculptor in all his previous knowledge of her. She described herself as springing from English parentage, on the mother's side, but with a vein, likewise, of Jewish blood; yet connected, through her father, with one of those few princely families of southern Italy, which still retain a great wealth and influence. And she revealed a name, at which her auditor started, and grew pale; for it was one that, only a few years before, had been familiar to the world, in connection with a mysterious and terrible event. The reader—if he think it worth while to recall some of the strange incidents which have been talked of, and forgotten, within no long time past—will remember Miriam's name.[1]

"You shudder at me, I perceive!" said Miriam, suddenly interrupting her narrative.

"No; you were innocent," replied the sculptor. "I shudder at the fatality that seems to haunt your footsteps, and throws a shadow of crime about your path, you being guiltless."

[1]One of the passages of teasing mystification in the romance. If Hawthorne has a specific allusion in mind, it may be to the Praslin murder case, as Nathalia Wright suggests in "Hawthorne and the Praslin Murder," *NEQ*, 15 (1942), 5–14.

"There was such a fatality," said Miriam; "yes; the shadow fell upon me, innocent, but I went astray in it, and wandered—as Hilda could tell you—into crime."

She went on to say, that, while yet a child, she had lost her English mother. From a very early period of her life, there had been a contract of betrothal between herself and a certain marchese, the representative of another branch of her paternal house,—a family arrangement between two persons of disproportioned ages, and in which feeling went for nothing. Most Italian girls of noble rank would have yielded themselves to such a marriage, as an affair of course. But there was something in Miriam's blood, in her mixed race, in her recollections of her mother,—some characteristic, finally, in her own nature,—which had given her freedom of thought, and force of will, and made this pre-arranged connection odious to her. Moreover, the character of her destined husband would have been a sufficient and insuperable objection; for it betrayed traits so evil, so treacherous, so wild, and yet so strangely subtle, as could only be accounted for by the insanity which often develops itself in old, close-kept breeds of men, when long unmixed with newer blood. Reaching the age when the marriage contract should have been fulfilled, Miriam had utterly repudiated it.

Sometime afterwards had occurred that terrible event to which Miriam alluded, when she revealed her name; an event, the frightful and mysterious circumstances of which will recur to many minds, but of which few or none can have found for themselves a satisfactory explanation. It only concerns the present narrative, inasmuch as the suspicion of being at least an accomplice in the crime fell darkly and directly upon Miriam herself.

"But you know that I am innocent!" she cried, interrupting herself again, and looking Kenyon in the face.

"I know it by my deepest consciousness," he answered; "and I know it by Hilda's trust and entire affection, which you never could have won had you been capable of guilt."

"That is sure ground, indeed, for pronouncing me innocent," said Miriam, with the tears gushing into her eyes. "Yet I have since become a horror to your saintlike Hilda, by a crime which she herself saw me help to perpetrate!"

She proceeded with her story. The great influence of her family connections had shielded her from some of the consequences of her imputed guilt. But, in her despair, she had fled from home, and had surrounded her flight with such circumstances as rendered it the most probable conclusion that she had committed suicide. Miriam, however, was not of the feeble nature which takes advantage of that obvious and poor resource in earthly difficulties. She flung herself upon the world, and speedily created a new sphere, in which Hilda's gentle purity, the sculptor's sensibility, clear thought, and genius, and Donatello's genial simplicity, had given her almost her first experience of happiness. Then came that ill-omened adventure of the catacomb. The spectral figure which she encountered there was the evil fate that had haunted her through life.

Looking back upon what had happened, Miriam observed, she now considered him a madman. Insanity must have been mixed up with his original composition, and developed by those very acts of depravity which it suggested, and still more intensified by the remorse that ultimately followed them. Nothing was stranger in his dark career, than the penitence which often seemed to go hand in hand with crime. Since his death, she had ascertained that it finally led him to a convent, where his severe and self-inflicted penances had even acquired him the reputation of unusual sanctity, and had been the cause of his enjoying greater freedom than is commonly allowed to monks.

"Need I tell you more?" asked Miriam, after proceeding thus far. "It is still a dim and dreary mystery, a gloomy twilight into which I guide you; but possibly you may catch a glimpse of much that I myself can explain only by conjecture. At all events, you can comprehend what my situation must have been, after that fatal interview in the catacomb. My persecutor had gone thither for penance, but followed me forth with fresh impulses to crime. He had me in his power. Mad as he was, and wicked as he was, with one word he could have blasted me in the belief of all the world. In your belief too, and Hilda's! Even Donatello would have shrunk from me with horror!"

"Never," said Donatello; "my instinct would have known you innocent."

"Hilda and Donatello and myself—we three would have acquitted you," said Kenyon, "let the world say what it might. "Ah, Miriam, you should have told us this sad story sooner!"

"I thought often of revealing it to you," answered Miriam; "on one occasion, especially, (it was after you had shown me your Cleopatra,) it seemed to leap out of my heart, and got as far as my very lips. But finding you cold to accept my confidence, I thrust it back again. Had I obeyed my first impulse, all would have turned out differently."

"And Hilda!" resumed the sculptor. "What can have been her connection with these dark incidents?"

"She will, doubtless, tell you with her own lips," replied Miriam. "Through sources of information which I possess in Rome, I can assure you of her safety. In two days more—by the help of the special Providence that, as I love to tell you, watches over Hilda—she shall rejoin you."

"Still two days more!" murmured the sculptor.

"Ah, you are cruel now! More cruel than you know!" exclaimed Miriam, with another gleam of that fantastic, fitful gayety, which had more than once marked her manner, during this interview. "Spare your poor friends!"

"I know not what you mean, Miriam," said Kenyon.

"No matter," she replied; "you will understand hereafter. But could you think it? Here is Donatello haunted with strange remorse, and an immitigable resolve to obtain what he deems justice upon himself. He fancies, with a kind of direct simplicity, which I have vainly tried to combat, that, when a wrong has been done, the doer is bound to submit himself to

whatever tribunal takes cognizance of such things, and abide
its judgment. I have assured him that there is no such thing as
earthly justice, and especially none here, under the head of
Christendom."

"We will not argue the point again," said Donatello,
smiling. "I have no head for argument, but only a sense, an
impulse, an instinct, I believe, which sometimes leads me right.
But why do we talk now of what may make us sorrowful?
There are still two days more. Let us be happy!"

It appeared to Kenyon that since he last saw Donatello,
some of the sweet and delightful characteristics of the antique
Faun had returned to him. There were slight, careless graces,
pleasant and simple peculiarities, that had been obliterated by
the heavy grief through which he was passing, at Monte Beni,
and out of which he had hardly emerged, when the sculptor
parted with Miriam and him beneath the bronze pontiff's outstretched hand. These happy blossoms had now reappeared.
A playfulness came out of his heart and glimmered like fire-
light on his actions, alternating, or even closely intermingled,
with profound sympathy and serious thought.

"Is he not beautiful?" said Miriam, watching the sculptor's eye as it dwelt admiringly on Donatello. "So changed,
yet still, in a deeper sense, so much the same! He has travelled
in a circle, as all things heavenly and earthly do, and now
comes back to his original self, with an inestimable treasure
of improvement won from an experience of pain. How wonderful is this! I tremble at my own thoughts, yet must needs
probe them to their depths. Was the crime—in which he and
I were wedded—was it a blessing, in that strange disguise?
Was it a means of education, bringing a simple and imperfect
nature to a point of feeling and intelligence which it could
have reached under no other discipline?"

"You stir up deep and perilous matter, Miriam," replied
Kenyon. "I dare not follow you into the unfathomable abysses
whither you are tending."

"Yet there is a pleasure in them! I delight to brood on

the verge of this great mystery," returned she. "The story of the fall of man! Is it not repeated in our romance of Monte Beni? And may we follow the analogy yet farther? Was that very sin—into which Adam precipitated himself and all his race—was it the destined means by which, over a long pathway of toil and sorrow, we are to attain a higher, brighter, and profounder happiness, than our lost birthright gave? Will not this idea account for the permitted existence of sin, as no other theory can?"[2]

"It is too dangerous, Miriam! I cannot follow you!" repeated the sculptor. "Mortal man has no right to tread on the ground where you now set your feet."

"Ask Hilda what she thinks of it," said Miriam, with a thoughtful smile. "At least, she might conclude that sin—which man chose instead of good—has been so beneficently handled by omniscience and omnipotence, that, whereas our dark enemy sought to destroy us by it, it has really become an instrument most effective in the education of intellect and soul."

Miriam paused a little longer among these meditations, which the sculptor rightly felt to be so perilous; she then pressed his hand, in token of farewell.

"The day after to-morrow," said she, "an hour before sunset, go to the Corso, and stand in front of the fifth house on your left, beyond the Antonine column. You will learn tidings of a friend."

[2]The transformation of the Faun is now complete. Here Miriam, and later Kenyon, suggest the theme of the *felix culpa*—the "happy fault" of man's sin which brought about the Incarnation. The term comes from the Exsultet, or canticle from the Easter Vigil liturgy, in which the deacon proclaims the Resurrection of the Lord. The term occurs in the following context: "O certa necessarium Adae peccátum, quod Christi morte delétum est! O felix culpa, quae talem ac tantum meruit habére Redemptorem!" ("O truly needful sin of Adam, which Christ's death blotted out! O happy fault, which required so great a Redeemer!") The degree to which Hawthorne endorses the *felix culpa* view is uncertain; both Miriam and Kenyon merely suggest such an interpretation.

Kenyon would have besought her for more definite intelligence, but she shook her head, put her finger on her lips, and turned away with an illusive smile. The fancy impressed him, that she, too, like Donatello, had reached a wayside paradise, in their mysterious life-journey, where they both threw down the burden of the before and after, and, except for this interview with himself, were happy in the flitting moment. To-day, Donatello was the sylvan Faun; to-day, Miriam was his fit companion, a Nymph of grove or fountain; to-morrow,—a remorseful man and woman, linked by a marriage-bond of crime,—they would set forth towards an inevitable goal.

On the appointed afternoon, Kenyon failed not to make his appearance in the Corso, and at an hour much earlier than Miriam had named.

It was carnival time.[1] The merriment of this famous festival was in full progress; and the stately avenue of the Corso was peopled with hundreds of fantastic shapes, some of which probably represented the mirth of ancient times, surviving through all manner of calamity, ever since the days of the Roman empire. For a few afternoons of early spring, this mouldy gayety strays into the sunshine; all the remainder of the year, it seems to be shut up in the catacombs or some other sepulchral storehouse of the past.

Besides these hereditary forms, at which a hundred generations have laughed, there were others of modern date, the humorous effluence of the day that was now passing. It is a day, however, and an age, that appears to be remarkably barren, when compared with the prolific originality of former times, in productions of a scenic and ceremonial character, whether grave or gay. To own the truth, the carnival is alive, this present year, only because it has existed through centuries gone by. It is traditionary, not actual. If decrepit and melancholy Rome smiles, and laughs broadly, indeed, at carnival time, it is not in the old simplicity of real mirth, but with a half-conscious effort, like our self-deceptive pretence of jollity

[1] Like his characters, Hawthorne spent two Carnivals in Rome, in 1858 and 1859. He enjoyed the second one much more than the first, especially since Una was experiencing a remission from her four-month siege of Roman fever.

at a threadbare joke. Whatever it may once have been, it is now but a narrow stream of merriment, noisy of set purpose, running along the middle of the Corso, through the solemn heart of the decayed city, without extending its shallow influence on either side. Nor, even within its own limits, does it affect the mass of spectators, but only a comparatively few, in street and balcony, who carry on the warfare of nosegays and counterfeit sugar-plums. The populace look on with staid composure; the nobility and priesthood take little or no part in the matter; and, but for the hordes of Anglo-Saxons who annually take up the flagging mirth, the carnival might long ago have been swept away, with the snow-drifts of confetti that whiten all the pavement.

No doubt, however, the worn-out festival is still new to the youthful and light-hearted, who make the worn-out world itself as fresh as Adam found it on his first forenoon in Paradise. It may be only age and care that chill the life out of its grotesque and airy riot, with the impertinence of their cold criticism.

Kenyon, though young, had care enough within his breast to render the carnival the emptiest of mockeries. Contrasting the stern anxiety of his present mood with the frolic spirit of the preceding year, he fancied that so much trouble had, at all events, brought wisdom in its train. But there is a wisdom that looks grave, and sneers at merriment; and again a deeper wisdom, that stoops to be gay as often as occasion serves, and oftenest avails itself of shallow and trifling grounds of mirth; because, if we wait for more substantial ones, we seldom can be gay at all. Therefore, had it been possible, Kenyon would have done well to mask himself in some wild, hairy visage, and plunge into the throng of other maskers, as at the carnival before. Then, Donatello had danced along the Corso in all the equipment of a Faun, doing the part with wonderful felicity of execution, and revealing furry ears which looked absolutely real; and Miriam had been alternately, a lady of the antique régime, in powder and brocade, and the prettiest peasant-girl of the Campagna, in the gayest of costumes; while Hilda, sitting demurely in a balcony, had hit the sculptor with a single rosebud,—so sweet and fresh a bud that he knew at once whose hand had flung it.

These were all gone; all those dear friends whose sympathetic mirth had made him gay. Kenyon felt as if an interval of many years had passed since the last carnival. He had grown old, the nimble jollity was tame, and the maskers dull and heavy; the Corso was but a narrow and shabby street of decaying palaces; and even the long, blue streamer of Italian sky, above it, not half so brightly blue as formerly.

Yet, if he could have beheld the scene with his clear, natural eyesight, he might still have found both merriment and splendor in it. Everywhere, and all day long, there had been tokens of the festival, in the baskets brimming over with bouquets, for sale at the street-corners, or borne about on people's heads; while bushels upon bushels of variously colored confetti were displayed, looking just like veritable sugar-plums; so that a stranger would have imagined that the whole commerce and business of stern old Rome lay in flowers and sweets. And, now, in the sunny afternoon, there could hardly be a spectacle more picturesque than the vista of that noble street, stretching into the interminable distance between two rows of lofty edifices, from every window of which, and many a balcony, flaunted gay and gorgeous carpets, bright silks, scarlet cloths with rich golden fringes, and Gobelin tapestry,[2] still lustrous with varied hues, though the product of antique looms. Each separate palace had put on a gala-dress, and looked festive for the occasion, whatever sad or guilty secrets it might hide within. Every window, moreover, was alive with the faces of women, rosy girls, and children, all kindled into brisk and mirthful expression by the incidents in

[2]Famous French tapestries, originally woven in the mid-15th century by Gilles and Jehan Gobelin. Hawthorne saw examples of this tapestry work in the Quirinal Palace.

the street below. In the balconies that projected along the palace fronts, stood groups of ladies, some beautiful, all richly dressed, scattering forth their laughter, shrill, yet sweet, and the musical babble of their voices, to thicken into an airy tumult over the heads of common mortals.

All these innumerable eyes looked down into the street, the whole capacity of which was thronged with festal figures, in such fantastic variety that it had taken centuries to contrive them; and through the midst of the mad, merry stream of human life, rolled slowly onward a never-ending procession of all the vehicles in Rome, from the ducal carriage, with the powdered coachman high in front, and the three golden lackeys clinging in the rear, down to the rustic cart drawn by its single donkey. Among this various crowd, at windows and in balconies, in cart, cab, barouche, or gorgeous equipage, or bustling to and fro afoot, there was a sympathy of nonsense; a true and genial brotherhood and sisterhood, based on the honest purpose—and a wise one, too—of being foolish, all together. The sport of mankind, like its deepest earnest, is a battle; so these festive people fought one another with an ammunition of sugar-plums and flowers.

Not that they were veritable sugar-plums, however, but something that resembled them only as the apples of Sodom look like better fruit. They were concocted mostly of lime, with a grain of oat or some other worthless kernel in the midst. Besides the hail-storm of confetti, the combatants threw hand-fuls of flour or lime into the air, where it hung like smoke over a battle-field, or, descending, whitened a black coat or priestly robe, and made the curly locks of youth irreverently hoary.

At the same time with this acrid contest of quicklime, which caused much effusion of tears from suffering eyes, a gentler warfare of flowers was carried on, principally between knights and ladies. Originally, no doubt, when this pretty custom was first instituted, it may have had a sincere and modest import. Each youth and damsel, gathering bouquets of field flowers, or the sweetest and fairest that grew in their own gardens, all fresh and virgin blossoms,—flung them, with true aim, at the one, or few, whom they regarded with a sentiment of shy partiality at least, if not with love. Often, the lover in the Corso may thus have received from his bright mistress, in her father's princely balcony, the first sweet intimation that his passionate glances had not struck against a heart of marble. What more appropriate mode of suggesting her tender secret could a maiden find, than by the soft hit of a rosebud against a young man's cheek.

This was the pastime and the earnest of a more innocent and homelier age. Now-a-days, the nosegays are gathered and tied up by sordid hands, chiefly of the most ordinary flowers, and are sold along the Corso, at mean price, yet more than such venal things are worth. Buying a basketful, you find them miserably wilted, as if they had flown hither and thither through two or three carnival days already; muddy, too, having been fished up from the pavement, where a hundred feet have trampled on them. You may see throngs of men and boys who thrust themselves beneath the horses' hoofs to gather up bouquets that were aimed amiss from balcony and carriage; these they sell again, and yet once more, and ten times over, defiled as they all are with the wicked filth of Rome.

Such are the flowery favors—the fragrant bunches of sentiment—that fly between cavalier and dame, and back again, from one end of the Corso to the other. Perhaps they may symbolize, more aptly than was intended, the poor, battered, wilted hearts of those who fling them; hearts which—crumpled and crushed by former possessors, and stained with various mishap—have been passed from hand to hand, along the muddy street-way of life, instead of being treasured in one faithful bosom.

These venal and polluted flowers, therefore, and those deceptive bonbons, are types of the small reality that still subsists in the observance of the carnival. Yet the government

seemed to imagine that there might be excitement enough—
wild mirth, perchance, following its antics beyond law, and
frisking from frolic into earnest—to render it expedient to
guard the Corso with an imposing show of military power.
Besides the ordinary force of gensd'armes, a strong patrol of
Papal dragoons, in steel helmets and white cloaks, were sta-
tioned at all the street-corners. Detachments of French in-
fantry stood by their stacked muskets in the Piazza del Popolo,
at one extremity of the course, and before the palace of the
Austrian embassy, at the other, and by the column of Antoninus, midway between. Had that chained tiger-cat, the
Roman populace, shown only so much as the tips of his claws,
the sabres would have been flashing and the bullets whistling,
in right earnest, among the combatants who now pelted one
another with mock sugar-plums and wilted flowers.

But, to do the Roman people justice, they were restrained
by a better safeguard than the sabre or the bayonet: it was
their own gentle courtesy, which imparted a sort of sacredness
to the hereditary festival. At first sight of a spectacle so fantastic and extravagant, a cool observer might have imagined
the whole town gone mad; but, in the end, he would see that
all this apparently unbounded license is kept strictly within a
limit of its own; he would admire a people who can so freely
let loose their mirthful propensities, while muzzling those
fiercer ones that tend to mischief. Everybody seemed lawless;
nobody was rude. If any reveller overstepped the mark, it
was sure to be no Roman, but an Englishman or an American;
and even the rougher play of this Gothic race was still softened
by the insensible influence of a moral atmosphere more delicate,
in some respects, than we breathe at home. Not that, after all,
we like the fine Italian spirit better than our own; popular
rudeness is sometimes the symptom of rude moral health. But,
where a carnival is in question, it would probably pass off
more decorously, as well as more airily and delightfully, in
Rome, than in any Anglo-Saxon city.

When Kenyon emerged from a side-lane into the Corso,

the mirth was at its height. Out of the seclusion of his own
feelings, he looked forth at the tapestried and damask-curtained
palaces, the slow-moving, double line of carriages, and the
motley maskers that swarmed on foot, as if he were gazing
through the iron lattice of a prison-window. So remote from
the scene were his sympathies, that it affected him like a thin
dream, through the dim, extravagant material of which he could
discern more substantial objects, while too much under its
control to start forth broad awake. Just at that moment, too,
there came another spectacle, making its way right through
the masquerading throng.

It was, first and foremost, a full band of martial music,
reverberating, in that narrow and confined, though stately
avenue, between the walls of the lofty palaces, and roaring
upward to the sky, with melody so powerful that it almost
grew to discord. Next came a body of cavalry and mounted
gensd'armes, with great display of military pomp. They were
escorting a long train of equipages, each and all of which shone
as gorgeously as Cinderella's coach, with paint and gilding.
Like that, too, they were provided with coachmen, of mighty
breadth, and enormously tall footmen, in immense, powdered
wigs, and all the splendor of gold-laced, three-cornered hats,
and embroidered silk coats and breeches. By the old-fashioned
magnificence of this procession, it might worthily have included his Holiness in person, with a suite of attendant Cardinals, if those sacred dignitaries would kindly have lent their
aid to heighten the frolic of the carnival. But, for all its show
of a martial escort, and its antique splendor of costume, it was
but a train of the municipal authorities of Rome,—illusive
shadows, every one, and among them a phantom, styled the
Roman Senator,—proceeding to the Capitol.

The riotous interchange of nosegays and confetti was
partially suspended, while the procession passed. One well-
directed shot, however, (it was a double-handful of powdered lime, flung by an impious New Englander,) hit the
coachman of the Roman Senator full in the face, and hurt

his dignity amazingly. It appeared to be his opinion, that the Republic was again crumbling into ruin, and that the dust of it now filled his nostrils; though, in fact, it could hardly be distinguished from the official powder with which he was already plentifully bestrewn.

While the sculptor, with his dreamy eyes, was taking idle note of this trifling circumstance, two figures passed before him, hand in hand. The countenance of each was covered with an impenetrable black mask; but one seemed a peasant of the Campagna; the other, a contadina in her holiday costume.

CHAPTER 49.   *A Frolic of the Carnival*

The crowd and confusion, just at that moment, hindered the sculptor from pursuing these figures,—the peasant and the contadina,—who, indeed, were but two of a numerous tribe that thronged the Corso, in similar costume. As soon as he could squeeze a passage, Kenyon tried to follow in their footsteps, but quickly lost sight of them, and was thrown off the track by stopping to examine various groups of masqueraders, in which he fancied the objects of his search to be included. He found many a sallow peasant or herdsman of the Campagna, in such a dress as Donatello wore; many a contadina, too, brown, broad, and sturdy, in her finery of scarlet, and decked out with gold or coral beads, a pair of heavy ear-rings, a curiously wrought cameo or mosaic brooch, and a silver comb or long stiletto among her glossy hair. But those shapes of grace and beauty, which he sought, had vanished.

As soon as the procession of the Senator had passed, the merry-makers resumed their antics with fresh spirit, and the artillery of bouquets and sugar-plums, suspended for a moment, began anew. The sculptor himself being probably the most anxious and unquiet spectator there, was especially a mark for missiles from all quarters, and for the practical jokes which the license of the carnival permits. In fact, his sad and contracted brow so ill accorded with the scene, that the revellers might be pardoned for thus using him as the butt of their idle mirth, since he evidently could not otherwise contribute to it.

Fantastic figures, with bulbous heads, the circumference of a bushel, grinned enormously in his face. Harlequins struck him with their wooden swords, and appeared to expect his immediate transformation into some jollier shape. A little, long-tailed, horned fiend sidled up to him, and suddenly blew

at him through a tube, enveloping our poor friend in a whole
harvest of winged seeds. A biped, with an ass's snout, brayed
close to his ear, ending his discordant uproar with a peal of
human laughter. Five strapping damsels[1]—so, at least, their
petticoats bespoke them, in spite of an awful freedom in the
flourish of their legs—joined hands, and danced around him,
inviting him by their gestures, to perform a hornpipe in the
midst. Released from these gay persecutors, a clown in motley
rapped him on the back with a blown bladder, in which a
handful of dried peas rattled horribly.

Unquestionably, a care-stricken mortal has no business
abroad, when the rest of mankind are at high carnival; they
must either pelt him and absolutely martyr him with jests, and
finally bury him beneath the aggregated heap; or else the
potency of his darker mood, because the tissue of human life
takes a sad dye more readily than a gay one, will quell their
holiday humors, like the aspect of a death's-head at a banquet.
Only that we know Kenyon's errand, we could hardly forgive
him for venturing into the Corso with that troubled face.

Even yet, his merry martyrdom was not half over. There
came along a gigantic female figure, seven feet high, at least,
and taking up a third of the street's breadth with the preposterously swelling sphere of her crinoline skirts. Singling out
the sculptor, she began to make a ponderous assault upon his
heart, throwing amorous glances at him out of her great goggle-
eyes, offering him a vast bouquet of sunflowers and nettles,
and soliciting his pity by all sorts of pathetic and passionate
dumb-show. Her suit meeting no favor, the rejected Titaness
made a gesture of despair and rage; then suddenly drawing
a huge pistol, she took aim right at the obdurate sculptor's
breast, and pulled the trigger. The shot took effect, for the
abominable plaything went off by a spring, like a boy's pop-
gun, covering Kenyon with a cloud of lime-dust, under shelter
of which the revengeful damsel strode away.

[1]Virgins.

Hereupon, a whole host of absurd figures surrounded him, pretending to sympathize in his mishap. Clowns and parti-colored harlequins; orang-outangs; bear-headed, bull-headed, and dog-headed individuals; faces that would have been human, but for their enormous noses; one terrific creature, with a visage right in the centre of his breast; and all other imaginable kinds of monstrosity and exaggeration. These apparitions appeared to be investigating the case, after the fashion of a coroner's jury, poking their pasteboard countenances close to the sculptor's with an unchangeable grin, that gave still more ludicrous effect to the comic alarm and horrour of their gestures. Just then, a figure came by, in a gray wig and rusty gown, with an inkhorn at his buttonhole, and a pen behind his ear; he announced himself as a notary, and offered to make the last will and testament of the assassinated man. This solemn duty, however, was interrupted by a surgeon, who brandished a lancet, three feet long, and proposed to let his blood.[2]

The affair was so like a feverish dream, that Kenyon resigned himself to let it take its course. Fortunately, the humors of the carnival pass from one absurdity to another, without lingering long enough on any, to wear out even the slightest of them. The passiveness of his demeanor afforded too little scope for such broad merriment as the masqueraders sought. In a few moments they vanished from him, as dreams and spectres do, leaving him at liberty to pursue his quest, with no impediment except the crowd that blocked up the footway.

He had not gone far when the peasant and the contadina met him. They were still hand in hand, and appeared to be straying through the grotesque and animated scene, taking as little part in it as himself. It might be because he recognized them, and knew their solemn secret, that the sculptor fancied

[2]The manuscript reads "to let him blood," but the "him" is probably just a slip of Hawthorne's pen for "his"; approaching Kenyon, the leech simply proposes to let his blood—a more idiomatic reading than "to let him blood." Bleeding and cupping were standard medical practice in 1860.

a melancholy emotion to be expressed by the very movement and attitudes of these two figures; and even the grasp of their hands, uniting them so closely, seemed to set them in a sad remoteness from the world at which they gazed.

"I rejoice to meet you," said Kenyon.

But they looked at him through the eye-holes of their black masks, without answering a word.

"Pray give me a little light on the matter which I have so much at heart," said he; "if you know anything of Hilda, for Heaven's sake, speak!"

Still, they were silent; and the sculptor began to imagine that he must have mistaken the identity of these figures, there being such a multitude in similar costume. Yet there was no other Donatello; no other Miriam. He felt, too, that spiritual certainty which impresses us with the presence of our friends, apart from any testimony of the senses.

"You are unkind," resumed he,—"knowing the anxiety which oppresses me,—not to relieve it, if in your power."

The reproach evidently had its effect; for the contadina now spoke, and it was Miriam's voice.

"We gave you all the light we could," said she. "You are yourself unkind, though you little think how much so, to come between us at this hour. There may be a sacred hour, even in carnival time."

In another state of mind, Kenyon could have been amused by the impulsiveness of this response, and a sort of vivacity that he had often noted in Miriam's conversation. But he was conscious of a profound sadness in her tone, overpowering its momentary irritation, and assuring him that a pale, tear-stained face was hidden behind her mask.

"Forgive me!" said he.

Donatello here extended his hand,—not that which was clasping Miriam's,—and she, too, put her free one into the sculptor's left; so that they were a linked circle of three, with many reminiscences and forebodings flashing through their hearts. Kenyon knew intuitively that these once familiar friends were parting with him, now.

"Farewell!" they all three said, in the same breath.

No sooner was the word spoken, than they loosed their hands; and the uproar of the carnival swept like a tempestuous sea over the spot, which they had included within their small circle of isolated feeling.

By this interview, the sculptor had learned nothing in reference to Hilda; but he understood that he was to adhere to the instructions already received, and await a solution of the mystery in some mode that he could not yet anticipate. Passing his hands over his eyes, and looking about him,—for the event just described had made the scene even more dream-like than before,—he now found himself approaching that broad piazza bordering on the Corso, which has for its central object the sculptured column of Antoninus. It was not far from this vicinity that Miriam had bid him wait. Struggling onward, as fast as the tide of merry-makers, setting strong against him, would permit, he was now beyond the Piazza Colonna, and began to count the houses. The fifth was a palace, with a long front upon the Corso, and of stately height, but somewhat grim with age.

Over its arched and pillared entrance, there was a balcony, richly hung with tapestry and damask, and tenanted, for the time, by a gentleman of venerable aspect, and a group of ladies. The white hair and whiskers of the former, and the winter-roses in his cheeks, had an English look; the ladies, too, showed a fair-haired, Saxon bloom, and seemed to taste the mirth of the carnival with the freshness of spectators to whom the scene was new. All the party, the old gentleman with grave earnestness, as if he were defending a rampart, and his young companions with exuberance of frolic, showered confetti inexhaustibly upon the passers-by.

In the rear of the balcony, a broad-brimmed, ecclesiastical beaver was visible. An abbate,[3] probably an acquaintance and cicerone of the English family, was sitting there, and

[3]An abbé; a priest-acquaintance serving as a tourist guide (cicerone).

enjoying the scene, though partially withdrawn from view, as
the decorum of his order dictated.

There seemed no better nor other course for Kenyon,
than to keep watch at this appointed spot, waiting for whatever should happen next. Clasping his arm round a lamp-post,
to prevent being carried away by the turbulent stream of
wayfarers, he scrutinized every face, with the idea that some
one of them might meet his eyes with a glance of intelligence.
He looked at each mask,—harlequin, ape, bulbous-headed
monster, or anything that was absurdest,—not knowing but
that the messenger might come, even in such fantastic guise.
Or, perhaps, one of those quaint figures, in the stately ruff,
the cloak, tunic, and trunk-hose, of three centuries ago, might
bring him tidings of Hilda, out of that long-past age. At times,
his disquietude took a hopeful aspect; and he fancied that
Hilda might come by, her own sweet self, in some shy disguise
which the instinct of his love would be sure to penetrate. Or,
she might be borne past on a triumphal car, like the one just
now approaching, its slow-moving wheels encircled and spoked
with foliage, and drawn by horses that were harnessed and
wreathed with flowers. Being, at best, so far beyond the bounds
of reasonable conjecture, he might anticipate the wildest event,
or find either his hopes or fears disappointed in what appeared
most probable.

The old Englishman and his daughters, in the opposite
balcony, must have seen something unutterably absurd in
the sculptor's deportment, poring into this whirlpool of nonsense so earnestly, in quest of what was to make his life dark
or bright. Earnest people, who try to get a reality out of human
existence, are necessarily absurd in the view of the revellers
and masqueraders. At all events, after a good deal of mirth at
the expense of his melancholy visage, the fair occupants of the
balcony favored Kenyon with a salvo of confetti, which came
rattling about him like a hail-storm. Looking up, instinctively,
he was surprised to see the abbate in the background lean
forward and give a courteous sign of recognition.

It was the same old priest with whom he had seen Hilda,

at the confessional; the same with whom he had talked of her disappearance, on meeting him in the street.

Yet, whatever might be the reason, Kenyon did not now associate this ecclesiastical personage with the idea of Hilda. His eyes lighted on the old man, just for an instant, and then returned to the eddying throng of the Corso, on his minute scrutiny of which depended, for aught he knew, the sole chance of ever finding any trace of her. There was, about this moment, a bustle on the other side of the street, the cause of which Kenyon did not see, nor exert himself to discover. A small party of soldiers or gensd'armes appeared to be concerned in it; they were perhaps arresting some disorderly character, who, under the influence of an extra flask of wine, might have reeled across the mystic limitation of carnival proprieties.

The sculptor heard some people near him, talking of the incident.

"That contadina, in a black mask, was a fine figure of a woman."

"She was not amiss," replied a female voice; "but her companion was far the handsomer figure of the two. Could they be really a peasant and a contadina, do you imagine?"

"No, no," said the other. "It is some frolic of the carnival, carried a little too far."

This conversation might have excited Kenyon's interest; only that, just as the last words were spoken, he was hit by two missiles, both of a kind that were flying abundantly on that gay battle-field. One, we are ashamed to say, was a cauliflower, which, flung by a young man from a passing carriage, came with a prodigious thump against his shoulder; the other was a single rosebud, so fresh that it seemed that moment gathered. It flew from the opposite balcony, smote gently on his lips, and fell into his hand. He looked upward, and beheld the face of his lost Hilda!

She was dressed in a white domino,[4] and looked pale and

[4]Face mask.

bewildered, and yet full of tender joy. Moreover, there was a
gleam of delicate mirthfulness in her eyes, which the sculptor
had seen there only two or three times in the course of their
acquaintance, but thought it the most bewitching and fairy-
like of all Hilda's expressions. That soft, mirthful smile caused
her to melt, as it were, into the wild frolic of the carnival, and
become not so strange and alien to the scene, as her unexpected
apparition must otherwise have made her.

Meanwhile, the venerable Englishman and his daughters
were staring at poor Hilda in a way that proved them altogether astonished, as well as inexpressibly shocked, by her
sudden intrusion into their private balcony. They looked—as,
indeed, English people of respectability would, if an angel
were to alight in their circle, without due introduction from
somebody whom they knew, in the court above—they looked
as if an unpardonable liberty had been taken, and a suitable
apology must be made; after which, the intruder would be
expected to withdraw.

The abbate, however, drew the old gentleman aside, and
whispered a few words that served to mollify him; he bestowed on Hilda a sufficiently benignant, though still a perplexed and questioning regard, and invited her, in dumb show,
to put herself at her ease.

But, whoever was in fault, our shy and gentle Hilda
had dreamed of no intrusion. Whence she had come, or where
she had been hidden, during this mysterious interval, we can
but imperfectly surmise, and do not mean, at present, to make
it a matter of formal explanation with the reader. It is better,
perhaps, to fancy that she had been snatched away to a land
of picture; that she had been straying with Claude[5] in the
golden light which he used to shed over his landscapes, but
which he could never have beheld with his waking eyes, till
he awoke in the better clime. We will imagine that, for the

[5]Claude Lorrain (1600–1682), a French landscape painter who settled in Rome in 1627 to work under the patronage of Pope Urban VIII.

sake of the true simplicity with which she loved them, Hilda had been permitted, for a season, to converse with the great, departed masters of the pencil, and behold the diviner works which they have painted in heavenly colors. Guido had shown her another portrait of Beatrice Cenci, done from the celestial life, in which that forlorn mystery of the earthly countenance was exchanged for a radiant joy. Perugino had allowed her a glimpse at his easel, on which she discerned what seemed a woman's face, but so divine, by the very depth and softness of its womanhood, that a gush of happy tears blinded the maiden's eyes, before she had time to look. Raphael had taken Hilda by the hand, (that fine, forcible hand which Kenyon sculptured,) and drawn aside the curtain of gold-fringed cloud that hung before his latest masterpiece. On earth, Raphael painted the Transfiguration. What higher scene may he have since depicted, not from imagination, but as revealed to his actual sight![6]

Neither will we retrace the steps by which she returned to the actual world. For the present be it enough to say that Hilda had been summoned forth from a secret place, and led we know not through what mysterious passages, to a point where the tumult of life burst suddenly upon her ears. She heard the tramp of footsteps, the rattle of wheels, and the mingled hum of a multitude of voices, with strains of music and loud laughter breaking through. Emerging into a great, gloomy hall, a curtain was drawn aside; she found herself gently propelled into an open balcony, whence she looked out upon the festal street, with gay tapestries flaunting over all the palace fronts, the windows thronged with merry faces, and a crowd of maskers rioting upon the pavement below.

Immediately, she seemed to become a portion of the scene. Her pale, large-eyed, fragile beauty, her wondering aspect, and bewildered grace, attracted the gaze of many; and

[6]For Guido, see note 1, p. 64; for Perugino, note 2, p. 208; for Raphael, note 1, p. 18.

there fell around her a shower of bouquets and bonbons—freshest blossoms and sweetest sugar-plums, sweets to the sweet[7]—such as the revellers of the carnival reserve as tributes to especial loveliness. Hilda pressed her hand across her brow; she let her eyelids fall, and, lifting them again, looked through the grotesque and gorgeous show, the chaos of mad jollity, in quest of some object by which she might assure herself that the whole spectacle was not an illusion.

Beneath the balcony, she recognized a familiar and fondly remembered face. The spirit of the hour and the scene exercised its influence over her quick and sensitive nature; she caught up one of the rosebuds that had been showered upon her, and aimed it at the sculptor. It hit the mark; he turned his sad eyes upward, and there was Hilda, in whose gentle presence his own secret sorrow and the obtrusive uproar of the carnival alike died away from his perception.

That night, the lamp beneath the Virgin's shrine burned as brightly as if it had never been extinguished; and though the one faithful dove had gone to her melancholy perch, she greeted Hilda rapturously the next morning, and summoned her less constant companions, whithersoever they had flown, to renew their homage.

---

[7]A somewhat inappropriate allusion, under the circumstances, to Gertrude's farewell to Ophelia at the tomb:

> Sweets to the sweet! Farewell. [*Scatters flowers.*]
> I hop'd thou should have been my Hamlet's wife;
> I thought thy bridal bed to have deck'd, sweet maid,
> And not have strewn thy grave.
>   SHAKESPEARE, *Hamlet*, V.i.229-332

The balcony setting also suggests *Romeo and Juliet.*

CHAPTER 50. *Miriam, Hilda, Kenyon, Donatello*

The gentle reader, we trust, would not thank us for one of those minute elucidations, which are so tedious, and, after all, so unsatisfactory, in clearing up the romantic mysteries of a story. He is too wise to insist upon looking closely at the wrong side of the tapestry, after the right one has been sufficiently displayed to him, woven with the best of the artist's skill, and cunningly arranged with a view to the harmonious exhibition of its colors. If any brilliant, or beautiful, or even tolerable effect have been produced, this pattern of kindly readers will accept it at its worth, without tearing its web apart, with the idle purpose of discovering how its threads have been knit together; for the sagacity by which he is distinguished, will long ago have taught him that any narrative of human action and adventure—whether we call it history or romance—is certain to be a fragile handiwork, more easily rent than mended. The actual experience of even the most ordinary life is full of events that never explain themselves, either as regards their origin or their tendency.

It would be easy, from conversations which we have held with the sculptor, to suggest a clue to the mystery of Hilda's disappearance; although as long as she remained in Italy there was a remarkable reserve in her communications upon this subject, even to her most intimate friends. Either a pledge of secrecy had been exacted, or a prudential motive warned her not to reveal the stratagems of a religious body, or the secret acts of a despotic government—whichever might be responsible in the present instance—while still within the scope of their jurisdiction. Possibly, she might not herself be

439

fully aware what power had laid its grasp upon her person.
What has chiefly perplexed us, however, among Hilda's adventures, is the mode of her release, in which some inscrutable
tyranny or other seemed to take part in a frolic of the carnival.
We can only account for it, by supposing that the fitful and
fantastic imagination of a woman—sportive, because she must
otherwise be desperate—had arranged this incident, and made
it the condition of a step which her conscience, or the conscience of another, required her to take.

A few days after Hilda's reappearance, she and the
sculptor were straying together through the streets of Rome.
Being deep in talk, it so happened that they found themselves
near the majestic, pillared portico, and huge, black rotundity
of the Pantheon. It stands almost at the central point of the
labyrinthine intricacies of the modern city, and often presents
itself before the bewildered stranger when he is in search of
other objects. Hilda, looking up, proposed that they should
enter.

"I never pass it without going in," she said, "to pay
my homage at the tomb of Raphael."

"Nor I," said Kenyon, "without stopping to admire the
noblest edifice which the barbarism of the early ages, and the
more barbarous pontiffs and princes of later ones, have spared
to us."

They went in, accordingly, and stood in the free space
of that great circle, around which are ranged the arched
recesses and stately altars, formerly dedicated to heathen gods,
but Christianized through twelve centuries gone by. The world
has nothing else like the Pantheon. So grand it is, that the
pasteboard statues over the lofty cornice do not disturb the
effect, any more than the tin crowns and hearts, the dusty
artificial flowers, and all manner of trumpery gewgaws, hanging at the saintly shrines. The rust and dinginess that have
dimmed the precious marble on the walls; the pavement, with
its great squares and rounds of porphyry and granite, cracked

crosswise and in a hundred directions, showing how roughly the troublesome ages have trampled here; the gray dome above, with its opening to the sky, as if heaven were looking down into the interior of this place of worship, left unimpeded for prayers to ascend the more freely: all these things make an impression of solemnity, which Saint Peter's itself fails to produce.

"I think," said the sculptor, "it is to the aperture in the dome—that great Eye, gazing heavenward—that the Pantheon owes the peculiarity of its effect. It is so heathenish, as it were —so unlike all the snugness of our modern civilization! Look, too, at the pavement directly beneath the open space! So much rain has fallen there, in the last two thousand years, that it is green with small, fine moss, such as grows over tombstones in a damp English churchyard."

"I like better," replied Hilda, "to look at the bright, blue sky, roofing the edifice where the builders left it open. It is very delightful, in a breezy day, to see the masses of white cloud float over the opening, and then the sunshine fall through it again, fitfully, as it does now. Would it be any wonder if we were to see angels hovering there, partly in and partly out, with genial, heavenly faces, not intercepting the light, but only transmuting it into beautiful colors? Look at that broad, golden beam—a sloping cataract of sunlight—which comes down from the aperture and rests upon the shrine, at the right hand of the entrance!"[1]

"There is a dusky picture over that altar," observed the sculptor. "Let us go and see if this strong illumination brings out any merit in it."

Approaching the shrine, they found the picture little worth looking at, but could not forbear smiling, to see that a very plump and comfortable tabby-cat—whom we ourselves

[1]Hilda paraphrases Hawthorne's own reflections while visiting the Pantheon on May 1, 1858. See *NB*, p. 187.

have often observed haunting the Pantheon—had established herself on the altar, in the genial sunbeam, and was fast asleep among the holy tapers. Their footsteps disturbing her, she awoke, raised herself, and sat blinking in the sun, yet with a certain dignity and self-possession, as if conscious of representing a saint.

"I presume," remarked Kenyon, "that this is the first of the feline race that has ever set herself up as an object of worship, in the Pantheon or elsewhere, since the days of ancient Egypt. See; there is a peasant from the neighboring market, actually kneeling to her! She seems a gracious and benignant saint enough."

"Do not make me laugh," said Hilda, reproachfully, "but help me to drive the creature away. It distresses me to see that poor man, or any human being, directing his prayers so much amiss."

"Then, Hilda," answered the sculptor, more seriously, "the only place in the Pantheon for you and me to kneel, is on the pavement beneath the central aperture. If we pray at a saint's shrine, we shall give utterance to earthly wishes; but if we pray face to face with the Deity, we shall feel it impious to petition for aught that is narrow and selfish. Methinks, it is this that makes the Catholics so delight in the worship of saints; they can bring up all their little worldly wants and whims, their individualities, and human weaknesses, not as things to be repented of, but to be humored by the canonized humanity to which they pray. Indeed, it is very tempting!"

What Hilda might have answered, must be left to conjecture; for as she turned from the shrine, her eyes were attracted to the figure of a female penitent, kneeling on the pavement just beneath the great central eye, in the very spot which Kenyon had designated as the only one whence prayers should ascend. The upturned face was invisible, behind a veil or mask, which formed a part of the garb.

"It cannot be!" whispered Hilda, with emotion. "No; it cannot be!"

"What disturbs you?" asked Kenyon. "Why do you tremble so?"

"If it were possible," she replied, "I should fancy that kneeling figure to be Miriam!"

"As you say, it is impossible," rejoined the sculptor. "We know too well what has befallen both her and Donatello."

"Yes; it is impossible!" repeated Hilda.

Her voice was still tremulous, however, and she seemed unable to withdraw her attention from the kneeling figure. Suddenly, and as if the idea of Miriam had opened the whole volume of Hilda's reminiscences, she put this question to the sculptor:—

"Was Donatello really a Faun?"

"If you had ever studied the pedigree of the far-descended heir of Monte Beni, as I did," answered Kenyon, with an irrepressible smile, "you would have retained few doubts on that point. Faun or not, he had a genial nature, which, had the rest of mankind been in accordance with it, would have made earth a paradise to our poor friend. It seems the moral of his story, that human beings of Donatello's character, compounded especially for happiness, have no longer any business on earth, or elsewhere. Life has grown so sadly serious, that such men must change their nature, or else perish, like the antediluvian creatures, that required, as the condition of their existence, a more summer-like atmosphere than ours."

"I will not accept your moral!" replied the hopeful and happy-natured Hilda.

"Then here is another; take your choice!" said the sculptor, remembering what Miriam had recently suggested, in reference to the same point. "He perpetrated a great crime; and his remorse, gnawing into his soul, has awakened it; developing a thousand high capabilities, moral and intellectual, which we never should have dreamed of asking for, within the scanty compass of the Donatello whom we knew."

"I know not whether this is so," said Hilda. "But what then?"

"Here comes my perplexity," continued Kenyon. "Sin has educated Donatello, and elevated him. Is sin, then—which we deem such a dreadful blackness in the universe—is it, like sorrow, merely an element of human education, through which we struggle to a higher and purer state than we could otherwise have attained? Did Adam fall, that we might ultimately rise to a far loftier paradise than his?"

"Oh, hush!" cried Hilda, shrinking from him with an expression of horror which wounded the poor, speculative sculptor to the soul. "This is terrible; and I could weep for you, if you indeed believe it. Do not you perceive what a mockery your creed makes, not only of all religious sentiment, but of moral law? and how it annuls and obliterates whatever precepts of Heaven are written deepest within us? You have shocked me beyond words!"

"Forgive me, Hilda!" exclaimed the sculptor, startled by her agitation; "I never did believe it! But the mind wanders wild and wide; and, so lonely as I live and work, I have neither polestar above, nor light of cottage-windows here below, to bring me home. Were you my guide, my counsellor, my inmost friend, with that white wisdom which clothes you as with a celestial garment, all would go well. Oh, Hilda, guide me home!"

"We are both lonely; both far from home!" said Hilda, her eyes filling with tears. "I am a poor, weak girl, and have no such wisdom as you fancy in me."

What further may have passed between these lovers while standing before the pillared shrine, and the marble Madonna that marks Raphael's tomb, whither they had now wandered, we are unable to record. But when the kneeling figure, beneath the open eye of the Pantheon arose, she looked towards the pair, and extended her hands with a gesture of benediction. Then they knew that it was Miriam. They suffered her to glide out of the portal, however, without a greeting; for those extended hands, even while they blessed, seemed to repel, as if Miriam stood on the other side of a fathomless abyss, and warned them from its verge.

So Kenyon won the gentle Hilda's shy affection, and her consent to be his bride. Another hand must henceforth trim the lamp before the Virgin's shrine; for Hilda was coming down from her old tower, to be herself enshrined and worshipped as a household saint, in the light of her husband's fireside. And, now that life had so much human promise in it, they resolved to go back to their own land; because the years, after all, have a kind of emptiness, when we spend too many of them on a foreign shore. We defer the reality of life, in such cases, until a future moment, when we shall again breathe our native air; but, by-and-by, there are no future moments; or, if we do return, we find that the native air has lost its invigorating quality, and that life has shifted its reality to the spot where we have deemed ourselves only temporary residents. Thus, between two countries, we have none at all, or only that little space of either, in which we finally lay down our discontented bones. It is wise, therefore, to come back betimes, or never.

Before they quitted Rome, a bridal gift was laid on Hilda's table. It was a bracelet, evidently of great cost, being composed of seven ancient Etruscan gems, dug out of seven sepulchres, and each one of them the signet of some princely personage, who had lived an immemorial time ago. Hilda remembered this precious ornament. It had been Miriam's; and once, with the exuberance of fancy that distinguished her, she had amused herself with telling a mythical and magic legend for each gem, comprising the imaginary adventures and catastrophe of its former wearer. Thus, the Etruscan bracelet became the connecting bond of a series of seven wondrous tales, all of which, as they were dug out of seven sepulchres, were characterized by a sevenfold sepulchral gloom; such as Miriam's imagination, shadowed by her own misfortunes, was wont to fling over its most sportive flights.

And now, happy as Hilda was, the bracelet brought the

tears into her eyes, as being, in its entire circle, the symbol of as sad a mystery as any that Miriam had attached to the separate gems. For, what was Miriam's life to be? And where was Donatello? But Hilda had a hopeful soul, and saw sunlight on the mountain-tops.

The End

CONCLUSION[1]

There comes to the author from many readers of the foregoing pages a demand for further elucidations respecting the mysteries of the story.

He reluctantly avails himself of the opportunity afforded by a new edition,[2] to explain such incidents and passages as may have been left too much in the dark; reluctantly, he repeats, because the necessity makes him sensible that he can have succeeded but imperfectly, at best, in throwing about this Romance the kind of atmosphere essential to the effect at which he aimed.

He designed the story and the characters to bear, of course, a certain relation to human nature and human life, but

---

[1]The first three American printings of *The Marble Faun* ended with the preceding chapter. Hawthorne "reluctantly" explained his purpose and method for the fourth printing and introduced himself as the narrator ("I") for the first time. His tone throughout this added conclusion is one of patient forbearance at the obtuseness of his public.

Several substantive variants exist between the Boston edition's "Conclusion" and the English edition's "Postscript." The Centenary Hawthorne (Ohio State, 1968) reprints the "Postscript" as probably having a later date of composition and thus more authority. Since their decision is based upon editorial speculation rather than on existing manuscripts, however, I have felt free to reprint the Boston "Conclusion."

[2]I.e., the fourth printing of the first Boston edition (1860).

still to be so artfully and airily removed from our mundane sphere, that some laws and proprieties of their own should be implicitly and insensibly acknowledged.

The idea of the modern Faun, for example, loses all the poetry and beauty which the Author fancied in it, and becomes nothing better than a grotesque absurdity, if we bring it into the actual light of day. He had hoped to mystify this anomalous creature between the Real and the Fantastic, in such a manner that the reader's sympathies might be excited to a certain pleasurable degree, without impelling him to ask how Cuvier[3] would have classified poor Donatello, or to insist upon being told, in so many words, whether he had furry ears or no. As respects all who ask such questions, the book is, to that extent, a failure.

Nevertheless, the Author fortunately has it in his power to throw light upon several matters in which some of his readers appear to feel an interest. To confess the truth, he was himself troubled with a curiosity similar to that which he has just deprecated on the part of his readers, and once took occasion to cross-examine his friends, Hilda and the sculptor, and to pry into several dark recesses of the story, with which they had heretofore imperfectly acquainted him.

We three had climbed to the top of St. Peter's, and were looking down upon the Rome we were soon to leave, but which (having already sinned sufficiently in that way) it is not my purpose further to describe. It occurred to me, that, being so remote in the upper air, my friends might safely utter, here, the secrets which it would be perilous even to whisper, on lower earth.

"Hilda," I began, "can you tell me the contents of that mysterious packet which Miriam intrusted to your charge, and which was addressed to Signore Luca Barboni, at the Palazzo Cenci?"

---

[3]Baron Georges Cuvier (1769–1823) was the first naturalist to classify the species of animals according to structural types.

"I never had any further knowledge of it," replied Hilda, "nor felt it right to let myself be curious upon the subject."

"As to its precise contents," interposed Kenyon, "it is impossible to speak. But Miriam, isolated as she seemed, had family connections in Rome, one of whom, there is reason to believe, occupied a position in the papal government.

"This Signore Luca Barboni was either the assumed name of the personage in question, or the medium of communication between that individual and Miriam. Now, under such a government as that of Rome, it is obvious that Miriam's privacy and isolated life could only be maintained through the connivance and support of some influential person connected with the administration of affairs. Free and self-controlled as she appeared, her every movement was watched and investigated far more thoroughly by the priestly rulers than by her dearest friends.

"Miriam, if I mistake not, had a purpose to withdraw herself from this irksome scrutiny, and to seek real obscurity in another land; and the packet, to be delivered long after her departure, contained a reference to this design, besides certain family documents, which were to be imparted to her relative as from one dead and gone."

"Yes, it is clear as a London fog," I remarked. "On this head no further elucidation can be desired. But when Hilda went quietly to deliver the packet, why did she so mysteriously vanish?"

"You must recollect," replied Kenyon, with a glance of friendly commiseration at my obtuseness, "that Miriam had utterly disappeared, leaving no trace by which her whereabouts could be known. In the mean time, the municipal authorities had become aware of the murder of the Capuchin; and from many preceding circumstances, such as his persecution of Miriam, they must have seen an obvious connection between herself and that tragical event. Furthermore, there is reason to believe that Miriam was suspected of connection with some plot, or political intrigue, of which there may have been tokens in the packet. And when Hilda appeared, as the bearer of this missive, it was really quite a matter of course, under a despotic government, that she should be detained."

"Ah, quite a matter of course, as you say," answered I. "How excessively stupid in me not to have seen it sooner! But there are other riddles. On the night of the extinction of the lamp, you met Donatello in a penitent's garb, and afterwards saw and spoke to Miriam, in a coach, with a gem glowing on her bosom. What was the business of these two guilty ones in Rome, and who was Miriam's companion?"

"Who!" repeated Kenyon, "why her official relative, to be sure; and as to their business, Donatello's still gnawing remorse had brought him hitherward, in spite of Miriam's entreaties, and kept him lingering in the neighborhood of Rome, with the ultimate purpose of delivering himself up to justice. Hilda's disappearance, which took place the day before, was known to them through a secret channel, and had brought them into the city, where Miriam, as I surmise, began to make arrangements, even then, for that sad frolic of the Carnival."

"And where was Hilda all that dreary time between?" inquired I.

"Where were you, Hilda?" asked Kenyon, smiling.

Hilda threw her eyes on all sides, and seeing that there was not even a bird of the air to fly away with the secret, nor any human being nearer than the loiterers by the obelisk, in the piazza below, she told us about her mysterious abode.

"I was a prisoner in the Convent of the Sacré Cœur, in the Trinità de' Monte," said she, "but in such kindly custody of pious maidens, and watched over by such a dear old priest, that—had it not been for one or two disturbing recollections, and also because I am a daughter of the Puritans—I could willingly have dwelt there forever.

"My entanglement with Miriam's misfortunes, and the good abbate's mistaken hope of a proselyte, seem to me a a sufficient clew to the whole mystery."

"The atmosphere is getting delightfully lucid," observed

I, "but there are one or two things that still puzzle me. Could you tell me—and it shall be kept a profound secret, I assure you—what were Miriam's real name and rank, and precisely the nature of the troubles that led to all those direful consequences?"

"Is it possible that you need an answer to those questions?" exclaimed Kenyon, with an aspect of vast surprise. "Have you not even surmised Miriam's name? Think awhile, and you will assuredly remember it. If not, I congratulate you most sincerely; for it indicates that your feelings have never been harrowed by one of the most dreadful and mysterious events that have occurred within the present century!"

"Well," resumed I, after an interval of deep consideration, "I have but few things more to ask. Where, at this moment, is Donatello?"

"The Castle of Saint Angelo,"[4] said Kenyon, sadly, turning his face towards that sepulchral fortress, "is no longer a prison; but there are others which have dungeons as deep, and in one of them, I fear, lies our poor Faun."

"And why, then, is Miriam at large?" I asked.

"Call it cruelty if you like, not mercy," answered Kenyon. "But, after all, her crime lay merely in a glance. She did no murder!"

"Only one question more," said I, with intense earnestness. "Did Donatello's ears resemble those of the Faun of Praxiteles?"

"I know, but may not tell," replied Kenyon, smiling mysteriously. "On that point, at all events, there shall be not one word of explanation."

LEAMINGTON, *March 14, 1860*

---

[4]A Roman citadel begun by Hadrian and completed by Antoninus Pius A.D. 139; it contains the ashes of emperors from Hadrian to Septimus Severus (d. A.D. 211). It was used as a prison from the 10th century until the end of the 18th. Several Popes and political prisoners were starved, poisoned, and strangled there.

Specimen Pages from the Holograph
Manuscript of
The Marble Faun
in the British Museum

Chapter I.

Miriam, Hilda, Kenyon, Donatello.

[Handwritten manuscript text of Hawthorne's draft, largely illegible]

FOLIO 7 (ADD. 44889)

Note "Hobson" penciled in at the top of the page. He was the first printer to set the manuscript up for Smith, Elder & Co., Hawthorne's English publishers. (The first American edition was set up from these proof sheets.) Note, too, how frequently Hawthorne punctuates. Six commas are omitted in the printing of page 1 alone (in lines 3, 4, 12, 12, 15, and 16 of Folio 7). The difference is roughly that between oral and written speech; Hawthorne seems to have thought orally as he wrote.

nymphs, satyrs, and the whole train of classic faith or fable, hardly took pains to hide themselves in the primeval woods; — ~~the lineage of Monte Beni~~ at that auspicious period, the lineage of Monte Beni had its rise. Its progenitor was a being not altogether human, yet partaking so largely of the gentlest human qualities, as to be neither awful nor shocking to the imagination. A sylvan creature, native among the woods, had loved a mortal maiden, and (perhaps by kindness, and the subtle courtesies which love might teach to his simplicity, or possibly by a ruder wooing) had won her to his haunts. In due time, he gained her womanly affection; and (making their bridal bower, for aught we know, in the hollow of a great tree) the pair spent a happy wedded life in that ancient neighborhood, where now stood Donatello's tower.

From this union sprung a vigorous progeny, that took its place unquestioned among human families. In that age, however, and long afterwards, it showed the ineffaceable lineaments of its wild paternity; it was a pleasant and kindly race of men, but capable of savage fierceness, and never quite restrainable within the trammels of social law. They were strong, active, genial, cheerful as the sunshine, passionate as the tornado. Their lives were rendered blissful by an unbought harmony with nature.

But, as centuries passed away, the Faun's wild blood had necessarily been attempered with constant intermixtures from the more ordinary streams of human life. It lost many of its original qualities, and served, for the most part, only to bestow an unconquerable vigour, which kept the family from extinction, and

FOLIO 257 (ADD. 44890)

The words crossed out in lines 3 and 4 are rewritten at the end of the sentence: "the lineage of Monte Beni had its rise."

Note the opening of the last paragraph: "But as centuries passed away...." Hawthorne's open *p* and his initial *s* in the double consonant suggest "raped" on hasty reading. We need not postulate the Rape of the Sabine Women and reread the chapter for its disguised myth, however; Hawthorne regularly made his *p*'s and *s*'s this way.

454

sweet Hilda with a crime which it was her unhappy fortune to witness, but of which, I need not say, she was as guiltless as the angels that looked out of heaven, and saw it too. No matter, now, what the consequence has been. You shall have your lost Hilda back, and — who knows? — perhaps tenderer than she was."

"But when will she return?" persisted the sculptor. "Tell me the when, and where, and how?"

"A little patience, I do not press me so!" said Miriam; and again temper was struck by the sprite-like characteristic of her manner, and a sort of hysteric gaiety, which seemed to be a Will o'the Wisp for a sorrow stagnant of her heart. "You have more time to spare than we. First, listen to something that I have to tell. We will talk of Hilda by-and-by."

Then Miriam spoke of her own life, and told facts that threw a gleam of light over many things which had perplexed the sculptor, in all his previous knowledge of her. She described herself as springing from an illicit parentage, on the mother's side, but with a vein, likewise, of Jewish blood, yet connected, through her father, with one of those princely families of southern Italy, which still retain a great wealth and influence. And she revealed a name, at which the auditor started, and grew pale; for it was one, that, only a few years before, had been familiar to the world, in connection with a mysterious and terrible event. The reader — if he think it worth while to recal some of the strange incidents which have been talked of, and forgotten, within so long time past — will remember Miriam's name.

"You shudder at me, I perceive," said Miriam, suddenly interrupting her narrative.

"No; you were innocent," replied the sculptor. "I shud.

FOLIO 472 (ADD. 44890)

The number 230 at the end of line 6 denotes the page in Add. 44890; the manuscript is bound in two vellum volumes.

Note the slip of the pen in line 15: "You have more time to spare than we." This edition, following the 1860 text, prints "I."

FOLIO 508 (ADD. 44890)

Clearly Hawthorne intended to end the novel here with Hilda's note of hope. (Note the printer's indication of the final gathering, "Sig 55 vol iii"; the English edition was printed in three volumes.)